She was an integr
that involved two p
an important clue to what appeared
to be a serial killer working in the
small town.

As he entered her hospital room, she turned to look at him and offered him a small smile.

The simple gesture shot a wave of unexpected heat through his belly. A job, he reminded himself. She was a tool he needed to use to complete a job and nothing more. For all he knew, despite the fact that she wore no wedding ring, she could have a husband or a family somewhere awaiting her return.

There was no way he could get caught up with her on a personal level.

Chapter 9

"Seth?" Jack stuck his head in the family room, where he'd last seen his son playing video games. He'd reached a stopping place in the bookkeeping files and had noticed the house was quiet. Too quiet. Where was Seth? The television was still on, but the game remote lay abandoned on the coffee table.

"Seth?" He called louder, glancing over the breakfast bar into the kitchen. Also empty.

He turned off the TV and was headed upstairs to check his son's room when a knock sounded on the front door. Turning to go back downstairs, Jack called out for his visitor to come in.

Brett poked his head inside, peering around the door, his expression unusually serious. "Got a minute?"

Jack eyed his brother in concern, imagining something having gone horribly wrong in the barn or in the fields.

"Sure. What's up?"

"It's Daniel." Brett removed his hat and cocked his head.

Jack frowned. "What about Daniel? Did something happen to him?"

"I overheard him talking to Kurt Rodgers a little while ago. He's gettin' real serious about this breeding program. He's been in touch with someplace called Kennedy Farms about their breeding program, and he's all hyped up about it."

Jack groaned. "Brett..."

"And it doesn't help matters that his assistant, Megan, came here from a large horse breeding ranch in California."

"Is this about buying that stud—what's his name—Geronimo?"

"Yes. No. I..." Brett huffed in frustration. "I'm telling you, Jack. If you don't let Daniel develop his horse-breeding business here as part of the Lucky C, he'll take it somewhere else. We'll lose both Daniel and the potential profits."

"We already had this conversation, and I made my position clear. I won't pressure Daniel to stay here if he feels led to go somewhere else. I won't guilt him into staying just because horse breeding is profitable—"

"Damn it, Jack!" Brett interrupted. "Why are you being so stubborn about this?"

He ignored him and continued, "What's more, I don't want to dilute the focus of the ranch from our tried-and-true business model. Big J entrusted me with the running of the ranch, and I take that responsibility seriously."

"Tell me about it," his brother grumbled, looking away.

"What's that mean?"

Brett squared his shoulders and turned fully to face Jack. "It means you used to be willing to take risks. You rode the wildest bulls at competition and took gambles in business most people wouldn't have the guts for. You weren't afraid to lose a few dollars in pursuit of a high-dollar payout."

"That's different. I was risking my own money, not the ranch's."

"You worked hard, drank hard and rode hard," his brother continued, getting more worked up. "You weren't afraid to try something new. What's happened to you?"

Jack huffed a quiet laugh and shook his head. "You know what happened. I became a father. I had to settle down to raise my son, especially after Laura walked out on us."

Brett looked unconvinced.

"And I took the reins as manager. That means some-thing to me. I won't let Big J down by screwing up his legacy or running the ranch into the ground."

Brett shook his head, giving Jack a narrow-eyed look. "Naw. I don't buy it. The change in you is more than a factor of new responsibility. Your spark is gone, man. You just don't seem…happy anymore."

"I'm plenty happy, Oprah. I have a good life and a great kid." He waved off that conversation. "What does this have to do with Daniel and the breeding program?"

Brett blew out a long breath, making his lips buzz. "Nothing, I guess. Only that ten years ago you would have been all over this horse-breeding venture. I know you would have."

"Maybe so. But that was then, and this is now. I hope I've made my point. I'm really not interested in debat-ing this again."

Brett continued staring at him speculatively. "It's Laura, isn't it?"

"What?"

"That's when the big change happened. Not when you

became manager or when Seth was born. You changed when Laura left."

Jack swiped a hand down his face as he groaned. "Don't you have something better to do than psycho-analyze me?"

"Why don't you date?"

Jack jerked his head up, sputtering a laugh. "What?"

"When's the last time you slept with a woman or so much as had a dinner date?"

Stomping down the last few steps, he crossed the foyer and yanked the front door open. "Goodbye, Brett."

"I know she hurt you, but you gotta stop living in the past, man."

He gritted his back teeth and gave Brett a warning glare. His history with Laura, and especially their divorce, was his absolute *least* favorite topic.

"I could fix you up with someone if you want," Brett said, undaunted by his brother's glower. "Or…hey, that Tracy McCain's a hot little number. I've seen the way she watches you. I think she's into you, bro."

The air in Jack's lungs stilled briefly, and a ripple of heat streaked through his veins. He'd been trying hard all morning to keep visions of Tracy's sleek legs, her wide blue eyes and her bowed lips out of his head. "I don't need dating advice, Brett."

His tone was darker than he intended, but the coil of lust that tightened inside him every time he thought about Tracy made him grumpy. Maybe he did need a night of no-strings sex with someone, just to work off the tension pounding through his blood. But not Tracy. Anyone but Tracy. He would not, could not get involved with Laura's cousin, of all people. For cripes' sake!

"Speaking of the lovely Miss Tracy…" Brett flashed a

simpering grin. "I saw her head out toward the bull pasture about an hour ago with Seth."

Jack stiffened. "What?"

He'd told her she wasn't allowed to be alone with Seth. And what was Seth doing, taking off somewhere without telling him? The heat of anger filled him and kicked his pulse up.

"You ought to head out there and spend a little *quality time* with her," Brett suggested with a waggle of his eyebrows.

"Oh, I'm going out there after them, all right," he said with a growl as he reached past his brother to retrieve his Stetson from the hat rack by the door. "If you'll excuse me…" He pushed his brother out the door as he exited. "I have to go collect my son and have a word with Miss McCain."

"Will you at least think about underwriting Daniel's horse breeding program?" Brett called after him.

"No!" Jack stomped down the porch steps and set off at a jog. "The subject is closed!"

I told Seth his mother died shortly after he was born. That's the story you need to stick to. Telling him anything else will only hurt him. It will lead to questions about where she's been, why she left…

Tracy dug her fingernails into her palms as she gazed at Seth's expectant face, and she swallowed hard. She searched for truths she could tell the boy that wouldn't violate her agreement with Jack. "Well…she was my cousin, and even though we were estranged for a number of years—"

Seth's head tilted, and his nose wrinkled.

Before he could ask, she said, "Estranged means we didn't get to see each other or talk to each other."

"Why not?"

She balled her hands tighter. *Because my husband was a selfish, controlling bastard.*

"Because…we, uh, both got busy with our lives and, uh, well…"

"Ms. Tracy?"

She stroked his hair, thankful for the reprieve from that question. "Yes, sweetie."

"I hope we don't get *stranged*."

Her insides turned to goo, and she pressed a kiss to the top of his sweaty head. "I hope not, too."

He picked at his tennis shoe again and murmured, "How did she die?"

Visions of shattered glass, crumpled metal and a tumbling landscape flashed in Tracy's mind's eye. She heard screams—Laura's and her own—smelled the leaking gas, tasted the tang of blood, felt again the pain that had streaked through her. And she remembered Laura's lifeless eyes, the wrenching realization that her cousin was dead.

Tracy drew and released a deep, cleansing breath. "She died in a car accident, sweetie."

Seth blinked and frowned as he scratched his arm. "Oh."

Tracy covered his hand with hers and squeezed. "Seth, the most important thing you need to know about your mom is that she loved you."

He raised a wide-eyed look to her as if this was news to him.

Tracy sighed with disgust. Of course it was news to him. Jack wouldn't have told him that, and obviously, none of the gifts or messages Laura had sent to her son had been delivered.

Tracy cupped his chin in her hand and met his bright

blue eyes evenly. "Your mother always wanted the best for you. She sometimes made bad choices, but her choices never changed the way she loved you. You were very important to her, and she was so very proud to be your mommy."

His eyes filled with tears, and Tracy pulled him close for a hug.

"I wish I knewed her," he said, his voice muffled against her shoulder.

She fought down the spike of pique toward Jack that swelled inside her. It served no purpose for her to hold a grudge against him for the past. Instead, she kissed Seth's head again and patted his back. "I wish you had known her, too."

Pulling out of her embrace, Seth swiped his arm over his eyes and nose and rose to his feet. "So, um, do you wanna see the fishing pond now?"

She knuckled away a tear from her own eye and flashed a smile. "Lead on, good sir!"

After fumbling down the ladder, a task that gave her a scraped knee and a splinter for her trouble, she followed Seth back through the wooded area. Once again, he set a brisk pace that forced her to jog to keep up. As she batted limbs out of her way, she kept an eye out for spiderwebs and snakes, certain such creepy crawlies were about somewhere.

A short distance later, they reached a stream, gurgling slowly toward a small pond before continuing its journey through a lower pasture. As they stumbled to a stop, Seth laughing while she wheezed and fought for a breath, she noticed hoofprints in the mud along the bank of the stream. "Is this...part of another...pasture?"

"Yep. The cows like to drink here. See? There's one." She turned her gaze the direction he pointed and found a rather stern-looking bull glaring at them. "Oh. Uh, that's a bull, not a cow. He doesn't look too happy to see us. Maybe we should move on?"

She took Seth's hand, and they started down the stream. Tracy picked her way carefully across rocks, trying to avoid the muck, and Seth traipsed contentedly through the shallow water, getting his shoes wet and muddy. Hearing a rustling noise in the trees near them, Tracy paused and glanced toward the trees. Two more bulls wandered in the shade of the wooded area, flicking their tails. Her heart kicked. *Hoo-boy.*

Distracted by the bulls, she stumbled a bit over a rock, and Seth squeezed her hand. "Careful, Miss Tracy. Don't hurt yourself. You're too heavy for me to carry home if you fall."

She snorted a chuckle, amused by his childlike bluntness. "So now I'm old and fat?"

He giggled. "Not fat. Just big like a grown-up."

"Okay." She ruffled his hair and had it on the tip of her tongue to ask him about his favorite TV shows when she spotted another impression in the mud. A footprint—man-sized.

"We shoulda brought fishin' poles with us. Have you ever been fishin', Ms. Tracy?"

"Nope. I'm a city girl. Remember?"

"Gol-ly!" Seth dragged the word out in dismay. "Never? In your *whole life*?"

Tracy grinned at the emphasis he put behind the question, as if she was ancient and the omission from her life was nothing short of tragic. "Not that I recall. But I—"

A loud cracking sound cut her off. She was hyper-aware of the bulls around them and paused to look for the source of the sound. Though it wasn't quite right to be a limb breaking under a bull's hoof, the noise was definitely out of place and sent a tingle up her spine. If a bull charged them, what would she do? Where would they go?

Seth hadn't waited for her when she'd stopped to listen, and now she hurried over the creek bank to catch up to him. "Wait for me, Seth. I—"

She gasped as her foot slipped on the wet, mossy rocks, and she went down. In the same instant, a loud, echoing bang shattered the calm. The gravel just past her hand scattered like shrapnel. For a stunned second, she simply stared at the spot where a large shiny rifle bullet gleamed in the sun.

"Miss Tracy! Are you okay?" Seth's frightened voice reached her through her shock as he scurried back to her. "That was a gunshot! And it was close!"

She shook herself from her momentary stupor, now fueled by adrenaline. By panic.

She reached for him, needing to feel him close to her, assure herself *he* was safe. "Yeah, I—"

Another cracking sound rode the wind, and she knew immediately what it was. A rifle cocking.

"Seth!" She grabbed his shirtfront and jerked him to her. Just as she threw them both down in the mud, another blast rang out. She screamed. Seth hollered. A bull bellowed and ran away, hooves thundering.

This time, Tracy didn't squander any time on shock and disbelief. The simple truth blared in her brain. Someone was shooting at them. On purpose. Someone was trying to kill them.

Jack trudged through the bull pasture, headed toward the pond where Seth liked to fish, fuming to himself about Tracy's defiance, Seth's disobedience and Brett's continued challenge to his business decision. He wasn't against making money. He wasn't against breeding horses at the Lucky C. He just didn't want to force Daniel's hand or guilt him into staying at the ranch if he felt a calling to go elsewhere. If Daniel came to him and said he wanted—

The blast of a rifle brought Jack's head up. The nearly simultaneous scream sent a chill to his bones and jacked his heart rate into overdrive. A fist of panic squeezing his throat, he spun to race in the direction the scream had originated.

"Miss Tracy!" he heard Seth shout.

"Run, Seth!" she answered, her voice taut with fear.

Another gunshot rent the air, reverberating in Jack's chest.

Tracy yelped. "Seth! Hurry!"

Horror punched Jack's gut as a frightening realization dawned. The shots were being fired *at Tracy. At his son.* Jack darted into the line of trees, scanning the area, desperately searching for Seth. His hand went to his hip, where he found only his cell phone. He thought of the handgun back at his house, cursed the fact he didn't have it with him. He glanced at his phone as he ran through the maze of trees and underbrush, thumbing the speed dial for Brett's cell.

Another shot was fired. He heard the terrified whimper of his son.

Brett answered his phone, and as he sped toward the creek, Jack panted, "Shots fired...bull pasture...call cops... bring my gun."

Chapter 10

Tracy seized Seth's hand as she scrambled for cover. Her feet slipped on the slick creek stones, and her ankle wrenched to an awkward angle. She ignored the bolt of pain in her shin. Her only thought was of protecting Seth. Finding shelter. Getting them to safety.

"Run!" She towed the boy behind her as she stumbled toward the trees. His frightened whimpers broke her heart, but they had no time for comfort. Her brain clicked in fast-forward, trying to find the best plan of retreat, the safest place to hide. A ditch? A tree? She discarded these ideas in rapid succession, even as she squeezed Seth's hand and clambered up a muddy bank and into the trees. Another shot whizzed past them, so close she felt the heat of the bullet just before it splintered the bark of a tree beside her.

Another scream slipped from her throat, and she dropped to the leaf-strewn ground, dragging Seth with her as she scuttled behind the tree.

"Miss Tracy, I'm scared!" Seth whispered, his voice shaking as much as her hands were.

"I know, sweetie. Me, too. But we're gonna be fine." She prayed she was right about that.

Groping in her pocket, she felt for her cell phone. Could she get a signal out here to call 911? Or should she call Jack? He was closer.

But her pocket was empty. She'd lost her phone somewhere when she fell or as they'd scrambled for cover.

As she gulped in air, her gaze searched the thin line of woods that bordered the pasture. If only they were nearer to the outbuildings or an old shack or... Her breath caught. "Your tree house!"

"Huh?"

"Come on, Seth. We gotta get to your tree house. It's the only shelter we have out here."

His eyes were round with fear, but he gave her a trusting nod. Shoving herself to her feet, she led him at a sprint through the tangled weeds and branches. Thorns clawed at her, limbs slapped her cheeks and her injured ankle throbbed. But she plowed on, determined to get Seth to the relative safety of his fort.

She could hear the rustle and snap of foliage behind them as their assailant pursued them. Another gunshot fired and another. She tried to weave as she ran, making herself and Seth harder targets to hit. Finally, they skidded to a stop at the base of the homemade ladder. She lifted him up the first several rungs, strengthened by the rush of adrenaline coursing through her. "Go!" she rasped. "I'm...right behind you!"

Seth scrambled up, and she placed her feet on the first rung. Her legs shook, her hands trembled and her heart beat so hard she could barely catch her breath. In her haste, her feet fumbled once, making her slide back down a rung and sending a fresh wave of pain through her twisted ankle.

Another blast of gunfire accompanied something hot searing her back near her shoulder. She cried out, frightened more than hurt. She knew she'd been hit, knew the next bullet could hit home, knew her next breath could be her last.

"Miss Tracy!"

"Seth, stay down!" She shook off the buzzing in her ears and put one hand, one foot after the other. Climbing. Hurrying. Praying.

As she reached the floor of the tree house, she rolled away from the ladder, hunkering low and away from the wall nearest the assassin. Seth clutched at her, hugging her and crying. She pulled his head to her chest and kissed his hair as she panted for oxygen. "It's okay. We're...safe."

A bullet pinged as it hit the corrugated metal and cracked the plywood. The walls of the little tree house would protect them only for a short while. They needed help. Rescue.

Jack.

Weaving through the underbrush at full speed, Jack spotted the flash of a muzzle. He skidded to a stop and used a tree for protection as he narrowed his sights on the area where he'd seen the flare of light. Approximately fifty yards ahead, he made out the hulking form of the shooter, a lever-action rifle lifted, and his attention focused on his target. Jack's mouth dried as he spotted Tracy at the foot of the ladder to Seth's tree house. He drew a deep breath to shout a warning to her but stopped it in his throat. Rather than draw attention to himself or distract Tracy in her escape, he needed to concentrate on the man with the rifle. He had to take the bastard down.

Moving with the stealth and silence he'd learned through years of hunting, years of hiding from his younger brothers, years of exploring these very woods, Jack crept closer to the gunman. He edged one careful step at a time, moving from tree to tree, avoiding anything in his path that would give his presence away. His footfalls were quiet, but the thump of his own heartbeat in his ears sounded loud enough to wake the dead. Holding his breath, Jack slipped to the last bit of cover he'd have before making his move on the shooter.

And, as if sensing Jack's approach, the gunman whirled around. Jack lunged. He shoved the barrel of the rifle up with his left hand, even as he swung at the man's jaw with his right fist.

The shooter's head snapped back from Jack's punch, but he recovered quickly. With a two-handed grip on the rifle, he jerked the weapon from Jack's reach, then swung it in an arc that crashed into Jack's head with a blinding force. Skull throbbing, Jack staggered and fell to his knees. From his peripheral vision, he saw the man level the weapon at him. The click of the lever cocking echoed in his ears, and rolling to his butt, he swept a leg toward the back of the shooter's knees.

His opponent swayed, and though the man didn't fall, the move bought Jack the time he needed to surge to his feet. Grunting, he plowed a shoulder into the trespasser's gut. They stumbled together, Jack shoving the man until his back came up against a cottonwood tree. When the shooter tried to reaim his weapon, Jack wrapped both hands around the rifle and jammed the fore stock against the man's throat. He held the gunman trapped against the tree and struggling for a breath.

"Who are you?" Jack barked. "Why are you here? Why are you shooting at Tracy and my son?"

The man gasped for a breath but made no effort to answer. He narrowed a glare on Jack while fighting for the leverage to push the rifle away from his neck.

Jack shoved harder, snarling at the man. "Who the hell are you? Who are you working for?"

His prisoner bit out a pithy and vulgar slur. Jack silenced him by shoving harder on the rifle, until the man's face grew red from lack of air.

"Help!" Seth cried from his tree house, the fear in his tone drawing Jack's attention.

That split second of distraction was all his opponent needed to lift a knee, land a glancing blow to Jack's groin, and shove the gun away from his throat. The groin strike hurt but wasn't incapacitating. As the man twisted away, he rammed an elbow into Jack's ribs.

In return, Jack swung a fist into the gunman's jaw. And they continued to trade blows until the shooter managed to break free of Jack's grasp and fled. Though winded from their fight, Jack gave chase. He followed the man through the knee-high grass of the bull pasture to a section of cut fence. There, the gunman mounted an ATV and sped away.

Jack bent at the waist, sucking in deep gulps of oxygen as his quarry escaped.

As he hurried back across the pasture, eager to check on Seth, a prickling awareness crawled through him. Tracy was sure she'd been targeted, been pushed when she fell into traffic earlier in the week. Now a gunman had sneaked onto Lucky C property and fired at her. Two incidents in one week. This was no random act of violence. Someone was determined to kill Tracy. But Jack was just as determined to find out why...and keep her safe.

* * *

"Miss Tracy, you're bleeding!" Seth's face was unnaturally pale as he gaped at the crimson smear on his fingers.

Tracy glanced over her shoulder to the spot on her upper back that stung like fire.

No shots had been fired in several minutes, but she kept Seth pinned down, her body protecting his until she could be sure the danger had passed.

For the past several minutes, she'd been singing to him in a whisper, trying to keep him calm...and ease her own nerves.

She could hear some sort of ruckus a short distance from them, but she didn't risk giving away their position or getting shot by stealing a peek. Taking slow breaths and struggling to stay calm, she examined her wound as best she could from her vantage point. She had a growing red stain on her shirt, but she gave Seth a half smile through her pain. "It's just a graze. I'll be fine. Are you hurt?" She ran a hand over his arms, turning him to check for injuries.

He shook his head, tears blossoming in his eyes. "I want my daddy."

Me, too, sweetie. She stroked a hand over his back and closed her eyes. "We're going to be okay, Seth. I promise."

She knew she had no right to make promises that were beyond her control, but she fully intended to protect Seth, even if it cost her her own life. They huddled together for long minutes while the wind soughed in the leaves and birds twittered overhead.

Laura's little boy sniffed and clung to Tracy, then jerked his head up. "Did you hear that?"

She shook her head. "Hear what?" Tracy had been focused on her own prayers that they'd survive the attack, and on the quiet sounds of nature.

Seth wiggled away from her, and she gasped, reaching for his shirttail to stop him. "Seth, no! Stay down!"

"I heard my dad." Before she could stop him, he cupped his hands to his mouth. "Help!"

"Seth!" she whispered, tugging his sleeve. "Get down! The shooter will see you!"

"But I heard my daddy. I know I did!" The earnest plea in his eyes broke her heart.

"Seth, you—"

Then she heard what the boy had. Voices. One was definitely Jack's. A staccato beat thumped in her chest.

"Stay down." She emphasized her order with a firm hand on his shoulder. "Let me look."

When she peered over the top of the tree-house wall, she carefully scanned the woods and pasture. In the distance, she spotted two men struggling, heard the harsh tones of arguing, saw the long-barreled gun that had no doubt been the one fired at them.

Identifying Jack was easy. His tall frame, shaggy hair and tightly muscled body were as familiar to her in just a few short days as if she'd known him for years.

The second man was also large. Frighteningly so. His hair was dark, heavily streaked with gray and cropped shorter than Jack's. A shiver raced through her, and as she watched, horrified by the scene, Jack's opponent broke free and ran. Within seconds, Seth's father was in pursuit.

While she couldn't be sure the shooter didn't have an accomplice, she knew she needed to get back to the ranch and get help. For her bleeding shoulder and for Jack. He might have been ably handling the gunman, but things could turn bad quickly.

"Okay, Seth." She pressed a hand to her stomach,

where acid churned. "We need to make a run for it. Get back to your house and find help." She didn't consider herself especially brave or heroic—after all, she'd cowered at her husband's intimidation for years—but to protect Seth, she'd mine every ounce of steel in her resolve that she could.

"I don't need to see a doctor. I just need to disinfect the wound and—"

"Too late. I've already called both Eric and Ryan to meet us here."

Tracy sighed, though she appreciated Jack's concern. He and Brett had showed up at his house a few minutes after she and Seth had. Once he'd seen for himself that Seth was safe and given his son a lingering hug, he'd been on the phone to Ryan at the Tulsa Police Department, then left a message for Eric at the hospital. While Brett had taken Seth into his bedroom to distract him with a video game, Jack had helped clean Tracy's bullet wound and given her the fifth degree. Who was the shooter? Did she recognize him? What had happened, and how did they escape?

She'd tried her best to answer all his questions, knowing she'd have to repeat everything for the police when they arrived. As they waited for his brothers, Jack held a sterile bandage over the injury to her shoulder, and with constant pressure to the ragged flesh, most of the bleeding had stopped. Tracy gripped her cell phone in her hand. Jack had handed it to her when she and Seth turned up back at the house, and she assumed he had found it in the woods.

His phone buzzed with a text from Eric saying he was headed into surgery and couldn't come.

"Good," Tracy said. "He won't be wasting a trip out here."

"Then we'll meet him at the ER again."

She growled in frustration. "Jack, I don't need a trauma surgeon for a little cut. You're the one who should be getting medical help!" She met Jack's gaze in the bathroom mirror. Already his right eye was purpling from a bruise, and his jaw and knuckles had swollen. Lord only knew what other injuries he hid under his T-shirt.

He waved her off. "I've had worse and survived. Don't worry about me."

"I've had worse, too," she told him, and his gaze darkened with understanding.

A deep voice called down the hall from his front room. "Jack? Where are you?"

"We'll be right there," he called back, still holding her stare. "That's Ryan." When Jack finally tore his lingering gaze away, he jerked open the cabinet and took a tube from the shelf. "Let me apply some antibiotic before we go out there."

She nodded and turned her injured shoulder to him. He dabbed the cool cream on her wound with gentle strokes, pausing to blow on the sting when she winced in pain, much the way she'd doctored Seth's wound more than a week ago.

When they met his brother in the living room a few minutes later, she took a seat on the sofa and carefully recounted the events of the afternoon. After she was finished, Jack gave his statement, detailing his description of the shooter.

"I'll arrange for a sketch artist to meet with you later today so we can get a composite together for the department," Ryan told his brother.

"Jack," Tracy said, a tremor low in her belly, "your

description sounds a lot like the one that woman gave of the guy who pushed me in town last week."

His jaw tightened and his eyes narrowed on her. "I thought of that."

"Whoa," Ryan said, eyeing them both. "What guy? Was there another incident like this?"

Taking a deep breath for patience and calm, Tracy explained to him about the man who'd pushed her into traffic. "And before you ask, I don't know why he would have done it. Jack already asked all those questions last week, and I have no answers."

Jack stroked his sore jaw and divided a look between Ryan and Tracy. "Whether she knows why or not, she's become someone's target. Someone wants her dead."

Tracy's already pale skin grew even more ghostly white. She closed her eyes slowly, and her shoulders drooped. Her nod was subtle and defeated, and Jack's gut wrenched. The urge to swallow her in his embrace and chase away the shadows of vulnerability in her expression nearly knocked him over.

"Sounds that way. In law enforcement, we don't believe in coincidence," Ryan said, folding his arms over his chest as he planted his feet in a wide stance. "I'll do everything I can to find out who is behind this and why, but I'll need your complete honesty and cooperation."

Tracy raised a startled look to Ryan. "I *have* been honest."

"But have you been completely forthcoming? I get the feeling there is something you are not telling us."

Jack had had the same sense many times with Tracy, but he didn't voice that opinion now. He simply watched the fragile-looking woman shrink farther into the cushions of his couch.

Tracy twisted the ring on her right hand with her left,

staring at her lap in silence for several minutes. Ryan said nothing, in turn. He let Tracy stew and the silence drag on. Jack was familiar with the interrogation technique. Eventually, the pressure of the quiet, the expectant and patient stare his brother had mastered, would crack even a hardened criminal.

Finally, she sighed and said softly, "The car accident that killed Laura happened when I was fleeing my marriage, running away from my husband."

"Running away?" Ryan repeated. "Why?"

But the truth was obvious. Jack had suspected it from the day he'd met Tracy and questioned her in the barn about her motives regarding Seth.

"He was violent. And...verbally abusive."

Even though he'd been expecting this truth, hearing it confirmed sent a blaze of fury and disgust through Jack. His hands fisted, itching to slam into a man he'd never met but loathed just the same.

"Laura had finally convinced me to leave him," Tracy continued, in a voice that shook with shame and regret. "She'd promised to help me find a new place to live, get a job and change my name." Tracy paused for a breath and knuckled away the moisture at the corner of her eye. Jack called on all his inner strength not to scoop her into his arms and kiss the tears away.

"But Cliff found out what was happening...somehow. He came home from work early. He showed up at the house just as we were leaving. Laura was driving. He chased us, and we ended up on a twisty road in the foothills not far from our house. He forced us off the road, then his car crashed into the guardrail. He was unconscious until the cops revived him and arrested him. Laura...was killed instantly."

"And you?" Jack asked, feeling tension vibrate in him like a tuning fork.

"I had a broken collarbone and internal bleeding. The air bag left bruising on my face." She frowned and waved her injuries away as if they were nothing. "My injuries don't matter, not compared to the price Laura paid to help me." She dropped her face to her hands, and her shoulders shook as she sobbed. "My only comfort is knowing she didn't suffer. The coroner said her neck broke. She died instantly. But it's my fault. She was saving me from a marriage I should have left years earlier."

"I'm not sure I see how this is relevant to what happened today," Jack said. "You told me Cliff was killed in prison."

"He was."

He flipped a palm up. "Then it clearly wasn't him who was shooting at you today."

She tipped her head, conceding the point. "No, but you asked what I had been keeping from you." She twisted her fingers together, fidgeting. "I didn't want to tell you about my marriage when I arrived because I wasn't looking for sympathy. And, to be honest, I'm still a little ashamed that I stayed with Cliff as long as I did. More ashamed that Laura died helping to free me from him."

Jack and Ryan exchanged a look.

"And?" Jack prompted.

Her brow furrowed. "And what? That's it. I've been completely open and truthful about everything else."

Ryan tapped a pen against a small notepad, his gaze hard and probing. "If someone is targeting you, as we believe, then there must be something in your past—"

"No," she said, shaking her head vehemently. "I really can't think of anything."

Jack paced to the window with a growing sense of

disquiet roiling through him. Knowing that somebody was trying to kill Tracy was bad enough, but not knowing who was gunning for her, not knowing where the threat was coming from, made the situation all the more untenable. Jack didn't do uncertainty. He hated feeling exposed. And he loathed the idea of someone innocent being harmed on his watch.

The primitive instinct to protect Tracy that had been simmering inside Jack since he met her roared to life. Despite any qualms or doubts he might still have about her, he knew he had to step up the safeguards around her, and he couldn't delegate the job of protecting her to anyone else.

"There's no one who has a personal beef against you or a legal dispute?" Ryan pressed, and Jack turned back to the room, eyeing the petite woman on the couch with renewed determination to keep her safe.

Tracy sat straighter, meeting his brother's gaze evenly. "I'm not the sort of person who goes through life making enemies at every turn. In fact, before today, I'd say the person with the most animosity toward me was you, Jack."

Ryan raised his dark eyebrows and shot his brother an openly questioning glance. "What's this?"

Guilt tripped through him, and Jack waved off his brother's curiosity. "My issues with Tracy have nothing to do with the shooter today. Just…personal business." He narrowed a hard look at Tracy, not quite ready to believe she wasn't still protecting a secret. "Is there anyone with something to gain if you were gone?"

"No. No one. Nothing," she repeated firmly, as she shook her head again.

"When Cliff died, did you inherit a large estate?" Ryan asked.

Her shoulders sagged, proof that she was growing weary of their questions. "He had a life-insurance policy, and we had some savings, but not enough that I would think it was worth murdering me over."

"So you don't think his family might be behind this?"

"Well," Tracy said, then hesitated, "there was no love lost between me and his parents. I think Cliff poisoned them against me soon after our marriage. They didn't think I was good enough for their little boy. In fact, his mother made many comments about how she thought Cliff would be better off without me." Her tone and expression made clear how this opinion hurt her. "But...I can't see Mrs. Baxter as a murderer."

"And his father?" Jack asked.

"I—" Tracy rubbed her forehead and closed her eyes. "I don't know. What would he have to gain from hurting me? This is all just so bizarre to me."

"Well, we can certainly start with Cliff's parents. I'll contact the Denver police department and have the Baxters questioned." Ryan flipped his small notebook closed and stashed it in his shirt pocket. "If you think of anything else let me know."

Tracy nodded wearily. "I will." With what seemed a tremendous effort, she pushed to her feet, swaying slightly. "So...it looks like you win, Jack. Clearly, I can't stay here if my presence is going to bring the threat to Seth and the rest of your family. I'll go back to the main house and pack my things to leave."

An uneasy thrumming started low in Jack's belly. "Sit down."

She angled a startled glance at him. "Wh—"

He aimed a finger at the couch. "You're not going anywhere."

Chapter 11

Tracy blinked at him, incredulous. "Excuse me?"

"I can't in good conscience let you leave the ranch knowing that there's a threat against you. In fact, I don't want you staying at the main house any longer. I want you where I can keep an eye on you." When she lifted an eyebrow in consternation, he added, "In order to protect you, not because I don't trust you."

"Does that mean you trust me now?"

Jack glanced away as if weighing his words. "Let's just say...I believe you have Seth's best interests in mind. He told me how you protected him when the shooting started, how you sang to him to calm him."

She flipped up a palm. "He's a little boy. I did what anyone would do."

"Maybe. But you took care of him, even at your own risk..." He tightened his mouth and held her gaze. "And I don't take that lightly."

Jack moved to the coatrack and took down his Stetson.

"When you're ready, I'll go back up to the main house with you and help you move your things."

"Jack, I'm not your responsibility." Tracy shook her head, surprising him with the starch in her back and the defiance in her tone. "I really think the best thing would be for me to leave the Lucky C. I don't want to put anyone in danger."

He glanced at Ryan, who lifted his eyebrows and gave him a mild this-is-your-fight-not-mine look. Jack's returned glare said, *Thanks for nothing, man.*

When Jack faced Tracy, he tried to maintain a calm, reasonable tone. "By leaving, you'd put *yourself* in danger. Is that what you want?" He shoved his hat on his head, then slid his fingers into his front jeans pockets. "Here on the ranch, you have a whole staff of ranch hands, not to mention Brett, Big J, Daniel and myself. There's not a one of us Coltons that's not a top-notch marksman." Surely she couldn't argue with that logic.

Tracy looked from Jack to Ryan and back again. "I appreciate everything you're doing for me, and I'll do anything I can to help catch the shooter. But I couldn't stand it if something happened to one of you because of me. Especially if something happened to Seth."

"It's my job to protect my son, and that's what I'm going to do." Jack infused his tone with the finality that ended arguments with his son, but Tracy persisted.

"We got lucky today, and he wasn't hurt. But if that man comes after me again…" Instead of finishing the thought, she nibbled her bottom lip and creased her brow.

Jack squared his shoulders, trying to ignore the heat that threaded through him as he watched her abuse her lip. He wanted to taste that mouth and knew he could distract her from her worries with a deep, lingering kiss. Clearing his throat, he growled, "If anyone comes after you again, I intend to be there. I'm making it my business to keep you safe until the shooter is caught." He paused and narrowed his gaze. "If you'd done as I asked about not spending time alone with Seth, I'd have been with you when the shooting started."

He knew he sounded peevish, but he didn't care. He'd been scared out of his wits earlier today when he'd thought about something happening to Seth. That same fear curled through him when he thought of the shooter gunning for Tracy, of the vicious ape returning to finish the job.

Her shoulders drooped in defeat, and she lowered her gaze to her lap. "All right, I'll stay."

Ryan opened the front door to leave.

"But—"

Ryan paused, and Jack groaned internally. He should have known she'd have conditions. He was in no mood to bargain, but he rested his hands on his hips and turned back to the couch. "But what?"

"As you said, Brett and Big J are skilled marksmen, and at the main house, I'll have them *and* the staff for protection. I'm settled there. There's no need to move me."

Except that *he* wanted to oversee her protection. Jack felt an overwhelming personal link to her, a duty to keep her safe, and a strange premonition that if he didn't take charge of her protection, something awful would happen to her. He didn't want to delegate this to his aging father and womanizing younger brother. Jack gritted his back teeth.

Ryan cleared his throat, and his eyebrow lifted as he moved out the door. "Jack, Tracy, I'll leave you two to figure out the logistics of your lodging. Meantime, I'll be down at the station making arrangements for a sketch artist and calling my Denver contacts." His gaze focused on Jack. "Meet me at my office soon as you can. We have work to do, and if I can arrange it with Denver, I'm going to fly up to assist with interviewing the Baxters."

Jack stiffened. "Tell me when you get that arranged. I'll go with you."

Ryan shook his head. "This is a police matter. You don't need to go."

"Maybe I don't need to, but I am going."

Ryan grunted. "If anyone should go with me, Tracy should. The Baxters are her in-laws."

Jack turned and narrowed a hard look on the fragile woman sitting on his couch. "You're right. We'll both go."

Tracy jerked her head up, her eyes wide with dismay, as his brother grated, "Hell, no. That wasn't my point. I wasn't inviting her to go."

"Maybe not, but she should be there. She may be able to give us valuable information during the interview, help us redirect our questioning or tell us when they are flat out lying."

Ryan poked Jack in the chest with his index finger. "What's all this 'us' business? Did you not hear me say that this is a police matter? The last time I checked, you don't carry a badge."

"Ryan, that sonofabitch took a shot at my son, on my property. I am going. And considering somebody seems to have a beef against Miss McCain, I intend to bring her with us. Not only will she be helpful during the interview, I can do a better job of protecting her if I keep her close."

"Excuse me," Tracy said, rising to her feet and sounding more than a little miffed. "Don't I get a say in this?"

Jack shot her another hard look. "Of course you do. The question boils down to whether you want to be of assistance catching the shooter like you said…or not."

She raised her chin a notch and pressed her lips in a thin line. "You know I want him caught."

"Then I guess you are going with me to Denver."

"Jack—" Ryan began, his face dark.

"Are you going to lock me in a cell down at the police station, Detective? Because that's the only way you're going to stop me. You have my word that I won't interfere with the official investigation, but I need to be there."

Ryan held his glare for several taut seconds. Finally, with an exasperated sigh, he shook his head and said, "Fine. Fly to Denver if you are so damn determined. But so help me, if you step one foot across the line during this investigation, I *will* lock you in a holding cell. *Capisce?*"

Jack jerked a nod. "Yeah, I understand."

After Ryan left for the police station, Tracy stayed at Jack's house. Even though he had already treated the wound on her shoulder and she had no good reason to linger, the thought of returning to the main house with all its cold marble and numerous large empty rooms left her oddly out of sorts. Brett wouldn't be back from the pastures yet and Greta was out of town, and she didn't look forward to sitting alone in the vast mansion. She much preferred the warm decor and cozy feel of Jack's ranch house. And if she were honest with herself, she felt safer being close to Jack. The crack of the shooter's rifle still echoed in her mind, sending rippling chills to her core.

Using the excuse that she felt a bit dizzy, she'd stayed to rest on the couch in Jack's family room. She managed to take a short nap, though her rest was fitful and filled with dreams of wild animals chasing her through the woods, their large teeth flashing and snapping at her.

When she woke, her forehead was damp with a cold sweat. She sat up and found that a lightweight afghan had been laid across her legs. The mantel clock read 6:30 p.m., and the scent of roasting beef told her Jack had already started dinner. Folding the crocheted blanket and draping it over the back of the sofa, she went in search of Seth and his father.

The tinny music and beeps of a video game led her to the living room, where Seth was engrossed in a cartoon car race, his thumbs flying over his game controller like a teenager texting gossip to his best friend. On the couch next to him, the barn cat—Sleekie, Seth had called her—slept curled into in ball. As she watched, Seth reached over and gave Sleekie a pat, and the feline woke to roll on her back and stretch, showing her fuzzy belly.

Tracy couldn't resist rubbing the cat's furry tummy, then ruffling Seth's hair. Sleekie chirped a greeting, but the little boy didn't even look up. Quirking a lopsided grin, she found her way down the short hall to Jack's study. She knocked softly on the door frame, and he lifted his head from his perusal of his laptop screen.

"Hi. Did you sleep okay?" Jack leaned back in his chair and laced his fingers together as he rested his hands against his chest.

"About as well as can be expected, I suppose, considering someone tried to kill me this afternoon." She stepped into the office and let her gaze take in the wood paneling and wall of bookshelves. Jack's desk sat in a corner of the room by a window, outside of which the early summer sun was sinking low on the horizon, casting the world in a golden glow. A highball glass with about an inch of amber liquid and ice sat on the corner of his desk near where he worked. The glass sweated, and condensation rolled down to puddle on a coaster.

"Are you hungry? I put a meat loaf in the oven a little while ago, and you're welcome to stay and eat with us."

Meat loaf was far from her favorite food, but sharing a meal with Jack and Seth sounded better to her than anything she might find to eat at the main house. She nodded and sent him a grateful smile. "Thank you. I'd love to. Is there anything I can do to help get dinner ready?"

"Now that you mention it, I was going to make a salad, but I got engrossed with what I was doing here."

"One salad coming up," she said, glad to have something useful to occupy herself.

"You should find all the vegetables you need in the refrigerator crisper." He told her where to find a chopping board and the knives she would need, then checked his watch. "The meat should be done in about twenty minutes. Give me a shout if you need any help."

Tracy returned to the kitchen and had a salad full of fresh summer vegetables ready ten minutes later. She peeked in the oven, checking on their entrée, before she went back down the hall to Jack's study.

She paused in the doorway and watched Jack sip his liquor for a moment without calling attention to her presence. Even small details about this man mesmerized her, enchanted her. He was every inch a man's man. His Adam's apple bobbed as he swallowed, drawing her attention to the muscled column of his neck and the small whorl of dark hair at the open V of his shirt. His long blunt-tipped fingers curled around his glass, and she imagined them stroking her. After he sipped his drink again, he licked a drop from the corner of his mouth. The sight of his moistened lips, his agile tongue, stirred more erotic images in her brain, and she caught a groan in her throat, stifling her lust.

But Jack must have sensed her attention, because without preamble, he said, "I've been doing a little checking on your ex in-laws."

"Oh?"

He waved her into the office and pointed to a chair, directing her to take a seat.

Wiping her palms on the legs of her jeans, she stepped into the room and perched on the edge of the high-backed chair he indicated. She clasped her hands in her lap and angled her head to see the computer screen. "Anything interesting?"

"I'll say. Did you know that Cliff's parents have business ties with Tony Rossetto?"

Tracy crumpled her nose in confusion. "No. Is that significant?"

"You don't know the name?"

"Should I?"

Jack laced his fingers behind his head and leaned back, making springs in his chair creak. "Maybe not, if you've been living under a rock recently."

She pulled a face and sent him a you're-not-funny glare. "Just tell me who he is. Why is it significant that Cliff's parents have ties to him?"

"Tony Rossetto stood trial in federal court last year for extortion, fraud, tax evasion, intimidation...and those are just the charges they could prove. I'm sure they wanted to try him for murder, money laundering and God knows what else. In short, he's a real bad dude, and even a preliminary search of public records shows that Cliff's parents were invested in a number of business operations that Rossetto also had his fingers in."

Tracy stared at Jack for a moment, trying to come to grips with what she was learning. "Th-that doesn't mean anything. Lots of people have the misfortune of investing with partners who prove to be bad apples. It doesn't make them criminals."

Jack snorted a humorless laugh. "Tony Rossetto is more than a bad apple. He's organized crime."

Chapter 12

Organized crime. Tracy's mouth dried. "You mean, like, the Mafia?"

He arched a dark eyebrow. "Not all organized crime is Mafia, but you get the gist." When his cell phone buzzed, he unclipped it from his belt and checked the caller ID. "It's Ryan. Hang on a minute, while I tell him what I've found, okay?"

She nodded numbly, too stunned by Jack's revelation to do more than gape. The Baxters had links to organized crime? She'd known they were wealthy and powerful in the business world, but she'd never imagined their sphere of influence came through illicit means. And while Cliff had been aggressive and cruel to her, she had a hard time imagining her ex-husband, who was so scrupulous about obeying traffic laws and abiding by neighborhood ordinances, being so bold as to flout the law in business matters.

You really are naive, aren't you? she could imagine Cliff saying with a sneer. A shiver ran through her, and she balled her hands into fists.

While Jack conducted a conversation in low tones with his brother, Tracy gathered her composure and forced herself to face facts. Cliff had not been the man she'd thought he was when she married him, and clearly, his parents had been just as deceitful.

Knowing how blind she'd been, a weighty sense of defeat pressed down on her. She slumped back in the chair and pressed her thumbs against her closed eyes. Was it possible that Cliff's parents were behind the attack on her yesterday? A greasy ball of guilt churned in her gut. She could never forgive herself if something happened to one of the Coltons from a danger she'd brought to the Lucky C.

"Tracy?" Jack's voice seeped through her thoughts on some level, but it wasn't until he grasped her wrist and shook her arm with a loud, "Tracy!" that she jolted from her fretting with a gasp.

"What?" She lurched upright in the chair, her gaze flying to Jack's worried frown.

"Are you all right?"

"I…yeah."

He leaned back, propping his elbows on his armrests and pressing his fingertips together. "Where did you go just then? I've been trying to get your attention for a full minute."

"Nowhere good," she mumbled, letting her shoulders slouch. Tipping a side glance up at him, she braced herself for more bad news. "What did Ryan say?"

"He's looking into the connections I found and will do more digging into the Baxters' business associates.

For now, you and I need to work out some ground rules to keep you safe."

"I still say, if there's a threat against me, I should leave the ranch. How can I stay on, knowing I could be putting the rest of you in danger?"

He drew a deep breath and expelled it slowly through his lips, allowing his cheeks to puff out. He lifted his glass for a sip before saying, "Try to see things from my point of view. How can I let you leave the ranch knowing you're in danger? That'd be like sending a lamb into a forest full of wolves. I'm not that callous."

"Jack, I appreciate your wanting to protect me, b—"

"Good." He set his drink on the coaster again, and the ice rattled as it settled. "Then we'll consider the matter closed." His level gaze brooked no resistance, and she was secretly relieved to acquiesce. Though she didn't like Jack's high-handedness—she'd had quite enough of that with Cliff—she hadn't been looking forward to going it alone while there was a killer stalking her. A jittery sense of unrest danced through her. She'd thought she was free of Cliff. Hadn't Laura paid the ultimate price in order to win Tracy freedom from this fear? The notion that her poor choice of husband could still be haunting her, putting other people at risk, was more than a little unsettling.

Unable to remain still, she rose to pace Jack's office. Distraction. She needed to think about something other than Cliff's disapproving parents, the crack of the shooter's rifle and the heart-wrenching sound of Seth's frightened sobs. Swallowing hard, she waved an unsteady finger at the room in general, asking, "Mind if I take a look around?"

He shrugged and bent over the laptop. "Knock yourself out."

With an encompassing glance, she cataloged the decor, the items Jack chose to surround himself with as he worked. She wanted to build a better mental image of who he was. As expected, he had numerous pictures of Seth at various ages scattered around the room, and she lifted one of a laughing toddler. Touched, she grinned back at the cherubic face. "Seth was a cute baby."

Jack gave a quiet hum that she took as agreement. When she glanced his way, she found his attention locked on the computer screen. His intent focus on the device reminded her of Seth's single-minded attention to his video game. *Like father, like son.*

As she moved on around the room, she trailed her fingers lightly over dusty book covers with titles by John Jakes, agriculture manuals and basic reference books—a dictionary, a thesaurus and a Farmer's Almanac—all with well-creased spines. She found the bottle of Kentucky bourbon, no doubt what he was drinking now, on a tray with an ice bucket and extra highball glasses.

"Help yourself. I'm sure after the day you've had, a drink might help calm you."

She shook her head. "Thanks, but I took something for pain. I'd best not add alcohol to the mix."

She continued her tour and found that his bookcase held a few rodeo trophies. Also not surprising. She recalled him mentioning his early start in the rodeo when they'd watched Daniel teaching Seth to ride around barrels.

She read the plaques at the base of the trophies. First Place, Bull Riding. First Place, Calf Roping. Second Place, Bull Riding. Her heart skipped as she imaged Jack in a rodeo arena, astride a bucking bull or charging after a calf on his horse, lariat raised. Dusty chaps and well-worn boots. Faded jeans and sweat…

Her mouth dried, and she shook her head to clear it. *Don't go there*, she warned herself. *You came to get to know Seth, not to fall for his father.*

Moving on, she noticed knickknacks made from re-purposed horseshoes, and a small box decorated with Magic Markers and glued-on macaroni. A formal framed portrait of all of the Colton siblings, minus Daniel, also held a prominent spot on the bookshelves. Her heart gave a sympathetic tug for Daniel, remembering how hurt he'd looked at Greta's party when Big J had excluded mention of him. Poor Daniel. She sighed as she studied the handsome faces, the similar smiles, the matching green eyes—although Greta's were much more hazel than her brothers'. The family dynamic was none of her business.

A tingle on the back of her neck told her Jack was watching her, even before he said, "That was taken three years ago as a Christmas present for our mother. She wouldn't have appreciated Daniel being in the shot."

She whipped her head around, startled that he'd so clearly read in her expression or body language where her thoughts had been. While his explanation gave the why behind Daniel's exclusion, it didn't soften the sympathetic ache for Jack's half brother.

"Daniel would be the first to tell you he's not looking for sympathy. He knows we count him as one of our own, regardless of Abra's opinion," Jack said, again reading her mind. But having seen Daniel's downcast face last week, she wondered how well Jack really knew his half brother's feelings about his place in the family.

Deciding it wasn't her place to argue the point, she gave Jack a nod of assent and strolled to the other side of the room as Jack got back to work. A glance at her watch told her the timer on the oven should be dinging in another two minutes.

She approached a glass-topped wood cabinet with ornate carvings on the face of the drawers, and she spied another picture that caught her eye. She picked up the small photo for a closer look. The man in the photo wore a white protective outfit and had a helmet with a face screen tucked under his arm. At first she thought the man was Ryan, due to the short hair, but upon closer inspection she realized it was Jack. The clothing seemed familiar, and she groped mentally to figure out what she was seeing. She turned back to Jack. "Do you keep bees?"

He raised his gaze, his forehead dented in confusion. "Bees?"

She angled the photo for him to see what she'd found. "Isn't this a beekeeper's protective suit you're wearing?"

He arched one eyebrow and chuckled softly. "No. It's fencing gear."

Jack couldn't have surprised her more if he'd tried. "Fencing?"

"You've heard of it, right?"

"Well, yeah. It's a sport. It's…sword fighting."

A disgruntled noise rumbled from his throat. "Maybe in the broadest terms. Sword fighting is about battle. Strength and physicality. The biomechanics of how to disarm and maim your opponent before they slice you up."

She winced at the brutal-sounding descriptive, and her bullet wound gave a throb of protest.

"Fencing," he continued as he pushed his chair back and crossed the floor to her, "is more civil. It's about subtle movements and skill." He took the picture from her and studied it himself. "This was taken at a tournament in New Hampshire. I was seventeen."

She'd started her prowl of the office hoping to learn

more about Jack but never thought she'd uncover such an intriguing tidbit. She lifted the corner of her mouth in amazement. "How in the world did a cowboy like you get interested in fencing?"

"Oh, I didn't care a fig about fencing when I started." Down the hall, the timer on the oven buzzed. He aimed a thumb toward the hall. "But I guess that story will have to keep."

She caught his arm as he turned to leave the room. "No, please. I want to hear it now. Dinner will keep a few more minutes."

"All right, but if your meat loaf is dry, remember... you asked."

"A risk I'm willing to take." She sent him a lopsided smile and leaned her back against the glass-topped cabinet.

Jack set the picture down and rubbed a hand against his stubble-dusted chin. "Well, let's see. When I was a kid, I wanted to be a pirate."

Startled by his explanation, she gave an indelicate snort of a laugh, earning an arched-eyebrow glance from him. "I'm sorry." She waved her fingers, indicating he should continue. "You were saying?"

"It started when I was ten, and I watched an Errol Flynn movie with Big J." Jack's deep voice warmed to his subject, and Tracy realized she was getting a rare peek beneath the tough surface of the normally taciturn cowboy. "All that swashbuckling appealed to the rambunctious kid I was. I spent months battling my brothers with plastic swords and broomsticks...pretty much anything I could find. Our nanny got tired of the inevitable roughhousing that would result— Eric and Ryan both thought wrestling was the best way to deal with my pirate obsession—so she told Big J to find me a better outlet for my new interest. Thing is, public schools in Oklahoma just don't teach sword fighting, and the closest he could come was fencing. Even then he had to drive me to Oklahoma City for private lessons. Like I said, fencing is similar to sword fighting, but it didn't quite satisfy me."

"Not swashbuckler-y enough for you, huh?"

"Something like that. I was looking for something more physical, more challenging. Well, Big J could tell I'd never really given up my first love, my real interest, so when he found these at an auction—" He nudged her aside with his hip and stepped up to the cabinet. Thumbing a latch open, he lifted the glass top "—he bought them for me."

Tracy peered down into the chest, where a pair of ornate swords were nestled in a red velvet bed, their blades crossed. She drew a sharp breath. "Oh, my word! Those are beautiful!"

She angled her head to glance up at Jack, and an unquestionable pride gleamed in the eyes. "Eighteenth-century small swords. They're from France. See the inscription here?" He tapped the engraved hilt of one sword, and she leaned closer for a better look.

"*L'Honneur ou la mort*," she read aloud. "Honor in death?"

"Close. Honor or death."

"Oh, right. My high school French is rusty."

"Anyway, the guy selling the swords asked Big J if he was a collector. Big J explained my interest in sword fighting, and the guy hooked me up with a friend of his who had trained in actual sword fighting."

"And you were able to take lessons from him?"

"For a while, yes. Meanwhile, I'd also gotten involved in the rodeo."

Her gaze traveled to the trophies on the shelf next to the horseshoe art.

"Bull riding and calf roping," she said, remembering the inscriptions on the awards.

His eyes widen briefly in surprise. "How did you—?" Without finishing the question, he turned and let his eyes follow hers. "Oh. Right. Anyway, rodeo started taking most of my time. For one thing, it had practical applications on the ranch. And that's where my friends all spent most of their time, and—" he cut a quick glance at her, his expression sly "—that's where the buckle bunnies were."

She wrinkled her nose. "I'm sorry? Buckle bunnies?"

His lips twitched. "Women. Rodeo groupies." He lifted one of the swords from the case, resting the blade carefully in one palm, the grip in his other while he stroked a thumb along the hilt. "When you're a testosterone-driven teenager, one thing always trumped all, and the buckle bunnies were happy to oblige."

Tracy felt her cheeks sting with a blush. "Took advantage of the admiring fans, did you?"

His eyebrows dipped. "Depends on what you mean by 'took advantage.' I was hellion in the past, no doubt about it. But Big J raised me to respect women. To know *no* meant *no*. I never preyed on a girl's vulnerabilities." He paused and handed her the sword. "But I never lacked for a date when I wanted one, either."

As she accepted the antique weapon, something deep inside Tracy squirmed uneasily at the thought of Jack with all those other women. Laura had told her Jack had been rather wild and sowing his oats before they married. As much as Laura had been suffocated by ranch life, Jack had chafed at the confines of marriage early on. Jack's attitude had changed when Seth was born.

Tracy kept these tidbits of insider information Laura

had shared to herself, though she found it hard to reconcile the image of Jack as an adrenaline-loving, risk-taking womanizer with the quiet, doting father and responsible rancher/businessman. Greta had said Laura broke Jack's heart, but had their divorce also broken his spirit?

"All of this work was done by hand, by an artisan in Paris around the time of the French Revolution." Jack's voice pulled her out of her thoughts as he waved a finger to the scrolled knuckle guard and elaborate engraving on the hilt.

She weighed the weapon in her hands. "It's heavy. Hard to imagine anyone wielding something like this as a weapon."

"But they did. The chinks here and here—" he pointed to the spots on the blade he meant "—are signs of use." He furrowed his brow as if in deep thought. "I like to imagine the circumstances of the battle or duel that put those chinks there." He scoffed lightly in dismissal. "Oh, well… That meat is getting drier by the minute."

He lifted the sword from her hands and placed it back in the velvet bedding.

"Have you ever used them? You know, for fun. A mock duel or whatever?"

"Not these. They're too valuable. But I have another small sword I use when I have time to indulge my hobby."

"Thank you…for showing these to me. They really are magnificent." She shook her head and grinned. "I'd never have guessed you had an interest in something so…unusual."

He lowered the top of the cabinet and paused with his hand resting on the display glass. "I'm not sure if I should feel insulted or complimented." He cast a side glance and cocked one eyebrow. "Are you saying you thought I was mundane?"

Hearing the teasing note in his tone, she laughed and curled her hand around his arm. "No…gosh, no! I'd never say that about you. I only meant…you were largely a mystery to me when I arrived, and what I've discovered about you this week has been…surprising."

He cocked his head. "As in, still waters run deep?"

His voice was as smooth and intoxicating as aged whiskey, and it rolled through her with a heady warmth. "Something like that."

When she started to remove her hand from his forearm, he covered it and wrapped his fingers around hers. "I have to admit, you've surprised me a bit, too."

Tracy was so startled by his touch, so enthralled by the scrape of his calloused palm against her skin, that she needed a moment to catch her breath. Heart thrashing in her chest, she croaked, "Oh? How?"

"You're tougher than I gave you credit for." His thumb stroked her wrist with the same gentle fondness he'd employed when he'd admired the decorative hilt. A low buzzing sounded in her ears, the sound of her blood pumping harder, faster in response to his mesmerizing touch and rumbling voice. "My first impression of you was that you were fragile. Like a doll that would break under pressure. But I realize now I was judging your character based on your appearance."

She forced her throat to swallow despite her rapidly drying mouth and worked to flash a smile that didn't tremble. "Now I'm not sure if I should feel insulted or complimented. You thought of me as a doll?"

He tugged her hand to bring her closer as he faced her and raised his free hand to her cheek. "A china doll, yes. Because you have that sort of delicate beauty. Big, innocent blue eyes and skin so pale I can see your veins." He tracked one of those veins in her throat with a fingertip, then lifted the same finger to brush her lips. "And a rosebud mouth."

Jack's voice had grown even softer, and his eyelids lowered as he focused on her lips. He dipped his head toward hers, nudging her chin up with a thumb as he cradled her cheek. Tracy's breath stuttered from her. She canted toward him, drawn to him by a force more powerful than common sense. She felt the moist heat of his breath as he exhaled a sigh of resignation, and angled his head—

"Dad?" Seth bellowed a fraction of a second before he crashed through the office door. "When's dinner? I'm starving!"

Tracy gasped and stumbled guiltily back a step. Disappointment speared her. Of all the bad timing! Or maybe it was providential that Seth had interrupted when he did. Becoming involved with her cousin's ex had never been part of her plan when she came to the Lucky C.

"We'll be in there in a minute. Meanwhile, you wash up and set the table." Jack's tone held none of the irritation or frustration that vibrated through her for their lost moment. When she turned a side glance to him, only the hint of color in his cheeks and dark pools of his pupils gave any indication how close they'd come to kissing.

Seth divided a look between the adults, then shrugged. "Okay."

"Hey! Turn the oven off, too. Okay, Spud?" Jack called as Seth trooped out.

Finally catching her breath, Tracy moved toward the door, pressing a shaky palm to the swirl of jitters and unsatisfied lust in her belly. "I'll help him."

But Jack caught her arm, stopping her. "There's something else you should know about me, Tracy."

She met his heated gaze, and her heart flip-flopped.

He drew her close again with a firm grip on her arm and a guiding hand at her hip. "I finish what I start."

With that, he captured her lips with his.

Chapter 13

Jack pulled her body flush to the whipcord strength and lean muscle of his, and Tracy's knees buckled as desire stampeded through her. Only his arm around her waist, cinching her to him, kept her upright. Once the shock of his kiss faded, heady sensations rolled through her and pooled low in her belly. A tiny mewl of pleasure escaped her throat, and she slid her arms around his neck, relaxing in his embrace.

Her fingers curled into the hair that brushed his collar. The silky wisps tickled her palm, while the stubble of his chin scraped lightly against her cheeks. His kiss tasted like the bourbon he'd been sipping, and his skin smelled like sweet hay, mellow leather and sensual man.

Jack took command of the kiss, holding her head pinioned with one hand splayed at her nape. While her body wallowed blissfully in his skill and seduction, a small voice in her head whispered a warning. Cliff had been demanding, unyielding, overbearing. His tyranny had become the source of her terror. *Don't make the same mistake*, her brain whispered.

Jack must have sensed the shift in her thoughts, because he broke their kiss and peered down at her. "You can tell me to go to hell if this isn't what you want."

"No, I—" Her voice cracked, and a tiny tremor shimmied through her. "You just…surprised me."

"Did I?" His fingers pushed a lock of her hair that had escaped her ponytail behind her ear. "Are you going to tell me you haven't felt the undercurrent of heat between us since the day you showed up at Greta's party?"

"I—" She swallowed audibly. She wasn't going to lie to him. Especially since she'd so obviously enjoyed his kiss. And because she desperately wanted his trust. "I have. I just…didn't want my purpose for being here, my wish to know Seth, to get tangled up in what I was feeling toward you."

"And I didn't want my desire for you to cloud my judgment of your purpose. But you showed me today—" he whispered as he trailed kisses along the line of her jaw and throat "—that you have an incredible core of strength. No matter how fragile…your appearance, you proved…you are no pushover."

Though his compliment warmed her heart, her gut tightened. She squeezed her eyes closed, feeling like a fraud. "I didn't feel strong," she admitted. "I felt horribly vulnerable." She tightened her grip around his shoulders as the chilling horror of those moments washed through her again. She buried her head under his chin, her ear pressed to his breastbone and shivered. "I did what I had to to protect Seth, but…I was scared to death."

Beneath her cheek, a hum of acknowledgment rumbled in his chest, and his arms tightened around her. "Fear doesn't determine your courage and inner strength. What you do in the face of fear does."

He angled his body away and tipped her head up with a hand under her chin. "Based on what you've said about your ex, I'd say you also showed that inner strength by breaking away from him."

She gave her head a little shake. "I couldn't have done it without Laura. She helped me get away, in so many ways. Not just by driving the car that day..." She let her voice trail off. The usual roil of unrest swirled through her, remembering Laura's death in the car accident, the high-speed chase that precipitated the wreck. But today, here, wrapped in Jack's arms, she felt safer than she had in months. In years.

He stroked the back of his hand along her cheek. "I stand by my assessment. What you did today— and when you left Cliff— took courage." He paused, his penetrating gaze locked on hers. "And I thank you for protecting Seth."

"Jack, I—"

He silenced her with another deep, toe-curling kiss, and Tracy forgot what she'd planned to say. She forgot everything but that cozy office and the cowboy holding her snug against him. She leaned into the kiss, parting her lips when his tongue sought entry to her mouth.

Falling for Jack may have been the farthest thing from her mind when she arrived at the Lucky C, but life was nothing if not full of surprises. She'd have never guessed a madman would track her to Tulsa and try to kill her, either. The dizzying speed of events, taking her life in directions she couldn't have predicted, left her mind spinning, the ground shifting beneath her feet.

Or was it the thorough, sultry way Jack took charge of

their kiss that made her legs rubbery and her head light? Some of each, probably.

"Now…how 'bout that supper?" he said, when he finally raised his head, and Tracy sucked in a shuddering breath. He gave her shoulders a squeeze before stepping back from her, his gaze still dark with desire.

With her heart drumming wildly, she nodded, not trusting her voice. Later, Tracy couldn't have said anything about the meat loaf, potatoes or salad that comprised their meal, because her mind kept straying to Jack's office, to his kiss. She didn't miss the intimate sense of family as they shared the meal. She savored the chance to watch Seth and Jack interact. To be included in the conversations about the ranch and Seth's video game. She marveled at Jack's loving reassurance when Seth mentioned the shooting, his ability to say just the right thing to calm the boy's fears without lying or evading.

He then explained to Seth about the plan to fly to Denver in the morning.

"Can I go?" Seth asked, his eyes wide with the excitement of a possible trip to a new city.

"This is business. You'd be bored. I've asked Brett to keep an eye on you."

Seth drooped in his chair, clearly disappointed.

"I want you to mind Brett and help him with chores. Understand?"

Seth nodded. "Yes, sir."

"Good boy. Now take your plate to the sink and get in your pajamas. I'll be up in a minute to read you a book."

"Can Tracy read to me tonight?" Seth asked, casting her a hopeful glance.

She consulted Jack, who dipped his chin in agreement, before sending Seth a broad smile. "I'd love to, sweetie."

Her heart clenched knowing that if Jack had his way,

she'd be living under the same roof with the father and son, sharing more dinners, more bedtimes, more familial moments in the coming days. How wonderful it would be to feel this warmth, this bond, the peaceful routine that was family life every day. A poignant longing tightened her chest, and she did her best to shove it down.

Before she could dream of home and hearth, she had to rid herself of the menace that had invaded her life. Her priority had to be keeping Seth and the rest of the Coltons safe from the assassin bent on killing her.

Early the next morning, Jack, Ryan and Tracy disembarked at the Denver airport and took a cab straight to the Denver PD station. The Baxters were being brought in for questioning, and according to Ryan's contacts in the department, the couple had immediately called their lawyer to meet them at the station.

"Interesting," Jack said, arching an eyebrow when Ryan relayed this tidbit.

"Actually, not so interesting. The Baxters are on a first-name basis with their lawyer. They don't scratch their noses without asking Mr. Rampart's legal advice." Now Ryan arched a dark eyebrow. "Are they paranoid or do they have something to hide?"

Tracy shrugged. "I don't know. Honestly, I tried to avoid spending much time with them. They're not exactly pleasant people to be around. But you'll see that for yourself soon enough."

Jack and Ryan exchanged a look but said nothing. As their taxi approached downtown Denver, Jack called Brett to check on Seth. While Edith would likely manage most of Seth's care while he was gone, Brett had promised to oversee Seth's protection in light of the gunman's attack. If there was trouble, Jack knew Brett could handle it.

"We're playing Sorry, and Seth is kicking my tail. Your kid is merciless, man!" Brett said, and Jack heard Seth's laugh in the background.

Jack tugged his cheek up in a half grin, and chuckled softly. "If you're gonna play, you might as well play to win." Assured that Seth was fine and all was quiet at the ranch, Jack signed off and clipped his phone back on his belt. He caught Tracy looking at him with a bemused expression and asked, "What's that look for?"

She blinked as if startled to have been caught staring. "I...uh, nothing." A tantalizing pink flush stained her cheeks. "I just...so rarely see you smile."

He wasn't sure what he'd expected her to say, but not that. He glowered at her. "I smile." He watched as Tracy and Ryan exchange a look and realizing his current countenance contradicted his assertion, he grumbled, "When it's warranted."

The taxi pulled up in front of the police department at that moment, and the subject was put on hold for the moment. But as Tracy swept past him into the bustling police station, she leaned close and said, "Perhaps you should consider what warrants a smile more often. Yours is quite stunning."

Her compliment was unexpected, and it rattled him. Discomposed was not a good state for the business at hand, but he couldn't deny the warmth that settled in his core as she tossed him a sideways grin and sashayed inside.

Was he really as dour as she made him sound? Granted, he didn't smile much. He'd found it hard to smile after Laura ditched him, Seth and the ranch, and perhaps he'd made little effort in more recent years. Seth had been his only source of real joy, his only reason to smile in the past few years.

Ryan showed his badge at the front desk, and a few minutes later, a plain-clothes detective with auburn hair and friendly smile appeared from the back offices to meet them. Ryan introduced the man as Detective Ron Hunnicutt, and Jack and Tracy both shook the detective's hand as Ryan gave their names. Genial questions about their flight and formalities concerning signing in to the police department and acquiring visitor tags were dispensed with in short order, and the group filed back toward the interrogation rooms.

"So here's how this will work," Detective Hunnicutt said as they walked, "I will question Mr. and Mrs. Baxter separately. Detective Colton will sit in and is free to ask any questions he has. My understanding of your case is you haven't any evidence they are tied to the shooting at your ranch. You are just looking for any information that might be helpful?"

Ryan nodded. "That's right. Ms. McCain had a contentious relationship with her in-laws before her husband died, and they are the only people she could think of who had any kind of beef with her."

The detective directed his next statements to Tracy. "So you understand, your in-laws are not under arrest. They are here voluntarily for questioning and are free to leave at any time. Without any evidence of their involvement, we have no legal grounds to hold them."

"It's a fishing trip, for sure," Ryan added, "but we have no other leads except the sketch of the suspect Jack helped us draw up last night."

"You're the only one saw the shooter?" Hunnicutt asked Jack.

"I saw him, too," Tracy volunteered, "but only from a distance. I had nothing to add to Jack's description that would be helpful."

Ryan paused long enough to open a satchel he'd brought with him and took out a file. Flipping the file open, he extracted a stiff sheet of paper. "I faxed this to you last night, but this is the original if you'd like to make copies."

Hunnicutt stopped walking and turned his attention to the sheet Ryan passed to him. Jack glimpsed the surly face of the man in the sketch the police artist had composed with his direction, and his gut soured. With his thumb, he stroked the still-sore and swollen knuckles of his opposite hand, remembering the hatred in the shooter's eyes. A killer's eyes. Jack had no doubt the man harbored no compunction for his crime, would feel no guilt for murdering Tracy and anyone else who got in his way.

He glanced at Tracy, whose face had paled since Ryan had produced the police sketch. "You don't recognize him at all? Have you thought of anything since last night?"

She tore her gaze from the image to face Jack. "No."

"You've never seen him before yesterday? You're sure?" Hunnicutt asked, handing the sketch back to Ryan.

She shook her head. "Never. I'd remember that face, those eyes. He looks...evil."

Tracy chafed her arms as if chilled, and the Denver detective twisted his mouth in thought. "Well, let's see if your in-laws recognize him."

"Ex-in-laws," Tracy corrected.

"You divorced your husband before he died?" Detective Hunnicutt asked.

"Well, no. But I'd left him...and since Cliff died, they've wanted nothing to do with me and vice versa."

A uniformed officer poked his head out of one of the doors along the corridor where they stood and announced, "We're ready when you are, Ron."

Hunnicutt nodded to the officer, then to Ryan. "Shall we?" Turning to Tracy and Jack, he aimed a finger further down the corridor and said, "There are some chairs down the hall where you can wait."

Jack squared his shoulders. "No."

Detective Hunnicutt blinked and angled his head. "Excuse me?"

"We came to observe the interview."

The Denver detective glanced at Ryan, whose jaw tightened.

"I'm sorry, that's not—"

"The interrogation room has an adjoining area where we can observe, doesn't it?" Jack interrupted. "We don't want to interfere with the questioning. We just want to observe."

Hunnicutt propped his hands on his hips and twisted his mouth again, dividing a look between Jack and Ryan.

"I told him before we left he wouldn't be allowed access to the interview room, but he insisted on coming."

Detective Hunnicutt appeared to be looking for the most tactful way to tell him to take a hike, when Tracy said, "Isn't it possible that I could have information that would assist in your interview? Or something they say may trigger a memory I'd forgotten, something that might help the investigation."

"If this were an official interrogation, my hands would be tied. I couldn't—" Hunnicutt fell silent and nodded a greeting as another officer passed them in the hall. When they were alone again, he finished. "You can watch from the observation room, but you may not do or say anything to influence the interview of either interviewee. And you will have Officer Grunnel in the room with you at all times." He marched to the next door and opened it.

"Got it." Jack placed a hand at the small of Tracy's back to usher her inside. "Thank you, Detective."

If the enticing presence of Jack's possessive hand at the base of her spine weren't unsettling enough, the sight of her former mother-in-law sitting behind the small table in the interview room, scowling, shook Tracy to the marrow. Irene's hair, a golden brown with subtle highlights, thanks to the help of her hairdresser, was worn swept up in a loose, stylish twist, and she'd accented her aqua silk pantsuit with chunky turquoise jewelry. Despite her advanced years, her cheeks were facelift-smooth and her makeup impeccably painted on. For all her style and attention to her appearance, she radiated a coolness that went beyond her glacial gray eyes.

The balding man in the crisp business suit next to her was equally menacing with his hard jaw and heavy brow over dark eyes. She'd met the Baxters' lawyer on more than one occasion, and each time she saw him, he seemed more intimidating than the last. Hovering at the edge of the crowd at her wedding, meeting with Cliff in their home behind closed doors and reading the terms of Cliff's will after the funeral. She remembered thinking at one point during her marriage that Rampart made Ebenezer Scrooge seem warm and cuddly.

Icy tingles nipped her neck as the ghostlike images flickered in her mind's eye. By sheer force of will, she held the flood of nightmarish memories at bay.

Wiping sweat from her palms onto her slacks, she moved closer to the one-way window.

She could imagine Jack and the uniformed officer in the observation room were both watching her closely, as if she were the suspect with something to hide. Taking a breath and digging up courage, she focused on the activity in the next room.

Detectives Hunnicutt and Colton entered and shook hands cordially with both Irene Baxter and her attorney, Joseph Rampart.

Once introductions were made, Joseph Rampart asked, "Would you mind telling us what this is about? Why have you dragged my clients down here?"

"Certainly. As I explained to Mrs. Baxter when I called her home, there was an incident at a ranch just outside Tulsa, Oklahoma, that we feel Mr. and Mrs. Baxter may be able to help us with."

"I haven't been to Tulsa in years, and neither has my husband! Whatever happened down there, you're barking up the wrong tree," Irene said, then pressed her mouth in a taut line of disapproval.

"I didn't say we thought you were there. As for your husband, we'll let him talk for himself when we interview him."

"About that," Irene snapped, "this business of separating us for questioning, like we were common criminals. It's insulting! I don't see why we couldn't be *interviewed* together." She infused the term with disdain.

"Standard procedure, ma'am. No insult intended," Hunnicutt replied with a patient smile. Hunnicutt pressed a button on the recording device on the table, then pulled out a chair and sat. Ryan remained standing, leaning against the wall by the door with his arms folded over his chest.

"Do you know a woman named Tracy McCain?"

Irene blinked, glanced to her lawyer for a nod of permission to answer, then narrowed her eyes with suspicion. "You know I do. That information is easy enough to obtain."

Tracy shook her head in disbelief. Irene was seeking guidance from Rampart about a question as basic as her acquaintance with her former daughter-in-law?

Hunnicutt rolled up a palm. "Again, just standard procedure. We need your response stated for the record."

Mrs. Baxter shifted her gaze to the recorder and wrinkled her nose in distaste as if the device were a foul-smelling baby diaper. "Tracy was my son's wife." She paused a moment before adding, "Though apparently the marriage meant so little to her, she didn't deign to keep my son's name after he died."

Tracy tensed. Irene was partially correct. Tracy had reverted to her maiden name after Cliff's death, but not because she didn't respect the sanctity of marriage. She had simply wanted a fresh start. She hadn't wanted the reminder of the years of agony that Cliff had put her through.

She glanced at Jack and found him watching her. She opened her mouth as if to defend herself, but before she could, Jack muttered, "Charming woman. Guess I'd change my name back and disassociate myself from her, too."

An odd warmth spread through Tracy's midsection. Jack had probably meant the comment as a throwaway, but Tracy appreciated the support underlying the snark. Pressing a hand to her swirling stomach, she returned her attention to the interview room.

"When's the last time you spoke with Tracy?" Hunnicutt asked.

Mrs. Baxter frowned, glancing to Rampart again. When he inclined his head, she wrinkled her brow in thought. "I don't know. Probably Cliff's funeral. Why?"

Hunnicutt flashed her a wry smile. "Mrs. Baxter, the

way this works is this—I ask the questions, and you give me concise honest answers. All right?"

Rampart sat forward and waggled a finger at Hunnicutt. "There's no need to be patronizing, Detective."

Hunnicutt raised a hand and flashed a quick smile. "My apologies. No offense intended."

Irene lifted her nose and gave a haughty sniff. "Fine. Get on with it then. I don't have all day."

Beside her, Jack grunted.

"Told you," Tracy said softly without looking at the imposing man beside her. Bad enough that his distractingly virile scent filled her nose and teased her with memories of their kiss.

"How would you characterize your relationship with Ms. McCain?" Ryan asked, drawing Irene's hostile gaze.

After consulting Rampart again, she said, "I wouldn't say we have a relationship at all. We were never close when she was married to my son, and I haven't spoken to her since his funeral. As I just said."

Hunnicutt laced his fingers, rested his arms on the table and leaned forward. "Would you say that the two of you are on good terms? Was there any bad blood between you?"

Irene, predictably, glanced to Rampart before she answered. He hesitated, then gave a subtle flick of his fingers. When she spoke, it was clear she was choosing her words carefully. "It was…indifferent. I know that sounds harsh, but—" she shrugged "—I really had very little chance to get to know her before Cliff was murdered." The hand Irene rested on the table fisted, and she drew her shoulders back. "I really don't know what you want me to say, Detective. I can't characterize our relationship because I really had none with her— good or bad."

Hunnicutt made no comment but kept a level gaze

fixed on Mrs. Baxter. When it was clear Irene would add nothing else, Ryan stepped forward and joined the group at the table, straddling a chair he'd turned backward.

"Mrs. Baxter," Ryan said, "yesterday afternoon, someone shot at Tracy McCain while she was visiting my family's ranch outside of Tulsa."

Chapter 14

Tracy swallowed hard, her eyes locked on Irene, and tried to interpret every subtle facial expression and gesture the woman made.

Mrs. Baxter's sculpted eyebrows shot up. Tracy would have sworn she saw the tic of a smug grin at the corners of Irene's mouth, but it was gone so quickly, she couldn't be sure. Or perhaps she was seeing what she expected to see.

Irene sat back in her chair, her eyes darting from one detective to the other before she pressed a hand to her chest, as if remembering the proper response to such news was shock or grief. A deep V furrowed her forehead, and she made the appropriate sounds of dismay in her throat. "Oh, dear. That's terrible! Have you caught the man responsible?"

Ryan kept his expression neutral. "I didn't say that the shooter was a man."

Irene flinched, then glaring at Ryan, snapped, "Surely you're not implying that you think I did it! I told you I haven't been in Tulsa for years. I was home all day yesterday. You can ask my husband."

Hunnicutt nodded. "We will. Were you with your husband all day yesterday?"

"Yes." Once again, Mrs. Baxter stiffened in the chair and lifted her chin. "We are well-respected members of this community," she added tapping the table top with a salon-perfect French-manicured fingernail. "It is preposterous to think that either of us could be responsible for anything as heinous as murder."

"No one is accusing you of murder, ma'am," Ryan said calmly. "In fact, I never said Ms. McCain was killed."

Irene shifted nervously on the chair, dividing a confused look between Ryan and Detective Hunnicutt. "Yes, you did."

"No," Ryan said shaking his head, "I said someone shot at her."

"I—" Mrs. Baxter shot a dubious glance to her lawyer.

"We can rewind the recording," Hunnicutt said, nodding to the gadget on the table, "and play it back for you, if you'd like proof." He scratched his chin and pulled a face that said he was intrigued. "I do find it interesting, though, that you assume that she was dead."

Irene turned back to glare at the two detectives, her chest heaving with indignation. "Do not play word games with me, Detectives, twisting everything I say, or this *interview* is over!"

"I've also noticed she has yet to ask how you are, how badly hurt you might be," Jack said, voicing Tracy's thoughts. He cut a side glance to her, and she met his gaze. Even in the dimly lit room, his eyes held a bright gleam that stole her breath.

"I know. Should I be offended that she doesn't care?"

In the interrogation room, Irene divided a hard look

between Ryan and Detective Hunnicutt. "So? Is she or isn't she dead?"

This time it was Officer Grunnel, in the observation room with them, that scoffed and muttered under his breath. "Cold."

Tracy shivered. She'd never known just how unfeeling and selfish Irene Baxter was until today. She shouldn't be surprised. She was Cliff's mother, after all. She felt more than saw Jack shift closer to her. She welcomed the warmth as his body heat wrapped around her in the confined, overly air-conditioned room.

"She survived the shooting," Ryan said cryptically, leaving it to Irene to inquire—or not—about Tracy's exact condition. Her eyebrows twitching and her mouth pinching slightly, Irene chose the latter.

Under normal circumstances, Tracy might have been hurt by the indifference, the lack of compassion shown by her late husband's mother. But things being what they were, she'd expected no more from Mrs. Baxter.

Detective Hunnicutt flipped open the file folder he'd brought in with him and pulled out the police sketch of the shooter. As he slid the sheet across the table, he asked, "Do you recognize this man?"

Irene dragged the picture closer for a better look, and Tracy noticed the woman's hand was shaking. Her ex-mother-in-law schooled her face as she examined the drawing. "I've never seen that man before in my life."

"Are you sure?" Hunnicutt asked. "Take your time."

"I said I don't know him." She shoved the picture back across the table and folded her arms across her bosom, shaking her head. "This is a waste of my time. Why are you asking me about this?" She focused her attention on Detective Colton, her thin eyebrows dipping low. "What did that girl say about us that brought you all the way up here?"

"By 'that girl,' may I assume you are referring to Ms. McCain?" Ryan asked.

"Of course, Tracy! Isn't she the reason we're here? Because someone tried to kill her?"

"Once again, ma'am," Ryan said, "you're putting words in our mouth. Why do you assume the shooter was trying to kill her?"

Mrs. Baxter's lips pursed, and she shifted in her chair, clearly growing agitated. "A natural assumption, gentlemen. Why else would someone shoot at her?"

Ryan lifted a shoulder. "There are as many reasons for a person's actions as there are people on this planet, ma'am. Maybe he simply wanted to scare her. Or he could have been a hunter who mistook what he saw and fired recklessly."

Mrs. Baxter's nostrils flared as she took a deep, aggrieved breath. "If you want to dicker over semantics, Detective, I suggest you do it on your own time. Either charge me with something or let me go home."

Hunnicutt rocked back in his chair and raised both hands. "Hey, like I said, you're not under arrest. You may leave any time."

"Good." She turned to her lawyer with a nod. "Joseph."

Irene and Rampart rose to their feet, and Tracy's heartbeat scrambled. "That's it?" She jerked a panicked look to Officer Grunnel for confirmation. "But they didn't—"

"Of course," Ryan said in the interview room, drawing Tracy's attention back to the one-way window. "I'd have thought you'd be more interested in helping find the person responsible for firing on a member of your family."

Irene paused, her hand on the strap of the purse she'd hung on the back of her chair.

"I know I want him caught and locked up. See—" Ryan leaned forward, his expression grave "—the man put my nephew at risk, too. Seth is only five, and I love him like my own son."

Tracy sensed the tightening of Jack's muscles as he drew his spine taller and his breath caught. A quick side glance to the spasming tendons at his jaw confirmed the tension gripping him. Without really thinking about what she was doing or why, Tracy reached for his hand and curled her fingers around his. He gave her a brief startled look before squeezing her hand and returning his gaze to his brother.

"I want the man responsible for the shooting," Detective Colton was saying, "if only to make him pay for scaring Seth and endangering an innocent little boy."

Irene's knuckles whitened as she gripped the back of the chair, as if she were realizing how callous she'd appear if she dismissed Seth's involvement in what had happened. Even if she could discount Tracy's. "You didn't mention the little boy before. Was the boy hurt?"

Ryan shook his head. "Not badly. A few scrapes as they scrambled for cover. Tracy protected him, for which my family will be eternally grateful."

Jack angled his head toward Tracy, and she met his gaze. His eyes were softer, reflecting a warmth that said he echoed his brother's sentiments. He gave her fingers another pulse-like squeeze, and something airy and magical fluttered in her chest. After being on the receiving end of Jack's hard-edged suspicion for days, this kinder, gentler Jack touched a part of Tracy that had been left raw and aching after Cliff's abuse.

"Not that Ms. McCain deserved to be frightened or put at risk herself," Ryan added. He waited a beat then stood like the others in the interview room. "We still need to talk to your husband, of course. If you would be so kind as to wait here, we'll let you know when we are through questioning him."

After whispering something to his client, Rampart straightened his tie and followed Hunnicutt to the door. Ryan and Rampart trailed out behind Hunnicutt, leaving Irene by herself. She pulled the chair back out and dropped into the seat with a huff and a glower at the closed door.

"I want to watch the interview of Mr. Baxter, too," Jack said, cutting a look to Officer Grunnel. "Will they question him in this same room?"

"No, I'll take you to the new observation room across the hall in a minute. Detective Hunnicutt didn't want the Baxters to see you or know you were on the premises."

"All right." Jack slipped his hand from Tracy's and moved it to her back, as if to show her out to the hall.

But Tracy's gaze stayed locked on Irene, fascinated by the woman's behavior once she thought she was alone. Mrs. Baxter rubbed her temples, her face puckered in an angry sneer. "Of all the incompetent…" she muttered before letting her hand drop to the table with a grunt of frustration.

Incompetent? Tracy puzzled over Irene's grumbled word choice. Who did she think was not performing up to standard? Rampart? Detectives Colton and Hunnicutt?

With an eerie sense of intuition, a chill slithered through her and pooled in her gut. "The shooter."

Jack hesitated by the door and turned back to her. "Did you say something?"

Tracy's throat felt dry, and she had to force herself to swallow before she could speak. "I said, 'the shooter.'" She flattened her hand over her jittery stomach. "After your brother and Detective Hunnicutt left the room, Mrs.

Baxter mumbled something. It sounded like she said, 'Of all the incompetent…'"

Tracy paused to draw a shuddering breath, and Jack walked back to her, his eyes narrowed and gleaming with an intensity that arrowed to her core. "And?"

"Well, I was trying to figure out who she could be talking about. It seemed unlikely she meant Mr. Rampart or the detectives. And when I thought about her reaction to the news that I hadn't been killed, I just…I don't know."

Jack angled his head to glare through the one-way glass at Mrs. Baxter.

"I'm just speculating, of course, but I had the weirdest feeling come over me, this odd insight that she meant the shooter." She rubbed the spot at her temple where her pulse was pounding, a throbbing headache building.

Officer Grunnel stepped closer. "Are you sure that's what she said?"

"Well, no. Like I said, she was kind of mumbling." Tracy glanced through the window to the interrogation room again. Mrs. Baxter continued to frown and tap her fingers restlessly on the tabletop. "But it sure sounded like that. I'm almost sure I heard her say 'incompetent.'"

Jack faced Grunnel. "Can we use this?"

"Not officially. It would be considered hearsay. But I'll let the detectives know what she heard, and perhaps they can use it to guide the conversation in new directions." Officer Grunnel returned to the door and stuck his head into the hall. He glanced back at Tracy and Jack and held his hand up. "Wait here a moment."

The officer stepped into the hall, closing the door behind him, and Tracy chafed the goose bumps that had risen on her arms.

"How are you holding up?" Jack asked, moving close and rubbing his wide palms along her arms. Rather than calm the jitters in her gut, his touch simply transformed the uneasy jangle. She flashed back to the last time he'd held her close—to the evening before, when he'd kissed the breath from her.

"I'm all right." She walked into his embrace, wrapping her arms around his waist. He pressed a light kiss to her forehead. "This is all just so surreal. Could Cliff's parents really be behind the attacks? Is it about money? I'll gladly give them Cliff's life insurance and savings. I don't want it."

Rather than answer her rhetorical questions, Jack tucked her under his chin and rubbed her back in small circles. A calm sank into her slowly, lulled by his caress and the security of his arms around her. After a moment, he moved a hand to her cheek and angled her face up to his. His intent blazed in his eyes, even before he dipped his head.

Heat curled through her blood, and she rose on her toes to meet his kiss. The hum of the busy police department beyond the closed door faded as she centered her attention on Jack. On his fingers threading through her hair. On his skillful lips possessing hers.

"So, new plan of attack," Ryan said as he burst through the door, then stopped short when he found his brother in a lip-lock.

Tracy tensed and would have jerked out of the embrace if not for Jack's firm grip cradling her skull with one hand and the small of her back with his other.

Lifting his eyebrows, Ryan sent them an amused grin. "Should I come back later? Or perhaps rent you a hotel room?"

Jack released Tracy and met his brother's quip with a scowl. "Save the jokes. What's the new plan?"

"In light of what Tracy heard the missus say, we're

going to go fishing again with her but using new bait," Ryan said, still eyeing his brother with a speculative gleam.

Movement in her peripheral vision caught Tracy's attention as Hunnicutt entered the interview room and took a seat at the table. "I've just talked with your husband and, well…I have one or two more questions for you, ma'am."

Mrs. Baxter gave Hunnicutt a peeved glare. "What now?"

The Denver detective made a show of shifting uncomfortably in his chair. "Well, you see…" He rubbed his temples and sighed.

"What is it? What did my husband say?"

Tracy stepped closer to the one-way glass to follow the exchange with rapt attention. She felt more than saw Jack step up behind her.

In the next room, Hunnicutt bowed his head and groaned. "I tell you, ma'am, there are a lot of things about my job that I don't like, but the two worst have to be making that house call to let someone know their loved one has died, and letting someone know a trusted friend or relative has betrayed them."

Irene flinched, and her face visibly paled. "What are you saying? What did my husband tell you?"

Hunnicutt shifted awkwardly again and sent her a frown. "Before we get into what your husband is saying—" he paused and gave Mrs. Baxter an almost apologetic look "—is there anything else you'd like to tell me about Ms. McCain or the attacks on her?"

Irene blinked rapidly and clutched her purse to her chest like a shield. "He's blaming me, isn't he?" Her face darkened. "That rat bastard… How dare he?" She raised a shaking hand to her throat. "I-I may have made the arrangements, b-but it was *his* idea."

A chill ran down Tracy's spine. Had Hunnicutt just gotten a confession?

Beside her, Tracy heard Ryan chuckle. "Brilliant."

"What?" Jack asked.

"Her husband's being even more tight-lipped than she was. Hunnicutt never said her husband rolled over on her, she just assumed that from his little speech and his little uncomfortable act. He played on her guilty conscience..."

"What was his idea?" Hunnicutt asked.

"Hiring someone to get rid of her." Irene's expression soured, and she leaned toward Hunnicutt, clearly caught up in defending herself. "She's the reason our Cliff was murdered. If the ungrateful bitch hadn't left him, the car accident would never have happened, and he wouldn't have been in that miserable prison where he was murdered. An inmate may have killed Cliff, but it was all Tracy's fault...and she has to pay!" Irene's deep, agitated breathing matched the thudding beats of Tracy's heart as she stared through the one-way glass in disbelief.

Hunnicutt nodded sympathetically and slid the picture of the gunman back toward her. "Okay. Is this the man you hired to get rid of Ms. McCain? Who is he?"

The woman barely glanced at the sketch. "You'll never find him. We hired him because he's the best. He stays under the radar and always completes his assignment. He's stealthy and thorough and very lethal."

"His name?" Hunnicutt repeated.

Irene lifted a shoulder, her voice bolder now as if she were relieved to have the confession off her chest. "I don't know. That's part of how he operates. No one knows his name. Our meeting was arranged through..." She cleared her throat. "Mutual associates."

Tracy cut her glance to Jack, and his expression said his thoughts were where hers were. The connections to organized crime Jack had discovered through his digging into financial holdings and public records.

"I simply think of him as The Wolf," Irene said.

"The wolf?" Hunnicutt repeated.

"Well, look at him." She flicked a finger toward the sketch. "Don't you think it fits?"

Hunnicutt didn't respond. Instead, he leaned forward and narrowed his eyes on Mrs. Baxter. "Can you have your...'mutual friends' arrange another meeting? To call off the hit? It would go a long way toward winning favor with the powers that be."

As if realizing for the first time that she had incriminated herself, Irene's eyes widened, and she sat back in the chair, once again clutching her purse against her as if it could protect her. "I've said too much. I want my lawyer, and I want to cut a deal."

Hunnicutt's chin dropped to his chest as if knowing he'd gotten all he'd get from Irene for the time being.

"I'll tell you what you want to know," the woman added, "but I want a guarantee of no jail time."

"Bingo," Ryan said. "If you'll excuse me, I need to make a call to the Denver district attorney." He exited the observation room, spilling light from the corridor into the dark space.

Tracy shivered, and Jack enveloped her in his warm arms from behind, whispering into her ear. "We'll get him, Tracy. I won't rest until we catch the man who shot at you, and I promise that the bastard won't get near you again."

"You won't stop him. I can't stop him." Upon learning his wife had cracked, George Baxter had started pouring out his guts, as if competing to be more forthcoming and win the better plea deal. "The Wolf will not stop until Tracy is dead. I have no way to reach him, and since he wasn't going to get the final payment until the job was done, he's all the more motivated to finish his assignment."

His assignment. Jack's gut churned. Meaning to murder Tracy and anyone else that got in his way, including little boys.

He glanced to Tracy, who had her arms wrapped around her middle as if to hold herself together. "Come on, Tracy. Let's get out of here."

She sent him an anxious look. "But they're not finished questioning the Baxters."

"Ryan will fill us in. We know the worst of it. Let me take you home." He held his hand out to her, and after a brief hesitation, she placed her cold fingers in his hand.

Her icy fingers worried him, because they spoke to her mental state, the stress and fear she had to be experiencing. Once the shock of learning her in-laws were behind the attack on her had passed, she'd grown increasingly pale and distraught looking.

Not that he could blame her. Knowing a professional assassin with connections to organized crime was gunning for her had shaken him to the marrow as well. And though Hunnicutt and Ryan had been grilling Irene and George Baxter for hours now, their story hadn't changed. The Wolf was invisible, unreachable, in the wind. And he wouldn't stop until he'd killed Tracy.

Chapter 15

Over my dead body. As he escorted Tracy out of the Denver police-department building and hailed a cab, Jack gritted his teeth. He swore silently to do whatever was necessary to keep Tracy safe. The Baxters might not know how to reach The Wolf and call him off, but he had faith in Ryan's detective skills. He and his team at the Tulsa PD would find this ghost and bring him in. And until they did, Jack would protect his family.

A jolt rippled through Jack when he realized that he included Tracy in that category. His *family.* She was Seth's cousin, so that made her family of sorts, but...

He balled his fists and exhaled deeply. Who was he kidding? The kiss they'd shared last night had rocked him to his roots. He hadn't felt a connection to a woman this strong, this pure and life changing since...since... hell, *ever.*

He was in unchartered waters, and that scared the hell

out of him. Because if loving Laura and having her leave him had hurt as badly as it had, how much would it cost him to lose Tracy? And how had he grown so attached to her in such a short time?

On the drive from the Tulsa airport back to the Lucky C, Jack revisited the idea of her moving from the main house to the old family house with him and Seth.

She nodded, too tired to fight him on the topic any further. "I'll move. In the morning. Tonight I just want to crawl into bed, pull the covers over my head and sleep for about twenty hours."

Jack reached for her hand and rubbed his thumb over her knuckles. "I know that today has been mentally and physically exhausting, but in light of what we've learned about who's after you, that he's a professional killer, I want somebody I can trust with your safety close to you at all times."

She massaged the growing headache in her temple with her free hand. "Don't you trust Brett for that?"

"Yeah, but I talked with Brett while you were in the ladies' room at the airport. He has Seth down at the bunkhouse, and he plans to sleep down there. Apparently Abra was complaining about the noise Seth was making, and she asked him to get Seth out from under foot."

Abra's attitude startled her, and she sent Jack a questioning look.

He shrugged. "This is the woman who spent most of my childhood in Europe, leaving me to be raised by nannies and Big J. She loves her family in her own way, but she has a very low threshold for noise and energetic children."

Tracy had suspected as much of Abra, and she experienced another pang of sympathy for Seth. He truly lacked a maternal influence in his life.

"If I have to," Jack said, leveling a hard stare at her, "I'll come in and pack you up myself. But I want you where I can protect you. Starting tonight."

She should have been annoyed by his high handedness, but in this case, Tracy appreciated Jack's concern and determination. The idea of the man they called The Wolf hunting her chilled her to the marrow. If she were honest, she was more than a little nervous about staying in the large mansion. The two miles from the main house to Jack's might as well have been one hundred. It was too far for him to reach her in time if there was trouble.

Jack parked his truck in the circular drive in front of the main house, and together they headed in to collect her belongings. The house was quiet and dark, evidence that Abra and Big J had already headed to their rooms for the evening. Greta was still in Oklahoma City, and Edith generally kept to herself after dinner, so the church-like silence wasn't surprising. But it did feel lonely...and somewhat eerie.

As Tracy trudged upstairs, keeping one hand on the railing for balance and putting one foot in front of the other with effort, she was glad Jack had insisted she move to the old ranch house tonight. The mansion, for all its grandeur, didn't have the warmth and sense of security that Jack's house did.

The throb of fatigue and stress that pounded in her skull turned her thoughts to the medicine bottle of Lorcet on her nightstand. Though she'd generally avoided taking the stronger painkillers Eric had prescribed, tonight she thought she might need the more powerful drug. The wound on her shoulder ached, and she was still sore from horseback riding and her tumble into the street earlier that week. But she couldn't complain. Not only was she still alive after two attempts on her life, but she was blessed to be getting to know Laura's son and his family. Lucky to have Jack's protection.

Despite the threat that hovered over her, she was free of Cliff's brutality. Laura had paid the highest price to give her that freedom, and Tracy could never take it for granted.

Jack placed a hand low on her back, as if he sensed she was struggling to mount the long flight of stairs. She recalled the last time they'd taken these stairs together, the way he'd swept her into his arms and cradled her to his broad chest. The memory caused a sweet quiver to race through her, and in response, Jack's fingers pressed more firmly against her skin.

"Tracy?"

She gave him a quick smile. "I'm fine. Just...not used to so many stairs."

When they reached the guest room, Jack slid her suitcase and toiletries bag out from under the bed. He handed her the smaller bag. "I'll start on your clothes while you pack in the bathroom."

She took the travel case from him and glanced to the small table beside the bed. Her novel was there, along with her hand lotion and a glass of water. But no pill bottle.

Tracy frowned. Had she moved the Lorcet to the bathroom and forgotten? Moving into the adjoining bathroom, she set the toiletries case on the counter top and scanned the area around the sink for the painkiller. She began packing her toothpaste, makeup and skin cleansers but still didn't find the bottle of Lorcet. She was puzzling over this when she noticed the small bag of jewelry items she'd brought with her was unzipped and had clearly been riffled.

Scowling, she checked the contents and discovered a

few of her better pieces were missing, including the two-karat diamond engagement ring Cliff had given her—no loss sentimentally but still quite valuable.

"Jack, have you ever had an issue with Edith stealing from the family?" she asked as she returned to the bedroom.

He raised his head from his careful work tucking her socks in the corners of the suitcase. "Edith? No. She's like family." He drew his eyebrows lower. "Why?"

"Well...some of my things are missing."

"Missing?" His expression darkened. "Like what?"

"Jewelry. And my Lorcet pills." She bit her bottom lip. "I'm not accusing her, but...well, who else could have taken them?"

He inhaled and slowly released a deep breath, stepping close to her. "I don't know, but I promise we'll get to the bottom of it in the morning."

After pressing a kiss to her forehead, he moved back to the dresser and opened the top drawer. Where she kept her panties and bras. An awkward flash of heat swamped her, and her pulse danced a nervous jig.

Jack, too, seemed caught off guard, and he stood for a moment simply staring at the collection of colorful lace bras and plain cotton bikini undies. Not until he reached for one of the frillier bras did it register that the undergarments were in an unkempt tumble.

"Jack," she said, catching her breath.

He paused with the pink bra dangling from his fingers and sent her a gaze, dark with desire.

She had to swallow twice to work loose the tangled knot of apprehension and lust that made strange bedfellows in her throat. Talking to him while he held her delicates in his callused hand left her off balance, but...

"My clothes...I—" she pointed at the rumpled disarray

"—I always keep things folded and in neat stacks. Someone's been rummaging in there. I'm sure of it."

Her first thought was that The Wolf had been in her room, searching for something or laying a trap. Planting a threat.

Clearly that was where Jack's thoughts went, as well, because he dropped the bra in order to conduct his own search of the drawer. After digging through the pink satin, lilac silk and white cotton garments, he turned a narrow-eyed look toward her. A muscle in his jaw twitched as he gritted his teeth and clamped his hands on her shoulders. "I assure you, whoever did this was not part of the house staff. Big J screens the help carefully, and most of them have been with the family since I was a kid. I don't know how anyone got up here unseen, but this only confirms my decision to get you out of here. I want you in the old house. With me."

With me. The emphasis he placed on the last words was underscored by the blaze in his blue eyes. His intensity stirred a tremor at her core. Before she could gather a coherent reply, he dragged her closer and crushed her mouth under his.

Her body reacted instantly, a fiery yearning flooding her limbs and melting her bones. When her knees buckled, she leaned into him, clutching his arms to steady herself. Her fatigue fled as he repositioned his lips to draw more deeply on hers, tracing the line of her mouth with the tip of his tongue.

A half whimper, half moan escaped her throat, and he answered with a hungry growl. Sliding his hands to her thighs, he lifted her so that her aching sex rode the thick ridge under his fly. In a couple of shuffling steps, he was at the edge of the guest bed. He hesitated briefly, giving her time to protest, then glancing at the door as if check to make sure it was closed.

Whether her defenses were low after the shocks and terror she'd experienced in recent days or whether Jack's kiss simply had her passionately mesmerized, a need burned in Tracy's blood unlike anything she'd experienced before. She wanted Jack Colton. Needed him. Here. Now.

She plowed her fingers into his thick, unruly hair and kissed him with a fervor that left no doubt what she wanted from him. Placing an arm across her back, he supported her as they tumbled to the mattress. She hooked her legs around his hips and gasped as he flipped up her skirt and simulated the sex act despite their clothes. The scrape of his jean-clad erection against her sensitized skin shot firebrands through her.

Jack slipped a hand under her bottom and squeezed. His intimate touch spun tendrils of pure pleasure through her, electrifying every nerve ending. His kiss was alternately demanding, then tender. He'd nip her bottom lip, then caress the fragile skin with a soft caress of his tongue. She'd never been kissed so thoroughly, so seductively. Her head spun, and she curled her fingers into his back. She had the sense of falling, of hurtling at a gallop over a cliff, and she clung to Jack for dear life.

When he skimmed his hand under her loosened blouse to her back, his fingertips strumming her ticklish spine, she sucked in a sharp hissing breath through her teeth. "Jack…"

"Tracy…I promise you," he murmured against her lips, "my intentions for taking you to my house are to protect you, not to get you into my bed." He feathered nibbling kisses across her cheek and down her throat, pausing at the V of her collar. "If this isn't what you want, tell me now. " He glanced up at her with eyes hooded with desire and a bright sincerity. "I would never take advantage of you."

His consideration was so unlike Cliff's merciless domination of her, she couldn't speak for a moment. Tears prickled her eyes, and her heart swelled with affection for her cowboy protector. "Yes. I want this. I want…you."

Rather than fumble for the words, she raised her mouth to his and anchored his head close with a splayed hand at his nape.

With a groan of satisfaction, Jack stroked his hand up her torso, setting her skin on fire. When he reached her bra, he dipped his fingers under the silky cup and covered her breast with his palm. She arched her back, savoring his touch and begging silently for more. His thumb flicked her nipple, while his mouth ravaged hers. While he rocked his body against hers, she groped with the buttons on his shirt, the zipper of his jeans.

Over the drumming of her heartbeat in her ears, she heard a loud thump from the wall behind them. Jack seemed not to notice, so she dismissed the sound and fought Jack's shirt out from his jeans. She found the hot, smooth flesh of his back and scraped her fingernails lightly over the ridges of muscle and sinew.

More noises reached her through the wall. A female voice. Abra's. Made sense. Abra's master suite was the next door down from her guest room.

Tracy tried not to let the voice distract her, but…

Something in Abra's voice disturbed Tracy. Although the words were indistinct, Tracy heard something in Abra's timbre that woke old demons. A note of confusion. Of *fear*. The word rippled through her as if an apparition had just passed through her. When a chilling sense of premonition choked her next breath, she stiffened and pulled away from Jack's kiss.

He lifted his head and frowned down at her. "Tracy? What's—"

A shriek rent the stillness. The sound of shattering glass. Abra screamed again, louder, her voice more horrified. "No! Please, no!"

Chapter 16

Jack shoved off the bed in an instant, scrambling to right his clothes.

Flashes of memory turned Tracy's insides to liquid. She saw Cliff hovering over her with a wine bottle raised. She felt the crashing blow of the decanter, saw the crimson liquid spread around her, mixing with her blood. She smelled the sweet port...

As Jack dashed for the door, more noises came from Abra's suite, shuffling and crashes.

"Mother!" Jack shouted as he disappeared into the hall.

Tracy's breath panted shallowly, panicked.

Past and present tangled. Adrenaline pounded in her ears, and she battled down the surge of bile that climbed her throat.

"Mother!" Jack's voice rang with agitation and dark concern, jolting Tracy from her paralyzing memories. Smoothing her skirt and blouse into place, she ran to the hall where she met Big J. His bathrobe loosely tied around him and hair mussed from sleep, he lumbered from his bedroom and scrubbed a hand over his face. "What the devil is going on out here?"

"It...it's Abra." She swallowed past the constriction blocking her windpipe. "Something's happened to her. I—"

"Call an ambulance!" Jack shouted from Abra's room, and Tracy watched the color leak from Big J's face.

"Abra? What—" Big J pushed past Tracy, hurrying into his wife's suite. "Abra!"

Tracy sucked in a reviving breath, knowing she'd already wasted precious seconds with her private fears and hesitation. Adrenaline fueled her feet as she hurried back to her room to find her phone and, hands trembling, tapped the screen to call 911.

Phone to her ear, she rushed to Abra's room and gasped when she saw the destruction. Abra's room had been violently trashed, mirrors broken, drawers emptied, furniture toppled and pillows slashed and gutted. In the midst of the chaos, Abra lay crumpled on the floor, face down, with blood pooling next to her head. Jack knelt beside her, gentling probing the wound on her head, pressing a strip of bedsheet to the gash on her scalp to staunch the flow of blood.

The emergency operator answered, asking for the nature of her call and her location.

"We need an ambulance. At the Colton ranch...the Lucky C..." Tracy's voice cracked when she spoke. She racked her muddled brain for the address until Big J snatched the phone from her hand and bellowed into the phone.

"My wife's been attacked! She's dying! Get someone out here. Now!" He spouted the address then demanded again that the ambulance, the police…anyone available, needed to hurry.

Spiders of dread skittered down Tracy's spine. Abra had been attacked. In her own bedroom. Ice filled Tracy's veins. Was no place safe? Was there no place sacred, private, secure…

A new horrifying thought occurred to her. Could the assailant still be there? The master suite was on the second floor, and they'd seen no one in the hallway…

Tracy swept her gaze around the room. She searched the vast room and every shadowed corner. No one was lurking there, but the French doors to her balcony stood ajar. The sheer curtains rippled in the warm night breeze.

Abra's suite was next door to her guest room. Had she been the real target and The Wolf entered the wrong room? Or had Abra discovered the assassin as he made his way toward Tracy's room and paid the price for the chance encounter?

Tracy knew the odds that this was a random attack were low. Nausea swamped her along with the guilt of having brought this calamity on her hostess.

"Abra!" Big J's pained tone shot to Tracy's core.

She held her breath as she crossed the floor to join the men. Abra lay motionless, her head bleeding and red marks swelling where she'd clearly been savagely struck.

"Tracy!" Jack's grave tone tripped through her. "Wake Edith. Speed dial five. Have her call the bunkhouse and alert Brett that there's an assailant on the grounds. And tell her to call Eric and have him meet us at the hospital." He shoved his cell phone at her, and she noticed the tremble in his hand. Not that she blamed him. Her whole body shook.

Tracy's heart contracted with the notion that she could be the reason her hostess had been hurt.

Big J glanced up at her. "Did you see anything? Who did this?"

"I don't know. I was in my room—" *About to make love to Jack...* A fresh wave of guilt rolled through her, and she took a shuddering breath. "I heard her talking to someone. She sounded upset. Then she screamed and—"

"And?" Big J prompted, his face pale. He still held her cell to his ear, his grip on the phone so tight his fingers were bloodless.

Tracy shook her head. "I don't know." She tried to swallow, but her mouth had grown arid. "I'm sorry. This is my fault. It must have been The Wolf...coming for me...I—"

Jack jerked his chin up and shook his head. "Don't blame yourself."

But how could she not? Every fiber of her being, her every instinct told her the attack on Abra had been intended for her.

"A wolf? What the hell are you talking about?" Big J asked.

"I'll explain later," Jack said.

The whine of distant sirens pierced the night, and Big J turned his stormy blue eyes to Tracy. "Will you go out front to meet the ambulance? Show them up? I don't..." He drew a shuddering breath. "I don't want to leave Abra."

She gave him a tiny nod and hurried to the stairs. Meeting the EMTs was the least she could do considering her certainty that her presence at the Lucky C had brought the lethal threat of The Wolf to the ranch residents. For that, she could never forgive herself.

Jack held Tracy against him, absorbing her tremors as Abra was put in the waiting ambulance. She flinched as the bay doors were slammed closed. He had to admit, the attack on his mother had him rattled, too. But he couldn't believe this was the work of a professional assassin. A pro like The Wolf would have no reason to search Tracy's or Abra's rooms, to steal from them and risk leaving trace evidence that would lead back to him. The Wolf would have realized quickly Abra was not Tracy and gotten away unnoticed. Wouldn't he?

But what he'd told Tracy was the truth. The household staff was trustworthy. This theft and attack must have been an outside job. But who? And why? Who would have a reason to hurt Abra, to steal Tracy's painkillers and jewelry and search for Lord-knows-what in Abra's suite?

Leading her by the elbow, Jack pulled Tracy back into the house and off to a corner of the foyer, away from the buzz of police officers searching the premises. He smoothed a loose wisp of her hair back from her face, tucking the silky strands behind her ear. "I think I'm going to fix myself a stiff drink. Can I get you something?"

She shook her head slowly, looking dazed, devastated.

Framing her face with his hands, he kissed the bridge of her nose. "This wasn't your fault."

"But I—"

"This *wasn't* your fault," he repeated, firming his grip. "Even if it turns out The Wolf did this, you can't blame yourself. Blame the cretin who attacked my mother. Blame the Baxters for hiring the bastard. Hell, blame *me* for being so focused on making love to you that I didn't realize what was happening in the next room until too late."

He paused and inhaled slowly, his gut quivering at the memory. The sweet taste of her kisses, the satiny feel of her skin and tantalizing whisper of her panting breaths had entranced him. Worked him to a fevered frenzy, wanting only to bury himself inside her. Even now his body quaked with unspent passion and need that he forced aside in deference to the more serious matters at hand. He rested his forehead against hers and said in a rasping murmur, "But do *not* blame yourself."

She bobbed her chin in agreement, but her expression said she was unconvinced. The bleak look in her eyes and uncharacteristically wan color of her cheeks told the story of her fatigue and stress. The sooner he could get her away from the main house for some rest, the better. But they'd been warned not to leave the area until the police dismissed them.

"I'm going to get that drink now and call to check on Seth. Why don't you sit down in the living room? You look ready to drop."

Her eyes widened and her lips parted at his mention of Seth, but before she could say anything, a police officer approached them and cleared his throat.

"I was told you two were the first on the scene. We need to take a full statement from each of you for the report."

Reluctantly, Jack released her, and he nodded to the officer. "Yes. Fine."

But he wasn't fine at all with letting Tracy go. He wanted to hold her until the pink glow returned to her cheeks, until the fear left her eyes…until he could be certain she was completely safe. As she followed the officer into the next room, she cast a glance over her shoulder that said her wishes echoed his.

The two of them were separated for questioning, much the way Irene and George Baxter had been earlier today. Basic procedure, he knew, but he didn't like it.

Ryan had arrived shortly after Jack's interview started, but his involvement, for now, was limited to observation. Jack could see Ryan's edginess, though. He sensed his brother's desire to dive into the investigation from the way he paced the floor and gritted his teeth, fire leaping in his gaze.

The police interviews lasted about thirty minutes, and when they were allowed to leave, Jack wasted no time collecting the last of Tracy's possessions from the guest room and trundling her down to the old homestead.

Eric had called from the hospital to report that Abra's condition was dire. Her doctors had decided to put her in a medically induced coma, giving her body time to heal the head wound while protecting her brain from further stress and damage. Eric had tried to get Big J to return to the ranch and rest, but he'd refused. Brett, too, had stayed at the hospital at Abra's bedside.

Due to the late hour, Seth was allowed to finish the night sleeping in Edith's quarters on the first floor of the main house.

After parking behind the house and unloading Tracy's suitcases from the truck bed, Jack led her in the back door, through the mudroom, piled high with Seth's dirty clothes and boots, and into the kitchen.

"Can I get you anything to eat?" He waved a hand toward his refrigerator. "We never got any dinner earlier."

"No," she said, her voice little more than a sigh. "I just want to go to bed." She heard the sudden catch in his breath and knew immediately where his thoughts had gone. Despite the tragic turn of events tonight, her mind had not strayed far from thoughts of the intimacy she'd shared with Jack in the guest room. Or where things would have led if Abra hadn't been attacked.

And now they were alone in his house...

"Jack, I…" She wet her lips, not sure what she wanted to tell him, but knowing something should be said about the new direction their relationship had taken. Did she want to sleep with Jack? Yes. Definitely.

Could she give herself to him and not put her heart at risk? Definitely not. Was Jack worth a broken heart? She studied the rugged lines of his square jaw, met the concern for her that burned in his bright green eyes and remembered the loving devotion he showed his son. A tender ache flowed through her, twisting a knot in her chest that stole her breath. Oh, yes. Jack was worth any pain she might experience down the road.

Drawing her shoulders back, she tried again. "About what happened earlier…when we…"

Dropping her bags with a thump, Jack closed the distance between them in two steps. He cradled the back of her head with one large splayed hand and angled her head up. Whispering her name, he bowed his head and kissed her gently. His lips were warm, their caress toe curling and sweet. Then he released her and stepped back, lifting her suitcases again.

"Follow me." He turned and strode toward the stairs.

Follow him? Oh, yes. To the ends of the earth. She was in deep. So deep it frightened her a bit. Jack Colton was so…very…

He was just *so very.*

Her pulse thundered in her ears and, moving like an automaton, she fell in step behind him. He showed her upstairs to a room at the far end of the hallway and laid her suitcase on top of a four-poster double bed with an ivory eyelet bedspread. Tracy sent an encompassing glance around the surprisingly feminine room and set her purse on the oak dresser.

"You should like this place. Laura decorated it, and I never saw any point in changing anything," Jack said.

Tracy jerked a startled glance toward Jack. She shouldn't be so surprised to learn that Laura had put her fingerprint on the guest room. What surprised her was that Jack hadn't seen fit to erase the traces of his ex. She cast a fresh eye to the room appreciating the feminine touches. A sky-blue and mint-green quilt was folded at the foot of the bed and small pillows trimmed with coordinating ribbons adorned the top. Sheer ivory curtains framed the windows, and dried flower arrangements sat atop the chest of drawers and bedside table. A set of pictures featuring turn-of-the-century women enjoying a picnic hung on one wall and a mounted piece of needlepoint in a floral design was displayed next to the window.

Tracy felt a tug at her heart, and a lump swelled in her throat. Standing in that bedroom, seeing all of the personal touches her cousin had chosen, she felt closer to Laura than she had in many months. "It's lovely. Thank you."

Jack gave a small nod of acknowledgment before striding to the door. "If you need anything, if there's...*trouble*, my room is across the hall."

Trouble. An image of Abra's body, blood puddling under her head flashed in Tracy's mind. The warmth she'd felt, being surrounded by the pretty things her cousin had chosen for the guest room evaporated in a chill. The terror of being hunted like an animal shimmied through her.

The Wolf will not stop until Tracy is dead. George Baxter's words reverberated in her head, in her heart. Jack was right. She stood little chance of surviving on her own. She'd thought staying on the ranch, having Jack's protection would be enough to keep her safe until The

Wolf was caught, but the attack on Abra changed things. How many more people would be hurt before The Wolf was caught? Was her death the only thing that would save the rest of the Coltons from the assassin's murderous mission?

The next morning, after helping Jack and Kurt Rodgers with ranching chores, Tracy accompanied Jack to the hospital to visit Abra in ICU. Though she wasn't allowed into the room with Jack's mother, she watched through a large window as Jack placed a chaste kiss on his mother's bandaged head.

"I hate seeing her like that."

She turned to find Big J standing behind her clutching a cup of coffee. Dark circles under his eyes stood out from his unnaturally wan skin and haggard expression. The man who'd seemed so robust and jocular when she'd met him at Greta's engagement party a couple weeks earlier, seemed to have aged ten years overnight.

Tracy touched his arm in sympathy. "I'm so sorry. Is there anything I can do?"

He heaved a weary sigh. "Just…pray."

She nodded. "Of course." When he continued to stare blankly through the glass to his wife's bed, Tracy asked quietly, "Big J, have you been here all night?"

He nodded weakly. "I can't leave her. She's…fragile. I have to take care of her…"

Her heart broke for him, knowing there was nothing he could do and how desperately he must have wanted to help her. "I know you want to be close to her, but…you need to rest, too."

He didn't react to her comment. He just stared into near space, swaying on his feet.

"Big J? Do you want to sit—"

"She wasn't happy here, you know. She never really loved the ranch the way I do."

Tracy blinked, not knowing how to respond.

"She spent most of her time in Europe when the boys were small. Recuperating." He sighed forlornly. "She spent more time at home with us after Greta came, but she…wasn't happy. I'd hurt her…with Daniel's mother… but her doctors had her depression under control…and Edith helps manage her on her worst days…"

Tracy shifted her weight, uncomfortable with the deeply personal nature of Big J's comments. He was overtired, rambling, feeling guilty and grief stricken.

Jack emerged from Abra's room and divided a glance between Tracy and his father. "Big J? Are you all right?"

The older man raised a hand and shook his head. "I'm not going home, so don't even start on me."

Tracy gave Jack a worried look that was reflected in Jack's eyes.

"Her doctors have said they intend to keep her in this medically induced coma for several days at least. She won't be coming to—"

"But she'll know if I leave!" Big J insisted. "I won't let her down by leaving her alone." He shuffled toward the window and pressed his hand to the plate glass. "Case closed."

Jack raked his hand through his rumpled hair and blew a deep breath through pursed lips. "Have it your way. I'll let Eric know you're staying, and he can check on you from time to time."

Big J lifted a gaze that flashed with emotion. "I'm not the one who needs attention. Your mother is!"

Jack opened his mouth, then snapped it closed. He jerked a nod and motioned for Tracy to follow him. "If anything changes with her condition, call me at the ranch office. I'm backlogged on paperwork and plan to be there most of the day."

Tracy fell in step beside Jack as he started for the elevator. "That's it? You're going to leave him here?"

"Coltons have their own brand of stubbornness and determination, Tracy, and Big J has Colton obstinacy in spades. I wasn't going to convince him to leave her once he'd made up his mind."

She cast another concerned glance over her shoulder as they arrived at the bank of elevators. "Maybe I should stay with him. He's—"

"No." Jack's tone brooked no argument. "Have you forgotten there's a hired killer after you? You're not leaving my side today."

"But—"

The ding of the elevator bell signaled its arrival. As the doors parted, Greta stepped off, and seeing Jack, she threw her arms around her brother and heaved a broken sob. "Oh, Jack! I got here as fast as I could. Why didn't anyone call me last night? How is she? What happened? Was the intruder caught? What did Eric say about her injuries?" she asked, not even pausing to take a breath.

After giving her a firm hug, Jack gripped his sister's shoulders. "There was nothing you could do last night, so Brett and I decided to wait until this morning to call." He summarized what had happened with the attacker, the police investigation into the break-in and assault, and the doctor's assessment of their mother's condition.

"I'll sit with Big J," Greta said, swiping a tear from her cheek. "I still wish you'd called me last night."

They left the hospital in silence, each absorbed in worrisome thoughts about Abra's condition and the killer who was on the loose, lurking somewhere in the area of the Lucky C. And if Jack's theory was correct, and the person who'd attacked Abra wasn't The Wolf, then there was *another* threat to the Colton family to worry about.

Chapter 17

Tracy leaned her head back, watching the ranch and farmland outside of Tulsa whiz past the passenger window of Jack's truck, and she rubbed the bridge of her nose. "What are you going to tell Seth?"

Creases of fatigue bracketed Jack's eyes and worry lined the corners of his mouth. "I don't know. The truth, but a scaled-down version of it. I don't want to scare him. He's only five, after all. But I won't lie to him, either."

"What does he know now about what happened and where we went this morning?"

His cell phone rang before he could answer. After checking his caller ID, Jack said, "It's Ryan." Lifting the phone to his ear he answered the call with, "Please tell me you have good news."

Tracy studied Jack's reactions for clues to what his brother was saying. The disgruntled twist of his mouth said his hope for good news was unmet.

"Hang on, I'm going to put you on speaker. I'm with Tracy. We're in the truck, headed back to the ranch after seeing Abra. No, no change. Greta's with Big J. Yeah, hang on." He handed her the phone to hold as he thumbed a button to switch the call to speaker mode. "Okay, whatcha got?"

"We've got some prelim test results back on the infant skeleton y'all found," Ryan said. "The baby was a male. Died approximately six years ago. Was African American."

Tracy snapped her chin up in surprise, her pulse kicking.

Jack's eyebrows drew together sharply, and he gave her a puzzled look as if asking if she'd heard what he did. "Come again?"

"A black infant boy. Five to seven years post-mortem." Ryan's tone was flat and matter-of-fact. But then he'd had time to digest this unusual bit of information.

"Why would he be buried in our family cemetery?" Jack gave his head a little shake. "That makes no sense."

"Which, in and of itself, is a clue. It's likely the bones weren't buried here originally. We're checking to see if any local cemeteries have reported a grave robbery or a theft from a medical school or lab."

"Are you thinking someone from the ranch stole the baby's bones and buried them out there? What would be the point in that?" Tracy asked. She clutched the phone tighter, this strange twist making her uneasy. How did this fit with the attack on Abra? With the Baxters' hiring an assassin to kill her?

"We haven't gotten as far as identifying who could have dug the grave," Ryan reported. "There were dozens of fingerprints on the handle of the shovel. I'm guessing everyone on the ranch has used it in the last couple weeks, so it's not proving helpful."

"So someone dug that grave and left the bones there for us to find… Why?" Jack asked, "To scare us? To send a message?"

"That's yet to be determined but…unofficially—" Ryan paused "—that'd be my guess."

"Who would do that? Why? That's…sick! It's just…" Tracy shuddered.

"Tracy," Ryan said with low, scoffing sigh, "ninety-nine percent of what I deal with in my job is sick and deranged."

"What else do you know?" Jack asked. "Anything new about last night's break-in and the attack on Mother?"

"Not much. Considering some jewelry and prescription drugs were stolen, we have to explore the possibility that this was a simple robbery gone bad. Abra was just in the wrong place at the wrong time."

"But—" Jack started, and Ryan interrupted.

"But…considering what we know about The Wolf and the contract on Tracy, we're definitely not dismissing the possibility this was a premeditated act."

Jack tapped his thumb restlessly on the steering wheel. "Keep us posted," he said, his tone grave.

"Of course. And Tracy?"

Her heart beat a little faster when he addressed her. "Yes?"

"I know you don't like being cooped up with Jack and feeling like you're under his thumb, but considering the circumstances, I think it's what's best. Listen to Jack and do what he tells you. I know my older brother's bossy, but if I had to choose one person to watch my back, it'd be Jack. He'll keep you safe."

Jack cut a startled glance toward his phone and arched one eyebrow, as if his brother's assessment of his skill surprised him.

Tracy didn't bother to explain that under Jack's roof was exactly where she wanted to be or that she agreed with Ryan's appraisal of Jack's capacity to protect her. Instead she simply said, "Thank you, Ryan, for all you're doing." She swiped the screen and disconnected the call.

Jack clipped the phone back on his belt, then signaled his turn onto the long drive leading to the main house.

Seth must have been watching for them, because he bolted out the front door as soon as they entered the circular drive.

Edith emerged from the house at his heels. "How is your mother?"

"No change," Jack said, as he slid out of the truck and crouched to greet his son.

"Dad!" Seth cried as he threw himself into Jack's arms. "What happened to Grandmother? Why is she in the hospital?"

Jack stroked his son's head and clutched him tightly. Finally, he sighed, and lifting Seth as he stood, he carried his boy inside the main house.

Tracy followed, not really wanting to return to the site of last night's vicious assault on Abra. The cold marble and formal decor of the main house didn't welcome and warm her the way Jack's house did, and she found herself longing for the homey, safe comfort of the old homestead.

After sending Edith to gather Seth's things, Jack sat down on the living room couch with Seth on his lap. "Well, Spud, she hit her head. And because it hurt her brain, the doctors put her into a deep sleep, so that her head could heal."

Seth wrinkled his nose in thought. "How did she hit her head? Was she playing too rough? Like when Brett and I wrestle, and you say to be careful 'cause someone could get hurt?"

Seth's youthful innocence twisted in Tracy's chest with a bittersweet pang. She grinned sadly, imagining a scene where Seth roughhoused with his uncle and Jack called them out.

"No, she wasn't playing," Jack said.

"Then what?" Seth's eyes, so like his father's in color, shape and attentiveness, widened in dismay and curiosity."

Jack raised a glance to Tracy that asked for her help. This was where the explanation got dicey.

"She was in her bedroom," Tracy volunteered, "and no one in the family was with her, so we don't really know, for sure, what happened."

Jack's face said the vague, dodging answer would suffice. He gave a curt nod.

Tracy exhaled a cleansing breath and sat beside Jack, taking Seth's hands in her own. "The important thing for you to know is, your grandmother has the best doctors taking care of her. She's in good hands, and she just needs time to get better." She prayed that was the truth. Until the doctors said otherwise, she intended to stay optimistic about Abra's prognosis. The answer seemed to satisfy Seth, who tucked his head under his father's chin and muttered, "Can we go home now?"

Edith returned with a Spider-Man backpack and a half-empty bottle of water. "Can I get either of you anything to eat? Greta called to say she and Mr. Colton would be at the hospital through lunch, but if either of you would like a sandwich or a reheated plate of brisket—"

Having no appetite, Tracy shook her head at the same time Jack said, "No. Thank you, Edith, but I'll wait till I get back to the house to eat something. I just want to get this little guy settled in at home and catch up on returning phone calls. I'll find something to eat after I see what's been happening with the ranch this morning."

Once they reached the old homestead, Jack parked in his usual spot behind house. As the three of them trudged into the house, Tracy glanced across the ranch yard, her attention snagged by a flash motion near the corner of one of the outbuildings. She caught a quick glance of a tall woman with dark brown hair just as the woman ducked into the shadows behind the bunkhouse.

Had she not known that Greta was at the hospital with her mother, she would have sworn that was who she'd seen. Remembering that she'd seen someone who looked like Greta from the upstairs window of the main house the week before, she asked, "Jack, do you have a lady on staff who is tall and dark-haired like your sister?"

He gave her a puzzled look. "I'm sure we have several people who fit that general description. Why do you ask?"

"I keep seeing someone around the ranch who looks like Greta."

"Maybe it is Greta."

"No. It's always when I know Greta isn't here. Like just now. I saw the woman in question out by the bunk-house as we came inside, but I assume Greta's still at the hospital."

Jack's brow dented in concern. "Spud, why don't you build a spaceship for me out of your Legos?"

Seth gave his father a long uncertain look. "Will you help me?"

"I'll help you," Tracy volunteered. "I think your dad has work to do."

He ruffled his son's hair. "Tell you what, pal. You start working on that spaceship with Tracy, and I'll check on you in a few minutes, okay?"

After giving his father one last wary look, Seth took Tracy's hand. "Come on. I'll show you my room."

Jack strode back to the door he'd just locked behind them. "It's probably nothing, but I'll go have a look, just in case. Relock the door behind me."

She nodded and did as he directed, then let Seth tow her upstairs to his toy-strewn room. Half an hour later, Jack joined them, answering her unspoken question with a shrug. "I didn't find anyone and none of the hands saw anything."

A prickle of apprehension scraped down her spine. "I know I saw someone."

"You sure it wasn't one of the hands? Ralph Highshaw is kinda slim and has dark hair."

Tracy huffed her frustration. "No. I saw a woman. I'm almost sure…"

"Almost sure?" Jack's direct gaze questioned her, and her own wording had her doubting.

Had she seen a woman? It made more sense that it had been one of the hands. She'd never met this Highshaw person. But the figure's dark hair had been to the shoulders like Greta's.

"Look, Daddy. It's a fighter spaceship. See the guns?"

Seth's enthusiasm as he showed his father the creation he'd been building chased most of the odd jitters from Tracy's bones. She had enough to worry about with The Wolf, the Baxters' hired assassin, hunting her without conjuring mysterious women lurking on the ranch.

"Hey, that's impressive, Spud." Jack settled on the floor next to her, his arm draping loosely around her shoulders as they spent the next several minutes listening to Seth explain the design of his fleet of Lego aircraft. If she closed her eyes and pushed her doubts and worries aside, Tracy could sink completely into a domestic fantasy where Jack was her husband and Seth their son. She could pretend this life was hers and no one was trying to kill her. The peaceful tranquility of that moment, and the childish excitement in Seth's voice as he teased with his father warmed her heart. She longed for the boy's resilience from his recent traumas, clearly based in his complete faith that his father would protect him. That once the danger had passed, he had nothing to fear, nothing to doubt in his life.

Reaching for that same level of confidence and trust in Jack, Tracy snuggled closer to the green-eyed cowboy. She leaned her head against his shoulder, and he gave her a reassuring squeeze.

That night, Tracy reveled in the chance to assist in Seth's bedtime ritual. After Jack assisted with his son's bath and the boy was in his pajamas, Tracy cuddled next to him on his bed to read several books together. The barn cat, Sleek, had sneaked inside at some point that afternoon and was curled at the foot of the bed. Tracy used her bare toes to rub the cat's cheek and elicit a purr while Seth stumbled through reading *Go, Dog, Go.* She took many opportunities to kiss Seth's head and inhale the fragile scent of his freshly shampooed hair. When the books were put away, she knelt with him beside the bed and listened to his innocent but earnest prayers.

"Dear God," he said, eyes clenched shut and hands clasped tightly, "thank you for my Daddy and Pooh and Sleek. Thank you for my house and our food and my Legos. Help Grandmother get well and please make Ms. Tracy my real mom. Amen."

Tracy's heart swelled to bursting and with tears in her eyes, she raised a startled look first to Seth, who climbed back into bed, oblivious to her surprise, and then to Jack, who looked as poleaxed by his son's prayer as she. Gathering her composure, she tucked Seth in, wished him a good night and waited in the hallway while Jack did the same.

"Oh, Jack," she whispered as he came out and closed Seth's door. "I promise I never said anything to him about—"

"Shh." He touched a finger to his lips and motioned with a jerk of his head for her to follow him farther down the hall. When they stood between his bedroom door and the one to the guest room, he faced her. Putting a hand at her waist, he drew her close and threaded his fingers through her hair.

"I never said anything to him about being his mother. I swear!" she finished in a hushed tone.

He lifted one dark eyebrow as he caressed her cheek. "Are you saying you wouldn't want to?"

Her eyes widened. "No! I—I'd love to be his mother." Realizing how that sounded and not wanting to appear pushy, she backpedaled. "I mean…Seth is a great kid. Anyone would be lucky to have a boy like him to call their own."

Jack's cheek hiked in a lopsided grin. "I'm not accusing you of anything. But I'm not blind. I see the rapport you have with him. You'll be a great mother someday."

His compliment wound through her, warming places left cold and dead by Cliff's heartlessness and insults. She lowered her gaze, her pulse racing like a wild stallion on the open range. She tried to reply, but forming a cohesive thought was hard while Jack was touching her.

When she flattened her palm against his chest, she felt the strong, drubbing beat of his heart, and that steady, life-affirming thud was one of the sweetest, sexiest things she'd ever experienced. Because it was Jack. Because his powerful presence was reassuring. Because she remembered so vividly having that pounding heartbeat pressed tight against her own just last night.

"About last night," he started, as if reading her thoughts. And why wouldn't he know what she'd been thinking? She'd always been told her face was an open book. But more important, she'd sensed from her first day on the ranch that she and Jack had a unique connection. A link that went beyond the spark of passion that crackled when they were close.

"Jack…" she whispered, and he silenced her with a soft kiss.

"I haven't forgotten where we were, what we'd started when…" he left his sentence trail off.

When Abra was attacked and left for dead. The unspoken words hung between them, and a shiver raced through her. His arms tightened around her, pulling her closer, chasing away the chill of fear.

"Do you remember what I told you earlier this week… in my office?" he whispered, his breath a warm tickle in her ear.

"You said a lot of things in your office." Her lips twitched with a teasing grin.

"Let me help you remember, then." He trailed light kisses along her cheek to the tip of her nose, and her breath snagged in her lungs. "I said that I finish…" he nibbled at her lips. "…what I start."

His meaning dawned on her as he deepened his kiss, and her heart jolted. He caught her tiny gasp with the caress of his mouth on hers. Even as her body melted against his, the heat and sweet tension of desire coiling in her core, her head rebelled. How could she make love to Jack and not end up with a broken heart? He hadn't said he loved her. He'd made no promises beyond protecting her until the Baxters' assassin was stopped. How could she deepen the bond she felt for him, give him her body, and not lose her heart to him?

But, oh mercy, she wanted him. She knew she'd regret it if she didn't seize this chance to be held and loved by this tender and passionate man. Every woman should know how it felt to be cherished and fully aroused by a loving man at least once in her life. Shouldn't they? And she'd certainly never had that kind of gentle intimacy with Cliff.

As if sensing her hesitance, Jack lifted his head and peered deep into her eyes. "Tracy?"

She swallowed hard and listened to the whisper of her heart. "Yes, Jack. Make love to me."

In the days that followed, the home-like family atmosphere the three of them shared and the lack of disturbance to the ranch's routine made it easy to picture herself as part of Jack's family. By day, she helped nurture Seth, cooked their meals and shared the ranch chores. By night, she slept with Jack, made love to him until they were both spent, then slipped back into her own guest bed before dawn, so that Seth wouldn't find them together should the boy wake early and sneak into his father's room.

It was a comfortable, blissfully simple life, and she was with two people she'd grown to love. What could be better?

She tried hard to quiet the voice of doubt that said Jack was merely using her body because she was convenient. He'd still given her no pledge of love, no promises of the future. She wanted to just enjoy this time on the ranch for what it was. A glorious, happy time. A respite before she had to return to her real life and her empty apartment in Denver. But with every day that passed, she fell deeper in love with Jack Colton and his son. Leaving them, when the time came, would be the hardest thing she'd ever done.

For all the joy she felt with each new day, the specter of danger lurked at the edges of every thought, every horseback ride, every family meal. She couldn't forget that a killer still hunted her, and she spent her days looking over her shoulder, jumping at shadows.

Abra's attack remained at the fore as well. Every day, after the work of the ranch was done, the three of them would drive in to the hospital to check on Abra and Big J. Jack's father refused to leave his wife, choosing instead to eat, sleep and shower at the hospital, despite his family's urging to get some rest at home. Day after day, Abra remained in the drug-induced coma, her condition stable but serious.

On the afternoon of her eighth day of living at Jack's house, Tracy stepped out of the shower, having needed a second one that day thanks to a messy incident involving a rambunctious little boy and a muddy holding pen. The house was eerily quiet, and she was anxious to dry off, re-dress and find Jack and Seth.

She spotted Jack near the stable from the guest room window as she toweled dry her hair, and once she'd put on a fresh pair of shorts and sandals, she headed out to meet him.

Jack greeted her with a brilliant smile and kiss. "Have I ever told you how great you smell?"

She chuckled. "No. But it's not hard to smell better than most of the things on this ranch."

"True," he said, taking another deep whiff of her newly shampooed hair and hugging her tight.

"Where's Seth? Doesn't he need a bath, too? Last I saw him, he was pretty muddy."

"I hosed him off behind the barn."

She gave an indelicate snort. "Hosed him off? Like he was livestock?"

"He's only going to get dirty again before dinner." Jack turned back to the saddle he was oiling. "He rode out to the north pasture to help Brett and the hands with sorting, vaccinating and branding calves."

She drew a sharp breath. "Branding? Isn't that rather a…harsh thing for him to witness?"

Jack lifted a shoulder. "It's part of ranching. Something he needs to learn. He'll be fine."

She opened her mouth to disagree but snapped it closed again. Jack loved his son and raised him by different methods than she would, but that didn't make his ways wrong.

Jack moved closer to her and rubbed a thumb over the crease she hadn't realized she'd made between her eyebrows. Lifting the corner of his mouth in a grin that was becoming a familiar part of his repertoire, he repeated, "He'll be fine."

She returned a grin and nodded. "All right. I trust you."

His grin grew more amused, and he shifted his hand to cup the back of her head. "So I have your approval to raise my son as I see fit?"

An awkward flush prickled in her cheeks. "I only meant—"

He silenced her explanation with a slow and sultry kiss that she felt all the way to her toes. When he stepped back, he tweaked her chin. "What if we headed out to the branding pen ourselves and gave them a hand?"

"Me?" She blinked rapidly. "How would I help?"

"Plenty of ways." He gave her a raised-eyebrow look that sent a silent challenge. "Assuming you don't mind getting your hands dirty again."

"You couldn't have told me this before I showered?"

He flipped up a palm. "You didn't ask."

"Branding, huh?" Tracy squared her shoulders and jerked a firm nod. "Bring it on." Then glancing down at her shorts and peasant top and sandals, she added, "Let me go change into work clothes, and I'll be right back."

She stood on her toes to give him another quick kiss, gave Sleekie a scratch on the cheek as she passed the straw bale where the cat napped and marched across the ranch yard toward Jack's house.

Tracy inhaled the sweet scent of hay that was carried on the June breeze and smiled up at the wide blue Oklahoma sky. She noticed she had a bounce in her step that matched the delight that filled her chest. It surprised her to realize that she, a city girl, was truly happy here at the ranch. Sure, she was still getting used to the early hours, the hard work and the dirty jobs that went along with ranching, but when she tumbled into bed at night, achy and exhausted, she had never felt as satisfied and accomplished.

After years of teetering on a precipice because of Cliff, she finally was beginning to feel as if her feet were on solid ground.

Her cell phone buzzed in her pocket, and she pulled it out to check the message. She read the message from her landlord in Denver, asking when she planned to return and reminding her that her rent was due in three days.

Her heart gave a painful throb at the thought of leaving the ranch once the police caught The Wolf and she was safe to return to her home in Denver. While she'd formed the bond she'd hoped to with Seth, she hadn't counted on falling in love with the little boy's father.

What if—

A heavy object struck a sharp blow to her head. Pain exploded through her skull. Her knees crumpled, and as she slid toward the ground, a muscled arm caught her around the waist. A smelly rag was slapped over her nose, the bite of some pungent chemical burning her nostrils.

Jack, help! her brain screamed, but she couldn't make her mouth form the words. Her vision grew fuzzy, dimming. Her last images were of the world tilting as the brute hefted her up. Tossed her over a meaty shoulder. Then everything went black.

Chapter 18

Jack finished saddling Mabel for Tracy, tidied up a corner of the stable where Sleekie or some other critter had knocked over the bottles and cans on a storage shelf, then checked his watch for the third time. What was taking Tracy so long to change clothes? He knew women took a while to dress when they were getting gussied up to go out, but how hard was it to put on jeans and a work shirt? He'd tried calling her cell phone, but it went to voice mail.

"Dang it," he grumbled, stashing his mobile phone back on the clip at his waist. A niggling fear twisted through him. Could something have happened to her? Should he have accompanied her back to the house? The distance to his house was short enough, with hands typically milling about the ranch yard, so he hadn't deemed the precaution necessary. But…most of the ranch hands were helping with the vaccinations and branding of the calves.

Disquiet needled him. Damn it, he should have gone with her! As unlikely as it was that the gunman could have gotten this far onto the property without being noticed, The Wolf had gotten onto the ranch before, even if just an isolated pasture.

And *something* had delayed Tracy. With a huff of agitation and self-censure, he headed toward the house. He swept his gaze around the yard, looking for signs of trouble, a strange vehicle or tire tracks on the dusty ground. The afternoon sun glinted off something dark near the base of the front-porch steps. Heart pounding, Jack jogged over to the reflective item.

Tracy's phone.

Acid gushed in his stomach, and panic spiked in his blood.

He scooped up her cell phone and rushed into the house. "Tracy!" There was no answer. "Tracy!"

His own phone beeped, and he whipped it out, checking the caller ID. Tom Vasquez. He pressed ignore. He'd have to get back to the ranch hand later.

Replacing his mobile phone, he hurriedly searched every room in the house, calling for Tracy. His voice grew more desperate with every passing minute. She simply wasn't there.

Hands shaking, Jack pulled his phone back out and dialed Ryan's number. Knowing time was of the essence, he flew down the steps and raced out to the front porch, while his brother's line rang in his ear. And rang. "Come on, Ryan!"

Finally his brother answered with, "Colton."

"It's Jack. Tracy's gone." Speaking the words made it real, and viselike pressure clamped his heart. His voice was hoarse and strained when he added, "I think that Wolf bastard has her."

Jack heard shuffling sounds through the phone that told him Ryan was on his feet and leaving his office, even as they spoke. "Talk to me. Where are you? How long has she been gone?"

"I'm at my house. She's only been gone a few minutes. Maybe ten? Fifteen?" *Too long.* Anything could have happened in that amount of time. It only took a few seconds to slit someone's throat and have them bleed out. His gut roiled at the possibility Tracy could have been hurt. But the more he considered it, the more likely it seemed. If she hadn't been injured or incapacitated, she would have screamed or called out for help.

Ryan fired more questions at Jack, and he answered as best he could.

No, he saw no signs of a struggle.

No blood to indicate violence.

He'd heard nothing, seen nothing.

He didn't have any damn clues where she might be. They couldn't even track her phone, since she'd dropped it.

"I'm on my way, and I'm bringing backup. We'll find her."

But reaching the ranch, even driving at top speeds with lights and sirens, would take Ryan twenty minutes or more. "What do I do in the meantime? I can't just sit here!"

"Nothing rash. Keep looking for anything to tell us which direction they went. There has to be *something.*"

Jack gritted his teeth in frustration as he disconnected. He knew basic tracking. All of the Colton kids had learned how to read telltale clues to track lost cows. He circled the house slowly, his gaze trained on minute details. The incoming text signal sounded on his phone. Vasquez again. He swiped his thumb across his screen intending to close the message menu when the first word of the text caught his eye. *Tracy.*

Tracy woke to a splitting ache in her head. When she blinked her vision into focus, her view of the world was upside down, and her body was being roughly jostled. *What the...?*

In an instant, fear charged through her. She was draped over the back of a horse. Her hands were bound in front of her with rope, and a foul-tasting rag had been shoved in her mouth.

An angry-sounding voice barked at the mare. "Come on, you stupid animal! Move it!"

Pounding fear flashed through her in a hot wave. Tracy twisted and flailed, trying to right herself. For her efforts, she earned a stinging slap on her buttocks.

"Stop squirming! You ain't going nowhere," the man, whose lap she was across, growled.

A whimper of fear swelled in her throat, but she determinedly muzzled the sound. Inhaling slowly, she fought to calm her jangling nerves and keep a level head. Her only chance of escape depended on thinking rationally, planning. Not panicking.

The horse slowed again, taking a few side steps, then tossed his mane and snorted, clearly agitated.

"Damn nag! Go!" The kidnapper kicked the horse in the ribs, but his brutality only upset the horse further. Grumbling under his breath, the man shoved her away from his legs so that he could dismount. Once on the ground, he grabbed a fistful of her hair and yanked her head up. "Don't try anything stupid, or you'll be dead before you take two steps."

Pinpricks of pain shot through her scalp, and she recoiled when she met the chilling gray glare of the man's feral eyes. *The Wolf.* His moniker suited him. Frighteningly so. His breath stank of cigarettes, and her stomach soured at the acrid stench.

She tried to swallow, but the dirty rag in her mouth left her tongue dry, her throat arid. Despite her fear, she narrowed her eyes in a defiant stare. She was through with cowering for bullies. She'd let Cliff push her around, intimidate her and ruin her life far too long. But in the few days she'd spent with Jack, she'd seen how a real man treated a woman. He'd showed her respect, patience, tenderness. He'd encouraged her to find her inner strength and fight for what she wanted from life.

And what she wanted was Jack. She wanted a chance to make a family with Jack and Seth. She wanted the happiness she'd found here at the Lucky C.

Because she loved Seth…and Jack. The realization flowed through her like warm honey and filled her with the will to fight.

"Come on, damn you!" The Wolf screamed at the horse.

Despite angling her head, Tracy couldn't see what had upset the horse and made it stall, but she knew enough from her few riding lessons that The Wolf's abuse and harsh tone were upsetting the horse further. Good. Any delay had to work in her favor, didn't it?

How long would it take before Jack worried about her and came looking? And once he did realize she was missing how would he find her? She had to do something to help him find her. But what?

Tracy kidnapped. Horse stolen. In pursuit on foot. East.

Jack read the text message twice, his heart in his throat. Though his worse fear was confirmed, at least he had a lead where Tracy had been taken. And someone was already following her. God bless Tom Vasquez. The ranch hand would definitely be getting a bonus in his next paycheck.

Regrouping, Jack ran toward the garage where the utility vehicles were stored, praying the hands didn't have all of the ranch's transportation at the branding pen.

East. Jack mentally pictured the terrain east of the ranch buildings. Mostly idle pastures and old, unused buildings from his grandfather's time. An equipment shed in bad repair. A dilapidated barn where hay bales were stored. Fields where they grew the hay.

He skidded to a stop at the garage and threw open the side door. The bay was empty except for an older SUV with two flat tires.

Damn it!

Wasting no time, he raced toward the stable, remembering he had Buck and Mabel saddled and waiting. Not as good as a motorized vehicle, but faster than racing after the kidnapper on foot.

As he ran across the ranch yard, he redialed Ryan's number. He quickly relayed what Tom had reported. "I'm headed that way...on Buck."

"Jack, don't do anyth—" Ryan started, but Jack disconnected and dialed Tom's number.

"Where are you now?" he asked without preamble when a breathless voice answered. "Any sign of her?"

"I can see them...ahead of me...but they're moving too fast...for me to...keep up."

"Where? Give me a landmark." Jack grabbed the saddle horn with his free hand and swung up on Buck's back.

"Miller's creek. They're near...the old hay barn."

"Can you tell..." Jack's lungs tightened, and dread speared his gut. "Is she hurt? Can you tell if she's..." *Dead.* His throat closed, not allowing him to say the word.

"I can see…her moving, struggling…to get free," Vasquez wheezed.

Relief flooded Jack so hard and fast that his head spun.

"I can't follow…anymore. I'm sorry. I—" Jack heard Vasquez retch.

"On my way." Pausing only long enough to tap out a quick text to Brett, alerting him to the kidnapping, he headed out. With a slap of his reins, he and Buck bolted toward the eastern fields. Silently he prayed he wouldn't be too late. If The Wolf was headed toward the old barn, did Jack have time to get there before the assassin carried out his mission to kill Tracy? He didn't like the odds.

Fear twisting through him, he gave Buck a kick, urging his mount to run faster.

The Wolf reined the stolen horse to a stop and shoved Tracy off his lap so that she tumbled with a jarring thud to the ground. Hands bound as they were, she hadn't been able to break her fall and ended up biting her tongue. The metallic taste of blood filled her mouth, adding to the nausea and anxiety that roiled inside her. After finally coaxing the horse to cooperate, The Wolf had set off at a gallop, unmindful of how the pace bounced Tracy in her awkward position. The only good thing she could say about the jolting ride was that she'd been able to work the rag out of her mouth and spit it out as they raced along. Her head reeled, and her ribs throbbed from the assault, but she shoved thoughts of her pain aside, focusing only on how she could escape.

She glared up at the man who towered over her, his imposing brow and menacing eyes sending icy trepidation down her aching spine. "They know who you are, you know. You won't get away with this. The Baxters confessed everything. The cops are looking for you even now."

Her news earned a brief hesitation, and the quirk of one dark eyebrow. "Oh, they did, did they? Well…" He scoffed. "I'll take care of them when I finish here."

He stalked toward her, and she scuttled back on her bottom as best she could with her encumbered hands. "No! Get away from me!" She kicked her legs, aiming for his knees, his crotch, any vulnerable area she thought she could hit.

Her captor managed to dodge all but a few cursory blows. "Stop it, bitch!"

"Help!" she screamed as loud as she could from her bruised chest. "Help me! Someone!"

A slinging slap found her cheek, and her head snapped back. Her ears buzzed from the force of the blow.

"Shut the hell up!" he snarled in her face, his cigarette breath making her gag.

For a moment, she flashed to the few times Cliff had let his temper turn violent, and her instinct was to curl inward, to protect herself and end the threat faster by becoming submissive. But a new stronger voice in her soul shouted down that first instinct.

This man intended to kill her, and she refused to go meekly to her death. Not when she now had so much to live for. Jack, Seth, a fresh start in life.

"Get up," he barked and caught her under her armpits. As he dragged her to her feet, she scrambled mentally for some way, *any way* to call for help, to signal her location or free herself from his grasp. He was too strong to overpower him. Her hands were tied, limiting her ability to fight. But she hadn't seen a weapon yet. If he was unarmed, then how…?

Her brain shied away from finishing that question, but

the sentiment remained. Where was his weapon? Was there any chance she could snag the weapon from him and use it to defend herself?

She scanned his body with a frantic gaze, looking for a telltale lump that might be a hidden gun or knife. The only obvious bulge she saw was at his chest pocket, where he'd clearly stashed his cigarettes. Her spirits wilted. Small paper-wrapped sticks of tobacco would hardly be helpful in freeing herself.

"Let's go." With a biting grip on her arms, he shoved her towards a dilapidated barn. He'd been so purposeful in bringing her here, she realized he must have planned it out. She knew he'd been on the ranch property before when he'd shot at her and Seth. The idea that he could have been lurking nearby all these weeks, learning the territory and plotting her murder sent a chill through her.

There was a sick logic to bringing her to this old barn. By killing her here, away from the main ranch property, he could make his escape before anyone found her body. Did that mean he also had his weapons stashed here? Would he kill her outright or torture her first? The man seemed sadistic enough to want to watch her suffer.

The hinges of the barn door screeched as he pushed her inside. Her heart thumped wildly, and she continued her frenzied search for a plan. She stumbled through the barn door and blinked as her eyes adjusted from bright sun to the dim light. Was there something close by she could use as a weapon?

The ground was primarily hard-packed dirt except for an animal stall with a thick layer of rotting straw where rusting farm equipment had been abandoned in a back corner. Dust motes swirled in the thin beams of sunlight that seeped through cracks in the roof. Disturbed by their presence, a bat swooped low then fluttered near the rafters before resettling in the shadows. A bent saw, some baling wire and a pair of pliers were hung on a Peg-Board on one wall, but they were too far away for her to reach.

He aimed a finger at the floor. "Sit down."

She didn't budge. If she was going to have a chance, she needed to stay on her feet, stay mobile. "Didn't you hear what I told you before? The Baxters gave you up. You won't get paid for killing me, so why not let me go?"

"Because I have my own reasons to want you dead."

His reply stunned her. "What reasons? I've never met you before. What could you possibly have against me?"

"You cost me thousands of dollars."

She shook her head, baffled. "How?"

He curled his lip in a sneer. "I had a business arrangement with your husband. Now that he's dead, that source of income is gone. Word on the street is he was chasing his runaway wife down when he was the arrested."

"What kind of b-business arrangement?" she rasped.

"We were selling Girl Scout Cookies," The Wolf said, his curled lip matching his sarcastic tone. His expression soured further, and he glared darkly at her. "What difference does it make, seein' as how he's dead, and it ain't going to pay off no more."

"Look, i-if it's money you want, I'll pay you."

"Only one form of payment I'd want from you." He looked her up and down with a leer that made her skin crawl. "Don't think I haven't considered having a taste of what you've got before I off you." He licked his lips like a hungry dog, and an oily revulsion rolled in her stomach.

"No," she rasped, her body trembling despite her efforts to be brave.

"If only I had more time…" He dismissed the idea with a lifted shoulder, then stuck his nose in her face and bared his teeth. "Now, *sit down*."

With that, he grabbed her shoulder in a painful grip and shoved her toward the floor. Weak with fear, her knees buckled, and she crumpled. Without use of her hands, she again landed hard and toppled onto her side, her face pressed to the dusty floor. The low rumble of a male laugh penetrated the swoosh of blood past her ears. She gritted her teeth as fury, humiliation and determination spiked in her, a triumvirate of rebellion and refusal to be subjugated again.

You have a core of inner strength, Jack had told her, and feeling her choler rise, she believed him. *Fight back*, the long-buried warrior inside her whispered.

Drawing a deep breath for courage, Tracy rolled to her back and sat up, working her legs under her.

Eyeing her with dark purpose, The Wolf bent at the waist and tugged up the leg of his pants. She saw the grip of the handgun poking from the top of his boot, and cold terror slithered through her. She was out of time, out of options. She had to act *now*, do *something*! Or die like the submissive wimp Cliff had convinced her she was.

She tensed, ready. And the instant The Wolf's gaze shifted from her to the gun, the second he reached for his weapon, she lunged. With a primal roar that shocked even her own ears, she pounced on him. Her tied hands clawed at his face, her feet swinging for his shins. Like a rabid wildcat, she attacked, flailing, leaping on his back, biting…whatever outlet she found she used in a whirlwind of desperation and anger. She'd caught him off guard, which gave her the upper-hand for a few precious seconds, and she battled for all she was worth.

But his superior strength and size soon turned the tide. His arms snaked around her thrashing body, and he pinned her arms down, her body facing his. He grabbed a fistful of her hair and jerked her head back. When she quit struggling, in deference to the painful grip he had on her hair, he jammed the handgun into her face, growling, "That's going to cost you, sugar. Do you know how many nonlethal holes I can put in you before I finally end your suffering?"

She moaned involuntarily, the lightning pain in her scalp making her eyes water.

"Here's a hint. This here PX4 Storm SubCompact holds ten rounds." He jerked her closer, snarling, "That's ten holes, sweetcakes."

Tracy seized what might be her last chance. She sank her teeth into the fleshy part of his gun hand, just below his thumb and bit down. Hard.

The Wolf howled in pain, pushing her away and flinging his hand to shake her off. And losing his grip on his weapon.

Seeing the gun spin across the dirt floor, she dove for it, her bound hands grappling in the straw until she held the gun between her shaking palms.

Hand in his mouth, sucking on the bloody wound she'd inflicted, he glared at her. "You won't shoot me. You don't have the guts."

Her breath shuddered as she took aim. "You sure about that?"

"You won't be able to live with the guilt." He inched toward her, and she scuttled back. "Have you ever seen a man die? It's not pretty."

Her heart clenched. She'd seen Laura die. She'd watched the life ebb from her cousin after their car crashed. Laura hadn't given her life, winning Tracy's freedom, just to have her cousin die months later at the hand of a hired assassin.

But Tracy's mind recoiled from the notion of killing a man in cold blood. She swallowed the bitter taste of bile that rose in her throat and scrambled for her next move. The Wolf continued to close in on her. He crept steadily toward her as if knowing a sudden move might make her panic and pull the trigger. She met the feral, chaotic gleam in his eyes and shivered. His hair was disheveled from her attack. His shirt pocket was ripped and dangling by a few threads. His cheeks bore long red scratches, and blood from his hand had smeared on his lips and chin. He looked like his namesake animal after a vicious hunt. Wild, ferocious, predatory.

Her back bumped the rusted old hay baler, preventing any further retreat. In a few more steps, he'd be on her, would overpower her and reclaim the gun. A cold sweat beaded on her lip. Either she shot him now, or...

The flicker of light, as the bat stirred again in the hayloft, drew her attention upward. Tracy followed a gut instinct, a rash idea. Just keep the gun away from him.

Swinging her tied arms between her legs for more heft, she flung the gun up and forward.

"Hey!" he roared as the gun sailed toward the upper loft.

The weapon discharged when it landed in the hayloft, startling the bat from its perch.

The Wolf blinked once, clearly startled by her move, then his face contorted in an ugly snarl. "You bitch!" He rushed her, grabbing a fistful of her shirt and shaking her like a rag doll. "All you've done is delay me. And piss me off!"

She gasped as he seized her wrists and dragged her to the end of the hay baler.

Unknotting the rope binding her arms, he looped the ends through a large-toothed iron gear wheel and quickly retied the knots. He jerked the ends hard so that the rope cut into her flesh. "I'll be back, bitch. And it won't go well for you."

Her stomach filled with acid, the bitter taste rising to the back of her throat, but she held his glare, fighting the urge to cower. She was through being anyone's punching bag or foot mat.

He stalked away, climbed to the loft using a half-rotten wooden ladder and began searching the piles of hay for his weapon.

Tracy knew she had precious little time to think, to plan, to come up with her next move. Frantically, she twisted her wrists, trying to angle her fingers so that she could loosen the knotted rope. But the binds were so tight, she was already losing feeling in her hands.

Next she scanned the hay baler, looking for a sharp edge she could use to fray the rope, but saw nothing within her limited reach. Shifting her gaze to check The Wolf's progress, a glint of metal on the dirt floor caught her eye. Next to the scattered pack of cigarettes that had fallen from his shirt pocket when she tore it, a sunbeam glimmered off a silver butane lighter. A throb of anticipation and hope skittered through her. If she couldn't cut her wrists free of the rope, could she burn through them?

Her mouth dried knowing she'd burn her wrists, but weren't burns better than surrendering to him and inevitable death? And he'd all but sworn to torture her first.

Sliding as far down to the floor as her tied wrists allowed, she stretched her leg toward the lighter. The toe of her sandal nudged the lighter closer, then a few more inches. Her awkward position strained her wrists, the binding knots gouging and pinching her skin, but she refused to give up. Every bit of pain was worth it if she could save herself. For the first time in many years, she had a future she looked forward to. A relationship with Seth, the opportunity to build a career of her own…and Jack. She'd only just realized that moments earlier, just before The Wolf grabbed her, and she hadn't had the chance to tell him her feelings. How would he react to her feelings? Would he ever give marriage a second chance?

She gave her head a brisk shake. That was a debate for another time. She had to focus on freeing herself, surviving her current ordeal.

The lighter was only a few inches from her now, but with her hands tied to the baler, she couldn't bend to get it. With a glance to check on her captor's progress, she kicked off her sandals. The Wolf was grumbling bitterly in the loft, clearly not having any luck finding his gun in the mounds of molded hay. Using her toes to grip the lighter, she wiggled and lifted her foot as high as she could. She dropped it once and had to start over, but finally got the lighter close enough to her fingers to clasp it between her hands. Working slowly, her hands trembling, she tried to flick the igniter. After a couple attempts, a flame danced up, and she exhaled the breath she'd been holding. Careful not to let the flame go out, she wrenched her arms to an awkward angle hoping to touch the ropes to the small flicker.

A few of the fibers glowed red as the rope struggled to catch fire. Tears of frustration and pain filled Tracy's eyes as she continued to hold the flame against the rope with only marginal success. Singed fibers dropped from the smoldering rope onto her skin, and she fought the instinct to flinch, to jerk her hands back from the heat. Her progress was slow, but the rope was burning, bit by bit. *Please, please, please!* This had to work. She had no other ideas, no other options, and no more time.

The Wolf's footsteps thudded as he crossed the wooden floor of the hayloft, still searching for his gun.

"I have other ways to kill you, ways that are less merciful than a bullet." When he came to the edge of the loft and shouted down at her, she curled her fingers around the lighter to hide it from him. "You think you've won a victory, but this only means you'll suffer more."

He drew his dark eyebrows into a frown and lifted his nose to sniff the air like a predator scenting his prey. "What's that smell? Something's burning. What—" His gaze narrowed on the ropes around her wrists.

Tracy glanced down. The spot she'd been burning smoldered, trailing a thin wisp of smoke.

"Like fire, do ya?" The Wolf cast his gaze around the old barn. "You're right. This place would go up like a tinderbox, all this weathered wood and straw." His grin was pure evil. "And you with time to think about burning up like a campfire marshmallow..."

An anxious whimper escaped her throat, the sound loud to her own ears. Loud enough that she almost missed the shout from outside. The voice of her salvation. Jack!

"Tracy!" He was clearly still a good distance away, but...he was coming after her!

She stretched her body trying to see out the nearest window. Fresh tears of hope rushed to her eyes. "Jack! Help me!"

The Wolf, too, moved to a spot in the hayloft where he could look out through one of the many gaps in the dilapidated walls. Growling a bitter curse, The Wolf headed back toward the ladder. Then, as if having second thoughts, he changed direction and disappeared into the shadows of the loft.

Tracy's anxiety ratcheted up a notch. Not knowing where The Wolf was and what he could be doing was somehow more frightening than his looming presence.

"Tracy!" Jack's voice was closer now, accompanied

by the pounding of hooves. Though she still couldn't see Jack, the jangle of reins drifted in from just beyond the barn door.

"Jack!" Her heart almost burst with a surge of relief when the barn door crashed open.

Rather than race into the barn, he hovered by the door, sweeping the interior with a keen gaze and leading with a gun clenched between his hands. Clearly he'd realized who'd kidnapped her, but he was walking into an unknown situation.

"Jack, look out!" she called in warning as he zeroed in on her and hurried inside the barn. "He had a gun... in the lo—"

Before she could finish, a large dark figure pounced from above. The Wolf landed on Jack's back, knocking him to the ground and causing him to lose his grip on his gun.

A startled scream slipped from Tracy's throat, and her anxiety spiked as the Wolf lobbed a punch into Jack's chin. Her cowboy's head snapped back, and his attacker snaked an arm around Jack's neck.

Tracy held her breath, her heart in her throat, as she watched the two grapple. Jack grunted with effort, his face reddening from lack of air as The Wolf held his forearm tight across Jack's windpipe.

A sob welled inside her, seeing the abuse The Wolf unleashed on Jack. If anything happened to Jack, how could she forgive herself? He'd come to rescue her, and now his life hung in the balance.

Chapter 19

Despite the viselike grip of the arm that choked him, Jack managed to find his footing and renewed leverage. Bracing his feet, he threw his head back into The Wolf's face. The assassin howled in pain as blood spurted from his broken nose, hitting Jack's neck in a warm spray. Jack followed with repeated blows from his elbow to the man's ribs.

Under counterattack, The Wolf cringed in defense, and his hold on Jack's throat loosened. With a twist of his body, Jack wrenched free of his opponent's grip. He stumbled to his feet and gulped air into his burning chest.

His gun. Where had his gun landed when he fell?

While The Wolf clutched his broken nose and sucked shallow gasps into his bruised lungs, Jack cast a quick glance around the floor his feet. He spotted the pistol about two yards away at the same time his opponent lunged for it.

Jack hefted his boot into the man's jaw just as The Wolf's hands closed around the barrel of the handgun. Determined to keep the weapon out of his assailant's hands, Jack stomped with all his weight on The Wolf's wrist.

The assassin shouted in rage and grabbed Jack's ankle with his free hand. Yanking hard, The Wolf managed to pull Jack off balance. Oxygen whooshed from him as he crashed to the hard-packed dirt, but he continued to kick, battering The Wolf with blows, striking him in the head and face with the heel of his boot. Though blinded by Jack's barrage of kicks, the assassin fumbled the pistol into his fingers. The Wolf aimed in the general direction of his opponent and fired. The heat of the bullet streaked past Jack's cheek. A sting on his ear told him he'd been knicked.

"Jack!" Tracy screamed.

When The Wolf rolled to his back and shifted the weapon toward her, Jack landed one last resounding kick to the assassin's gun hand. The jolt knocked the pistol from his hand, and the gun skittered toward Tracy. Out of his reach, but also out of The Wolf's reach. Good enough. That evened the odds.

Gathering his focus and strength, Jack sprang to his feet, ready for The Wolf's next attack.

He didn't have to wait long. The dark glare of the hired killer narrowed as he surged toward Jack. But the man's hands weren't empty. He'd found a piece of steel rebar and swung it at Jack's head.

Jack ducked, just in time, and flicked a fast look askance as he dodged the next arc of the swinging bar. Finding the stack of rebar, he grabbed one himself and met The Wolf's attack with a practiced parry and riposte.

A *Prise de Fer* and *remise*. Jack met The Wolf's startled look with a smug grin. "Come on, bastard. Bring it."

Tracy gasped as Jack's gun landed a few feet from her. She might be tied to the baler, but she had to do something to try to keep the gun out of The Wolf's hands. As she had in retrieving the lighter, Tracy scrunched low and extended her foot as far as she could. She toed the gun closer, closer...

The clank of metal brought her head up, her attention back to Jack's battle with The Wolf. Her gut roiled seeing the heavy bar the assassin swung toward Jack. A blow from the steel rod could do serious damage, could even be fatal if it struck him in the head. She bit her bottom lip, willing herself not to cry out and distract Jack. After a moment, she realized Jack had the upper hand in this battle. His moves and countermoves were skilled and effective in both tiring The Wolf and landing strikes that diminished his opponent's ability to fight back.

A strike to the arm, a jab in the gut, a blocked thrust.

She flashed back to her recent visit to Jack's home office and the small swords he kept in the display case. *Of course.* Fascinated, she followed his moves, his footwork.

An optimistic buoyancy lightened the pressure in her chest. Jack was in his element.

Monitoring the fight with half her attention, she went back to her pursuit of the gun. Another couple inches. And again...

Finally she was able to twist and pick up the weapon, but in doing so the lighter slipped from her hands. Didn't matter. Jack was here. He'd free her once he handled The Wolf.

A loud curse and groan yanked her focus to the men. The Wolf clutched his chest and crumpled on the dirt floor. Jack stepped back, panting, and eyed his quarry critically. The Wolf coughed, spitting out blood, and his eyes rolled back as he hugged his ribs.

Jack pulled the rebar away from the downed man, then cut a glance to Tracy. "Are you hurt?"

"Not much." She showed him the gun she'd retrieved. "Here."

"Good girl," he said, lifting a corner of his mouth as he strode toward her, the rebar swords still in his fist. When he reached her, he tossed the bars into a corner of the barn and pulled her head close for a kiss. "Thank God you're all right. If anything had happened to you…" Rather than finish the sentence, he kissed her again.

She closed her eyes, relief rushing through her and weakening her knees. "I was so scared."

He took the gun, slid it in the waist of his jeans at the small of his back, then took a small folding knife from his pocket. "Let's get you out of here."

Tears filled her eyes as she watched him saw on the ropes binding her hands. "How did you know—"

A sudden movement, a scuffling drew her gaze and Jack's across the barn. Too late.

The Wolf had seized another steel bar from the original stack and lunged, staggering toward them. He swung the steel rod in a downward arc at Jack.

His hands occupied with cutting her ropes, Jack's reaction was a fraction of a second too slow. The rebar cracked a glancing blow to his head, but he fell backward and didn't move.

"Jack!" Tracy sobbed, her heart plummeting to her toes.

Still swaying on his feet and holding his side, The Wolf cast his gaze around, clearly looking for the gun. When he spotted the lighter, he stooped and scrabbled it off the floor. "This was a gift…" he paused and wheezed a gurgling breath "…from my father."

Grabbing a handful of straw from the stall, he lit the stalks and let the flaming tinder land on the pile.

Horror streaked through Tracy as the flames caught and the hay ignited in a bright, fast fire.

This place would go up like a tinderbox, all this weathered wood and straw. And you with time to think about burning up like a campfire marshmallow… The Wolf's taunt replayed in her mind, and her heart galloped. The smoke was already making her cough and gag.

The Wolf backed toward the barn door, his steps weaving and his grin pure evil. "Time to go."

Tears prickled her eyes. From fear. From smoke. From guilt. Bad enough that her in-laws' assassin would kill her today, but Jack…

Her chest squeezed. Seth would be an orphan. Both of his parents' deaths would be blood on her hands.

"Jack?" she called, nudging him with her foot. *Please, please wake up!* She had to revive him before the smoke overwhelmed them both. Before the flames crept any closer or blocked their only exit.

When Ryan got the call about Tracy's kidnapping and Jack's pursuit of the assassin, he'd had already been planning a trip to the ranch, bringing his latest intel on The Wolf. The killer had been identified as Wayne Parnell and a partial fingerprint of Parnell's had been found at a service-station restroom where he'd been ID'd from security-camera footage. Now, minutes later, after driving at top speeds with lights and sirens, he'd commandeered a ranch four wheeler and was bouncing across the fields to the old hay barn. He had a rifle with a sniper scope strapped to his back in addition to his department-issued side arm.

He'd just picked up Tom Vasquez, who'd abandoned the pursuit after Jack galloped passed him. An asthma attack had left Vasquez winded, but he was able to direct Ryan where they needed to go. Their destination became all too clear when a billow of smoke rose over the horizon, just past a large hill. Ryan's gut pitched. If that was the old barn burning, as he feared, the aged building would be ashes in minutes. God help anyone trapped inside. And *anyone* could be Tracy. Or Jack.

Fresh urgency whipped through him, and he squeezed the throttle.

"Hang on!" Ryan told the ranch hand who rode behind him. He gunned the engine, and it whined with effort as they shot up the incline.

Thick smoke filled the barn quickly. Within minutes, Tracy's skin stung from the heat of the flames, and her throat and lungs were raw and scorched. Her eyes watered as she tried again to revive Jack, rasping, "Please! Please, Jack, wake up!"

Her head felt muzzy from lack of oxygen, but she fought the pull of unconscious oblivion, knowing she had to get Jack out. Even if she was going to die here. "Jack…please!"

She poked him weakly with her toe again, the effort almost more energy than she had left to give. Finally he stirred, coughing and raising a hand to his head wound. *Thank God!*

"Jack, you…" *cough* "…have to get out!"

He blinked up at her, in confusion for a fraction of a second before clarity lit his gaze and alarm filled his eyes. "Not without you!"

Groaning and choking on the thick smoke, he rolled to his hands and knees, scanned the floor until he found the pocketknife he'd dropped when he'd been attacked, and began sawing again at the ropes.

"Leave…me…" she said, then gave over to a fit of racking coughs.

"Like hell," he said, his voice a low scrape. "I lost…one woman I loved…and didn't fight for. I won't lose…you."

Ryan spotted Jack's horse and a brown gelding prancing restlessly outside the barn as he crested the hill. He scanned the area carefully looking for his brother, for Tracy…and for The Wolf. Wayne Parnell. A man with a lengthy rap sheet and a brutal history of merciless killing.

"Jack!" he shouted over the roar of the ATV.

A movement in his peripheral vision caught his attention at the same time that Tom Vasquez aimed a finger toward the same tree-shaded ravine a hundred yards down the other side of the hill. A tall, dark-headed figure lumbered and lurched into the shade of the trees. Ryan brought the ATV to a skidding halt. "Check the barn," he barked to Vasquez, as he swung off the four-wheeler and pulled the rifle from his back. "Jack and Tracy have to be around here somewhere."

The ranch hand hurried toward the burning barn, covering his mouth and nose with his shirt.

After checking the rifle and chambering the first cartridge, Ryan crouched low and took up a position from which he could monitor Parnell's movement.

"Do you see them?" he called to Vasquez.

"I think so. But the fire's too hot to go in the front." Vasquez raised his arm to shield his face from the heat and stumbled away from the flames licking the barn door.

Ryan set his jaw. No way in hell was he letting his

brother perish in that fire without even trying. "Then we have to create a way for them to escape out the back."

"Ideas?" the ranch hand asked.

Ryan's gaze darted to the four wheeler and the tow chain mounted on the rear. "Let's rip a hole in the wall."

I won't lose you.

Tracy heard the words, and her heart gave a light flutter of recognition, but her eyelids drooped. Staying awake took too much strength. He legs were rubbery. The only thing keeping her upright was the rope that bound her to the baler, and it cut into her flesh as her weight sagged against the constraint.

The smoke was so dense. Jack was awake. She could just...

"Tracy!" he growled when her head lolled. "Stay—" *cough, cough* "—with me!"

"Can't..." The ropes tugged at her wrists as he cut. "I love...y—"

The ropes dropped loose, and she toppled toward the floor. Muscled arms caught her. Lifted her.

She curled weakly against Jack's chest, her breathing no more than a feathery wheeze. Beneath her cheek, his chest heaved and rumbled when he coughed.

I love you, Jack. She longed to say the words, but her head was too fuzzy, her body too weak.

Jack had started for the front door of the barn, before realizing the fire blocked the exit. Tracy lay draped in his arms, limp and unresponsive. A bitter ache lashed his heart at the thought of losing her.

Hang on, darling. I'll get you out of here. I promise. Just hang on a little longer!

Adrenaline fueled his legs as he changed direction,

searching for another way out. Without protection from the smoke for his mouth and nose, he was rapidly succumbing to the acrid cloud filling the barn. He had just turned, searching the dark recesses for an alternate escape route, when he heard a familiar voice shouting his name. Relief and gratitude pricked the bubble of tension swelling in his chest, but he didn't call back. He saved his oxygen for rescuing Tracy.

Ryan was there, but could his brother do anything to help them get out? And what about The Wolf? Was the killer lying in wait to pick them all off as they fled the burning barn?

He heard a distant roar, a loud screech and a crash. A large piece of the back wall tore away, and bright beams of sunlight streamed in through the dense smoke. Weaving through the maze of flames, Jack rushed towards the gaping hole. Fingers of fire reached for him and floating embers scorched his skin, but he didn't slow his step. His only thought was of getting Tracy out that barn and reviving her.

"Jack!" Tom Vasquez shouted. "Bring her over here!"

Sucking in fresh air as he emerged from the conflagration, Jack staggered to the shade of a nearby tree where Tom met him.

"Tracy!" His voice was choked by emotion and phlegm as he set her carefully on the ground. He slapped her cheeks lightly to rouse her, and she blinked against the blinding sunlight that peeked through the branches above her.

She groaned hoarsely, her head rocking side to side in distress. "Jack…" she whispered, her voice crackling roughly.

He pressed a kiss to her forehead and shushed her. "Easy, darling. You're safe now."

Her body convulsed as she coughed and wheezed, and Tom helped her sit up.

Jack, too, cleared his lungs as best he could, spitting out the dark taste of ash that lined his throat, before turning back to Vasquez. "Where's...The Wolf?" he asked between gasps for breath.

"Down in that ravine," Tom said, aiming a finger past the idling four wheeler. "Your brother is watching him."

Jack rubbed his gritty eyes, which stung from the smoke, and narrowed his gaze on the dark figure huddled under the trees in the ravine. He drew his gun from the small of his back and rose from his knees. "Stay with her, will you? I have unfinished business."

He stalked past the blazing barn and dropped weakly on the ground beside Ryan.

His brother gave him a side glance. "You okay?"

Jack nodded and coughed.

"Tracy?"

"Alive, but..." He drew a rattling breath. "She needs medical attention."

"You both do. Go. I've got this." Ryan peered through the sniper scope. "He's not going anywhere."

At that moment, The Wolf dashed from the cover of the trees, charging them. Jack didn't wait for permission. He aimed his pistol. Fired.

A second shot blasted at the same time. Ryan's rifle.

The Wolf dropped, writhing on the ground, holding his leg.

Ryan glared at Jack. "I said I had it."

Jack slumped with fatigue and relief, raising a hand to his aching head.

His brother grunted and hitched a thumb over his shoulder. "I'll take it from here. I have backup on the way. You get out of here. Get Tracy and yourself to a hospital."

At the foot of the hill, The Wolf had stopped moving, his eyes in a fixed stare. Assured that the killer was no longer a threat, he jerked a nod to Ryan and stumbled back to Tracy's side.

Wide blue eyes met his as he dropped to his knees next to her. "W-Wolf," she rasped, grabbing his hand.

Jack stroked her cheek. "We got him, Trace. He's dead."

Chapter 20

His living room resembled Grand Central Station.

Having heard about the incident at the old hay barn, Jack's heroic rescue of Tracy and the death of the assassin who'd been stalking their guest, every Colton and hired hand had assembled in Jack's living room.

"I'm fine," Jack assured Big J for the tenth time when his father cast him a worried glance. "Eric said the CT scan showed no concussion. I have a hard head apparently."

Tracy, too, had been treated for minor wounds at the ER and released. Now, she sat on his sofa with Seth on her lap and Greta hovering beside her. Jack wanted to be the one keeping vigil over Tracy, but his turn would have to wait until his sister, Brett, and half of the ranch's staff including Edith, who was a force of her own, finished buzzing worriedly about her.

"I know you probably could use something stronger,"

Tom Vasquez said, handing Jack a glass of iced tea, "but your brother says alcohol doesn't mix with whatever painkiller he gave you at the ER."

Jack smiled his thanks, keeping half of his attention focused on Tracy even as he answered questions for the curious hands who surrounded him.

"You're all being so kind," Tracy said, squeezing Greta's hand and tugging Seth close for another one-armed hug. "Really, all I need is a good night's sleep. I'm just glad the ordeal is over, and none of you were hurt." Her eyes lifted to Jack's then, and he read in her gaze the same fear that had shaken him to the core when he'd learned she'd been kidnapped. The bone-deep terror of losing her.

"So now that the threat to your life has been eliminated, will you move back to the main house?" Greta asked.

Tracy hesitated, drawing a slow deep breath. Her expression darkened, Jack's only warning before she said, "Actually, I think the time has come for me to leave. I've already imposed on your hospitality and protection far too long."

Jack's gut swooped, and his muscles tensed. She was *leaving*?

"What?" Greta said, frowning.

"No, Miss Tracy! Stay here!" Seth whined, tugging her sleeve.

"I'm sorry," she said, "I never intended to stay this long. If not for the threat I was under and Jack's insistence that I stay here, I'd have gone last week."

"You're not an imposition. We've all loved getting to know you," Greta said.

"Thank you. Really, but I must. There are things back in Denver I have to—"

"Nooo," Seth groaned again, tears welling in his eyes. The hurt and disappointment on his son's face left a hard, cold pit inside him. Everything he'd tried to protect Seth from when Laura left, everything he'd felt when his wife had abandoned him and their son, everything he'd tried to repress for five years so that he could make a happy home for his boy came crashing down on him in that instant.

Tracy said something quietly to Seth he couldn't hear over the roar of blood in his ears. His fingers tightened around his tea glass, and he gritted his back teeth so hard his molars ached. A tremor started low in his belly and worked its way outward until his limbs trembled. He turned without speaking to anyone and stalked outside. He needed air. He needed distance. He needed to punch something.

He'd opened his home, his life, his heart to Tracy. And she was walking away.

Tracy's gaze followed Jack as he stormed out of the living room, and her heart sank. She'd hoped for a chance to talk to him privately and explain her decision before telling the rest of the family, but when Greta asked, she'd been honest with her new friend about her plans. What she hadn't told Greta, what she couldn't put into words even in her private thoughts was the devastation she'd felt when she'd seen Jack crumple on the barn floor. In those moments when she thought they'd both burn to death, when she considered the danger and anguish she'd unwittingly brought to the Colton ranch, her guilt and despair had been a vicious animal gnawing her soul. She was jinxed. She had been responsible for her cousin's death and nearly cost Jack his life. Tragedy followed her, and she wouldn't allow the train wreck of her life to hurt anyone else she loved.

She would keep in touch with Seth, as she'd promised, but lingering at the ranch any longer, allowing the little boy to grow more attached to her—and vice versa—would be selfish and cruel, knowing she couldn't stay permanently.

And Jack...

Jack would be the hardest to leave. She'd fallen in love with him. Losing him from her life would be like ripping out her heart. Like living underwater with no air to breathe. Already the pain was suffocating.

Maybe things could be different if she thought he loved her. If he'd ever said anything about a future together. If he'd asked her to stay—not because she had to to save her life, but because he wanted her there.

But his silence was deafening. Shattering. Conclusive.

Even the small hope she clung to that he was waiting for the crowd of relatives and friends to clear out of his house to speak his mind proved futile. He was decidedly closed off, sullen and terse with her as they prepared Seth for bed.

He remained withdrawn the next morning as she packed her bags. When she tried to broach the topic of her departure, he'd brushed her aside and stalked outside to the stable. He remained hidden in the shadowed stalls with the horses, even when she sent Seth with a message for him that she was ready to go.

"He said to tell you he was busy, but to have a safe trip," Seth reported when he returned.

Brett and Greta had both turned out to wish her well and say their goodbyes, and Jack's siblings exchanged a look of disbelief.

"Tracy, I'm sure he just—" Greta started.

"No, it's okay. I understand," she said as bravely as she could and flashed them all a smile she didn't feel.

She cast one last look toward the stable, and the crack in her heart widened. With a sigh of resignation and heartache, she pulled Jack's son into her arms for a final hug. "I'm going to miss you, sweetie. But I'll call, and we can Skype, and you can visit me anytime you want."

Seth's chin quivered. "Bye, Miss Tracy. I…l-love you."

"Oh, Seth, I love you, too." She gave his rumpled hair a kiss, fighting not to lose her composure in front of the child, then hurriedly climbed into the rental car and closed the door.

Jack moved with stiff, jerky motions as he worked in the stable, killing time until he heard the engine of Tracy's rental car rev and the tires crunch over gravel as she drove away. He slammed things down with more force than needed and smashed his finger in a stall gate.

Spitting a curse out under his breath, he stuck his injured finger in his mouth and sucked on the throbbing wound. If only he could find a similar balm for his seared heart.

He heard the thud of booted steps and glanced up to see Brett striding toward him with his mouth set in a grim line. "You're an idiot and a bastard, Jack Colton!"

Jack fisted a hand and returned his brother's glare. He didn't want to punch his brother, but he was itching to hit something, and if Brett provoked him… "Leave me alone."

"You couldn't even come out and tell her goodbye? That's more than rude, man. That's just…" Brett flattened his mouth again and shook his head in disgust.

Self-preservation, Jack finished mentally.

"Cold," Brett said. "And pathetic."

Jack heaved an exasperated sigh. He felt bad enough about Tracy leaving without his brother heaping on guilt.

He grabbed a rake and started shuffling straw around the stall floor. "If you have a point to make, do it. I'm kinda busy here."

Brett seized the rake handle and yanked it from Jack's hands. "Did a bull kick you in the head, bro? Why did you let her leave?"

"Let her?" He scoffed. "I can't keep her here against her will. That's called imprisonment, and it's illegal. Ask Ryan."

"She wanted to stay!" Brett waved a hand toward the stable door. "Anyone with eyes could see that."

"Really? Fine way of showing it. I thought packing her suitcases and hopping in her rental car at her first opportunity said she was eager to leave." He stepped closer to his brother and put his hand on the rake, trying to grab it back. Brett held tight.

"Well, from what I can tell, you didn't put up even a token resistance. Does she know how you feel about her? Did you tell her?"

Jack stilled, and his insides grew cold. "I don't know what you're talking about."

Brett laughed without humor, shaking his head. "Man, you *must* have been kicked by a bull." He stared at Jack for a few seconds with an incredulous look furrowing his brow. "Is it because of Laura? Are you going to let Tracy walk out of your life without a fight because you think this is somehow a repeat of what happened with Laura?"

Jack heard the quaver in his inhaled breath, felt the sting of moisture in his eyes. "Leave me alone, Brett," he gritted through his teeth.

His brother released the rake and curled his fingers in the front of Jack's shirt, tugging him close enough to stick his nose in Jack's face. "It's not the same. Don't screw this up because you're scared of what you're feeling for her."

Jack couldn't breathe, couldn't make his lungs loosen enough to take in oxygen. He held Brett's stare and fought the surge of emotion that stampeded through him.

"She was happy here. You'd have to be blind not to see that. You made her happy." Brett cocked his head. "She loves you, Jack. Hell, even I could see that!"

"He's right."

Jack jerked his gaze to Greta, who'd sneaked up on them undetected.

"Listen to him, Jack. Our bonehead brother is making sense. I saw it. Tracy blossomed in the last couple weeks, even with the threat of that killer hanging over her. Because of you. And Seth. She's leaving because she's scared, too."

"Maybe I'm letting her go to protect Seth," he said defiantly.

"Bull," Brett said with a snort. "She loves Seth, and he loves her. You let her go to save your own sorry hide. From what, I don't know, because it's pretty obvious she's perfect for you."

Greta stalked closer. "Jack Colton, if you love her, go after her. Don't let her leave here thinking you don't care."

Jack's pulse ramped into high gear. Laura had left because she didn't belong on the ranch. The life of a rancher didn't suit her, and she never loved him enough to overcome her unhappiness. But Tracy *had* taken to ranching, messy chores and all, like she was born to it. She'd smiled when she woke in his arms, excited for a new day. Despite the stress she was under from The Wolf.

And *he'd* been happy, damn it! As happy as he'd been in a long time.

His stomach bunched as he cast a glance toward the ranch yard where Tracy had just driven away. "It's probably too late to stop her. She must be to the highway by now."

Greta squeezed his arm. "Maybe not. She was going to stop at the main house to tell Maria and Edith goodbye."

Blowing out a nervous puff of breath, Jack pushed past his sister and tugged Buck, saddleless, out of his stall. If he wanted to catch up to Tracy, he'd have to hurry.

Tracy sat at the entry gate to the ranch, wiping away tears as fast as they filled her eyes. She couldn't read the rental car's GPS device for the moisture blurring her vision.

Where do you want to go? the screen read.

The ache in her chest swelled. "I want to turn around and go back," she said with a sniff. "But I can't."

Fumbling for the rental car papers, she looked for the address of the rental agency where she would return the vehicle. She started tapping the address onto the electronic keyboard when a low thundering noise rumbled through her open window. She raised her head and checked for storm clouds, but the Oklahoma sky was a bright, clear blue. The sound got louder, and as she scanned the highway for hot rods or large trucks, a movement in the rearview mirror snagged her attention.

A horse was galloping up behind her at a full run. The rider's head was down, and he hunched forward over the horse's neck, clutching his mount's mane. Startled, and somewhat alarmed by the sight, she blinked hard to clear her eyes. Everything about the horse's speed and the cowboy's tense position screamed trouble.

Then she recognized the gelding, the black cowboy hat, the dark, unruly hair of the rider.

"Jack..." she whispered with a shuddering breath. What was wrong? Why—?

"Tracy!" he shouted as he rode past her and reined Buck in front of the car, blocking the driveway.

Limbs trembling, she clutched the steering wheel and gaped at him in dismay. What in the world? He'd ridden bareback, not even bothering to saddle Buck, and now he swung off the gelding in a smooth motion and rushed to the driver's-side door.

"Tracy!" he gasped, out of breath from his jarring pursuit. "Don't...don't go." He snatched open the car door and pulled her arm to coax her out.

Unsnapping her seat belt, she slid out of the front seat and narrowed a concerned gaze on him. "Jack, what's wrong? What's happened?"

"Not wrong..." he panted. "Right. I fell..." He paused as he swallowed hard and dragged in a lungful of air. "I fell in love with you."

"I— What?" She felt fresh tears fill her eyes, and she held her breath, almost afraid to move for fear she'd shatter the moment and it would be lost.

"Stay." His fingers gripped her shoulders, and the desperation and sincerity that lit his eyes stirred a flutter under her ribs.

"Wha—"

"You belong here. You belong with me."

Her eyes widened in surprise, and her mouth opened in a silent question.

Jack grunted in frustration and scrubbed a hand over his face. "Let me start over." He drew and released a cleansing breath. "I don't want you to leave, Tracy. I love you. Seth loves you. You belong with us, not in Denver."

"But..."

"You were happy here. Weren't you?" For the first time a flicker of uncertainty flashed in his gaze, and she quickly nodded, assuaging his doubt. Even as she admitted the truth, though, her own uncertainty lashed at her.

"B-but…I'm jinxed, Jack. I've brought trouble and tragedy to everyone I love. You were almost killed because of me. I can't bear the idea of anything happening to you or Seth because of me."

He scowled at her and shook his head. "Don't be crazy. There's no such thing as a jinx. What you brought me and my son was a second chance to be a complete family. You brought love and happiness and laughter. We need you, Tracy. Don't go."

"I don't want to leave, but—"

"But nothing, Trace." He framed her face with his hands and pressed his forehead to hers, their bodies touching head to boots. She felt the tremor that rolled through him as he feathered kisses across her cheeks. "Say you'll stay. Say you'll be part of our family and grow old with this stubborn, surly cowboy."

The shock and joy of the moment overwhelmed her. Her emotions tangled and knotted in her throat, choking her voice, while happy tears spilled from her eyes.

When she didn't answer, he leaned back from her, a dent of worry in his brow. "Tracy?"

Again her mouth opened and closed without a sound.

His hands slid from her shoulders to grasp her hands, and whipping off his cowboy hat, he dropped to one knee. "Tracy McCain, I love you and want you in my life. Please say you'll stay. Say you'll marry me."

Joyful laughter bubbled up from her soul, and despite the grip her happy tears had on her throat, she squeaked out, "yes!"

* * * * *

Don't miss the next book in
THE COLTONS OF OKLAHOMA *series,*
COLTON'S COWBOY CODE by Melissa Cutler,
available July 2015 from
Harlequin Romantic Suspense.

And if you loved this novel, don't miss other
suspenseful titles by Beth Cornelison:

THE MANSFIELD RESCUE
PROTECTING HER ROYAL BABY
THE RETURN OF CONNOR MANSFIELD
COLTON CHRISTMAS RESCUE

Available now from Harlequin Romantic Suspense!

COMING NEXT MONTH FROM

HARLEQUIN

ROMANTIC suspense

Available July 7, 2015

#1855 HOW TO SEDUCE A CAVANAUGH

Cavanaugh Justice • by Marie Ferrarella

Kelly Cavanaugh and Kane Durant could barely be friends, much less partners, and never in a million years lovers. But while working together to solve a series of seemingly random home invasions, whatever chill existed between them transforms into a sizzling passion...

#1856 COLTON'S COWBOY CODE

The Coltons of Oklahoma • by Melissa Cutler

Pregnant and desperate, Hannah Grayson never expects to face the baby's father at a job interview! Cowboy Brett Colton gives her the position and vows to protect her and their unborn baby, but when long-buried secrets turn deadly, no one on the ranch is safe.

#1857 UNDERCOVER WITH A SEAL

Code: Warrior SEALs • by Cindy Dees

Eve Hankova demanded answers from the Russian mob about her missing brother, thereby adding herself to their list of enemies. Her only shot at answers—and survival—lies with her reluctant rescuer, a burned-out and far-too-appealing navy SEAL.

#1858 TEMPTING TARGET

Dangerous in Dallas • by Addison Fox

After priceless jewels are discovered in the floor of a prominent Dallas bridal boutique, a detective and the alluring wedding caterer he's protecting race to find the villain plotting to recover the gems...and perhaps they'll give in to a simmering attraction, which might necessitate a walk down the aisle!

YOU CAN FIND MORE INFORMATION ON UPCOMING HARLEQUIN® TITLES, FREE EXCERPTS AND MORE AT WWW.HARLEQUIN.COM.

HRSCNM0615

REQUEST YOUR FREE BOOKS!

2 FREE NOVELS PLUS 2 FREE GIFTS!

⊕ HARLEQUIN®

ROMANTIC suspense

Sparked by danger, fueled by passion

YES! Please send me 2 FREE Harlequin® Romantic Suspense novels and my 2 FREE gifts (gifts are worth about $10). After receiving them, if I don't wish to receive any more books, I can return the shipping statement marked "cancel." If I don't cancel, I will receive 4 brand-new novels every month and be billed just $4.74 per book in the U.S. or $5.49 per book in Canada. That's a savings of at least 12% off the cover price! It's quite a bargain! Shipping and handling is just 50¢ per book in the U.S. and 75¢ per book in Canada.* I understand that accepting the 2 free books and gifts places me under no obligation to buy anything. I can always return a shipment and cancel at any time. Even if I never buy another book, the two free books and gifts are mine to keep forever.

240/340 HDN GH3P

Name _____ (PLEASE PRINT) _____

Address _____ Apt. #

City _____ State/Prov. _____ Zip/Postal Code

Signature (if under 18, a parent or guardian must sign)

Mail to the **Reader Service:**
IN U.S.A.: P.O. Box 1867, Buffalo, NY 14240-1867
IN CANADA: P.O. Box 609, Fort Erie, Ontario L2A 5X3

Want to try two free books from another line?
Call 1-800-873-8635 or visit www.ReaderService.com.

* Terms and prices subject to change without notice. Prices do not include applicable taxes. Sales tax applicable in N.Y. Canadian residents will be charged applicable taxes. Offer not valid in Quebec. This offer is limited to one order per household. Not valid for current subscribers to Harlequin Romantic Suspense books. All orders subject to credit approval. Credit or debit balances in a customer's account(s) may be offset by any other outstanding balance owed by or to the customer. Please allow 4 to 6 weeks for delivery. Offer available while quantities last.

Your Privacy—The Reader Service is committed to protecting your privacy. Our Privacy Policy is available online at www.ReaderService.com or upon request from the Reader Service.

We make a portion of our mailing list available to reputable third parties that offer products we believe may interest you. If you prefer that we not exchange your name with third parties, or if you wish to clarify or modify your communication preferences, please visit us at www.ReaderService.com/consumerschoice or write to us at Reader Service Preference Service, P.O. Box 9062, Buffalo, NY 14240-9062. Include your complete name and address.

HRS15

SPECIAL EXCERPT FROM

⬥ **HARLEQUIN**
™

ROMANTIC suspense

*Pregnant and desperate, Hannah Grayson never
expects to face the baby's father at a job interview!
Cowboy Brett Colton vows to protect them, but someone
dangerous is stalking the ranch...*

Read on for a sneak peek at
COLTON'S COWBOY CODE by **Melissa Cutler**,
the latest in Harlequin® Romantic Suspense's
THE COLTONS OF OKLAHOMA *series.*

"You, Brett Colton, are as slippery as a snake-oil salesman."

"I prefer to think of myself as stubborn and single-minded. Not so different from you."

The suspicion on Hannah's face melted away a little bit more and she closed her lips around the fork in a way that gave Brett some ideas too filthy for his own good.

He cleared his throat, snapping his focus back to the task at hand. "When my parents remodeled the big house, they designed separate wings for each of their six children, but I'm the only one of the six who lives there full-time. You would have your own wing, your own bathroom with a big old tub and plenty of privacy."

For the first time, she seemed to be seriously considering his offer. Time to go for broke. He handed her another slice of bacon, which she accepted without a word.

"Where are you living now?" he said. "Can you look me in the eye and tell me it's a good, long-term situation for you and the baby?"

She snapped a tiny bit of bacon off and popped it into her mouth. "It's not like I'm living in some abandoned building. I'm staying with my best friend, Lori, and her boyfriend, Drew. It's not ideal, but with the money from this job, I'll be able to afford my own place."

"And until that first paycheck, you'll live at the ranch." He pressed his lips together. That had come out a smidge more demanding than he'd wanted it to.

Their gazes met and held. "Are you mandating that? Will the job offer depend on me accepting the temporary housing?"

Oh, how he wanted to say yes to that. "No. But you should agree to it anyway. Your own bed, regular meals made by a top-rated personal chef, and your commute would be five minutes to the ranch office. The only traffic would be some overly excitable ranch dogs."

"I know why you're doing all this, but I really am grateful for all you're offering—the job and the accommodations. In all honesty, this went a lot better than I thought it would."

"The job interview?"

"No, telling you about the baby. I thought you'd either hate me or propose to me."

Brett didn't miss a beat. "I still might."

Don't miss COLTON'S COWBOY CODE
by Melissa Cutler, part of
THE COLTONS OF OKLAHOMA *series:*

COLTON COWBOY PROTECTOR by Beth Cornelison
COLTON'S COWBOY CODE by Melissa Cutler
THE TEMPTATION OF DR. COLTON by Karen Whiddon
PROTECTING THE COLTON BRIDE by Elle James
SECOND CHANCE COLTON by Marie Ferrarella
THE COLTON BODYGUARD by Carla Cassidy

Available wherever Harlequin® Romantic Suspense
books and ebooks are sold.
www.Harlequin.com

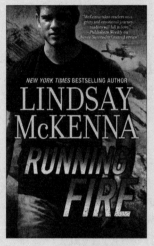

HARLEQUIN®

A *Romance* FOR EVERY MOOD™

JUST CAN'T GET ENOUGH?

Join our social communities
and talk to us online.

You will have access to the latest
news on upcoming titles and special
promotions, but most importantly,
you can talk to other fans about your
favorite Harlequin reads.

Harlequin.com/Community

 Facebook.com/HarlequinBooks

 Twitter.com/HarlequinBooks

Pinterest.com/HarlequinBooks

THE WORLD IS BETTER WITH

Romance

Harlequin has everything from contemporary, passionate and heartwarming to suspenseful and inspirational stories.

Whatever your mood, we have a romance just for you!

Connect with us to find your next great read, special offers and more.

 /HarlequinBooks

@HarlequinBooks

www.HarlequinBlog.com

www.Harlequin.com/Newsletters

CARLA CASSIDY

SCENE OF THE CRIME: DEADMAN'S BLUFF

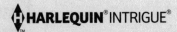

Recycling programs
for this product may
not exist in your area.

ISBN-13: 978-0-373-69681-9

SCENE OF THE CRIME: DEADMAN'S BLUFF

Copyright © 2013 by Carla Bracale

Printed in U.S.A.

ABOUT THE AUTHOR

Carla Cassidy is an award-winning author who has written more than fifty novels for Harlequin Books. In 1995, she won Best Silhouette Romance from *RT Book Reviews* for *Anything for Danny*. In 1998, she also won a Career Achievement Award for Best Innovative Series from *RT Book Reviews*.

Carla believes the only thing better than curling up with a good book to read is sitting down at the computer with a good story to write. She's looking forward to writing many more books and bringing hours of pleasure to readers.

Books by Carla Cassidy

*The Recovery Men

CAST OF CHARACTERS

Seth Hawkins—The FBI agent was looking for a vacation and instead finds himself embroiled in a murder investigation with a beautiful woman at the center.

Tamara Jennings—She'd just been passing through the small town of Amber Lake but finds herself buried in the Deadman's Sand Dunes on the edge of town. Saved from death by Seth, she has no memory of who she is or what has happened to her.

Henry Todd—He's a successful restaurateur, but does he also have an appetite for murder?

Deputy Raymond Michaels—He has a reputation as a bully. Has that character trait progressed into something more deadly?

Sam Clemmons—The young college dropout who rides the Deadman's Dunes every day and has been present at the discovery of each body. Does he enjoy burying women in his playground?

Mark Willoughby—Seth's sister's ex-husband. Had the contentious divorce turned him into a woman-hating monster?

Chapter One

The sand dunes were nearly blinding in the late-June sunshine, but that didn't stop the surge of adrenaline that raced through Seth Hawkins as he pulled his pickup to a halt and cut the engine.

Deadman's Dunes. It had been almost a year since he'd been back here in the small Oklahoma town of Amber Lake to enjoy not only the company of his sister and niece, but also the thrill of conquering the dunes.

Seth pulled on a pair of goggles against the sun's glare and then got out of his truck. As far as the eye could see the dunes rose up like an alien landscape located seven miles outside town.

In the distance he could hear the roar of quad and other ATV engines and knew he wouldn't have the dunes to himself. Not that it mattered, there was plenty of room for everyone.

He'd driven here from his home in Kansas City early that morning and had a leisurely lunch with Linda and Samantha, his sister and niece, but he'd been eager to get out here on the dunes where nothing mattered but the throttle beneath his hand and the elemental challenge between man and nature.

It took him only minutes to unload his dirt bike from

the back of the truck. As he strapped on his protective equipment and then pulled on his helmet, he drew in a deep breath of the fresh warm air.

For the next week he wasn't FBI Special Agent Seth Hawkins—he was simply Seth on vacation, visiting with his only relatives and enjoying some much needed downtime from the job.

He climbed on the dirt bike and kick-started it, the thrum of the engine filled him with a teenagelike excitement. It felt as if in the past couple of years there had been nothing but work, no time for anything but murder and mayhem. He needed this vacation and he intended to spend each and every moment of it just having fun and relaxing.

With this thought in mind, he released the clutch and shot forward, the sand shifting ever ominously beneath his tires as he approached the first dune and after that miles of more dunes that would eventually lead to the large hump that was Deadman's Bluff.

A hairpin turn at the crest of the hill had to be maneuvered with precision. Otherwise the rider would fly off the bluff and to the sand fifteen feet below. More than one rider had tasted that sand at the bottom of Deadman's Bluff, although Seth himself had never had the unpleasant experience.

As he flew over the first mound, exhilaration spiked and he would have grinned, but knew that gesture would only get him a mouthful of sand.

He saw the tracks that others had left before him and saw in the distance several riders on quads who were obviously riding together.

Seth hadn't visited Amber Lake often enough over

the years to get to know the locals. He tried to come and visit his sister every six months or so, especially since her contentious divorce five years ago, but most of the time it was just an overnight visit.

But he was here now for a wonderful week and intended to take full advantage of having nothing more on his mind than dinner and dunes.

He'd been riding about a half hour when he spied the other three riders in the distance, all stopped and off their vehicles near an area referred to as the whoop-ti-doos, tiny bumps set so close together they rattled your brain. The young men looked like they were freaking out, two of them jumping around while the third stood as if frozen into a statue.

Was the young man who wasn't moving hurt? Had he taken a tumble and was now in a state of shock? Seth turned his bike to head toward them and as he drew closer he could hear two of the male voices shouting above the whine of his engine.

Seth pulled up, cut his engine and pulled off his helmet and goggles. "In the sand…" It was a short, dark-haired young man who shouted at Seth. "There's a dead woman in the sand."

What? Seth dropped his helmet on the ground, wondering if this was some kind of stupid prank the three were playing on him. He walked over to where statue man stood staring down at the sand just in front of him. Seth followed his gaze and gasped in shock.

A pale face in the sand, a woman's face, partially visible with her eyes closed. Obviously a dead woman, Seth's brain processed as the shock quickly passed.

"Any of you have a cell phone?" he asked, having left his own in his truck.

"It's freaky," the blond boy exclaimed as he wore a path back and forth in the sand. "Jeez, who would do something like that?"

"A phone," Seth barked. "Anyone have a phone?" The tall, frozen man stumbled back a couple of steps and pulled a phone from his pocket.

"Call for help," Seth commanded as he took a step closer to the body. "All three of you get over there by my bike."

The last thing he wanted was for everyone to trample what was obviously a crime scene. Whoever the woman was, she hadn't willingly lain down in the sand and buried herself. However, as an FBI agent he wanted to get closer, assure himself she was dead despite the obvious.

"The sheriff is on his way," one of the guys said.

As Seth approached the woman, he was vaguely aware of the three others talking among themselves, their voices all holding a barely contained edge of hysteria.

There was no question the scene was disconcerting. There was no indication of her body beneath the sand, simply a face half-emerged from the sandy surface, like some art sculpture left behind by a mentally ill artist.

Careful not to step where he assumed her body must be, Seth knelt down at the side of the face and swept away some of the sand that covered her closed eyes.

In all of his years as an FBI agent working violent crimes, he'd never seen anything like this, and he'd certainly seen a lot of evil things.

He brushed a bit more sand away from her eyes and

froze as he thought one of her eyelids twitched. A trick of the sun? He touched her skin. Warm…warmed by the heat of the day or by blood still flowing through her veins?

Quickly he dug through the sand by her neck, seeking the place where he might find a pulse. It took him only seconds to find her pulse point and place his fingers against it. He nearly yelped in surprise as he felt the beat of life throbbing there.

"She's alive," he yelled. "Get over here and help me. We've got to get this sand off her."

Two of the three ran to help Seth as he began to scoop sand away from her neck and her chest. As he worked on her upper body the other two men worked on her thighs and legs. The tall young man appeared to be in some state of shock still, standing like a robot in front of Seth's dirt bike.

"Hey, call the sheriff back and tell him we need an ambulance," Seth instructed the robot. "And tell him to hurry."

"This is so freaky…so freakin' freaky," the dark-haired man said as he uncovered a jean-clad leg.

"Are you sure she's alive?" the other one asked as he worked on getting the last of the sand off her other leg.

It all felt like a weird dream to Seth. As she was freed of the sand, his mind clicked off details. She was dressed in worn jeans and a blue T-shirt. One foot wore a gold sandal, the other one was bare. Her hair was dark, although it was so embedded with sand it was hard to discern an exact color.

"Sheriff Atkins is here," one of them said in relief.

Seth didn't look up from the woman. Once again he

sought the side of her neck to assure himself that she was still breathing. At that moment her eyes flew open.

Bright blue, they connected with Seth for one long moment. Before Seth could react, she skittered backward like a crab, her pupils dilating as her eyes filled with an abject terror Seth knew he'd never forget.

"It's okay. You're safe now," Seth said as she continued an attempt to escape, her eyes darting around wildly, like a crab seeking a rock to hide under.

As she moved she made sounds that no human being should ever make, the sound of terror too great for words. She got about three feet away from them and then with an audible moan, she collapsed.

By that time the sheriff had joined them. "FBI Agent Seth Hawkins," he said quickly. "We called for an ambulance," he added curtly. "We've got a crime scene and a live victim here who needs immediate medical care."

"We only have two ambulances who serve this area and both of them are currently working a four-car pileup on the other end of town," the sheriff said as he raked a hand through his salt-and-pepper hair.

Seth immediately assessed that the man appeared not to know exactly how to proceed. "We've got to get her to the hospital now." Seth took control.

"Hey." He focused on the dark-haired young man who'd helped uncover the victim. "You know where Linda and Samantha Willoughby live?" He shook his head, but the taller blond nodded. "I do," he replied. Seth threw him his truck keys. "Load my bike and drive my truck to their place. Put the keys under the floor mat."

Seth turned to the sheriff. "We're going to put her

in the back of your car and you're going to drive us to the emergency room as quickly as possible. And you might want to contact some of your men to cordon off this scene so there's no more contamination."

He didn't wait to see if anyone followed his orders. Instead he approached the unconscious woman and bent down next to her. He was aware that by picking her up, that by transporting her in the back of a car, he might be doing more harm than good, but her pulse had been weak and thready and he didn't want to wait around for an ambulance that might never come.

He saw no visible wounds on her, no blood to indicate she had been wounded with a knife or by a gunshot. He knelt down beside her and gently scooped her up in his arms and then stood.

She was a tiny thing, short and slender and even though she was deadweight in his arms, he had no problem carrying her to the sheriff's car.

The local lawman hurried in front of him and opened the back door to his cruiser. Once Seth and the woman were in the backseat, the overweight sheriff quickly made his way to the driver's side.

He slid into the car and started the engine and only when they were driving away from the dunes did he radio in location and instructions for somebody named Raymond to grab a couple of men and get their butts out there as quickly as possible to protect the crime scene.

As he talked on the radio, Seth stared down at the woman in his arms. What had happened to her? How had she come to be buried in the dunes?

Despite the sand that clung to her, she was very pretty, with long dark lashes and a hint of cheekbones and shapely lips that at the moment hung slack and partially open.

He thought he'd never forget that moment when her eyes had first opened, when for just a moment her gaze had connected with his. In that first instant, he'd felt electrically charged, as if her eyes had held an appeal he had to answer.

It had lasted only a heartbeat before the terror of whatever she'd endured had obviously coursed through her, momentarily stealing away anything human inside her. She'd been a wild animal seeking escape.

"By the way, I'm Sheriff Tom Atkins," the older man said from the front seat. "What's an FBI agent doing in my town?"

"I'm here on vacation visiting my sister and niece, Linda and Samantha Willoughby. I just got into town this morning."

"Hell of a way to start a vacation," Atkins said.

"This woman is definitely having a worse day than me," Seth replied. "Do you know her?"

"I don't recognize her and this is a pretty small town where most faces are familiar to me."

Seth once again looked down at the broken woman in his arms. "Hopefully when she comes to she'll be able to tell you who she is and how she came to be buried in the sand. I'm assuming you'll question thoroughly the boys at the scene. They are not only potential witnesses but also potential suspects, as well."

"They'll be brought in for questioning." That was all Atkins said as they pulled up to the emergency room entrance. Seth lifted the woman out of the car and carried her in where he was relieved of his burden by an orderly with a cart.

Within seconds, the woman was taken back behind doors that forbade Seth's entry. Sheriff Atkins had disappeared, probably headed back to the crime scene.

Seth sank down in one of the plastic chairs in the waiting room and drew a couple of deep, steadying breaths. He felt as if he'd been flying on a sickening surge of adrenaline since the moment he'd seen that haunting face in the sand.

He looked up as he saw his sister hurrying down the hallway toward him, her blue scrubs looking crisp and clean. Linda worked as a nurse and had left for her shift here at the hospital when Seth had left her house for the dunes.

"Hey," she said as she approached.

"Hey yourself," he replied with a soft smile. At thirty-eight Linda was three years older than him, but the two siblings had always been unusually close, especially since Linda had gone through her divorce from her domineering, verbally abusive husband, Mark.

She sat down next to him. "I heard the strangest story in the break room a few minutes ago. I heard that you went out dirt-bike-riding and wound up here with a woman you dug out of the sand."

He nodded. "Strange, but true."

"A couple of months ago another young woman was found dead in the dunes," Linda said. Seth sat up straighter in his seat, his questions obvious in his eyes as Linda continued. "Apparently some of the teenagers in town decided to have a party out there. From the story I heard there was a lot of booze, some drugs and at the time that the woman was discovered Sheriff Atkins thought it was some kind of a freak accident resulting from partying."

Seth frowned. "This today definitely wasn't an accident." His frown deepened as he thought about the scene. "She couldn't have been there that long before I got to the dunes. It was almost like she'd been intended to be completely buried but something or someone chased the killer away before he could deliver the final shovelful of sand onto her face." He wondered if perhaps the three young men who had arrived at the dunes before him had interrupted the murderer or had buried her themselves.

Linda reached over and patted his hand. "Go home, Seth. This isn't your crime scene. Remember, you're on vacation." She stood. "And I'm not, so I've got to get back to work. I'll see you at home late tonight."

He nodded absently and watched as she disappeared back down the hallway. She was right. This wasn't his job. He'd done what he needed to do and there was nothing to keep him from walking away.

Except those startling blue eyes and that moment of connection he felt with her before she'd freaked out and then had passed out. He couldn't just head home and forget about all of this. Besides, he thought with a touch of humor, he had no way to get home.

He had no doubt that the kids from the dunes would see to it that his truck and bike got back to Linda's okay. This was a small town and if they screwed with his rides, there would be no place for them to hide.

Still, despite the fact that he was on vacation, he couldn't walk away from this until he had some answers. He wanted to know her condition, assure himself that she was physically okay. He wanted to know her name. He needed to know what had happened to her.

He jumped up from his chair as his cell phone rang. Seeing on the caller ID that it was his boss, Director Forbes, calling from Kansas City, he answered and walked with the phone outside the building doors and into the early-evening sun.

"Hope you've enjoyed the first few hours of your vacation because it's officially over," Director Forbes said. "I just got a call from Sheriff Atkins requesting your aid in the investigation of a serial killer who is burying women in sand dunes. Apparently you're already a part of the most recent case."

"A serial killer?" Seth felt as if he were missing a significant piece of a puzzle. Linda had mentioned one woman whose death had been ruled some sort of an accident, but nothing else.

"The sheriff has managed to keep the details of the other two murders under his hat. This woman you found is apparently the third victim in as many months. Since you're already there in town Sheriff Atkins would like you to assist his team, and it sounds like you need to be there. Three women buried in the sand sounds like a case where the locals might be in over their heads. They definitely could use your help."

"Yes, sir," Seth replied, fighting an overwhelming irritation that the sheriff had gone directly to his boss before mentioning to Seth what he intended to do, and he'd neglected to tell Seth that this wasn't the first woman found buried in the sand dunes.

As the conversation ended Seth noticed with dismay

that the wind was picking up. A little wind out on the dunes would destroy any hope of collecting any evidence that might have been there.

He went back into the waiting room and within half an hour Sheriff Atkins showed up once again. "Any word on the victim?" he asked.

"Nothing so far. The only thing that's happened is that I got a call from my director indicating that I'm now on this case. Why didn't you tell me while we were in your car that this was the third woman found buried in the sand dunes?"

Sheriff Atkins winced, the lines on his face appearing to deepen into bone-weariness in the span of a heartbeat. "I wasn't sure what I had going on here until you found this woman today. This makes number three and that officially makes it bigger for me to handle. It's obviously a serial killer at work and I know as FBI you'd have more experience with this sort of thing."

Whatever else he might have said was interrupted as a doctor came into the room. "Tom." He greeted the sheriff with a nod.

"And this is Special Agent Seth Hawkins," Sheriff Atkins said. "Doctor William Kane. How is she?"

"Other than being a bit dehydrated and showing some sand abrasion, she appears to be surprisingly fine physically. Her vitals are stable, but we're giving her fluids and we've drawn blood for a tox screen."

"Is she conscious?" Seth asked. "Has she said anything?"

"She's conscious and we've moved her to a regular room, but she came to so agitated we had to give her a mild sedative. She's calm now but so far she hasn't said a word to anyone," Dr. Kane replied.

"Can we see her?" Seth asked.

Dr. Kane hesitated a moment and then nodded. "But I have to warn you that she appears to be emotionally fragile. I don't want her upset. I understand that you have questions and want answers, but right now my main concern is her health and welfare."

"Understood," Sheriff Atkins agreed.

"Room 223."

Seth took the lead down the long corridor that would take him to her room. He told himself his eagerness to see her, to talk to her was because she was now his case. It was official business.

Room 223 was in semidarkness, the curtains pulled across the windows to shield the late-day sun, and only a small light illuminated the area just above the bed.

Seth nodded in surprise at his sister, who rose from a chair next to the bed at their entrance. "We did the best we could to clean her up, but there's still a beach-full of sand in her hair," she said in a soft whisper. "I think she's asleep right now, but it's hard to tell. She hasn't made a sound since you brought her in."

Linda moved away from the bed as Seth stepped closer. Sheriff Atkins remained just inside the doorway, as if perfectly happy to take a secondary role to Seth.

Seth gazed at the woman in the bed and then looked up at the sheriff. "You sure she isn't a local?" he asked, his voice low and soft.

"Fairly sure," Tom replied.

Seth sank down into the chair that Linda had vacated, satisfied to simply sit and watch until the mystery woman woke up. He had no idea how long Sheriff Atkins was willing to stand in the doorway, but Seth was committed to sitting all night if that's what it took.

It didn't take all night. They'd only been waiting about fifteen minutes when she drew a deep intake of breath and opened her eyes. Almost instantly the tension level in the room shot through the ceiling.

She half rose from her prone position, eyes wild until her gaze landed on Seth and then she appeared to relax a little bit and leaned back into the pillow.

"You're safe now," he said softly. "You're in a hospital and nobody is going to hurt you again." He realized her eyes weren't just a simple blue, but had silver shards around the pupils, giving them a depth that drew Seth in.

"Can you tell us your name?" Tom asked as he stepped up to the foot of her bed.

She looked at the sheriff and then back at Seth and tears began to fill her eyes. She clutched the sheet that covered her and Seth noted that her fingernails were medium-length and polished with a pretty pink gloss that had dulled slightly, probably from sand abrasion.

Still, no broken nails, no obvious defense wounds, no wounds at all on her. So, what had happened to her and who had attempted to bury her in the sand?

"Can you tell us your name?" Seth repeated gently, aware of the tremor that had begun to show on her face, in her shoulders.

Slowly, she shook her head and closed her eyes, as if seeking the numbness of sleep once again. Seth and the sheriff remained in the room for another fifteen minutes or so and then left her room and stood just outside it in the hallway as Linda resumed her seat next to the sleeping woman.

"We found nothing at the crime scene," Sheriff Atkins said as they began to walk down the hallway. "The wind started howling out there and sand was blowing everywhere." He released an audible sigh. "I was hoping we'd get some answers by talking to her tonight."

"She's obviously still traumatized. We'll probably get some answers in the morning. She needs to rest tonight." Seth was as frustrated as the sheriff, but nothing could be done for the remainder of the night. "I would like to get the files from the other two crimes that you believe are linked to this one."

"You're staying at your sister's house?"

Seth nodded. "It looks like I'll be there until we get this mess cleaned up."

"I'll have one of my men bring you the files sometime this evening."

"One more thing, I'd like the names of the young men who were out there on the dunes with me when our mystery woman was found," Seth said.

"The short one with the dark hair is Jerome Walker. He's nineteen and home for the summer from college. The blond is Ernie Simpson, also nineteen and works at the hardware store."

"And the tall one?" Seth asked, thinking of the kid who had stood as if frozen in shock while all the activity had gone on around him.

"Sam Clemmons. He's twenty-one, spends his evenings working part-time as a bartender at a tavern on Main and most of his days out at the dunes riding."

Seth mentally took note of each name, intending to

check them all out. Just because they'd been there to help him didn't mean they'd had nothing to do with how the woman had gotten into the sand. It was possible they'd been burying her and had only stopped and pretended to discover her when Seth had shown up. At this point everyone in Amber Lake was a potential suspect.

"I'm glad to have you on board," Sheriff Atkins said as they stepped out into the waning light of day. "The first young woman I just assumed was some kind of freak party accident. When the second one showed up a month ago I had a bad feeling. And now this…" He allowed his voice to trail off and then continued, "I'm just glad your director allowed you to join me on this."

"I'll meet you at your office at seven tomorrow morning and then together we'll head over here to see if our Jane Doe can wrap things up for us. If this is some kind of a serial killer at work, then she might be able to give you a description, some information that will lead to an arrest."

Sheriff Atkins raked a hand through his hair. "I hope so. You need a ride back to your sister's place?"

"No, thanks. We're close enough that I can just walk there." Linda's house was only three blocks away and Seth needed to expend some of the adrenaline that still coursed through him. The walk would do him good.

"Then I'll see you in the morning."

Seth watched as the sheriff got into his cruiser and pulled out of the hospital parking lot. Only when the cruiser had disappeared from view did he begin the walk to Linda's place.

It's just a job, he told himself, like so many he'd worked before in his career. But, even though that was what he thought, he knew it was more than that. Something had happened in that split second of eye connection they'd shared, something that made him decide long before he'd been officially assigned to the case that he was in until the end.

Chapter Two

She awoke in increments of consciousness, first aware of the sharp smell of antiseptic and then the feel of the stiff mattress beneath her. A hospital. Full consciousness came to her like a slap in the face, bringing with it a spill of memories that were too strange for her to want to claim as her own.

Sand...and sun...and a terror so huge she couldn't now embrace what she knew she'd felt before. Safe. She was safe now. Her head filled with a vision of a handsome, dark-haired man with soft gray eyes. He'd told her she was safe and she'd believed his low, calm voice, the steady assurance of his gaze.

She heard the approach of a rattling cart in the hallway, smelled the scent of coffee and bacon and realized she was ravenous.

A hand control allowed her to raise the head of her bed at the same time a nurse came in. "Ah, good. You're awake," she said cheerfully. "And just in time to enjoy Amber Lake Memorial Hospital's finest cuisine." With an efficiency of movement, the nurse pulled out a table and swung it across the center of the bed and then placed a tray on top.

She looked at the nurse with her short, curly dark

hair and eyes that were a blue-gray and remembered her from the night before. She'd been kind.

"My name is Linda," she said as she pulled the cover from the tray, exposing a plate of bacon and eggs and toast. There was a cup of coffee, a carton of orange juice and a small fruit cup, as well.

Linda smiled at her once again. "It was my brother, Seth, who found you yesterday."

So, Gray Eyes had a name. Seth. Even just hearing his name took away some of the knot of anxiety that pressed tight against her chest.

"I don't know if you remember or not, but we got you off the IV in the middle of the night. Your vitals are all good and the doctor should be in later this morning to see you. I know Seth and the sheriff are going to be here anytime, so you'd better enjoy your meal in peace and quiet before they get here and start bothering you with questions." Linda's smile faded into a look of concern. "Is there anything else I can do for you now?"

Tell me this is all a dream, she thought. *Tell me I'm going to wake up soon and all of this has just been a crazy nightmare.* She shook her head to indicate that she was fine and then picked up her fork.

As she began to eat, Linda hesitated a moment at the door. "Can you tell me your name this morning?"

Her hand trembled slightly as she shook her head.

Linda offered her a reassuring smile. "It's okay… maybe later." She left the room. The scrambled eggs were cooked perfectly and the bacon was crisp. The coffee was a bit strong, but it warmed her a little bit as she drank it. And she needed the warmth, for there seemed to be a cold hand clenched around her heart that refused to release its hold.

She focused solely on the meal, not wanting to think about anything else, afraid to delve too deeply into her own mind until she figured out some things.

She ate everything on the plate and then swung the table away so that she could get out of bed. She needed to use the restroom. She moved her legs to hang off the side of the bed and sat up, wanting to make sure there was no dizziness that would create a potential fall.

As she got to her feet, she was grateful that the IV was gone and pleased to discover that she felt strong. She quickly made her way into the bathroom, the green-flowered hospital gown swimming around her small frame.

The reflection that greeted her in the mirror was that of a stranger. The knot of anxiety that had momentarily subsided grew bigger, tighter in her chest.

She didn't recognize the woman in the mirror with her blue, widened eyes and her dark hair hanging limp and dirty to her shoulders. She reached up to scratch her itchy scalp and her fingers came away with tiny granules of pale sand beneath the nails.

Sand…everywhere, pressing in on her, suffocating her. She couldn't move as she heard the scrape of a shovel, felt the weight of the sand covering her. As the strange memories shot through her she slapped a hand over her chest to keep her rapidly banging heart from beating right out of her skin.

She whirled away from the mirror, took care of her needs and then quickly exited the bathroom and got back into the bed. *Safe, you're safe now.* The words re-

verberated through her head, finally slowing her heartbeat to a more normal pace, and the trembling that had
taken hold of her eased.

She wasn't in bed long before an aide came in. She
looked like a teenager and chirped a cheerful greeting
as she removed the breakfast tray and then disappeared
out of the room.

Linda came back in the room, carrying a pair of
lightweight blue jogging pants and a matching T-shirt
and underclothes. "Do you feel up to a shower?"

She nodded eagerly. There was nothing she'd love
more than to wash the sand out of her hair, to feel clean
again. Maybe a shower would better prepare her for
whatever happened next.

Even though she needed no help, Linda offered her
an arm to lean on as they walked to the bathroom. This
time she consciously avoided looking in the mirror and
leaned against the wall as Linda started the water in the
small shower enclosure.

"I brought you some clothes," Linda said. "Actually,
they belong to my daughter, Samantha. She's sixteen
and you look to be about the same size. Shampoo…
soap, it's all in the shower. Take as long as you need
and I'll be back to check on you in just a few minutes."

Moments later she stood beneath a warm spray of
water and scrubbed the shampoo into her hair. It took
three shampoo-and-rinses before she felt as if all the
sand and grit were finally gone.

She'd wanted to thank Linda for the clothes, for her
kindness, but she was afraid to speak, afraid that somehow the sound of her own voice would make this all
frighteningly real. And she didn't want it to be real.

There was toothpaste and a toothbrush, a hairbrush and a comb on the sink and she used them all before finally leaving the bathroom. She almost felt human again…almost.

As she returned to the bed and sat on the edge, the knot of anxiety returned, make her feel half-breathless. Amber Lake Memorial Hospital. The name was every-where. But where exactly was Amber Lake, and how had she gotten here?

At that moment the sheriff and Seth walked into the room. Linda entered as well, leaning against the wall and out of the way.

She immediately looked into Seth's eyes, seeking the same kind of calmness she'd found there the night before. She wasn't disappointed.

"Well, you look much better this morning than when we left you last night," the sheriff said with obviously forced cheerfulness. "How are you feeling?"

She knew an answer was required from her, but her mouth would form no words, and her diaphragm re-fused to work to allow her any speech.

The sheriff frowned. "Are you up to a few ques-tions?"

She hesitated a moment and then nodded.

"What's your name?" he asked.

Tears began to press hot at her eyes. Sand…it was everywhere, stifling her ability to draw a deep breath, filling her mouth and making it impossible for her to speak, to move.

"Ma'am? Can you tell us who you are?" the sher-iff asked.

She was aware of the tears beginning to trek down

her cheeks as she remembered the weight of the sand on her body, the sound of the shovel scooping up more… more sand to throw on top of her.

She couldn't seem to get past those moments of sheer terror. She couldn't access any other information. She was trapped in that moment, her mouth, her brain filled with sand, unable to move forward from the experience.

Seth stepped closer, his chiseled features softened. "You know you're safe now." She hesitated a moment and then nodded. "Can you talk to us?" She paused again and then slowly shook her head negatively as the tears fell faster down her cheeks.

"Maybe we should try this again later in the day," Linda suggested, her concern for her patient obvious.

Seth's gaze never left hers as he reached out for her hand. Again she hesitated and then slipped her cold hand into his warm one. He squeezed slightly. "Will you talk to us later?"

She wanted to please him, this man who'd saved her life. She wanted to be able to give him whatever it was he and the sheriff needed to know, but she couldn't. Slowly, she once again shook her head.

"She needs more time," Linda said. "She's obviously still traumatized."

Seth released her hand and stood, a frown tracking across his handsome forehead. "We met Dr. Kane on the way in. He gave me the name of a counselor for her to see if necessary and told told me she's free to go, that he intends to release her."

"Release her to where?" the sheriff asked.

Once again her heart began to bang a sickening rhythm. Where would she go? What would happen to her now? At least here in the hospital she knew where she was, she knew she was safe. But safe from what? Safe from who? Who would try to kill her by burying her? Why would anyone want to do that to her? She shoved the horrifying questions to the back of her mind and instead focused her attention on the conversation between the sheriff and Seth.

"We're a small town. We don't have the resources to put her up someplace until we can get some information from her," the sheriff said.

"She'll come to my house," Linda replied smoothly. "Seth is there, she'll be safe there and I'll be able to look after her whenever I'm home."

"Are you sure about this?" Seth asked.

"Positive. You can bunk on the sofa and I'll give her the guest room." Linda smiled at her. "Would you be okay with that? Staying at my place and giving yourself a little more time?"

She nodded. She had no reason not to trust the kind nurse and the man who had rescued her. And she was terrified by any other alternative.

"If you could just tell us your name then we could find out where you live, maybe call some relatives to let them know you're here." The sheriff took another step closer, his frustration wafting off him. "Just your name. Can you just tell me your name?"

She'd love to do that, but the problem was she didn't know her name. She didn't know who she was or where she lived. It was as if the sand where Seth had found her had given birth to her. She had absolutely no memories before that time and it was that particular horror that kept her from speaking.

She had nothing to say that could help them and she'd rather they thought her mute from trauma than admit that she had no idea who she was or where she belonged.

IT WAS JUST AFTER TWO in the afternoon when Seth went back to the hospital to pick up Jane Doe and take her home to Linda's place. Since their early-morning visit with her, Sheriff Atkins had taken her fingerprints to see if anything would pop up in the system to identify her.

His deputies had searched the area for a car, scoured the dunes in hopes of finding a purse or a wallet that might let them know her name. But at the moment she remained Jane Doe.

Seth only hoped that with a little more time she'd trust them all enough to tell them who she was and exactly what had happened to her.

He'd spent most of the night before poring over the files of the two crimes that had occurred in the past two months. Deputy Raymond Michaels had dropped them off about seven the night before.

Seth could understand how the sheriff might have convinced himself that the first young woman, nineteen-year-old Rebecca Cook, had been the victim of some kind of a freak accident.

There had been a party on the dunes, and according to eyewitness reports, things had gotten pretty wild. Rebecca had attended the party but it had been the next day when a couple of riders had come out to enjoy the dunes that they'd discovered her body buried in the sand with only the tips of her toes showing.

The second victim, Vicki Smith, had been a relative

newcomer to town. She was thirty years old at the time
of her death and had been found almost exactly a month
later, buried in a different area of the dunes. There was
no way to write off her death as anything but what it
had been…murder.

And here they were almost a month to the day after
the last murder with a victim who had lived through
sheer luck alone. Three months…three women, and Seth
was aware that if the killer stayed on the same pattern
that meant the clock had already begun ticking down
for the next victim.

Time. It could be the biggest hindrance in solving
a crime. The more time that passed the more opportunity a killer gained to cover his tracks or to manufac-
ture an alibi. And the more time that passed, the closer
they would get to the time when the killer would feel
the need for a new victim.

Hopefully Sheriff Atkins would get a hit from the
fingerprints they'd taken from the woman in the hospital and they would soon know her name. With that
information they could attempt to retrace her footsteps
just before she wound up buried in the sand and hopefully find some information that would lead to an arrest.

He hoped by now the Sheriff had interrogated the
three young men who had been on the dunes when Jane
Doe had been found. As far as Seth was concerned they
were all persons of interest in the crime.

As Seth parked his truck in the hospital lot, he found
it ridiculous how eager he was to see Jane again. There
was no question that something about her drew him.
Maybe it was the helplessness and slight hint of need he

saw in her eyes when she looked at him, but he'd never been attracted to any such women in his past.

He was usually attracted to strong, independent women who invited him into their lives, into their beds, because they wanted him, not because they needed him. Of course, it had been over a year since he'd been in a relationship with any woman. Too much work and no play, was it any wonder a sexy little slip of a woman with bright blue eyes would fire off some testosterone?

When he'd first walked into her hospital room that morning he'd been stunned by her cleanup. Her hair had been a shiny dark curtain hanging below her shoulders and her eyes had held not just fear, not just need, but also an intelligence and awareness that had entranced him.

Unfortunately, something was keeping her from communicating. He had to trust Linda and hope that it was just a matter of time. He reminded himself it had only been twenty-four hours since he'd dug her out of the sand dune.

Her inability to speak might be some sort of self-preservation instinct until she fully processed what had happened to her. He knew she was capable of at least making sounds…he'd heard the inhuman cries issuing from her when she'd come out of the ground and had tried to scramble away. He knew he needed patience, but it was difficult to be patient under the circumstances.

Linda greeted him in the hall just outside her room. "She's all set. She seems to be okay with the plan to stay at my house for the time being. I don't want you browbeating her with a bunch of questions, Seth. She's fragile. We don't know what happened to her before she was found in the sand. The fact that she isn't speaking attests to the depth of trauma she's undergone."

Seth smiled at his sister with affection. "Hey, sis, this isn't my first rodeo. This is what I do for a living."

"You catch killers for a living," Linda countered. "And I just don't want you focused so solely on the endgame that you forget you have a real, living victim here."

"I promise I'll be gentle with her," he replied.

"Pinky swear," Linda demanded and held up her hand.

Seth laughed and linked his little finger with hers. "Pinky swear," he agreed.

"Samantha knows what's going on and has promised to help however she can."

"Then there's nothing left for me to do but get Jane to your house and hope we can build some trust that will get her talking as quickly as possible." Even though Seth had promised to be gentle with her, he couldn't lose sight of what they needed from her.

She was an integral part of a puzzle that involved two previous deaths, an important clue to what appeared to be a serial killer working in the small town.

As he entered her hospital room she stood with her back to him, looking out the window into the sun-filled June afternoon. Despite the fact that she was short and slender, she had a good figure with a nice shapely butt.

He shook his head to dispel this totally male thought. "Jane." She turned to look at him. "Since we don't know your real name, we're going to call you Jane. Is that okay?"

She nodded and offered him a small smile. The simple gesture shot a wave of unexpected heat through his belly. A job, he reminded himself. She was a tool he needed to use to complete a job and nothing more. For all he knew, despite the fact that she wore no wedding ring, she could have a husband or a family somewhere awaiting her return.

There was no way he could get caught up with her on a personal level, despite the beauty of her smile, in spite of the simmering emotions that radiated from her eyes.

"So, you know the plan? You're coming with me to hang out at my sister's place until we have a better idea of what's going on?"

Once again she nodded and stepped closer to him, close enough that he could smell the scent of clean shampoo and soap. "You're in Amber Lake, Oklahoma. Does that sound familiar?"

She frowned and shook her head. "Then let's get you out of here," he said. Together they left the hospital and he led her to his pickup. He opened the passenger door and she stepped up into the cab.

As Seth slid behind the steering wheel he wondered how on earth this was going to work. He'd never spent any time with a woman who couldn't…or wouldn't talk. Usually he complained about having the opposite problem…hooking up with women who wouldn't let him get a word in edgewise.

Seth was accustomed to being the strong, silent type but that obviously wasn't going to work in this particular situation.

The good news was that Samantha would probably be home and she was a typical sixteen-year-old chatterbox. Linda would be home around five to help with what suddenly felt like a babysitting job for a trauma-tized victim who intrigued him like no other woman had done in a very long time.

Just a job, he reminded himself as he pulled into the driveway of Linda's neat three-bedroom ranch-style house. Atkins had told him earlier in the day that he'd posted signs that Deadman's Dunes were off-limits to everyone for the time being.

But Seth knew there was no way Sheriff Atkins and his team could monitor all of the dunes day and night in an attempt to prevent another burial. He glanced at the woman seated next to him staring out the passenger window. She held the keys to catching the killer. Hope-fully she would be able to give them the information they needed before another woman died.

"Here we are," he said. He realized he hadn't said a word on the short ride home from the hospital.

She turned and looked at him. As he saw the grati-tude in her beautiful eyes, a surge of unexpected pro-tectiveness rose up inside him. "It's going to be okay," he said softly. "You're going to be just fine."

Her eyes darkened and at that moment Samantha ex-ploded out of the house, her short dark curls bouncing and a bright smile of welcome on her beautiful face. She halted at the edge of the driveway as Seth and Jane got out of the truck.

"Hi, Uncle Seth," she said as she beelined to Jane. "Hi, I'm Samantha, and I'm so glad you're here. Mom explained to me that you're not talking right now, but it's okay, I talk enough for two people. If you need to borrow any of my clothes, you're welcome to them. Clothes, makeup, whatever you need I've got."

Seth could almost feel the tension leaving Jane as Samantha's friendly chatter filled the air. He guessed that Jane was probably in her mid to late twenties, probably ten years older than Samantha, but Samantha could charm the birds out of the trees when she wasn't having a typical teenage hormonal moment.

He watched as Samantha took Jane's hand. "Come on, I'll show you to your room and then if you want you can help me with supper. I'm hoping if I have it all ready to eat when Mom gets home I can talk her into getting a puppy."

"Good luck with that," Seth said dryly as he followed the two into the house.

"I've been working on her for the past month. I think I've almost got her convinced. You should help me, Uncle Seth. You know having a puppy would teach me responsibility and keep me from doing drugs and partying."

"You don't need a puppy to keep you from doing drugs," Seth replied. "If I even think that's an issue you'll have to contend with me."

Samantha smiled at Jane. "Don't worry, he sounds like a big tough guy but he's got a really mushy center."

Seth watched as Samantha led Jane down the hallway and the two disappeared into the spare room. Knowing at least for the moment that Jane was in good hands, he walked into the kitchen and pulled a cold soda from the fridge.

If this had been a usual case, Seth would have been holed up in the sheriff's office, leading a new investigation not only into this latest crime, but also reinvestigating the two that had occurred previously.

He'd have all the players reinterviewed, check and double-check alibis, and set up a task force to specifically work on it. But this wasn't a usual case, and he forced a smile as the biggest clue of the case came into the kitchen with Samantha.

"We're having meat loaf and mashed potatoes for supper. The meat loaf is already cooking, but I've got to peel the potatoes and get them boiling," Samantha said.

Jane pointed to herself, indicating that she'd peel the potatoes. Within minutes she was at the sink working as Samantha got out salad makings from the fridge and talked about the events of her day.

Jane appeared perfectly at ease, responding to Samantha with smiles and head nods. Maybe Samantha with both her teenage angst and cheerful natural exuberance was just what they needed to open up Jane.

Seth remained in the kitchen, seated at the table and out of the way as the two worked side by side to finish preparing the evening meal.

Dr. Kane had done a quick exam of Jane's throat and had found no physical reason why she wasn't speaking. Seth had already known that she was capable of talking. He would never, for the rest of his life, forget the sounds that had come from her throat in those moments when she'd tried to scrabble away from him...from the sand that surrounded her.

It was simply a choice that she refused to say a word. Her words were probably trapped inside the trauma and somehow they needed to break through.

By six o'clock Linda arrived home, pleased that her daughter had the evening meal ready and that Jane seemed to be settled in just fine.

"Mom, even Uncle Seth agrees that a puppy is a good idea," Samantha said once they were all seated at the table.

"Whoa." Seth held up both hands. "Don't get me in the middle of this argument." Samantha glared at him and Jane laughed.

Time seemed to freeze at the low, pleasant sound. Jane's eyes widened and then she quickly focused on the food on her plate as Linda and Samantha began their discussion about a puppy.

Seth scarcely heard the conversation going back and forth. He was focused on Jane and the beautiful sound of laughter that had escaped her.

It wasn't much, but it was a start, and hopefully by the end of the evening she'd be able to give him more... she'd be able to at least tell him her name.

Chapter Three

Amnesia was a terrible thing, Jane thought as she showered early the next morning. She had no memories to draw upon, no place to go inside her head where she felt safe. She didn't even have a name.

And yet somebody had tried to kill her. Somebody had tried to bury her in a sand dune where she'd remain until some dirt-bike riders had discovered her body. Why? And who? The two questions screamed inside her brain.

How had she gotten here in Amber Lake, Oklahoma, and how had she hooked up with a killer? Who would want to hurt her and why? So many unanswered questions screamed inside her head.

She stood beneath the warm water and thought of the night before. As sexy and handsome as she found Seth, all evening she'd felt like he was a praying mantis poised to spring should she show any sign of weakness.

She knew he wanted her help, desperately needed her to talk about what had happened to her, but she had absolutely nothing to offer him. She didn't know anything about herself or what events had transpired to put her in that sand dune where he'd found her. Right now being in the blankness of her own head was a frightening place to be.

Finished with the shower, she stepped out of the stall and grabbed the thick fluffy towel that awaited her. She was thankful that Linda was a kind and gracious hostess, and Samantha was an absolute doll. It was obvious that Seth loved them both very much.

Seth. If she were in a position to speak she had a feeling he'd make her tongue-tied. His broad shoulders, slim hips and long legs made her feel both safe and yet in just a little bit of danger.

The danger she felt wasn't for her physical being, but rather her emotional state. She was acutely attracted to him, but she knew she'd be a fool to even entertain thoughts of any kind of a relationship with him.

Although she didn't know her own name, she knew for certain she wasn't a fool. He was an FBI agent seeking a killer and she just happened to be his best chance at finding that person. Besides, without knowing who she was, she didn't even know if she already had a man in her life, somebody who was frantically seeking her at this very moment.

She dressed in a pair of jean shorts and a T-shirt that Samantha had provided her. Samantha had won the battle of the dog. Today was Linda's day off and the plan was for all four of them to head to the pound and pick out a puppy.

Jane was looking forward to the outing, hoping that something she saw in the small town would release a flood of memories that would not only answer her questions about herself, but also give Seth what he needed to arrest a madman.

He'd told her briefly the night before about the two murders that had occurred before she'd been discovered, and she'd gone to bed with the thought of those two women's deaths weighing heavy on her soul.

Remember. She had to remember, and yet the harder she tried the more fleeting any memories became. She felt as if they were a word on the tip of her tongue and the more she tried to bring that word into focus the deeper it hid inside her mind.

She quickly ran a brush through her long hair and then pronounced herself ready to face whatever the day might bring. As she left the bathroom she met Samantha in the hallway. The teenager grabbed Jane by the hands and twirled her around.

"Today's the day," she said with excitement. "After months of driving my mom insane, today I get my puppy."

Jane grinned, unable to help the positive flood of energy that filled her at Samantha's happiness. Together they went down the hallway to find Seth and Linda in the kitchen, a cup of coffee in hand.

"Help yourself," Seth said and pointed to the coffeemaker on the cabinet.

Jane nodded and tried to ignore how hot he looked with the early-morning sun shining on his thick dark hair and clad in jeans and a navy T-shirt that stretched across his broad shoulders.

"I hope you slept well," Linda said as Jane joined them at the table. Jane nodded. "I guess the plan is to go to the Amber Lake Animal Pound today and get a puppy." Linda's enthusiasm was definitely less apparent than that of her daughter.

Amber Lake. Although the town sounded vaguely familiar, Jane couldn't imagine why she'd been here… Amber Lake, Oklahoma. The place evoked no emotional response inside her. It was obvious she didn't live in the small town because nobody had recognized her. And how on earth had she been buried in the Deadman's Dunes?

Breakfast was a dog affair, with Samantha and her mother discussing all the things they'd need to buy for the new member of the family. Seth sat silently, his gaze lingering for long periods of time on Jane, making her feel both half-breathless and self-conscious.

She was grateful when the time came for them to go to the pound. Maybe getting out for some fresh air and sunshine would make her feel less like a science specimen and ease some of the tension Seth's gaze coiled inside her.

Besides, Samantha's excitement was contagious and drove away the edge of anxiety that threatened to take hold of her whenever she tried to think too hard about everything she didn't know.

It was just after nine when they left the house, the sun already hot overhead. Seth and Jane got into his pickup while Linda and Samantha got into Linda's car. They planned to stop by a pet store on the way home and get some supplies. Seth's plan was for him and Jane to leave the pound and then take a tour of the town in an effort to stir something of Jane's missing memories.

It felt more than a little surreal to have been buried in a sand dune two days before and now be on the way to the pound to pick out a puppy.

To her surprise Seth kept up a steady stream of

conversation as they drove through the small town of Amber Lake to reach the pound on the other side.

"Linda and I were always close as kids but since my parents are both gone and since her divorce we've gotten really close," he said. "Do you have brothers or sisters?"

She shrugged, wishing she knew the answer, wishing she could voice something, anything to him.

"Samantha is a pip, isn't she?" His voice was filled with affection and Jane smiled and nodded at him.

"Linda's had a rough time since her divorce from her husband, Mark. He was a real control freak and of course because of Samantha he's still in Linda's life."

As he talked, Jane looked out the window, trying to find a building, a place on the sidewalk, something that would jog her absent memory. But there was nothing, and by the time they pulled up to the large, flat building on the outskirts of town that comprised the Amber Lake Animal Shelter and Pound, Jane fought against a sweeping discouragement.

Linda and Samantha parked next to them and as they all got out of the car a young man clad in a khaki uniform stepped out of the building. He had an open face, round blue eyes and light brown hair cut neatly. He appeared ill at ease, standing at attention as if guarding the animals within his care was the most important thing in his life.

"Hi, Steven," Samantha greeted him. "We're here to adopt a dog."

He shot a quick glance at Seth and Jane and then gazed back at Samantha. "The place is nearly full, so you've got plenty to pick from."

"Steven, this is my brother, Seth, and his friend

Jane," Linda said. "And this is Officer Steven Bradley, the man in charge of all things animal in Amber Lake."

"Nice to meet you both," Steven replied. He visibly relaxed and smiled at them all. "I usually don't let people in until noon so I haven't had a chance to clean all the cages yet, but you can come on in. The air conditioner stopped working yesterday and the city is supposed to be sending somebody out here today to fix it. If they don't get out here soon, it's really going to get unpleasant in there."

Steven turned and led them into the building where the smell of dog and cat was nearly overwhelming in the heat that was already building inside.

Cage after cage filled the space, and the barking was nearly deafening. "Quiet," Steven shouted and almost immediately the dogs either stopped barking or muted to soft whines.

"That's pretty amazing," Seth said in the ensuing relative silence.

Steven opened the door to a nearby cage where a small terrier immediately rolled on his back to show his belly. "Dogs need four basic things—consistent discipline, shelter and food and plenty of love." He scratched the terrier's belly and then closed the cage door.

"I could tell you some real horror stories about the conditions I've found some of these animals living in," he continued as they made their way down a narrow aisle. "People just bury their head in the sand when it comes to animal abuse. They don't want to hear about it, they don't even report it when they see it going on."

He shook his head and then smiled at Samantha. "I think I've got just what you want in the back…a litter of poodle-mix puppies that are just now old enough for adoption."

Jane listened to all this absently, fighting an overwhelming desire to run from the building. The air felt oppressive…suffocating, like the sand where she'd been buried. The animal scent was thick, making it hard for her to breathe.

She pushed forward, wanting to see the puppies, but her anxiety grew with each step she took. She couldn't breathe. Her chest ached with the effort. It was just like it had been in the sand. She felt as if she were dying.

Out.

She had to get out.

She turned and bumped into Seth's broad chest. She pushed him aside and slid past him and ran for the exit. She had to get out of this place.

She hit the outdoor air and gulped in deep breaths. Spying a bench nearby, she walked over to it on unsteady feet and sat, lowering her head and hoping the sense of impending doom would pass as quickly as it had claimed her.

Sand and suffocation, being buried alive—her chest tightened with the memory of helplessness.

"Jane?" Seth's soft voice sliced through the panic as he sat next to her on the bench. "Are you okay?"

A moment of utter clarity filled her mind. She raised her head and gazed at him. "My name is Tamara. I'm Tamara Jennings." Her heart filled with the certain knowledge of her statement.

Seth sat back on the bench in surprise. "Why haven't you told us that sooner?"

"Because I didn't know sooner. I didn't know my

name until this very moment, and that's all I know. I'm Tamara Jennings and I don't know where I belong or what happened to me. I don't know anything about myself except my name." To her horror she began to weep.

SETH WAITED FOR HER to get her emotions under control, fighting the impulse to reach out and pull her into his arms. He had two initial thoughts. He liked the sound of her low, sexy voice, and the trauma she'd suffered obviously went far deeper than any of them had initially realized.

"So, since I pulled you out of that sand dune you've had complete amnesia?" he asked once she'd stopped crying and had straightened her shoulders to meet his gaze.

She nodded. "I've been so terrified by it. That's why I didn't talk. I had nothing to say and somehow I felt like if I did say something it would make all of this real, rather than some horrible nightmare. But, it is real, isn't it?"

"I'm afraid so," he replied, his mind still working to take in the ramifications of what she'd just told him. It had to be some sort of a temporary amnesia brought on by whatever ordeal she'd gone through.

"The good news is that with a name we can search DMV and find out where you're from—that is if you have a valid driver's license somewhere."

She frowned. "But the bad news is I can't help you."

"Maybe not at this moment, but I'm hoping with a little time and maybe a little prompting we can get the rest of your memories back, and in those memories will be the information we need to arrest a killer."

She released a tremulous sigh. "A little prompting? Does that involve electric shock?"

It took him a moment to realize she was joking. "Out here in Oklahoma we prefer the cattle prod method," he replied, keeping a straight face and pleased by her ability to joke under the circumstances.

"Amber Lake, Oklahoma." She frowned. "It sounds oddly familiar but not in any real, meaningful way."

"Maybe we should check out that counselor Dr. Kane referred you to," he suggested.

"Not yet." She frowned. "I'm hoping with just a little more time I'll be fine."

At that moment Linda stepped outside. "Everything okay?" she asked worriedly.

"Everything is okay," Seth assured her. "Jane has found her voice and her name is Tamara." He stood and held out a hand to Tamara. "I'm taking her back to the house so we'll see you there when you're finished with the puppy stuff."

He motioned his sister back into the building, not wanting the two women to waste time with small talk. He needed to get in touch with Sheriff Atkins to tell the man that Jane Doe had a name, and with that a true investigation could begin.

Minutes later the two of them were back in his truck and he was deep in thought. With a name they could discover where she lived and from there they could gain all kinds of information in order to retrace the steps she'd taken that had led her to Amber Lake.

Regular people thought they moved through life with anonymity, but in this day and age that wasn't true. If you used an ATM, your picture was taken. Security cameras could be found in parking lots and convenience stores. Traffic cameras were at various intersections. Photos were snapped of people all the time without them knowing…good for victims and officers of the law, not so good for the average criminal. Unfortunately, Seth believed the man they sought wasn't average.

He glanced over to Tamara, who peered out the window as if seeking a point of reference. "Maybe tomorrow we'll do some driving around town to see if anything knocks on your memory."

She turned to look at him. "I'm sorry about my amnesia issue. I know you were hoping that once I started talking you'd have all the answers you needed."

"Don't apologize. Right now your mind is protecting you from whatever happened to you out at Deadman's Dunes. Hopefully once you have some time and we convince you that you're truly safe, then your memories will all come tumbling back."

"I hope so. It's terrible not knowing anything about yourself. I don't know where I live or how old I am. I have no idea what I do for a living or how I got here. I mean, did I take a bus? Did I drive here? And if I did then where is my car?" The questions bubbled out of her.

"I know you didn't take a bus here. There's no service here in town. And by the end of the evening I should be able to answer most of those questions. I've got a lot of resources at the FBI to use to get us information about you now that we know your name."

She gave him a rueful smile. "Most people don't want the FBI anywhere near their personal lives."

"True," he agreed. "But most people know about their own lives."

Once again she directed her gaze out the window. She looked fragile, as if she was just now fully embracing the amnesia she'd been afraid to speak of.

She hadn't spoken of the questions he knew must be screaming in her mind...who had tried to kill her and why? Had somebody driven her to town and dumped her at the sand dunes? Was that why they hadn't found a vehicle? He frowned. That didn't make sense considering there had been two women before her, two victims who had been local.

Once again Seth fought the need to reach out and touch her, to take the darkness from her eyes and watch them fill with the light of laughter.

Instead he focused on all the things he intended to do, all the people he needed to contact when they got back to Linda's place.

With the information he could gain, it would be time to get to work. He'd spent the past twenty-four hours with Tamara hoping she'd speak, hoping she'd be able to give them a starting place.

Now he had one, and he needed to get together with Atkins and discuss their plan of action for finding this killer and taking him off the streets. What he didn't need to think about was how silky Tamara's dark hair looked, how her full breasts pressed against her T-shirt and how long it had been since he'd been with a woman.

Just his luck, that the one woman who sparked his interest, who stirred a physical response just by her nearness was a victim in a heinous crime. Getting involved with a victim was kind of like trying to find love on a reality show...rarely successful.

Whatever he and Tamara might share now had nothing to do with real life. Any feelings that might arise between them would be based on too many other emotions...need, fear and, for him, the desire to do his job.

He'd seen other agents get embroiled on a personal level with victims and witnesses and it never worked out. Besides, he reminded himself, he wasn't looking for anything romantic in his life.

Linda's dismal marriage to her husband and her subsequent contentious divorce had been enough for Seth to reconfirm his commitment to remaining a lone wolf.

It was just after ten when they returned to Linda's and Seth immediately got on his cell phone to begin the process of tapping into the resources he had at his fingertips.

He sat at the kitchen table with his laptop and phone and Tamara slid onto the sofa. The open floor plan of the house allowed him to watch her as he made his calls.

It must be terrifying to not know anything about yourself, to not have memories or images of any past, of any part of your life to identify what kind of a person you were, where you fit in the world.

It took him almost an hour to put into motion the people and programs that would give him all the information they needed about Tamara Jennings.

When he'd made all his calls and set up a meeting with Sheriff Atkins for later in the day, he got up from the table and went to join Tamara on the sofa.

He sat several inches away from her, but could still

smell the clean, fresh scent of her. "Are you doing okay?" He seemed to be asking her that a lot.

"As well as can be expected, I suppose, considering I just learned my name, I'm in a town I don't know and you dug me out of a sand dune." She smiled and raised her chin a notch. "But at least I know my name now and hopefully by the time I go to bed tonight some more of my memories will return or you'll be able to fill in some of the blanks." Her smile fell. "Tell me more about the other two victims."

He told her what he knew about the young Rebecca Cook, found after the wild party on the dunes and the second victim, Vicki Smith, who had recently moved to town and worked as a waitress in one of the local restaurants.

He watched the play of emotions sweep over her face. Sympathy, horror and the relief that she hadn't become a third victim found dead in the sand, it was all there in her eyes, on her features. There was also a hint of guilt there, the guilt of survival, the guilt that so far she'd been unable to help them identify the killer.

She tucked a strand of her long silky-looking hair behind an ear and gazed at him thoughtfully. "So, don't you FBI people work up a profile of some kind on the killer?"

Seth nodded. "We also work up a profile on the victims. But a profile is only as good as the facts of the crimes, and in these cases there are few facts to go on. Unfortunately two months ago when Rebecca Cook was discovered Sheriff Atkins made an error in judgment writing it off as a freak accidental death instead of investigating it like a homicide. Then a month later

Vicki Smith was found and he knew he had a killer somewhere in town."

"Does he have any suspects?" she asked. She shifted positions and once again he caught a whiff of her clean fresh scent.

"A few, although nobody who is at the top of a fairly pathetic list," he admitted. "I intend to revisit all those suspects and reinterview everyone who had any part of the initial investigations. Hopefully I can pick up on something the sheriff and his men missed."

"Was I drugged? Maybe that's why I can't remember anything? At least that would explain how I got in the sand and apparently didn't fight my attacker."

"Maybe, but doubtful. The tox screens for both of the previous victims came back clean for drugs. Rebecca's showed a bit of alcohol but not enough to render her mentally or physically impaired. Dr. Kane should have your initial blood tox report back sometime today, but if it's like the others, it won't show any drugs."

Her gaze remained locked with his and he could almost see that she was working to process everything he had told her. Her eyes had grown darker in hue, and the silver shards around her pupils looked more pronounced.

"So, Rebecca Cook's body was found in the dunes in April. Almost thirty days later Vicki Smith was found, and then thirty days after that you found me. So, it appears that the killer is on some sort of thirty-day timeline," she said thoughtfully. "Since I survived, does that mean he's already hunting for a new victim or will he wait thirty days to act again?"

Seth released a sigh. "I can't answer that. I don't have enough information to know what he will do next."

Worse than that, he couldn't know if the killer would just choose another victim or if he'd try to finish what he'd begun with Tamara.

Chapter Four

It was just after six when Sheriff Atkins arrived at Linda's house. Linda had left for her shift at the hospital an hour earlier, Samantha and the new puppy, Scooter, were in her bedroom, and Tamara, Seth and the sheriff all sat down at the kitchen table.

It had been a strange afternoon. Once Linda and Samantha had come home, Tamara had spent most of her time with Samantha playing with the new little black fur ball.

Seth had taken his cell phone, the files from Atkins and his laptop into the guest room where Tamara had slept the night before and worked through the afternoon. He'd tried not to get distracted by the sight of the bed where she'd slept the night before, the faint clean scent of her that lingered in the air.

He'd thought that by working in another room from where she was located, he wouldn't be so distracted, but he'd been wrong. The thought of her long dark hair spilled over the white of the pillowcase distracted him. He didn't want to entertain thoughts of how warm and soft her body would be against his underneath the bedsheets.

He just wanted to figure out what had happened to

her and get her back where she belonged. He didn't want to think about how lush-looking he found her lips, how much he liked the sound of her voice and how she created an ache inside him that he hadn't felt in a very long time.

She now looked at Seth from across the table, obviously eager for him to share the information he'd gathered about her throughout the afternoon, information he hoped would kick-start her memory and lead them to their killer.

Atkins appeared tired, but also anxious to hear what he had to say. Seth had a legal pad in front of him and once he'd offered the sheriff a cup of coffee and they were settled in, he began.

"Tamara Jennings, thirty-two years old, you live alone in an apartment in Amarillo, Texas. You were married briefly but divorced two years ago. You were fairly easy to find by a driver's license and the photo on the license was good enough to make the identification." He paused and looked up at her, waiting for some kind of an aha moment.

Her hair shone like black silk with the early-evening sunshine streaming through the window. She shrugged with a frown. "Nothing rings a bell. You could be talking about anyone." Her eyes grew slightly glassy, as if she was fighting back tears, but she nodded for him to continue.

Seth glanced back at his notes. "Nothing criminal in your past, not even a speeding ticket. I couldn't find any living relatives. According to your neighbors in the apartment complex where you live you don't socialize with anyone in particular, you're friendly but pretty much stay to yourself. Nobody I spoke to could give me the name of a boyfriend or even a close friend. You own a successful business designing and maintaining websites for a variety of businesses and work out of an office in your apartment."

Once again Seth looked at her, hoping to see something, anything in her eyes that might indicate a glimmer of memory, but there was nothing in the blue depths but the swimming start of tears.

To Seth's surprise it was Atkins who reached out and patted the back of her hand. "It's all right. It will all come back to you in time. You're just going through a rough patch, that's all."

Tamara cast him a grateful smile and Seth wished it had been he who had reached across the table to comfort her, he who had been the recipient of her smile.

He clenched his jaw muscles and looked back down at his notes. "According to DMV records you own a blue Ford Focus. It isn't currently parked at your apartment building in Amarillo."

"So, I probably drove it here to Amber Lake."

Both Seth and the sheriff nodded. "I've got my deputies looking everywhere for the car, but so far it hasn't turned up," Tom said.

"I checked your ex-husband out," Seth said. "He's a real estate investor who moved to California months after your divorce." He'd mostly gotten details about her ex out of curiosity, but he wasn't about to admit that out loud. "He hasn't been out of the San Diego area since the time you've been missing from your apartment. I ruled him out, but we all know that the killer we're looking for is probably right here in Amber Lake."

He turned his attention to Tom. "I don't want to step on toes here, but I'm starting at the beginning with a reinvestigation into Rebecca Cook's and Vicki Smith's murders."

"You aren't stepping on my toes," Tom replied. "I welcome the help and you know you have my full force at your disposal. Just tell us what you need and we'll see that it's done."

"The first thing I want from you is your gut instinct," Seth replied. "Is there anyone you've investigated so far that shot off any alarms in your head? Somebody that you felt might be guilty but had no evidence?"

Tom frowned and shook his head. "I wish I could tell you a name, but I can't imagine anyone in this town having the capacity to do what's been done to these women."

Seth glanced over to Tamara, who appeared lost in thought, a delicate frown etched into her forehead. "Tamara, we really have no reason to hold you here. If you want to return to your home in Amarillo, then you can. We can't keep you here, but I'd like for you to stick around here and see if we can find something or somebody here in town to shove past your amnesia. Right now you still remain our best lead to getting this guy."

She turned her bright blue eyes toward him, hers holding the faint edge of inner haunting. "I'll stay. The life you just told me about, the woman who lives in Amarillo, doesn't feel like they have anything to do with me. I need my memories not just to help you and Sheriff Atkins, but so that I can truly get back where I belong, and I think the key to unlocking them is here in Amber Lake."

Seth didn't try to analyze why her decision to stay pleased him. He told himself it was simply because she was their best hope for catching a killer.

"So, what's our plan?" Tom asked.

"Right now my plan is to get Tamara out first thing tomorrow and take her around town to see if anything strikes a chord with her. I also intend to reinterview everyone who had anything to do with the first two victims."

Tom nodded. "We have a lot of abandoned barns and buildings in the area and we'll start a grid search to find the missing car. It's got to be somewhere not too far away and maybe it will hold some clues. And I'll be glad to make available anyone you want to talk to at my office."

"I appreciate it," Seth replied. Once again he looked at Tamara, who stared out the nearby window where the light of day had begun to turn the golden hues that occurred just before twilight.

He wished he knew her well enough to be able to guess what she was thinking, although it didn't take a rocket scientist to know that she had to be feeling lost and so alone.

Half an hour later he walked Sheriff Atkins to the door and then returned to the kitchen to find Tamara in the same spot at the table, her gaze appearing to be captured by something in Linda's backyard.

She turned to face him as he walked over to the coffeemaker on the countertop. "Want a cup?" he asked.

"Please."

He poured them each coffee and then once again sat across from her at the table. She cupped her hands around the mug, as if seeking the warmth from the liquid within.

Before they could say anything Samantha appeared in the doorway with her pooch in her arms. "Scooter and I are going to my friend Amy's for a couple of hours. Don't worry, I already checked in with Mom and she said it was fine. I'll be home by ten." She flew out the back door without waiting for a response.

"I feel like I'm intruding into everyone's lives here," Tamara said once Samantha had left the house. "You're sleeping on a sofa instead of a bed and I'm taking advantage of your sister's generosity."

"Nonsense," Seth replied. "First of all, I've slept on a lot of sofas in my lifetime and Linda's is one of the most comfortable. Second, you aren't taking advantage of anyone. You're an invited guest in this house."

"And a useless key to a serial killer," she exclaimed in obvious frustration.

"Maybe a little useless now," he agreed, "but you never know when your memory is suddenly going to return and hopefully with that you'll know a face, remember a detail that will give us what we need."

She raised her mug to her lips and took a drink and then set the mug back on the table. "All I remember right now is sand...sand everywhere and the scrape of a shovel."

"The scrape of a shovel?" He looked at her in stunned surprise. She hadn't mentioned that before. "You were aware enough to hear a shovel while you were being buried?"

"I guess so." Her eyes went a midnight-blue. "My only memory is of sand, covering me, suffocating me and the noise of a shovel digging and scraping nearby. I couldn't move, but I know I was conscious while I was being buried." A shiver shook her shoulders and she stood, as if unable to sit while those horrible images swept through her mind.

Seth stood as well, wanting…needing to lighten the darkness in her eyes, steal away some of the horror that lingered there. Without thinking about right or wrong, Seth reached for her and she came willingly into his embrace.

She leaned heavily against him, the top of her head fitting neatly beneath his chin as her body continued to shiver against his. He wrapped his arms more tightly around her, as if he could somehow absorb whatever darkness flowed through her.

She didn't cry and finally the shivering that had swept over her halted, but still she remained in his embrace as if he were her lifeline in a sea of the unknown.

And wasn't that just what he was right now for her, he reminded himself. But she did feel good against him, her feminine curves melting into him as her arms reached around his neck.

He tried to maintain his objectivity. He tried to think of her only as a victim who needed comforting, but it was as a man he smelled the sweet fragrance of her hair, felt the press of her breasts against him, and he felt himself responding as a man. Fearing that she might notice, he released her and stepped back from her, needing some distance before he completely embarrassed himself.

As good as she felt, as much as he might want her as a man, he needed her more for what was locked inside her head. Somehow, someway, he had to crack her memories open as quickly as possible, before another body wound up buried in the sand.

They returned to the table where once again she sat and cupped the mug in front of her, her gaze not quite meeting his.

"I'm sorry I can't help you right now," she said softly.

She finally looked up at him and once again in her eyes he saw a haunting fear. "I want to help you, but there's a small part of me that's afraid of my memories. I'm afraid that if I remember who put me in the sand and why, if I remember every sensation, every moment of my time with my killer, I'll go crazy. There's a part of me that's scared that by helping you, that by remembering, I'll lose myself to complete madness."

TODAY WAS THE DAY SHE might face the person who tried to kill her, the monster who had buried her in the sand dunes. Tamara checked her reflection in the bathroom mirror, grateful that Samantha had a generous spirit and an awesome wardrobe. Today Tamara was clad in a pair of jeans and a bright yellow T-shirt. She'd hoped that by wearing the color of beautiful sunshine some of her nerves might calm, but so far it wasn't working.

She turned away from the mirror, knowing that Seth was waiting for her in the living room. They'd all eaten breakfast together an hour earlier, then Samantha had left with friends and Linda had gone to bed after her night of working. Now it was time to leave the safety of this house and venture out on a treasure hunt for her memories.

She reached for the bathroom doorknob to leave,

but paused for just a moment, remembering the brief, but wonderful time the night before that she'd spent in Seth's embrace.

He'd told her she'd been married, but she couldn't remember ever feeling so safe, so secure in a man's arms as she had last night with Seth. In fact, whenever she thought about her marriage, a knot of new anxiety formed in her stomach.

What kind of a man had she married? And why had they divorced? And why did thinking about it all make her feel so anxious and unsettled? She gave a mental shrug and left the bathroom. Until she remembered her past, there was no point in speculating about anything. All she knew about herself were the facts that Seth had managed to discover.

He rose from the sofa as she entered the living room. As always, her breath caught in her chest at the sight of him. He was so handsome, and as his gaze flicked over her from head to toe, a warmth grew inside her and she remembered how quickly he'd stepped away from her last night, but not before she'd realized he was aroused.

"Yellow is definitely your color," he said. "You look bright and cheerful."

"Good, then my disguise worked," she replied drily.

"Nervous?"

She nodded. "I want my life back, the memories of who I am, but when I really think about remembering the minutes before my near death, the back of my throat closes up and I feel like I'm suffocating."

"Trust me, there will be no suffocation in your life while I'm around." He pulled his truck keys from his pocket. "Ready for the town tour?"

"I wish I could say I was looking forward to it."

He frowned. "But you want to get your memories back. You need to know your past, to know who you are and what your life consisted of before all this. Without your past I'd think it would be difficult to have a future."

"You're right, of course," she agreed as they stepped out the front door and into the warm June sunshine. "I just hope that when I do get my memories back I don't discover that I was a thief or something terrible."

He opened the passenger door for her and grinned. "Tamara, if you were something terrible we'd all know it by now. If you were a criminal, it would have come up in my background search. If you were a mean, hateful woman, your true colors would have bled through by now."

She climbed into the truck seat and watched as he rounded the front of the vehicle to get to the driver's side. She didn't know what kind of evil wind had blown her into the sand dunes and to her near death, but fate was definitely smiling on her when it had been Seth who had found her.

She wasn't sure where she'd be at this instant in time if not for Seth and his family. The fact that they'd taken a risk allowing her into their lives without knowing anything about her wasn't lost on her.

"Just relax," Seth said as he climbed behind the steering wheel and started the engine. "I have a feeling this is something that the harder you work at, the less success you'll have." He cast her another one of his killer smiles. "The sun is shining, you're healthy and safe and best of all, you're with me."

A bubble of laughter escaped her at his obvious stab

at mock conceit, but the laughter quickly faded. "Samantha told me yesterday while you were on the phone that you'd come here for vacation. I guess I screwed that up for you."

"Vacations are highly overrated," he replied easily as he backed out of the driveway. "I like my work and really had only decided to take a vacation because I wanted to spend some time with Linda and Samantha."

"They're wonderful. Are your parents alive?"

"No. They died in a car accident eight years ago."

"I'm sorry," she said, at the same time wondering when her parents had died. If she'd mourned deeply for them. The fact that after speaking with her neighbors he couldn't even come up with the name of a friend pierced her with sadness. "Surely I had a cell phone. Can't it be pinged or whatever to locate it?"

"If you had a cell phone it must have been a pay-as-you-go, and without a phone number we have nothing to ping," he replied.

As he turned onto what was obviously the main drag of the small town, Tamara focused her attention out the window and tried to relax her mind.

Amber Lake was a quaint small town that displayed touches of community pride here and there. Trees had been planted in the sidewalk at regular intervals, providing shade to the shoppers who found themselves out in the heat of the day.

There were the usual stores—hardware, grocery, a discount apparel shop as well as a dress boutique—some fast-food places, a café and a fancy restaurant called the Golden Daffodil.

Yes, it was a nice, quaint little town, but nothing

looked even vaguely familiar, nothing jogged a single piece of her memory.

"Nothing," she said dispiritedly after several minutes.

"Don't be so impatient," he replied easily.

"I'm trying not to be, but I was hoping that something that I saw would at least spark a tiny piece of memory." She sighed in frustration.

Seth pulled into a parking space at the south end of Main. "Why don't we get out and take a little stroll. It's a nice morning and maybe you'll see something in a shop window or somebody you'll recognize."

"Sounds like a plan," she agreed. Moments later they walked together down one side of Main with the intention of returning to the truck by walking on the opposite side of the street.

They walked at a leisurely pace, small-talking about the weather and Samantha and the newest member of the household as Tamara took in each store window they passed, every person who nodded and smiled as they went by.

"I'm assuming you aren't married," she said after they'd walked for a few minutes.

"You've got that right," he replied.

"What about a significant other?"

"Nope, nobody. All I've had in my life for the past couple of years is work. Besides, after watching what Linda went through with her divorce from her husband, I decided for sure that I never wanted to get married."

"Bad divorce?"

"Terrible," he replied. "I didn't like her husband,

Mark, when they married and I liked him a hell of a lot less by the time the divorce was finalized."

"Does he live here in town?" she asked.

"Two blocks away from Linda." He drew a deep sigh. "As much as I find him an arrogant, controlling ass, I have to give him props for being a good father to Samantha. She spends most of her weekends at his place and she adores him."

"That's important. Girls need their fathers in their lives." She frowned. "But you shouldn't allow your sister's experience to deter you from having a family. I've seen how you are with Samantha and you'd make a great dad."

He laughed, a deep, full-bodied sound that swept pleasurable warmth through her. "It's easy to be a favorite uncle, but I'm not so sure that I'd be good dad material, and in any case it doesn't matter. I have no intention of ever getting married."

"I wonder why I got divorced?" Tamara asked, although she knew he had no answer. She found it difficult to imagine herself a married lady, but then she found it impossible to know exactly what kind of a woman she'd been before Seth had dug her out of the sand.

"Hopefully you'll know soon," Seth replied.

Although he said it easily, Tamara felt the pressure to remember, the need to help him find the person who had already killed two women and had tried to kill her, a man who could at any moment decide to claim another victim.

"How about an early lunch?" Seth suggested when they reached the Amber Lake Café.

"Sure," she agreed.

As they walked into the front door of the restaurant a jingle of wind chimes sounded and Tamara had a visceral sense of déjà vu.

She said nothing as she followed Seth to a booth and slid across from him. The chimes sounded familiar, like a musical echo in the very back of her brain. She didn't want to get his hopes up, didn't want to jump to any conclusions.

She might have heard the same kind of wind chimes in another place, she might even possess some herself in her apartment in Amarillo. A single noise wasn't enough to indicate that at some point in the past she'd visited this particular café.

"Hey, folks," a blonde waitress with a name tag that read Lucy greeted them, with two menus. "Can I start you off with something to drink?"

"I'd like a diet cola," Tamara said.

"And a glass of iced tea for me," Seth replied.

"Be back in a jiffy," Lucy said as she left their booth.

Tamara opened her menu and made her decision, then looked at Seth as a thought occurred to her. "Since we know who I am and where I live is it possible I can access my bank account and get out some cash?"

"I don't see how that can be done without us driving into your bank branch and somehow explaining the situation to them. You don't have a bank card and I'm assuming you wouldn't know your pin number. Is there something you need?"

"A loan?" she ventured. She felt the warmth of a blush fill her cheeks. "I'd like to buy some clothes for myself instead of borrowing everything from Samantha. I'd just feel better if I had a few things to call my own."

"I should have realized how difficult it has been for you." Seth smiled at her. "Just tell me how much you want and I'll get it for you when we pass by the bank."

"Maybe a hundred dollars?" she said tentatively.

"We'll make it two hundred and if you need more than that I want you to come to me." He leaned forward across the table, his eyes like a gray bank of calming fog. "And it's not a loan. We'll consider it living expenses for a material witness in a murder investigation."

"A material witness who can't remember anything," Tamara said dispiritedly.

At that moment the waitress returned with their drinks and they placed their orders. "So, I guess if we're going to small-talk over lunch we're going to have to talk about me," Seth said teasingly.

"Actually, I'd like that topic of conversation," she replied lightly. "You can tell me all about your work for the FBI and about your life in Kansas City."

"I don't have a life in Kansas City," he said drily, "but I love talking about my work."

And he did. While she ate a club sandwich and he wolfed down a double cheeseburger he talked about the cases he'd worked in the past and the evil he'd seen over the years working as a profiler.

Tamara found everything about him fascinating, from what he did for a living to the way the left corner of his mouth moved upward to begin one of his sexy smiles. She found it fascinating the way his eyes went from soft dove-gray when he talked about things he cared about to a cold steel color when he spoke of things he didn't like.

It would be easy for her to develop a little bit of a crush on FBI Special Agent Seth Hawkins, even though she knew it would also be foolish.

For all she knew there was a man somewhere in Texas worried sick about her, a man who loved her, a man she loved to distraction. But, if there was such a man, then why couldn't she even remember him? And why wasn't he looking for her? Surely she would have some sense of loving…of being loved.

Why when she tried to remember her former life, before the sand dunes, before Amber Lake, did a tight squeeze of anxiety grip her stomach? Had she fled her apartment in Amarillo because of something bad? Because of something sad?

She was attracted to Seth but when she looked into his eyes she not only saw a man's attraction, but also an FBI agent's need…the need for answers she didn't have at this time.

As they finished up the meal she once again cast her gaze around the café. It was like a hundred cafés that the Midwest sported, homey and warm and filled with people who had grown up together, who were friends and neighbors and gathered here on a regular basis.

Hanging on the wall behind the counter was a large picture of a piece of pie with the caption Enjoy A Piece of Amber Lake Café's Famous Caramel Pie.

Sparks shot off in her head. She remembered that sign, and she'd had a piece of that pie. Her mouth filled with the solid memory of the flaky crust, of the gooey richness of caramel.

"I've been here." The words whispered out of her as she turned to stare at Seth. "I've eaten here before," she exclaimed as a wave of excitement washed over her.

"Are you sure?" Seth sat up straighter in his seat, his gaze intense as it held hers.

She leaned back against her seat and once again stared at the sign advertising the pie and as she did snippets of memories snaked through her head. "A plump waitress, a chicken salad sandwich, the shadows of twilight filtering in through the front windows and a piece of caramel pie and coffee for dessert," she said softly. "I was definitely here."

"Twilight, that means you were probably here for dinner." Seth's voice brought her out of the kaleidoscope of flashing snippets of memories.

"The plump waitress was a redhead. She served me," she replied, once again looking around the café for a flame-haired waitress. She pointed to a woman working the other side of the café. "I think that's her."

Seth shot out of the booth and approached the waitress. Tamara could see the energy that wafted from him, felt the energy drumming inside her own veins. Remembering eating a piece of pie wasn't much, but it was something and gave her the hope that more would follow.

Seth returned to the booth with the waitress, who wore a name tag that read Annie. She smiled at Tamara and shoved a strand of her crimson hair behind one ear. "Sure, I remember her," she said. "She was in for dinner Monday night and I waited on her."

"Was she alone?" Seth asked.

"Ate alone, left alone," the waitress replied.

"Did I mention where I was going, what I was doing here in town?" Tamara asked.

"I've got to be honest with you, hon. I don't remember making any small talk with you. You ordered. I brought your food and that was it. Sorry I can't be more helpful, and now I've got to get back to my customers." With an apologetic smile she hurried back to her side of the café.

Seth sank back down in the booth, his eyes bright with hope. "This is good. This is very good. Maybe this is a sign that your memories are starting to break loose. Now we know you were here and ate dinner on Monday night and you were found at the dunes on Tuesday. This is the beginning of solving the puzzle, Tamara." He reached across the table and took hold of her hand.

She clung tightly as she held eye contact with him. She had a feeling that if this was just the beginning, then she knew she'd probably have to go to hell and back as the rest of her memories returned.

Chapter Five

It was well before dawn when Seth sat at the kitchen table with a cup of coffee at his elbow and the files of the two murders in front of him. Sleep had been difficult and he'd finally decided to forget even trying to get up.

There were so many things about these cases that bothered him, starting with his number-one witness. Although no other memories had returned to Tamara for the rest of the day, he'd been pleased by the little bit of progress they'd made during lunch.

They'd finally returned home at dinnertime after having walked most of Main Street several times. By the time they'd gotten back here and eaten dinner Tamara had pled exhaustion and a headache and had gone to her room.

Seth had almost been grateful that she'd removed herself from his presence. He'd been far too aware of her all day, smelling her scent, watching the play of emotions that crossed her beautiful features. He'd fought a simmering desire for her all day long and had felt like he drew his first real deep breath when she went to her room.

He had to stop looking at her as an attractive female

and instead stay focused on her as a potential victim and the best opportunity they had to catch a killer.

He took a sip of his coffee and studied the file containing everything about Rebecca Cook's murder. There was no question that Sheriff Atkins and his team had had their work cut out for them investigating the young woman's death. Most of the teenagers and young adults in town had been at the party at the dunes.

There were reams of pages of interviews contained in the file and Seth flipped through each one, unsurprised to find that the three young men who had been on the dunes the day Tamara had been uncovered had also been party attendees.

As he moved on to the file with notes and interviews and the official reports on Vicki Smith, two things caught his attention. The first was that Sam Clemmons, the young man who had been like a frozen statue at the scene with Tamara, had also been present when the other two women had been found at the dunes. What were the odds of him being there when three bodies were uncovered? He knew the sheriff had interrogated the boys after Tamara had been found, but he hadn't seen the interview transcripts yet.

Vicki Smith had been a pretty, thirty-year-old brunette who had worked as a waitress at the Golden Daffodil and at the time of her death had been dating the owner of the restaurant, Henry Todd. Todd had been questioned but despite his intimate relationship with the victim the authorities had been unable to tie him to Vicki's murder or find any kind of a connection between Todd and Rebecca.

The only thing all three victims had in common was

dark hair. The first two victims had been natives of Amber Lake and so far it appeared that Tamara had simply been passing through.

What had happened to her between the hours when she'd had dinner in the café and the next day when she'd been found in the sand dunes? What horrors was her amnesia attempting to protect her from remembering?

Linda had spoken to him for a little while the night before about post-traumatic stress and all that it could entail for Tamara.

She'd even suggested it might be healthy for Tamara to meet with the professional the doctor had recommended to discuss her amnesia and whatever else she might be experiencing due to her trauma. Seth intended to ask Tamara this morning if she needed to see a counselor or somebody else, even though so far she'd declined.

In the meantime, he intended to pick apart each and every report and interview from the two murders and make a list of people he intended to reinterview personally.

There were only two official entrances to Deadman's Dunes that provided a small parking area for the off-riders to park. On the day that Seth had arrived and gone to the dunes, he'd parked at the main entrance on the north side. The other way in was on the west side of the sand.

Rebecca's body had been found almost directly in the center of the dunes, where the area was a flat run for riders to test their speed before hitting the hilly mounds again.

Vicki's body had been found close to the west entrance and Tamara's on the east side of the dunes. It didn't matter what any of it meant to Seth. What he needed to find out was what the dunes meant to the killer.

At six-thirty, he got up from the table, grabbed some of his clothes from the hallway closet where he'd moved them from the guest room and then headed for the bathroom to get ready for the day.

Minutes later as he stood beneath the shower spray his thoughts returned to Tamara. It was strange, he knew nothing about her past, nothing about the life experiences that had made her who she was, and yet he felt as if he knew a wealth of information about her just from the hours they'd spent together.

Her political beliefs jived with his, she had a wicked sense of humor that he enjoyed and there was softness to her spirit that made him want to be strong for her.

He liked the way she tucked her hair behind her ear when she was nervous, how her eyes lit up just before a smile curved her lips.

They'd spent part of yesterday at the discount store where she bought a basketful of clothing and miscellaneous items to call her own. If you could tell a woman's personality by the things she bought, then Tamara was definitely low maintenance.

Seth had paid for everything and she'd insisted that when she had access to her bank account again she would make it right with him.

He didn't care if she ever paid him back. She hadn't spent that much money and the pleasure that had ridden her features as she picked out things for herself had been worth every penny.

He stepped out of the shower and grabbed the awaiting towel. As he dried off he thanked the stars that he'd packed a pair of dress slacks and a short-sleeved dress shirt. Today he wasn't going into the sheriff's office as Seth Hawkins on vacation in jeans and a T-shirt, but rather as Special Agent Seth Hawkins, dressed for business. He'd already let Sheriff Atkins know that he meant business when he'd called him the night before to set up a meeting with Atkins's team.

Dried and dressed, he clipped his badge onto his belt, added his shoulder holster and gun and then pulled on a lightweight jacket. He not only wanted the local law enforcement to know that he was ready to roll, but also everyone he interviewed that day that they were facing a professional.

He nearly yelped in surprise as he opened the bathroom door and almost ran over Tamara. He grabbed her shoulders to steady her and then together they headed for the kitchen where they wouldn't disturb the others who were still sleeping.

"You're up early," he said, noticing that the blue-and-white blouse she wore emphasized not only the bright blue of her eyes, but also her small waist. A pair of white shorts showcased the length of her slender legs and Seth felt a slow burn begin in the pit of his stomach.

"I should be up early," she replied as she headed for the coffeepot. "I went to bed at the crack of dusk last night."

"Did you sleep well?"

She finished pouring herself a cup of the coffee and then turned to face him. "I'd love to tell you I tossed and turned with memories whirling all through my brain, but the truth is I slept hard and deep and without any dreams, at least none that I remember."

She took a sip of her coffee and above the cup her gaze slid over him. "You look quite official this morning," she observed as she lowered the cup from her mouth.

"I'm heading into Atkins's office for the day. I'm meeting with his entire team and going to do some interviewing."

"Do I need to be there?"

He shook his head. "Not today. Are you comfortable just hanging around here with Samantha and Linda? It's Linda's day off, so you won't be alone."

"I'll be fine," she assured him.

"Linda has my cell number. You'll call me if you think of anything new?"

"You mean like the name and address of the killer?" she asked wryly. "I promise you'll be the first to know."

He grinned at her. "Good, and I'd like to officially invite you to dinner tonight at the Golden Daffodil."

"Is this someplace I might have been?" she asked.

"Or where someone you might have encountered is," he replied. He watched the apprehension that raced across her features. "But it's not all business," he hurriedly added. "The food is supposed to be excellent there and I'd like to have you as my dinner date."

The apprehension on her face transformed to something pretty, something half-yearning. "I'd love to be your dinner date," she said, her cheeks with slightly more color than normal. "What time should I be ready to go?"

"Why don't we plan on around six-thirty." He backed

toward the kitchen door. "And now, I've got to get out of here and down to the sheriff's office. I'll check in later."

He escaped out of the house and into the fresh early-morning air, wondering what in the world he had just done pretending he and Tamara were going out on a date tonight, wondering why the idea of being out on a date with her filled him with the same kind of wistful longing he'd momentarily seen in her eyes.

He started his truck and clenched the steering wheel with a sense of determination. For the past couple of days he'd felt more like a babysitter than an investigator. As much as he enjoyed spending time with Tamara, as much as he hoped she'd regain her memories and solve the crime for them all, they couldn't just sit around and wait and hope that that might happen.

It was time to get to work…the tedious grunt work that usually solved crimes. They couldn't depend on Tamara another minute. They needed to attempt to find the killer the old-fashioned way until Tamara was at a place where she could help them.

If he discovered that Atkins's team couldn't keep up with him, that they weren't up to his kind of investigation, then he would contact Director Forbes and request a couple more men to form a task force. He was hoping to work well with the locals, but he wouldn't hesitate to call in reinforcements if necessary.

As he stepped into the low, flat building that served as the sheriff's headquarters, he smiled at the woman behind the desk at the same time that he heard Tom Atkins's voice coming from a back room. The sheriff didn't sound like a happy camper.

"You can go on back," the woman said as Seth flashed

his badge. "They're all there waiting for you in the conference room…last doorway on the left."

As Seth walked down the long corridor that led to the back of the building, he realized from the sound of things that Tom Atkins was definitely having a temper fit.

Seth opened the door to the conference room and a dozen pairs of eyes turned his way. The dozen deputies were seated in chairs at a long conference table and Atkins stood at the head of the table, his chubby face flushed with residual anger.

"Agent Hawkins," he greeted Seth. "Please, join us."

Seth slid into a chair next to Deputy Raymond Michaels, the man who had brought him the files the other night.

"Have you seen the morning paper?" Tom asked Seth.

Seth shook his head. Linda didn't have the local newspaper delivered and Seth hadn't ventured out to find one that morning. A paper was slid in front of him and he stared at the front page in irritation. The headline read: The Sandman Attempts to Bury Another. There was also a grainy picture of Tamara being lifted out of her sandy grave by Seth. He scanned the accompanying article, his irritation growing as he realized it named not only Tamara but also himself and the fact that he was in town visiting Linda. The article had been written by Jeff Armando, reporter at large.

He looked back at Tom. "It would appear there's a mole in the room."

"And there's nothing I hate more than moles," Atkins replied as he directed his gaze to his men. "And if

I find out one of you talked to Jeff, then I'm going to have your hide."

"Have you spoken to this Armando to see how he got the information?" Seth asked.

Atkins's frown deepened. "He has a right to protect his sources and all that First Amendment crap. Now, let's get to work, but don't think I intend to let this news item go. I'll get to the bottom of it one way or another. Now, reports."

A young man with sandy-colored hair spoke up. "Deputy Aims and I spent all day yesterday checking out all the motels and anyplace that rents rooms to see if Tamara had registered anywhere to spend Monday night here in town. She wasn't registered anywhere."

"So, she either intended to just pass through or check into a nearby motel without a reservation," Atkins said.

Another deputy spoke next. "Jack and I checked out all of the abandoned buildings, barns and sheds on the north side of town for the missing car. Obviously we didn't find it. We plan on doing the south side today."

Tom nodded and looked at Seth. "When you called me last night Tamara had remembered eating at the café. Has she remembered anything else?"

"No, but I've been thinking about the timeline on her particular case. We know she ate dinner at the café and then was found the next afternoon in the dunes. What we need to find out is if she was seen anywhere else in town by anyone during those hours."

He glanced toward the sandy-haired deputy who'd reported earlier. "We know now that she didn't register at any of the motels and we can assume that she meant to leave town after dinner. But if she was taken by somebody immediately after she ate at the café, that means somebody kept her someplace alive until he took her to the dunes the next afternoon." Seth didn't even want to think about what might have happened in those missing hours.

"So we need to check around and see if anyone saw Tamara after the café," Raymond said. "Can't we get her driver's license photo copied to pass around?"

Atkins nodded. "Already done. I have photos up here for all of you to carry throughout this investigation."

Seth's admiration for Tom grew a notch. Initially when he'd met Tom on the dunes Seth had feared Tom was an ineffectual small-town putz who didn't know his butt from his elbow, but Tom was proving Seth wrong. So far, Seth was impressed with both the sheriff and his team of deputies.

Seth listened as Tom gave his men their duties for the day and then the room cleared, leaving only Tom and Seth. The lawman moved from the head of the table to sit across from Seth.

"Surely you knew that you couldn't keep two murders and another attempted one out of the public eye forever," Seth said.

Tom raked a hand through his thinning hair. "Nah, I knew it would eventually all become public. But it ticks me off that it's possible one of my men talked. The article had too much inside information for me to think anything else. It even mentions the amnesia thing."

Seth looked down at the newspaper. "That information could have been leaked by somebody at the hospital. The photo looks like it was probably taken with a cell phone. Have you talked to the three guys who were there when she was found?"

"I did an initial interview with all of them, but I've got them all scheduled to come in today to talk to you. I figured you'd want to interview each of them so Ernie Simpson is going to be here at nine. Jerome Walker is coming in at noon and Sam Clemmons is scheduled for three. I'll set up more interviews with some of my other potential suspects for tomorrow."

Seth leaned back in his chair and frowned. "The Sandman. I hate it when the media gives the killer a moniker. Usually makes the perp feel more powerful, more important."

"I hate everything about this case," Tom replied.

"According to the reports I've read on the other cases, Rebecca Cook had only been dead four to six hours before her body was found early afternoon on the day after the party. We don't know for sure when she went missing from the party."

Tom nodded. "She lived with two roommates who said it wasn't unusual for Rebecca to hook up with somebody and not come home for a night, so they didn't think anything about it when she didn't come home after the party."

"And we don't know how long Vicki Smith was missing before she was found in the dunes." It was more a statement than a question.

Once again Tom nodded. "True. She lived by herself. She worked her shift on a Saturday night and Sunday was her day off. Nobody saw her on Sunday and her body was found Monday in the early morning. The coroner set her time of death sometime Sunday night."

"So, it's possible our perp kept her someplace for a while before he took her out to the dunes," Seth said thoughtfully. "Tamara had to have been kept someplace, too, before she wound up in the dunes. We need to figure out a place where a person could keep another without anyone knowing about it. Tamara remembers hearing the scrape of a shovel in the sand. She remembers the sound of being buried alive." Seth's heart twisted as he thought of what she'd endured.

Tom's eyebrows rose in surprise. "Oh, God, that's horrible. Does she remember why she didn't fight back? Why we didn't find any defensive wounds on any of the victims? I mean, how does a man get a woman to simply lie down in the sand and be buried?"

"I don't know, it's got to be a drug of some sort, like succinylcholine or something like that," Seth replied.

"Succinylcholine?" Tom frowned.

"It's a drug that paralyzes the muscles. The victim would remain conscious and mentally alert, but would be unable to move. The body breaks it up quickly so it wouldn't be evident in a blood test. Unfortunately, it's also a drug that stops the heart after several minutes, so that can't be the method he uses. These women were paralyzed but their hearts were still beating."

"So we need to add everyone who works at the hospital or in the medical field in town to our list of potential suspects," Tom said, a new weariness in his voice.

"Not necessarily," Seth replied. "Although it makes sense that the killer would have some sort of medical background. Still, you can learn about and obtain almost anything on the internet these days."

"I just hope Tamara gets her memories back soon.

Otherwise I've got to be honest with you, I'm not sure we'll solve these murders before he hits again," Tom said.

"It does appear he's on a timeline of thirty days or so," Seth agreed.

"And we don't know if his miss with Tamara will make him act again soon or if we have the luxury of three weeks or so before another body shows up."

"Hurry up, you little punk." Deputy Raymond Michaels's deep voice drifted in from the corridor.

"Stop pushing me," a younger voice complained. "I'm not doing anything wrong so keep your hands off me."

Tom stood. "It sounds like your first interview subject has arrived. You know when I interviewed the three boys from the dunes on the night Tamara was found they all were tested for any kind of trace evidence, but we found nothing unusual on any of them."

"I know, and I hope you don't take offense of me needing to speak to them again for my own investigation."

"No offense taken," Atkins replied.

Seth stood as well, ready to try to find answers that might stop a killer, the answers that might free Tamara from her amnesia and allow them both to get on with their lives.

He didn't think about why that thought caused a vague sense of dissatisfaction to slide through him. He was an FBI agent and this was nothing more than an assignment. He wouldn't allow Tamara to mean anything to him except as part of a case that needed to be solved.

THE GOLDEN DAFFODIL was dimly lit at a quarter to seven when Tamara and Seth walked in and were greeted by an attractive blonde working as hostess.

"Table for two?" she asked with a smooth, practiced smile. Seth nodded and she grabbed a couple of menus from beneath her desk and motioned for them to follow her.

Samantha had insisted Tamara borrow a little black dress and a pair of high-heeled sandals for the meal out and now seeing the upscale interior and the formal attire of the waiters and waitresses, Tamara was grateful that she'd dressed up. She was also conscious of some of the other diners eyeing her with interest as they made their way to the table.

Seth had come home from his day at the sheriff's office with just enough time to quickly shower and change his clothes before leaving for dinner. They'd scarcely had a chance to talk and she was eager to hear over dinner what he might have discovered during the day.

The hostess led them to a smoke-glass-topped table that boasted a slender vase with a bright yellow daffodil in the center. "Your waitress will be here shortly," she said as she handed them each a menu.

"You look very nice," Seth said once they were alone.

"You clean up pretty well yourself," Tamara replied. Seth wore a pair of black slacks and a short-sleeved gray dress shirt that made his eyes almost silver in the dim room.

That was the sum of their conversation when the waitress stepped up to their table. "Good evening," she said with a bright smile. "My name is Kelly and I'll be your server for the evening. Can I start you off with an appetizer?"

"No, thanks, but how about two glasses of the house wine?" Seth said with a look at Tamara for confirmation. "Red or white?"

She nodded. A glass of white wine sounded wonderful.

As the waitress left to get the wine, Tamara opened her menu, but her gaze remained on Seth. "You had a long day."

"Definitely. Let's get our orders in and then I'll tell you all about it."

Fifteen minutes later, with orders placed and wine delivered, Tamara looked at Seth expectantly. "Let's talk about your day first," he said. "I need to take a few minutes to decompress before I tell you about mine."

She took a sip of the wine and then set the elegant glass back on the table. "I had a fairly quiet day. Linda and I had a nice lunch together and then she showed me some of the photos in your family album. You were a cute kid. I played with Scooter and Samantha for a lot of the day. Your niece is a sweetheart and that puppy is just too sweet for words. The only real excitement that happened all day was when Steven Bradley stopped by."

Seth frowned. "Steven Bradley?"

"You remember, the young guy in charge of all things animal in Amber Lake," she replied with a grin. "He said he just wanted to check in to see how Scooter was adjusting to his new home, but I have a feeling he might have a bit of a crush on your niece."

Seth's frown deepened. "He's got to be in his mid-twenties. He'd better not have a crush on Samantha."

Tamara smiled at his instant protectiveness. "I don't think you have to worry, Samantha definitely isn't interested. If she were, then you'd have cause to be concerned. Anyway, he was only there a few minutes. He played with Scooter, asked Samantha about his appetite and some other doggy questions and then left."

"Did you see the paper this morning?" he asked.

"I saw it, not my best angle." She shot a quick glance around the restaurant and then looked back at Seth. "I think probably most of the people in here saw the morning paper. I feel a bit like I'm on display."

Seth's jawline clenched. "Yeah, Tom wasn't happy with all the information that was in the article. He thinks there's a leak in his department."

"From what I read, I'd say he's right." It had been strange that morning when Linda's neighbor had brought the morning paper by. Seeing the photo of herself, being the front-page story had been unsettling.

"The Sandman." She shook her head. "The monster now has a name. Unfortunately the biggest thing that happened today was what didn't happen…no more memories resurfaced."

"If I had my way you'd never have to remember what happened to you," Seth said softly. "We'd solve this crime without you, you'd get all your memories back except the horrible ones and life would go on. And you'd never have to think about the sand or Deadman's Dunes or Amber Lake again."

Her heart squeezed at his words and for a moment she couldn't speak around the lump that formed in her throat. There was such a wealth of caring in the senti-

ment he'd just voiced and it shot straight to the hollow-
ness in her heart.

"Thanks," she finally managed to say, "but I doubt
if it's going to work that way unless you got a bunch
of clues during the day today." She could tell by the
expression on his face that it probably hadn't been a
productive day, but before he could reply their meals
arrived, delivered by a handsome, dark-haired man who
introduced himself as Henry Todd, the owner of the
restaurant.

"I couldn't help but recognize you," he said to Tamara as he set her plate before her. "I just wanted to
personally come out and tell you how sorry I am for all
that you've been through. Our town obviously hasn't
been nice to you." Tamara fought the urge to squirm
beneath his intense gaze.

He stood too close, invading her personal space and
she was grateful when he finally stepped away from her
side and turned his attention to Seth. "And I understand
I have an appointment with you tomorrow morning at
ten to discuss some things."

"That's correct," Seth replied and Tamara noticed
that his eyes were slightly narrowed and the color of
hard flint. "But in the meantime we're both starving
and I've heard the food here is amazing."

Henry smiled in obvious pleasure. "I personally oversee the menu and everything that leaves my kitchen.
This might be a small town, but everyone deserves the
best that food has to offer." He took another step back.
"And now, please enjoy. Your meal is on me tonight."

"That's not necessary," Seth replied coolly.

Henry smiled at Tamara. "For the beautiful lady, I insist."

Tamara watched as he sauntered back toward the kitchen, pausing long enough to stop and put his arm around their waitress and say something to her before disappearing into the kitchen.

She felt Seth's gaze on her and turned to look at him. "He's a real smarmy charmer," she said drily. "I wonder if he makes all the women he's around feel like they need to shower off?"

"Not your type?" he asked as he picked up his fork and knife to cut into the steak on his plate.

"I like my men with a little less swagger and a lot more substance."

He raised a dark eyebrow. "You could tell that he's arrogant and superficial just by that brief meeting with him?"

Tamara picked up her own fork and knife to begin damage on the beef fillet in front of her. "Must be a woman thing," she replied. "He reminds me of my ex-husband, Jason."

Her utensils clattered to the table as she stared at Seth. "Oh, my God, Seth, I remember Jason." She paused a moment, allowing her mind free rein. "I remember bits and pieces of my marriage."

She leaned back in the chair and closed her eyes as memories assaulted her, flashing in her mind so fast, so furiously she felt ill.

THE SANDMAN. HE LIKED the name they'd given him. It sounded mysterious and, in this case, crazy scary. It sounded like the stuff of nightmares for children, but there were no kids in the town of Amber Lake who needed to fear him. In fact, he liked kids, unlike his old man who had hated kids…hated him.

He could still hear the sound of his father's boots on the front steps when he got home from work. He could tell by the weight of those footsteps against the wood if it was going to be a good night or a bad one…and most nights were bad.

Any small infraction of one of his father's endless household rules resulted in a beating. It was rare they completed a meal without his father backhanding him for one thing or another.

It was funny, when he'd finally grown up and left his mother and father's house, he'd realized he hated his father, but he hated his mother far more.

Mothers were supposed to love and protect their children, and she'd done nothing to protect him. She'd turned a blind eye to the abuse, leaving him to feel afraid and powerless in a volatile childhood.

But now he had all the power. He was the Sandman and nobody could touch him. When he'd first seen Rebecca Cook, he'd recognized his destiny. There had been something about her that had reminded him of his mother when he'd been young and the rage that he'd fought against for most of his life had finally reached maturity.

Rebecca had been his first and Vicki Smith had been his second. He hadn't known the name of the dark-haired beauty he'd encountered at the rest stop just outside Amber Lake, but he'd known the moment he'd seen her that she would be his third.

He should have taken her right to the dunes that

night, but he hadn't. He'd waited until midafternoon to take care of her and it had been his first mistake...one he wouldn't make again.

That mistake had allowed her to live. Tamara Jennings. He hadn't known her name when he'd buried her in the sand, but he knew it now. He also knew she had amnesia. It was an interesting dilemma...he couldn't be sure what she saw or heard during her time with him, couldn't know for certain if she could identify him or not.

It really didn't matter. He intended to rebury her as soon as the opportunity presented itself to him. He didn't want to give her time to remember. She had been his chosen third victim, the woman with dark hair and something special that had ignited memories of his mother.

Yes, she was his chosen one and nothing had happened since then to change his mind.

Chapter Six

"This is a good thing, right?" Tamara asked as she picked up her fork and knife once again. "Each time I remember something I put another piece in the puzzle and eventually I'll have all the pieces back."

Her eyes shone bright and while Seth wanted to share in her excitement he couldn't help but be afraid for her, afraid that when she had all the pieces she'd never find her smile again, she'd never get over the trauma of whatever had happened to her in those missing hours, might never recover from the fright of being inside the dunes.

He was ambivalent about her getting her memories back. He wanted her to retrieve any information that might help him get a killer behind bars, but he was also aware of the fact that once she had the puzzle of her past back together, it would be time for her to return to her life, and he was surprised to discover that he wasn't ready to say goodbye to her yet.

"Seth?" She looked at him expectantly and he realized he hadn't replied to her.

"Yeah, I guess it's good that your memories are coming back to you," he agreed as he sliced into the steak in front of him. "So, you remember your ex-husband and your marriage?" He wasn't sure why but he was intrigued to know what kind of a man she'd married and why that marriage hadn't worked.

"I do." She reached for the salt and pepper and topped her baked potato with both. "Jason Jennings, hotshot real-estate investor and womanizer extraordinaire."

"Is that why the marriage broke up? He was a cheater?" Seth asked. He couldn't imagine a man stupid enough to cheat on a woman like Tamara.

"That, among other things," she replied. "Jason and I were an ill-fated match from the beginning. He loved people and parties and I preferred quiet nights at home. He liked flashy cars and big houses and I didn't care about those kinds of things. I just wanted a couple of kids and a loving husband. We were married about a year when I realized he also liked other women."

She took a sip of her wine and then frowned. "That's all I remember," she said curtly, but her eyes had gone the dark blue of unpleasant thoughts, memories she apparently wasn't ready to share with him or hadn't yet fully accessed.

"To be honest, the divorce was a relief for both of us and we parted ways as friends," she finally continued. "It's funny, I can remember my marriage and my brief life with Jason, but I can't remember what finally broke us apart for good or what my mother and father looked like. I don't know what my apartment looks like or why I left it to come here."

"It will all fall into place," Seth replied in an attempt to calm her. "And if it doesn't, there's always that therapist you can see."

She shook her head. "I'm not ready for that yet. My

memories are coming back on their own. I don't think it will be long before I'll have them all."

Their conversation was interrupted by the appearance of Deputy Raymond Michaels and a thin, nervous-looking woman at his side. "Agent Hawkins, Ms. Jennings," he greeted them with a smile. "I see you two have found the best place to eat in the area." He threw an arm around the brunette next to him. "This is my wife, Sue. We're here celebrating our fifth anniversary."

"Congratulations," Tamara and Seth said at the same time.

Michaels squeezed his wife close to his side. "Thanks. Enjoy the great food and I'll see you in the morning at the office," he said to Seth.

Seth watched the two of them as they left to follow the hostess to their table. "You don't like him," Tamara said.

He looked at her in surprise. "What makes you think that?"

"Your eyes have gone flat and I can feel some tension coming from you."

He grinned at her. "You'd make a good cop."

She returned his smile. "No, I've just been hanging around you long enough to recognize some of the subtle signals you give off. Why don't you like him?"

"I interviewed the three kids that were on the dunes with me when you were found today and all three of them complained about Michaels being a bully." Seth found it disconcerting and not in an unpleasant way that she'd been able to read him so well. "He just strikes me as the type of man who swaggers around town during the day and then goes home and beats his wife and kicks the dog to pass the evening."

Tamara flashed a glance at the couple. "She looks like a woman who either doesn't have a voice or is afraid to find one."

"I'd bet on the latter."

She reached for a piece of the fresh-baked bread and slathered it with butter. "Did the guys you talked to today give you any information you didn't already have?"

"Nothing about the crime but a little bit about their personal lives. Jerome Walker seemed like a nice kid from a good family. He's home for the summer from college and wants to graduate with a business degree. Ernie Simpson works at the hardware store and, although he didn't mention it, Tom told me Ernie's father is the town drunk."

"And the other young man?"

"Sam Clemmons." Seth frowned as he thought of Sam. "Hates his parents, lives by himself in a shanty he rents at the edge of town. His whole life seems to be riding the dunes."

He'd found Sam hard to read, with a touch of a temper when pushed hard. "Sam has been at the scene each time a woman has been discovered."

Tamara's eyes widened. "So, is he a suspect in the murders?"

"I'm calling him a person of interest at this point." She had such beautiful eyes. If he looked into their blue depths for too long he wanted to fall into them. He wondered what they'd look like darkened with passion or lazy with sexual contentment.

He grabbed a piece of the bread, irritated by his wayward thoughts. "Anyway," he continued, "tomorrow I'm interviewing Henry Todd, who was dating Vicki Smith at the time of her murder and a couple of the kids that were at the party with Rebecca Cook before her death."

Tamara leaned back and gazed at him thoughtfully. "It must be rough to work all day dealing with the darkness of murder and then go home where there's nobody to talk to, nobody to share your day with."

"Most of the women I've dated in the past don't want to hear about my day at work," he replied.

"Then you're dating the wrong kind of woman," she replied. "I find it all fascinating."

He held her gaze and for a long moment, their mutual attraction was palpable in the air. Her words forced him to think about those nights alone in his apartment, when he'd wished for somebody to talk to, somebody who might partner him through life.

Something about Tamara made him think about having a soft place to fall at the end of a long, difficult day and no other woman had ever made him think of such a thing before.

Thankfully after dinner as they lingered over coffee their conversation was light and easy with topics like the summer heat ahead and the antics of the adorable puppy, Scooter.

It was almost ten o'clock by the time they got back to Linda's place. A note on the table indicated that Linda had already gone to bed and Samantha was spending the night with a girlfriend.

The house was quiet and even though it was officially the end of the evening, Seth was reluctant to tell Tamara good night.

"One final nightcap?" he asked as he wondered how he managed to be standing so close to her.

He heard the hum of the refrigerator just behind him and smelled the floral scent of her perfume, felt the heat of her body radiating toward him as if to seduce him even closer.

"I don't think so. It's been a long day," she replied, but she didn't step back from him or make a move to go to her bedroom. "Thank you for the lovely meal and the company."

"I enjoy your company," he replied. He probably should be telling her that it had been all business, that he'd wanted her seen around town and that he'd wanted to get an initial impression of Henry Todd. He should not be telling her that he liked being with her for no other reason than she was who she was.

"Do you think the killer saw me tonight?" she asked, as if catching part of the wavelength of his thoughts. She took a step closer to him. He didn't know if it was because the thought made her afraid or if it was because she felt the simmering tension in the air, a tension he didn't want to feel but seemed unable to control.

"I don't know…maybe," he replied. Anything else he might have said stuck in his throat as she took another step closer to him.

"I don't know what I'd do without you, Seth." She moved close enough to him that her body was mere inches from his. Her cheeks grew slightly pink as she continued to look up at him. "I know it's probably not a good idea, but I want to kiss you…I really need you to kiss me."

"It's definitely not a good idea," he replied even as he reached to bring her body tight against his. She melted into him, all warm curves and fragrant softness. "In fact, it's probably the worst thing we could do," he said as his lips touched hers. With that simple touch, he knew he was in trouble.

She leaned into him and reached up to wrap her arms around his neck as she opened her mouth to him. As he followed her lead and swirled his tongue against hers, igniting a new fire of desire inside him, he knew he was taking advantage of her, of her vulnerable state, but at the moment he couldn't summon the strength to stop.

Instead he reached up and tangled his hand in her long silky hair and momentarily lost himself in the sweet pleasure of the heat of her mouth, the overwhelming presence of her so intimately against him.

He wanted nothing more than to carry her into the guest bedroom and make love to her. He wanted to see her naked against the sheets, wanted to move his own naked body against hers, into hers.

And that would be a huge mistake. This was a huge mistake. Although he didn't want it to stop, reluctantly he broke the kiss and stepped back from her, his heart beating more quickly than it should.

She stared up at him, her eyes slightly glazed and midnight-blue. Just by looking at her his desire heightened and his resolve to stop anything else that might transpire between them wavered.

She reached a hand up and tucked a strand of her hair behind her ear and he couldn't help but notice that her hand trembled. She wanted him. And he wanted her. And the situation they found themselves in couldn't be far more removed from real life.

"I'm not going to lie to you, Tamara." He shoved his hands in his pockets, as if afraid of what they might do if left to their own volition. "I find you ridiculously attractive and there's nothing I'd like better than to take you to bed and make love to you all night long. But it wouldn't be fair to either of us. When this is all over we both have lives to return to. I don't want to see either one of us get hurt."

"Logically I agree," she said and her voice held a huskiness of barely suppressed emotions. "But emotionally and physically I want you, Seth."

Although it was one of the most difficult things he'd ever done, he stepped toward her, kissed her on the forehead and grabbed her by the shoulders and turned her around to face the direction of the hallway.

"Go to bed, Tamara. I think that's the best thing for both of us, to go to bed alone and get a good night's sleep."

She looked back at him one last time, her beautiful eyes filled with the longing that he felt deep in his soul. He kept his features set and stern, refusing to give in to her, in to his own base needs.

"Good night, Tamara."

She released a small sigh of obvious dissatisfaction.

"Good night, Seth." As he released his hold on her shoulders, she walked down the hallway toward the guest bedroom.

She paused at the door and gazed back at him one last time and he fought the need to sprint down the hallway to her door. Instead he turned his back and walked to the hall closet where the top shelf held the sheet and pillow he'd been using to sleep on the sofa.

By the time he'd gotten his bed linens, she was gone and her bedroom door was closed. He was grateful for he knew another minute of seeing her in that clingy little black dress, another moment of thinking about the lush warm welcome of her lips against his and he'd lose all resolve to be smart.

Within minutes he was on the sofa, his gun within reach on the coffee table and his thoughts a mass of chaos that let him know sleep would be a long time coming.

Trying to keep his thoughts away from Tamara, he focused on the three guys he'd interviewed that day. They were just kids, trying to find their way through life, but that didn't mean that one of them wasn't a killer. Although he'd told Tamara that Sam was simply a person of interest, the truth of the matter was that all three of the kids were at the top of the suspect list and had been since the moment Tamara had been found.

Whoever the perp was, it was obvious, at least at this point in the investigation, that the only connection between the victims was the dark color of their hair, which probably meant he was playing out some sort of rage against a dark-haired woman who had negatively impacted his life.

It could be a mother, a sister or an ex-girlfriend. It could be a childhood friend or a woman who'd snubbed him in a way he found offensive. There was just no way of knowing at this point in the investigation.

He closed his eyes and tried to stay focused on the

crimes, but his mind filled with the way Tamara's eyes had sparkled in the dim light of the restaurant, of how easy and natural it had felt for the two of them to be out dining together.

It felt easy whenever they were together. Despite the fact that she had few memories of her past, they never ran out of conversation and he felt as if he could tell her almost anything and it would be all right.

Was that the way it had been with Linda and Mark when they'd first met? Had they felt a leap in their pulse each time they saw each other? Had they wondered what the other was thinking, feeling when they weren't together?

How could a couple who had appeared so in love when they'd wedded come to hate each other so much in the ten years of their marriage?

Seth had seen too many divorces in his lifetime to believe that there was such a thing as lasting love. In any case, even if he did change his mind, Tamara was the wrong woman at the wrong time.

He drifted off to sleep and dreamed of the dunes. They rose up in a moonlight setting like an alien world he didn't know. He wasn't on his dirt bike but rather was walking.

Ahead he saw Tamara lying in the sand while a dark figure shoveled sand over her prone body.

She yelled his name, her voice filled with terror and he tried to run faster but the earth beneath him was suddenly like quicksand, sucking him down with each step.

He jerked awake, heart pounding with adrenaline, assuming it had been his own cry of fearful frustration that had pulled him from the nightmare.

Then Tamara screamed.

Seth grabbed his gun and raced down the hallway. He opened her door and flipped the light at the same time. He took in the scene in an instant...the missing screen, the opened window and Tamara in the bed.

"At the window," Tamara managed to stutter. She clutched the sheet up tightly around her neck, as if the cotton was some magical material that could protect her from harm.

"Go to the living room," he said curtly and then turned and bumped into Linda in the hallway. "Get her to the living room and stay there."

He didn't wait for an answer, but stalked toward the front door, hoping he wasn't too late to find whoever had attempted to get into Tamara's bedroom.

The night air was warm and humid, the grass beneath his bare feet damp with dew. He headed toward the back of the house instinctively knowing the perp would have run back that way rather than toward the street where there was more light.

Linda's backyard wasn't fenced, nor were her neighbors', giving Seth a half a dozen options for pursuit. He jogged to the edge of the property and then stopped, listening to see if he heard the sound of running feet, sensed a presence hiding nearby.

Nothing.

As he gazed in all directions with narrowed eyes he figured the perp was long gone, having made tracks when Tamara had screamed.

God, that scream, coupled with his nightmare, still had the hairs on the back of his neck standing on end. He stood as still as a statue for several long minutes, then believing the danger passed, he walked back to the window to check out the damage. He stayed far enough away that he wouldn't be contaminating any evidence.

The screen was on the ground and the window was wide open. If Tamara had slept another minute longer the person would have been in the room and on top of her. It would have been easy for her to be overwhelmed, perhaps drugged and then dragged out the window and into the night.

Dammit. He cursed himself soundlessly. He'd been so stupid. With all the news in the media about the murders and her amnesia, with him parading her all around town, of course the killer had known exactly where to come to find her.

And it wasn't just Tamara he'd put at risk with his own thoughtlessness, but also Linda and Samantha as well, both brunettes and both potentially fitting the killer's profile.

He'd put everybody he cared about at risk by not anticipating that the killer would return for Tamara. Because nothing had happened so far he'd thought maybe the killer's focus had moved to somebody else, but this was proof he apparently had somebody in the house in his sights.

This had been a tragedy averted, but things had to change and they had to change immediately. The first thing he needed to do was check on Tamara and make sure she was okay. The second thing he wanted to do was call Tom and get somebody over here to dust the window for fingerprints or any evidence that might have been left behind.

He only hoped this near-miss might actually yield some clues.

THE FIRST THING TAMARA thought when Seth walked into the front door was that he looked lethal and hot in a pair of boxers with every muscle tensed and his gun in his hand.

"You both okay?" he asked, his gaze going to Linda and then to Tamara, who sat side by side on the sofa.

"Just shaken up a little," Tamara admitted. "Thank God I woke up when I did." She fought a shiver as she thought of that moment when she'd suddenly awakened and seen the dark shadow of a man at the window.

Seth walked over to the coffee table and picked up his cell phone. Tamara and Linda sat silently while he made a call to Sheriff Atkins.

"I guess you didn't see him outside," Tamara said.

"I didn't even know which direction to give chase," he replied. "You two stay here and don't open the door for anyone but Tom and I'm going to get dressed and head back to the bedroom to check out the window."

As he disappeared down the hallway, the shiver Tamara had tried to control swept over her. Linda leaned over and patted her hand. "How about a cup of hot tea? Maybe that would take away some of the chill."

Tamara nodded absently. Her thoughts were scattered. She knew she should be scared to death…and she was, but she also felt as if she was still trapped in a bad dream where nothing seemed quite real. There was a faint numbness that had swept over her through the past couple of minutes, a numbness that kept her from screaming once again in terror.

Seth returned to the living room, this time wearing a pair of jeans and a T-shirt. He frowned with concern at her. "Are you sure you're okay? He didn't hurt you in any way, did he?"

She shook her head. "He didn't even get inside the room. I don't know what woke me up, but I opened my eyes and he was there at the window and I just screamed."

At that moment a knock on the door indicated the arrival of the local law. Seth opened the door to admit both Sheriff Atkins and Raymond Michaels. As he led them back into the bedroom, Linda urged her to join her at the kitchen table for a cup of hot tea.

"You need anything else?" Linda asked sympathetically as Tamara sat across from her at the table and cupped her hands around the warmth of the mug. "You look a little shell-shocked."

Tamara forced a smile and glanced at the clock on the wall. It was just a few minutes after two. "Don't you feel a little of the same? I'm sure the last thing you expected was for some man to try to break into your house in the middle of the night. I think the best thing for me to do is head back to Amarillo first thing in the morning."

"Let's wait and see what Seth and the sheriff have in mind," Linda said, appearing unruffled by the middle-of-the-night chaos. "It's never any good to make decisions in the heat of the moment."

Tamara sipped her coffee, her thoughts scattered in every direction. Somebody had tried to get to her through the window. Seth had kissed her and thoughts of her previous marriage brought with them a sense of anxiety that made no sense. The kiss and the odd feeling concerning her marriage had kept her awake for a long time after she'd gone to bed.

It was easy to figure out why the kiss had kept her awake. Seth's lips against hers had fired a heat inside her that, despite her amnesia, she was certain she'd never felt before.

She knew he was right, that the two of them making love would only complicate what was already a muddled situation, but she'd so desperately wanted to be in his arms, to feel the warmth of his nakedness against her own. She'd wanted to leave this place with a single memory of making love to Seth to take with her back home.

She frowned and took a sip of the hot tea, knowing that her mind was focusing on Seth and what might have happened between them rather than what had just happened…somebody had tried to get to her, probably the same somebody who had already once buried her in the dunes.

The Sandman. It didn't take a brilliant scientist to make an educated guess that the person who had tried to get into the house was the serial killer, and that his goal was to finish the job he'd started.

Even the warmth of the tea couldn't stanch the shiver of horror that shuddered through her, a horror that eased somewhat as Seth came back into the room, followed by Tom and Raymond.

"Whoever it was must have worn gloves," Tom said. "Raymond here dusted the sill and screen and couldn't find any prints. You were lucky you woke up when you did. Another minute or two and he would have been on the bed with you."

Tamara nodded, tuning out of the conversation as

she felt the back of her throat close up and a tight pressure against her chest.

As the three lawmen moved into the living room, their voices became white noise as the scrape of a shovel against the sand filled her head. If she hadn't awakened…the words thundered in her brain. If she hadn't awakened when she did it was possible that by now she'd be buried in the dunes, without anyone knowing she'd been carried out of the house in the darkness of the night.

Hollowly she gazed at Linda. She'd brought danger to Linda's home. She'd brought danger far too close to a woman and her daughter, both of whom had been kind to her.

She needed to go. It didn't matter that she didn't have her memories back. She needed to return to the life she didn't remember and try to pick up the pieces. She had to do that in order to protect the people she had come to care about so very much.

SETH RETURNED TO THE KITCHEN alone and sat in the chair between his sister and Tamara. He reached for each of their hands and Tamara held on tight, feeling as if he was once again pulling her from the suffocating weight of a sand dune.

"So, we need to make some changes," he said, his voice calm in contrast to the utter chaos in Tamara's head. He turned and looked at his sister, his eyes gunmetal-gray. "We can't remain here and put you and Samantha in danger." He frowned, as if assessing the options.

"Actually, I have an idea of my own," Linda said.

"Next week Samantha had planned on staying with her dad for a couple of weeks. She does that every summer. I can talk to Mark tomorrow and I'm sure she can move right in over there. As far as I'm concerned I've got a friend in Oklahoma City who has been nagging me for the past six months since her husband passed away to come and stay with her for a while. I've got plenty of vacation time coming and I can be on the road first thing in the morning. Then the two of you can stay here and get things figured out."

Tamara pulled her hand out of Seth's grip. "Absolutely not. I can't let you be chased out of your house because of me," she protested. She wanted to weep, she felt so helpless and out of control.

"I'm not being chased out by you or anyone else," Linda protested. "I'm making a choice." She looked from Tamara to her brother. "It's the logical thing to do. Besides, if you move someplace else he'll just end up finding you again. At least you know the layout here. Seth knows how best to protect you in this house rather than someplace else in town."

Seth rubbed a hand across his forehead as if fighting back a headache. His frown was so deep it tugged his dark eyebrows close together as he gazed first at his sister and then back at Tamara. For the first time since she'd known him, he seemed to be at a loss for words.

"I should go home," Tamara whispered faintly, although she had the feeling that somebody or something bad awaited her there, as well.

"That's not the answer. Amarillo is the last place you need to be," Seth replied gruffly. "At least here you have me and the sheriff working on things. In Amarillo you'd be all alone until you get your memories back."

He looked back at Linda. "You can make all this happen tomorrow?"

She nodded with a certain resolve. "Without any problems at all."

"I just want you and Samantha someplace safe and Tamara and I will stay at the house. He knows she's here and I have a feeling he'll come back for her. I'd rather that happened where we can have some control and we can do that here."

Linda nodded and got up from the table. "I'll make the arrangements and Samantha and I will be out of here by noon tomorrow. And now that the excitement is all over, I'm going back to bed." With a tired wave of her hand, she headed out of the kitchen.

Tamara watched her go. Things were spinning out of control and she didn't know what to do about it. She hated the fact that she was forcing two people out of their home because she'd somehow had a run-in with a crazy killer.

"Maybe it was just a normal attempt at a home burglary," she said hopefully. "I mean, under normal circumstances that guest bedroom would be empty. Maybe some robber assumed it was empty and just decided to break in tonight."

Seth shook his head. "No, it was definitely him."

"How can you be sure?"

Seth hesitated a long moment, long enough for a knot of anxiety to twist tighter and tighter in her chest. "I can be sure because next to the window on the ground he left a miniature sand dune." He raked a hand through his hair. "If he'd been successful and I'd awakened tomorrow morning and found you gone, he wanted everyone to know for sure what had happened to you, who had taken you."

"The Sandman," she whispered. A new shiver of horror fluttered through her as she considered the fact that the next time he tried to get to her, he might succeed.

HE WANTED TO WEEP. He'd been close…so achingly close to her. Just a few more steps, a quick stab of a needle that would almost instantly render her helpless and then all he'd had to do was carry her out the window and get away.

He'd been so proud of the whole plan, so certain that they would never assume he'd be bold enough to attack there, right beneath an FBI agent's nose.

And he'd almost succeeded. If the bitch had just stayed asleep another two minutes he would have had her incapacitated and carried her away to the dunes… where she belonged.

It wasn't over, not by a long shot. So far he'd had two false starts, but he knew the old saying…third time was a charm.

Chapter Seven

The remainder of the night passed with Seth on high alert. He insisted Tamara move into Samantha's bedroom for the rest of the night and then he had half dozed in a chair in the living room, unable to completely relinquish himself to sleep as he thought about the days to come.

The mound of sand he'd found outside the window told him two things…that the killer had embraced the name the newspaper had given him, and that he was getting bolder. That could either work for them or against them in capturing him.

By the time morning came Seth made a pot of coffee to go along with his exhaustion. He definitely needed a major caffeine boost in order to do his interviews that day. And whatever he did, wherever he went, Tamara would go with him. There was no other option.

The coffee had just finished dripping into the carafe when Linda came into the kitchen and sat at the table. With her hair bed-messed, without makeup and clad in a pair of hot pink pajamas she looked ten years younger.

"You know, you don't have to do this," he said as he placed a cup of coffee in front of her. "I can pack up

Tamara and take her to the local motel until the investigation is finished."

Linda shook her head. "She's been through enough. I don't think it would be good for her to be moved someplace else at this time in her recovery. Besides, I've just wanted somebody to give me a reason to take some time off and visit Helen, and Samantha bunking in at her dad's place is no big deal. I think they have a camping trip planned in the next week or so. She and Scooter will be fine and so will I."

A wealth of affection rose up inside Seth for his sister. "You're the best, sis." He grabbed his coffee and joined her at the table.

She took a sip and eyed him over the rim of the cup. "I see the way she looks at you, Seth," she said as she set the cup back down on the table. "And I see the way you look at her."

"I don't know what you're talking about." He looked into his cup, unable to meet her gaze.

"Yeah, right," she replied drily. "You know how much I'd love for you to find a woman and fall in love and build a family, but you need to take care in this case. She doesn't know where she belongs, and for all we know there is a special somebody waiting for her return. I don't want to see her get hurt, but more important I don't want to see you get hurt."

"Don't worry about me. I just want to catch this freak, get him under arrest and then return to my life in Kansas City," Seth said.

Linda raised an eyebrow. "What life?"

Seth laughed humorlessly, knowing his sister believed he had no life except his work, which, of course, was true.

"I'm just telling you to tread softly. The attraction between the two of you is palpable, but you need to remember the circumstances of why she's here now and she'll be gone soon."

"Duly noted," he replied. Despite the kiss from the night before, a kiss that had rocked his world, he had no intention of taking things any further with Tamara.

By nine o'clock, Linda had taken off to drive to Oklahoma City to visit with her friend, Samantha had come by and packed two enormous suitcases for her time with her father and Seth had boarded up the window in the guest room with plywood he'd found in Linda's garage. Then he and Tamara were on their way to the sheriff's office.

"There's a break room in the back and you can hang out in there while I conduct my interviews," Seth explained. "We'll get somebody to run out and get you some magazines to read and there's a television in there, so you shouldn't be too bored."

"I'll be fine," she replied. "Although I probably would have been fine staying at home. If this creep lives up to his name, then the nighttime will be his playtime. The Sandman doesn't visit people during the daylight hours."

"I thought the Sandman was only supposed to sprinkle good dreams into the heads of sleeping children." Seth pulled up in front of the office, shut off the engine and turned to look at her.

"Apparently not this Sandman," she replied. Despite the short night she looked lovely with her long hair pulled back and clasped at the nape of her neck. She wore a pair of jeans and a white blouse with blue trim that complemented the color of her eyes.

"Apparently not," he agreed. "And whether we like it or not, he is focused on you, so there's no way I want you alone anywhere for now."

They both got out of his truck. The late-June heat was already hot on his shoulders and Seth had a feeling things were going to get even hotter for the people he intended to interview.

He needed to get this job done and the sooner the better because Linda was right, Tamara was getting to him, and the end result of anything that might happen between them was that somebody was going to wind up being hurt.

After seeing Tamara settled in the small lounge in the back of the building, Seth sat in the interrogation room with Tom. The short night showed on the sheriff's features. Tired lines raced down the sides of his face and Seth had a feeling he had the same kind of stress lines on his own.

"Henry Todd will be here in just a few minutes to talk to you and this afternoon I've got Casey Minter coming in. She was friendly with Vicki and although

open with you."

"Why didn't she open up to you?" Seth asked curiously.

"Probably because I've arrested her father a dozen times for public intoxication. I'm not exactly a favorite around the Minter household."

"I met Henry Todd last night. Tamara and I ate at

the Golden Daffodil and he came out and introduced himself to us," Seth said.

"Quite the Dapper Dan, isn't he?"

Seth smiled. "I believe Tamara mentioned the word *smarmy* after meeting him."

Tom's grin lasted only a moment. "After last night have you made alternate plans for where Tamara is going to stay?"

"No, she and I are remaining at the house, but I sent Linda and Samantha away for the next week or so."

Tom studied him for long moment. "You're hoping he'll attempt to take her from the house again?"

"Heck, I'm hoping I'll have the bastard's name by the end of the day," Seth retorted.

Tom stood. "I'll see to it that Tamara has whatever she needs so that you can focus on these interviews. I don't need to tell you how badly I want this guy in my jail."

"Trust me, I want him there just as badly," Seth replied.

As Tom left the room, Seth opened the file he'd brought in with him for the day of interviewing. Inside were not only copies of the original interviews, but notes that Seth had made as to what new questions he wanted answered.

As he waited for Henry to arrive, he couldn't help but think about Tamara and the kiss they had shared the night before. He'd wanted to take things further. He'd wanted to scoop her up in his arms and carry her to the bedroom and make love to her.

Thank God he hadn't followed through on his desire. His conversation with Linda that morning had confirmed his own beliefs, that getting that close to Tamara would be a big mistake for both of them.

He shoved thoughts of her away as Henry Todd was led by Raymond Michaels into the interrogation room. Seth stood and gestured the handsome man into the chair opposite him at the table. Coffee was offered and declined, small talk made to break the ice and then Seth got down to business.

"From the notes I've read I understand that you and Vicki Smith were something of an item before her murder," Seth said.

Henry smiled with a touch of condescension. "Vicki wanted us to be an item, but I just dated her a couple of times and that was it. Our relationship was only a big deal in her mind. There was no real relationship. Besides, I made it clear to her that we were done almost a month before she died."

"I'm guessing she wasn't happy to hear that?" Seth asked.

"To be honest, she was a real pain after that. She still worked at the restaurant, but she bad-mouthed me to all my staff and I think she keyed my car, although I never had any way to prove it. I'm telling you all this

didn't have anything to do with her murder." He gave Seth a charming grin. "Besides, you know what sand would do to a pair of expensive Italian loafers?"

Seth wasn't amused. The conversation lasted another thirty minutes, with Seth leaning on him hard, trying to break a weak alibi and fluster Henry enough to make a mistake and say something telling. But the restaurateur remained calm and collected and firm in his answers.

Seth finally told him he could go. Henry got to the doorway and then turned to look back at Seth. "Have you talked to your brother-in-law?" he asked.

"My brother-in-law?" Seth stared at him blankly.

"Mark Willoughby. I heard it through the grapevine that he and Vicki were dating in the days before her murder. They even came in for dinner at the Golden Daffodil right before Vicki's death."

Seth felt as if he'd been sucker-punched. Nowhere in the notes had Mark been tied to Vicki Smith. Mark hadn't even been interviewed in either of the previous investigations.

Once Henry left the room, Seth reared back in his chair, his stomach churning with a new anxiety and troubling thoughts.

There was no question that Mark hated his ex-wife, and Linda had dark hair just like all the victims. Seth had always believed his ex-brother-in-law to be many things, but he never would have suspected him capable of murder...until now.

He couldn't discount Mark because he'd been married to his sister for ten years, and yet he couldn't allow his personal distaste for the man to color the investigation in any way.

He directed Tom to make arrangements for Mark to come in that afternoon for an interview and then the rest of the morning was taken up by talking to teenagers who had been at the party on the dunes the night that Rebecca Cook had been killed.

Casey Minter had confessed to him that Rebecca had worked at the Golden Daffodil for two days, then had quit because she felt uncomfortable with her touchy-feely boss. According to Casey, Rebecca had thought Henry Todd was an old pervert who couldn't keep his hands off his young help.

As far as Seth was concerned the information was just another strike against Henry Todd. Did that make him the killer? Hard to tell. Did it make him a smarmy creep? Definitely.

It was just after noon when he went to the break room and discovered Tamara gone. A gossip magazine was open on the table and the television was tuned to the Lifetime channel.

He glanced toward the restroom. The door was open, indicating it was empty. So, where was Tamara? He'd told her not to leave this room until he returned for her.

His heart skipped a beat even as he told himself not to panic. But it was sheer panic that torched through him. Where in the hell was she?

Was it possible a deputy was involved with the killings? Had he missed something…had he unintentionally placed Tamara at risk by simply bringing her here where she should have been safe?

TAMARA STOOD IN LINE at the fast-food restaurant next to Deputy Raymond Michaels. He'd come into the break room a few minutes earlier and asked if she'd wanted to stretch her legs and walk with him to grab some lunch at the place next door to the sheriff's office.

Assuming Seth had sent him and eager to do anything to break the monotony of the long morning, she readily agreed. For the most part she'd been alone in the break room for the past couple of hours with nothing to occupy her except the television and a few magazines a deputy had brought in earlier in the day.

She'd had way too much time to be in her own thoughts, to attempt to sort out what had happened to her and how she felt about Seth. It bothered her that whenever she consciously reached for any memories of her former life she felt not only a knot of anxiety but also a sweeping grief that made no sense.

She was certain the grief had nothing to do with whatever had happened to her here in Amber Lake, but rather had its seed in the former life that she couldn't remember.

Although she wasn't sure what she thought about Deputy Michaels, she was grateful for him allowing her to get out of the little room that smelled of stale coffee and male for a few minutes.

"So, still nothing happening up here?" Raymond touched the side of his head.

"Nothing worthwhile," she confessed. "Just bits and pieces that don't help your investigation at all."

"But you are starting to remember some things," he replied.

She nodded. "A few, although nothing of consequence to the case."

"Who knows, maybe in just the blink of an eye it will all come back to you." His dark brown eyes held hers long enough that she was grateful that it was their turn at the counter to order.

She got a cheeseburger and fries and a diet cola while Raymond ordered one of the meals that had a sandwich with enough burger to make a full cow. She protested when he paid for hers, but he insisted he wasn't paying, that it was on the Amber Lake Sheriff's Department.

"You know you're our best chance for a break in this case," he said as they pushed out the door to walk back to the office. "At this point we don't have jack."

"We can't even be sure that when I get my memories back it will have the information you need to make an arrest," she replied. "It's possible that I didn't see the face of the person who attacked me."

"But it's also possible you did," he countered. "You've got to let us know when your memories come back. Anything you remember might be a clue and we need to know what's in that head of yours."

At that moment she saw Seth approach them from across the parking lot. He walked in long strides, his handsome features set with a rigid anger she'd never seen before. Even before he reached them she could feel the wave of rage that radiated from him.

"What's up?" Raymond asked.

"What in the hell do you think you're doing?" Seth asked the deputy as he drew closer. He barely shot a glance at Tamara and then once again glared at Raymond.

"What does it look like I'm doing? I got us some lunch." Raymond straightened his shoulders, obviously not liking Seth's aggressive tone. "It was after noon and I knew she hadn't had anything to eat."

"Deputy Michaels, this is my case and this is my witness. You don't talk to her without my permission. You don't even look at her unless I tell you it's okay, and you sure as hell don't remove her from safe custody to get some lunch."

"Take a chill pill, Mr. Fed Man," Raymond said with more than a touch of belligerence. "I just figured *your* witness might need something to eat and would like to take a short walk. I had it all under control. I wouldn't let anyone hurt her."

He didn't wait for Seth to reply, but with a sigh of disgust, he stalked away toward the office. Seth immediately turned to Tamara, his eyes the color of ice. "Are you all right?"

"Got my burger and fries, I'm golden," she said in an attempt to lighten his mood.

He raked a hand through his hair and motioned for them to follow after Raymond. "I went to find you and you weren't there. I…I freaked out. I thought maybe…" He allowed his voice to drift off as he drew a deep sigh.

She realized how fearful he'd been when he hadn't been able to find her and her heart cringed. "I'm sorry, Seth. I didn't mean to worry you. I just assumed you knew what was going on when Deputy Michaels invited me to take the walk with him to get lunch."

"It's all right," he replied as they began to walk. "I guess I hadn't realized how much on edge I've been until I walked into the break room and you weren't there." He kept his gaze focused on the building in front of them. "I didn't realize how important you are to me… to this case," he quickly tacked on as if in afterthought.

A dangerous spin of want whirled through her as she smelled the familiar scent of him, gazed at the handsome features now set in stone. Too close. They were definitely getting too close emotionally, and Tamara knew that was a mistake, but wasn't sure how to halt it from happening.

She was falling in love with Seth and that frightened her almost as much as the memories she kept repressed.

When they reached the office they went back into the break room. Apparently Raymond had decided to eat his lunch at his desk for they had the room to themselves.

"Want some of my fries?" she asked as she settled in at the table.

"No, thanks." He went to the vending machine in the corner and bought a soda and a prepackaged sandwich, then sat across from her. "Did Raymond give you a hard time?" he asked.

"Not at all. He asked me a bunch of questions about my memory, but I think he was just curious. Why?" She looked at him closely and noted that his features still looked harsh.

"There's something about him that I don't like." Seth unwrapped his sandwich and frowned at it thoughtfully. "I keep thinking what, other than being drugged, would make a woman lie down in the sand without putting up a fight? Maybe a sheriff or a deputy with a gun?"

Tamara gasped. "Are you telling me you don't trust the people you're working with?"

His frown deepened and for the first time his gaze met hers. Cold and distant, keen with intelligence, his gray eyes stared at her for a long moment before replying. "I'm telling you that at this moment there are only two people I really trust. Me and you, and that's it. Everyone else in this one-horse town is on my list of potential suspects."

Tamara picked up a French fry but suddenly discovered she'd lost her appetite. If she was to believe as Seth did, then she had nobody on her side, nobody she could trust except him, and that only made their emotional connection stronger.

One thing was certain. One way or the other she had a feeling that when it came time to leave Amber Lake she was going to be damaged. Whether that damage came from the memories of the crime against her resurfacing or from loving Seth, only time would tell.

Chapter Eight

Mark Willoughby was a burly man with dark hair and a chin that thrust outward as if he was expecting a fight at any moment. He eased down into the chair opposite Seth and even though his lips curved into a smile, it was obvious by the seething emotion in his eyes that he was ticked.

"You don't look happy to see me," Seth said as he leaned back in his chair across from his ex-brother-in-law.

"I wouldn't exactly call this a happy family reunion," Mark replied. "So cut the crap and tell me why I'm here."

"Vicki Smith." Seth watched intently Mark's reaction to the name.

The only response was a slight narrowing of Mark's green eyes. "What about her?"

"I understand you were seeing her at the time of her murder." Again Seth watched intently for any telltale subtle expression that might reveal something Mark didn't know he'd given away.

"Seeing her sounds a little more serious than what was going on. Vicki and I had dinner together a couple of times before she was killed. That's all, just a couple of casual dinners. She was still totally hung up on Todd. We were just friends, that's all."

He'd gone on long enough that it had begun to sound defensive. "Did you beat her like you beat my sister?" Seth asked.

Mark jerked up in his chair, his chin thrust forward as he fisted his hands on the top of the table. "You're out of line, Seth. I never laid a finger on your sister, never."

He unfisted his hands and appeared to relax against the back of the chair. "I won't deny that I made a lot of mistakes in my marriage to Linda, and I'm sorry every day for those mistakes, but I was never violent with her."

"But you hated her when the two of you divorced," Seth said.

"I didn't want the divorce. I wanted my family to stay intact more than anything. I've never gotten over Linda."

"And maybe that's why you're murdering dark-haired women who remind you of her?"

"Don't be ridiculous," Mark scoffed. "I know you've never liked me, that you never thought I was right for your sister, and I might have been a controlling ass when I was married to her, but I'm not a murderer. Jeez, Seth, how could you even think of me that way and allow me to have my daughter living with me half the time?"

"When was the last time you saw Vicki Smith?" Seth asked, trying to take the personal out of the conversation.

"Two nights before her murder. We had dinner together. Of course she insisted we eat at the Golden Daffodil. It was obvious she wanted Todd to see her with me, maybe make him realize what he'd thrown away."

"And after dinner?"

"I took her home, safe and sound. I don't know what happened to her after that. All I know for sure is that I had nothing to do with her murder. Besides, the way I hear it Vicki's murder is tied to Rebecca Cook's death. I didn't even know that kid and I sure had nothing to do with Tamara Jennings."

Seth asked a few more questions and then released Mark. After he left the interrogation room Seth remained seated at the table, his thoughts a chaotic mess.

Was it possible that Mark hid such a hatred for Linda that he'd come up with an elaborate plan for murder? Kill three dark-haired innocent women as a ruse and then attack the object of his rage, thus confusing the investigators? Somehow he wasn't sure Mark was smart enough, wily enough to come up with such a complicated plot. Besides, he and Linda had been divorced for years. If he was responsible, then why would he explode now? As far as Seth knew there had been no inciting incident, nothing out of the ordinary that would cause him to suddenly begin killing women. He and Linda seemed to have found a comfortable peace with each other, a peace that went beyond the sharing of their daughter.

And if his confusion about the crimes weren't enough he had to deal with his conflicted emotions where Tamara was concerned. His heartbeat caught painfully in his chest as he thought of those moments when he'd been unable to find her in the building.

Raw terror had raced through him, and it hadn't been the terror of an agent who had lost a key witness, but rather that of a man for a woman.

He didn't want to go there. He didn't want to feel the

kinds of emotions she evoked in him. It was emotional suicide for him to allow himself to think there could be anything real, anything lasting between them.

She had a life someplace else, a life that hadn't included him until somebody had buried her in a sand dune. He raised a hand and rubbed at his temple where a headache threatened to take hold.

He had two more interviews this afternoon and then he could call it a day. He expected nothing new to come from Rebecca's best friend or one of Vicki's coworkers, but he intended to leave no *t* uncrossed and no *i* undotted.

He'd even considered the possibility that the killer was a woman since there appeared to be no sexual motivation to the crimes. But he'd dismissed the idea almost as quickly as it had occurred to him. If the women had been basically comatose when taken to the dunes, it would have required a man's strength to get them from a parking area to the place of their burial.

It had to be a man. But who? And why? And would Tamara ever retrieve the hidden memories that might solve the case? Certainly he had some men who were topping his suspect list.

Henry Todd appeared a likely suspect for Vicki's death. It sounded like Vicki had become something of a stalker chick once Henry had moved on. Maybe she became such a pain he'd decided to get rid of her permanently. But that didn't explain his reason for killing Rebecca Cook.

It was just after six when he called it a day and found Tamara in the break room. Her face wreathed into a smile and he wasn't sure that she was glad to see him or just thankful her boredom was over.

It didn't matter. Her smile warmed him like the sun after a cloudy gray day. "You ready to break out of this joint?" he asked.

She popped up out of the chair. "I can't tell you how ready."

"I thought maybe we'd stop by the pizza place on the way home. Order a large supreme to go."

"Sounds like a great plan to me," she agreed.

They were quiet on the way to the pizza parlor. When they got there, they ordered the pizza to go and sodas to drink while they waited.

"Just so you know, I'm probably going to pick off most of the pepperoni and eat it," she said, finally breaking the long silence.

"Just so you know, I'm probably going to pick off all the black olives and eat them," he replied.

"That makes us good pizza buddies."

He smiled at her, knowing she was eager to hear what he'd learned during the day but also aware of the fact that she was giving him time to unwind.

She would make a perfect life partner. She seemed to know instinctively what he needed before he'd identified the need. She understood what he did for a living and that it was a large part of who he was as a man.

He took a sip of his drink and stared around the restaurant, willing away these kinds of strange thoughts. For years he'd told himself he was satisfied being alone, cooking for one and having his space to himself.

But Tamara made him think of dinners for two, of conversation to fill the long hours of an empty evening.

She made him think of making love to her before closing his eyes to sleep, awakening in the morning to share coffee across a kitchen table.

He was grateful when the kid behind the counter announced their pizza was ready for pickup. He grabbed the box and together he and Tamara headed back to his truck.

"We'll eat first, and then we'll talk about our days," he said as they pulled away from the restaurant.

"Does that mean you want me to keep my mouth shut unless it's open stringing mozzarella cheese?" she asked, her voice filled with the lightness of a tease.

He flashed her a fast grin. "No, it just means we only talk about pleasant things while we enjoy eating."

"Deal," she agreed easily.

Fifteen minutes later they were seated at Linda's table, the pie box open before them and each with a bottle of beer. "Nothing better than hot pizza and cold beer," she said as she reached for a slice.

"You've got that right." He smiled in amusement as she carefully picked off each piece of pepperoni and popped them into her mouth.

He grabbed his own slice and as they ate they talked about Linda and Samantha and about Kansas City and how much he loved it there.

"The best part is from the downtown area within a fifteen-minute drive you can be standing in the middle of a pasture. It's a great combination of big city and small town all rolled into one," he said.

"Sounds nice."

He nodded. "I can't imagine living anywhere else. Is Amarillo your hometown?"

"Born and raised there," she answered automatically and then her startled gaze met his. "Ah, that was sneaky, you tricked me into having more memories."

"I didn't mean to be sneaky," he protested. "I just asked a question."

He watched her as she chewed a bite of the pizza, her brow wrinkled with deep thought. "I remember Amarillo," she finally said. "And I remember my apartment. What I don't understand is why thinking about it makes my heart fill with a terrible grief? Why when I think about it, I don't want to go back there."

"But you know you'll have to sooner or later," Seth reminded her. "This time now, here in Amber Lake, is just a single moment in a million moments that make up your real life."

"But this moment feels so real," she replied softly.

"Eventually it will just feel like a dream." The conversation continued back to safe subjects as they finished up their meal. They cleaned up the kitchen and then moved into the living room where they shared the activities of their day while seated at opposite ends of the sofa.

"I leaned about the value of vitamin B on *The Doctors* and watched a couple of old reruns of *Everybody Loves Raymond,*" she said. "That was the high point of my day."

"Are you prepared to do it all over again tomorrow?" he asked.

"More interviews?"

He nodded and then told her what he'd learned from the interviews he'd conducted that day.

"So Henry Todd can be tied to both dead women,"

she mused as she kicked off her sandals and pulled her bare feet up beneath her on the sofa. "I told you I had a bad feeling about him."

"But is your bad feeling about him because you encountered him as a killer or because you think he's just an average slimeball?"

She leaned her back against the sofa cushion and released a sigh. "I don't know. The night that I apparently 'disappeared' I ate at the café. I can't imagine that I would have run into Henry anywhere else."

"Still, we don't know where you went after you left the café," he reminded her. "And we aren't sure Todd spends every minute of every night locked away in his restaurant."

She worried a hand through her hair, the silky lengths causing Seth's fingers to itch with the need to touch it. "It's strange that this here and now feels so much more real than the memories of my former life. I have a serial killer apparently hell-bent on burying me in a sand dune and I know probably the best thing I could do is leave town, but I'm not ready to go back to my half-remembered life yet."

"And I'm not ready to let you go yet," Seth said, then hurriedly added, "at least not until you have all your memories back and know exactly where you fit."

There she was again, messing with his mind, looking so soft and welcoming, forcing his thoughts to go places they had no business going.

"What if I never remember that night?" she said, bringing him back to the crime.

"With or without your memories, we're going to find this guy. Eventually he's going to make a mistake or we're going to find a clue. I'm not leaving Amber Lake until this killer is caught or killed." A swell of tension filled his chest as he thought of the man he sought.

He was obviously a planner…organized and bright. How many women would die before he made a mistake? How many bodies would be uncovered in the dunes before they finally got a break?

Just that quickly he was exhausted. The thought of the murders weighed heavy in his soul, as heavy as the thought of letting Tamara go.

Maybe it was best if Tamara headed back to Amarillo. She was right. If last night was any indication, she had a serial killer actively seeking to finish what he had begun with her. Surely she'd be safe in Amarillo even without all of her memories.

He gazed at her for a long moment, drinking in the sight of her lovely features, the long length of her shiny hair, and realized he was more than a little bit in love with her.

"Maybe it really is time for you to go home…back to Amarillo," he finally suggested tentatively, although they were the last words he wanted to speak.

Her eyes opened wide. "But I'm not ready," she replied, an edge of panic making her voice a bit higher than usual. "I don't remember enough. Besides, we know the killer wants me, otherwise he would have just taken another woman rather than trying to break into the window of the bedroom where I was sleeping."

Her lower lip began to tremble and her eyes filled with the sheen of tears. "You've all said he's smart and if he has any information at all then he already knows where I live in Amarillo. What's to keep him from following me there? Who says he has to adhere to his pattern of burying women in the Deadman's Dunes? What if he just kills me and buries me someplace outside Amarillo?" The tears spilled down her cheeks. "Please don't send me home, Seth." Her crying began in earnest, the sobs of a woman still terrified, still unprepared to face an uncertain future in a place she barely remembered.

He couldn't stand it. He couldn't stand her tears. Without thinking he reached out to her and she fell into his embrace. As she wept into the front of his shirt, he could feel her heartbeat banging against his own.

"Please, Seth. Please don't send me away yet." The words came from her as hiccupping sobs.

He stroked her hair and held her tight, unable to imagine what fears might reside inside her head, what anxiety must burn in her soul. This place and he was all she really knew. Was it any wonder that the idea of being sent away would upset her?

She did have a point about the killer. If he had any inside information at all, if he'd heard any idle gossip around town, then he knew she lived in Amarillo. The last thing he wanted to do was send her away from here and into the arms of a killer. If he were perfectly honest with himself he'd admit that the last thing he wanted to do was send her away from him.

"I won't make you go anywhere you aren't ready to go," he murmured into her sweet-smelling hair. He held her for several long minutes, until her tears had halted and the only thing he was conscious of was the soft warmth of her in his arms.

He released her, needing to separate, needing to draw

enough distance from her to inhale a full breath. "You know that sooner or later you'll have to go home."

"I know." She leaned back against the opposite side of the sofa and wrapped her arms around herself, as if shielding herself from something. "But every time I think about going back there I'm overwhelmed with grief and anxiety and I can't imagine why."

"Whatever it is, you'll have to face it sooner or later. That is your life, Tamara, and I'm sure there are plenty of good things and good people waiting for you there." At least that's what he wanted for her, that's what he hoped.

"Then where are all these good people? Why hasn't anyone been looking for me? You all can't even find anyone who knows much of anything about me."

It was true. Tom and his men had tried to find people who knew Tamara, but her life had obviously been one of isolation. Other than neighbors who professed to know her only superficially and people she'd worked with on webpages who had only known her professionally, nobody had come forward anxiously seeking her. No frantic boyfriend relieved she had been found. Seth didn't even want to examine why he was perversely pleased by this.

"I don't know," he admitted, his heart breaking more than a little for her. He glanced at the clock on the mantel. "We should probably call it a night. Tomorrow is going to be an early, long day."

She nodded and stood, but as she looked down the long hallway toward the guest room he felt the tension that filled her heart.

"There's nothing for you to be afraid of," he said

softly. "I boarded up that window this morning. Nobody is coming through it without a chain saw."

"Then I'll just say good night," she said.

She turned and he watched her walking slowly down the hallway. She broke his heart and revved his adrenaline.

She paused at the door of the bedroom and turned back to look at him. "Seth, if this is just a single moment of time in a lifetime of moments, I want to spend it with you. I want making love with you to be one of the memories I take away from this experience. I don't want being buried in the sand to be the most intense memory I have of my time in Amber Lake."

He stared at her and felt her longing wafting down the hallway with sweet seduction. His brain worked to process all the reasons why they shouldn't spend the night together, why if they did it would be an enormous mistake.

But his brain was trapped in a vision of her naked in the bed, in the sensation of her soft skin against his, in the fire of her lips kissing him.

He should be strong, but even as he thought it, he stood. He should be the one capable of denying temptation, but still his feet moved forward down the hallway toward where she stood.

His brain was in utter denial up until the time he stood face-to-face with her, up until the moment she took his hand in hers and only then did he completely surrender to his own desire, to his own need.

Chapter Nine

The instant Seth's hand slipped into hers, Tamara knew the rightness of this moment in time with this man. She pulled him into the bedroom and instantly their mouths found each other in a kiss that screamed of the hot desire that had raged between them for the past couple of days.

She didn't question her want for him. She merely accepted that he was something she needed, something that she couldn't live without…like food or air.

His mouth plied hers with a heat that filled her body and soul. His arms wrapped around her and pulled her tight against him and she could tell he was aroused. This fact alone only made her more certain that this was right and good.

She knew it wasn't forever. She was fully aware of the fact that tomorrow they might catch a killer, tomorrow she might be on her way back to her half-remembered life in Amarillo. But she needed tonight in his arms, a memory that would burn itself into her brain so vividly she'd never, ever forget it.

As their lips remained locked, he moved her toward the left side of the bed, where without breaking the kiss he took off his holster and gun and placed them on the top of the nightstand.

His lips left hers only to blaze a trail of fire down the length of her neck as his hand tangled in her hair and he pressed closer against her.

His scent, a half-wild fragrance of cologne and male infused her, and she knew that particular scent would always bring with it both a sense of excitement and utter security and safety.

"You are so beautiful," he murmured against her ear.

She dropped her head back, allowing his mouth access to the hollow of her throat. If she had been able to remember anything from her past, Seth's touch, his mouth would have chased it all away.

She didn't want to have a sudden explosion of memories, she just wanted to dwell in this moment of magic with the hot, handsome man who had saved her life. She wanted just this night with the man who stirred her not only on a physical level, but also on an emotional level, as well.

As he slid his warm hands up beneath her T-shirt to caress across her naked back, she knew she'd never, ever get enough of him.

It was possible this might be her only night with him, but she knew in her heart that she would want more even when morning dawned.

Impatiently he grabbed the bottom of her T-shirt and as he tugged it upward she raised her hands above her head to aid him, grateful that the bra she'd bought at the discount store was a sexy lace.

Once her shirt was gone he pulled his own over his head, exposing his sculpted, muscled chest as he tossed his shirt to the floor behind him.

They stood mere inches apart and simply stared at

each other. Tamara's heart fluttered rapidly, making her half-breathless. He breathed through his mouth, as if he, too, was finding it difficult to draw in enough air.

"You look amazing." His voice was deep, husky, as his gaze swept her from head to toe.

She laid a hand on his chest. "So do you."

She wasn't sure who moved first, but suddenly they were both on the bed, limbs tangled as his mouth once again sought hers. His tongue dipped inside, swirling with hers as their desire reached new levels.

She loved the feel of his sturdy long legs entwined with hers, his solid, muscled chest against her breasts. She couldn't get enough of the taste of him, the feel of him.

There was no thought of killers or repressed memories, there was nothing but Seth and the hungry desire that claimed her.

"I can't tell you how much I've wanted you," he breathed against her neck, causing shivers of delight to dance up her spine.

Had she ever felt this way with another man? She had no memories to pull from, but she didn't believe anyone had ever made her feel the way she did now in Seth's arms, with his lips tracing lazy circles against her neck, sliding down to mouth the tip of her breast above her bra.

Her breath caught at the erotic tug of sensation that rippled through her as her nipple rose in response. Not enough. So not enough, she thought as she half pushed him off her, reached behind and released the clasp on her bra.

When his mouth returned to her bare breast she

raked her fingers through his hair, wondering how she'd ever lived without his touch.

The rest of their clothes disappeared, his shoes and socks gone, jeans quickly shucked and both his boxers and her panties thrown to the side of the bed as they moved in a frenzy.

He was hard against her and she curled her fingers around his hardness, marveling at the velvet skin over taut muscle. She had only stroked him a couple of times when he hissed, "Stop...too soon." He smoothed a strand of her hair from her cheek. His eyes burned mercury-silver and wild. "I want to take my time with you. I want to hear you screaming my name with pleasure."

A new shiver whipped through her at the promise of the sexual delight in his words. As his hands began to explore the length of her body, stroking...teasing... coming closer and closer to the very center of her, she arched and moved in an attempt to capture his intimate touch.

He laughed, a low, sexy growl, as she moaned in obvious frustration. "Patience is a virtue," he said.

"Torture is a federal offense," she replied.

He laughed again and then his laughter died as his fingers found her moistness and moved with butterfly gentleness against her. She arched once again with a swift intake of breath as she felt an orgasm begin where he touched her and spread shuddering sensations outward to the tips of her fingers and toes.

She gasped his name as she rode the wave, and before she could catch her breath he moved between her thighs and eased into her.

He froze, his facial features set in stone as he gazed down at her. His struggle for control was evident in the taut chords of his neck and the glaze of his eyes.

Finally he moved, thrusting forward and she closed her eyes as he filled her up, moving against her in the ancient rhythm of lovemaking.

Tamara was lost to the feel of him, to the rising sensations that built inside her as they rocked together. In and out he stroked, first slow and then with a faster pace that had her panting and on the edge of yet another cliff.

Tears filled her eyes as he moaned her name and then she fell over the cliff, shattering apart as a second, more intense climax struck her. At the same time she was vaguely aware of him tensing against her and then gasping with his own release.

Time seemed to stand still as they remained embraced, him holding his body weight on his elbows as he looked down at her and grinned. "Now that's a vacation."

She laughed and then his grin fell and he shook his head. "Like a couple of horny teenagers with no thought of tomorrow and no thought of protection. We should both be shot."

"Can you wait until the glow leaves me before you shoot me?" she asked.

He smiled down at her. "You are glowing. You look gorgeous."

"It's the look of a sated woman."

"I like it." He finally disengaged and rolled to the side of her. "But we should have thought about protection."

"I'm sure it will be fine." She didn't want to think

about accidents or mistakes at the moment. There was no way she could consider getting pregnant by Seth a terrible mistake, and yet the thought filled her with an inexplicable anxiety. What kind of woman was she that the thought of having a child filled her with a whispering dread?

She rolled away from him and off the bed. "I'll be right back," she said. She padded into the adjoining bathroom and stared at her reflection in the mirror above the sink.

Who was she? She still only had bits and pieces of herself, not enough to remember what experiences she'd been through, what paths she'd taken in life that formed her.

All she really knew after the past thirty minutes in bed with Seth was that she was in love with him. And she had no right to be. As he'd reminded her earlier, this time they shared wasn't real life. Ultimately, no matter how she felt about him, no matter how much he wanted her, they both had separate lives to go back to.

The only thing she really had to remember was that she was a key witness and Seth was the FBI agent in charge of her case. And that there was still a serial killer who wanted her buried in the Deadman's Dunes.

SETH AWOKE LONG BEFORE dawn, his naked body spooned around Tamara's back. He fit perfectly around her, like the shell on a turtle.

He was in no hurry to leave the bed, to leave the comfort of her warmth, the fragrant scent of her or the memory of making love to her. He was in no rush to begin his day, hunting for a killer with little success, another day of utter frustration.

Maybe it was time for him to call in reinforcements. Maybe he needed to contact Director Forbes and have a couple more agents come to town to help work the case. Although he hated to admit defeat, he wasn't too proud to ask for help if he thought it was warranted.

The issue was he wasn't sure what any other agents could do that he and Tom and his men weren't already doing. He had a list of potential suspects, but nobody who popped to the top of the short, pathetic list, except perhaps Sam Clemmons, who could be picked up simply because he'd been at all three scenes. Still, Seth was reluctant to jump to obvious conclusions. There were too many players in the game.

A womanizing restaurateur, a deputy with a reputation as a bully, an ex-brother-in-law and a handful of dirt-bike-riding kids…not exactly the stuff that thriller movies were made of, and yet someone, perhaps one of those very people was burying brunettes in the sand dunes.

Somebody wanted Tamara to be the third victim badly enough to make a bold move and steal her right out from under Seth's nose. Thank God, the Sandman had been thwarted by Tamara's scream. But Seth knew deep in his soul that the misstep had probably only fired a new determination in the killer to take Tamara.

Reluctantly, he rolled away from her and out of the bed. It was easier to think about murder and suspects than it was to analyze his feelings for Tamara.

He padded naked from the guest bedroom and down

the hallway to the main bathroom and within seconds stood beneath a hot shower.

There was no question that last night had been a mistake, but what a wonderful mistake it had been. Even now he could still taste her skin, feel the heat of her body against his, hear the echoes of the cries she'd made in the throes of pleasure.

Making love to her once had been a mistake, but then he'd repeated it by making love to her a second time before they'd fallen asleep. That time they'd gone slowly, exploring each other with both the familiarity of old lovers and yet the sizzling excitement of new ones.

The greatest mistake he'd made of all was falling for her, for being sucked into feelings he'd never wanted to feel in his life. He'd allowed himself to get so close and now it was going to be difficult on them both when it was time for her to head back to her home, her life and anyone who might be waiting for her there.

It was a bit odd that she'd been gone for well over a week and yet nobody from Amarillo had filed a missing persons report. He knew from the information he'd gained that she'd been known around her neighborhood as a loner, but surely there was somebody somewhere who cared, who'd noticed that she was missing? And the idea that there wasn't anyone shouldn't affect his heart like it did.

He had to separate from her, he had to regain the relationship of investigator and potential victim. He had to get back on a more professional footing with her, not just for his own sake, but for hers, as well. It should be fairly easy today.

He'd be stuck in the interrogation room all day and

she'd be back in the lounge. Then when they got back home tonight they'd eat dinner and he'd set up his laptop on the kitchen table, a not-so-subtle hint that he intended to continue to work.

Once he was dressed he left the bathroom and headed to the kitchen to make the morning coffee. He consciously willed away any further thoughts of Tamara or the night before. He had to focus on getting this madman in jail as quickly as possible.

Minutes later as he stood at the window and watched the sun slowly peeking over the horizon, he sipped his coffee and once again ran over his list of suspects in his head.

Tom's men were checking alibis for both the murders and the night and morning of Tamara's near death. But people's memories were faulty, and at least in the case of the first two murders, alibis were tough to pin down definitively.

In the case of Rebecca Cook it was particularly difficult as the death was initially ruled a freak accident. All the young people in town knew where they had been that night…at the party on the dunes. But where had Henry Todd been? Where had Raymond Michaels spent his time on that night? And Mark…where had his brother-in-law been?

Hell, Seth couldn't come up with an unbreakable alibi for a particular night two months before. Days went by without specific incidents; nights were spent mostly at home alone.

While he was certain that Raymond's wife would alibi him for whatever time necessary, both Todd and Mark lived alone. None of them lived in an area that was remote enough to keep a woman alive for hours before dumping her at the dunes.

As he thought of that moment when he'd seen Tamara's face in the sand, frustration gnawed with sharp teeth at his gut. As he considered what Rebecca and Vicki had endured in the last moments of their deaths, he wanted to smash his fist into something…preferably the perp's face.

He was on his second cup of coffee when Tamara entered the kitchen. She'd showered and was dressed for the day in a pair of formfitting jeans and a turquoise tank top. Her dark hair was pulled up in a high ponytail, showcasing her delicate features to perfection.

He steeled himself against the automatic response he suffered at the sight of her, the desire to take her into his arms, the need to kiss her lips as he told her good morning.

"Morning," he said, the word more of a grunt than a real greeting.

"Good morning to you," she replied cheerfully as she walked straight to the coffeemaker on the counter. She poured herself a cup and then turned to face him. "I see morning regrets all over your face."

"Maybe a few," he admitted. He took a sip of his coffee and eyed her over the rim of the cup. Her cheerful smile slowly fell and she raised her chin a notch, as if anticipating a fight.

"I have absolutely no regrets, and you don't have to worry about last night having any long-term repercussions. I'm a big girl, Seth. I know the score. I know there's no future between us and I don't anticipate there ever being one. Still, there's no reason to regret what was a beautiful, wonderful night."

She carried her cup to the table and sat. "Now, tell me about the plans for the day."

Just that quickly the night was left behind and a new day had begun. They were at the sheriff's office by eight and within fifteen minutes Tamara was in the break room and Seth was interviewing another of Rebecca's friends.

The day passed with person after person brought in for Seth to interview and no answers forthcoming to aid in the breaking of the case.

He stopped at noon and ordered in lunch from a nearby Chinese restaurant for himself and Tamara. When the order arrived he carried it back to the break room where Tamara was sprawled in a chair, staring blankly at the television.

She straightened as he entered, eyeing the white bag he carried hungrily. "I was afraid I was going to have to hit up Deputy Michaels for another trip next door to get fed."

Seth scowled and set the bag in the center of the small round table. "I want you to stay away from him," he said as he began pulling out boxes of food.

She joined him at the table. "You can't really believe he has anything to do with the murders," she said in a low voice.

"I don't know what to believe about anyone," he replied.

They didn't speak again until they were seated at the table with a combination of Chinese fare on their paper plates. "These murders were about power," he finally said. "And I know from the scuttlebutt around town that Michaels wields his official power heavily. It just doesn't sit well with me, nor does the fact that he asked you so many questions about your amnesia yesterday."

She speared a piece of sweet-and-sour chicken. "Speaking of, I've had more of my memories return. Unfortunately, none of them will help you. I remembered that my parents are dead, that my life was mostly my web business and that I was lonely." She popped the chicken into her mouth and chewed thoughtfully.

When she was finished, she gazed at him, obviously troubled. "I wonder if maybe I'm not remembering what I need to because I don't want to go back to my former life." The words came from her slowly, as if they were a painful admission.

"I don't believe that," he replied. "Your memories are coming back to you as they should…the safe things first. The more painful things will try to remain repressed, but I can't believe that you'd even subconsciously not want to remember a killer who is going to kill again because you don't want to go home to a lonely life."

"I hope you're right." She grabbed another piece of chicken. "I want to remember that night in the dunes. I want to believe that I can help you put this monster away before he strikes again."

Their conversation turned to mundane things as some of the other deputies entered the room for their lunch break. The mood among them all was somber.

"I still think we should get Clemmons in jail and charged," one of the younger deputies said.

"We don't have enough evidence for the DA to even

be interested in charging him," Seth replied. "We can't find anyplace where he might have stashed the women before burying them. Sam rides those dunes almost every day and half the night. The dunes might be Sam's playground, but that doesn't make him a killer. A defense attorney would rip the case apart. We need more," Seth said in frustration.

Each and every day they were all waiting for another body to turn up, speculating that if the killer couldn't get to Tamara, he'd eventually be unable to stop himself from taking somebody else. Although the dunes were being patrolled as much as possible, they all knew it was impossible to keep a determined person from finding a place where nobody would see, where the body wouldn't be found until some errant dirt-bike rider kicked up the sand in just the right place.

Lunch finished, Seth returned to his duty and left Tamara once again. The afternoon crawled by in increments of the nervous sweat of the interviewees, Seth's growing frustration and the sweltering heat of summer filling the building.

He had to hand it to Tom. With the lawman coordinating the people coming in, the interviewing process was going relatively smoothly, just not yielding any kind of result that Seth could use.

By the time Seth decided to call it a day he was in a foul mood. Someplace inside him he felt the tick of a time bomb that could explode at any moment, resulting in another innocent woman's horrific death, but he wasn't any closer to finding the guilty party than he had been on the day he'd dug Tamara out of the sand.

Tamara must have read his mood for the ride home from the office was a silent one.

Seth was certain these murders were about power and control. He knew that the victim profile was brunettes and there was a reason that the killer was burying them in the sand.

The sand was important to the killer. But why? It was part of the ritual. Take a woman, somehow render her helpless and then bury her in the sand. The sand was the key, but what did it mean?

He cast a quick glance at Tamara, who stared out the window as if lost in thoughts of her own. He had to keep her safe. As long as she was with him nobody was going to touch her.

But that meant the killer would have to take another victim. He was already overdue, probably filled with the anxiety of the need of the kill. A bomb ready to detonate and nobody had the answers to stop the explosion of death.

Except perhaps Tamara.

They went to the drive-through at the burger joint to get dinner and now, back at Linda's, sat across from each other at the table to eat. "I'm going to gain a thousand pounds while I'm here if we keep fast-fooding it," she said, finally breaking what was quickly becoming an uncomfortable silence.

"I didn't figure you'd want to cook after a long day at the sheriff's office and I'm no good in the kitchen unless you can zap it in a microwave."

"I like to cook. I wouldn't mind making dinner each night when we got home."

"Linda has a freezer full of meat. Whatever we use

I'll replace." He shrugged. "Whatever you want to do is fine with me. I'm male, I'll eat anything and, to be honest, a home-cooked meal sounds good to me."

He finished his burger and wadded up the wrapper. "Have you given any more thought to seeing that therapist or maybe a hypnotist to help you retrieve the last of your memories?"

She stared at him as if he'd suddenly sprouted an order of French fries in the center of his forehead. She toyed with her straw in the diet drink, her gaze focused on the cup. "Honestly, I hadn't considered either option, but if you think that's what we need to do, then I'll do whatever is necessary."

Seth knew what he was asking of her, knew the damage that might come to her by forcing her to remember what her brain was protecting her from, but he was at a dead end, and so afraid of more bodies showing up. His heart broke with his suggestion, but his admiration for her grew by her immediate acquiescence.

He was unable to look at her as he told her he'd look into finding somebody to work with her the next day. Thankfully when they finished eating she went into the living room and turned on the television and he set up his laptop on the table and fed in notes and impressions from the day.

He consciously willed himself not to look at Tamara, not to feel the fear she must be feeling as she thought of being forced to remember the horrible moments just before he'd found her in the sand.

He didn't want to think about the night to come when there was nothing he'd like better than curl up in bed with her at his side, feeling the silk of her hair and smelling the scent that belonged to her alone. He was half in love with her and hated that he couldn't control the softening of his heart where she was concerned.

Still, she'd sleep alone tonight in the guest room and he would bunk on the sofa. With the window in the guest room boarded up there was no way anyone could get to her without Seth hearing them. She'd be safe, both from the killer and from any further deepening of the bond that she and Seth shared, a bond that shouldn't exist.

He wasn't surprised when at nine o'clock she got up from the sofa and turned off the television and announced that she was going to bed. He felt her questioning gaze on him but he didn't look up from his computer screen as he murmured a good-night.

He didn't look up until he sensed that she was gone and had disappeared into the guest room and only then did he realize he'd been holding his breath. He released it on a deep sigh.

Did he want her again? Absolutely. Was he going to follow through on his desire for her? Absolutely not. He frowned and stared at the screen in front of him where he had typed his list of persons of interest. Hell, he couldn't even call them suspects. There just wasn't any hard evidence to tie any of them to the murders. They didn't have enough to ensure the state a foolproof case and no self-respecting district attorney would go forward with what little they had.

He leaned back in his chair and released another deep sigh. Maybe he should call it a night, too. Last night sleep had been in short supply with the two bouts of lovemaking with Tamara.

And when he had finally fallen asleep he'd suffered nightmares of being stuck in sand, unable to save Tamara, unable to move as he heard the scrape of a shovel nearby.

The last thing he wanted to do was force Tamara to face her nightmares and even asking her to see somebody who would actively chase after them broke his heart. But that was Seth the man thinking.

With the growing anticipation of another kill at hand, he had to put his personal feelings aside and become Seth the FBI agent, who was tasked with finding and stopping a killer and using every resource available to him to get the job done.

He shut down his laptop and then got out of the chair and stretched with his arms overhead, working out kinks from sitting too long.

He checked the back door to make sure it was locked and dead-bolted and then walked to the living room to do the same with the front door. After checking it, he moved to the front window and pulled one of the curtains aside to gaze out.

Night had fallen…another night with no answers, no way to stop a killer from following his dark impulses again. He was about to move away from the window when something caught his eye…the figure of a man just behind the streetlamp post across the street.

Chapter Ten

It looked as if he were attempting to hide, to blend into the lamppost itself. Adrenaline shot through Seth. Why would anyone be across the street from this house after dark?

He left the window and as he went through the living room he grabbed his gun from the kitchen table. He didn't like things that didn't make sense and it didn't make sense that somebody was outside watching this house with Tamara inside.

As he approached the back door his heart pounded a hundred miles a minute. Maybe it was the killer, come back to look for a weakness in the house security that he could exploit in order to get to Tamara.

Quietly, Seth unbolted and unlocked the back door and slid out into the hot night air. His gun was a familiar, comforting weight in his hand and he wouldn't hesitate to use it if necessary.

With the stealth of a stalking cat, he moved slowly around the corner to the side of the house and then to the corner of the front of the house. He peered out and saw that the male figure was still there, although there was too much distance for Seth to specifically identify who he was.

He had no idea if the man was armed or not, but Seth had the element of surprise on his side. With a renewed burst of adrenaline he shot from the corner of the house and across the street. He threw himself at the person and tackled him to the ground as the man yelped in surprise.

Seth instantly got to his feet, the business end of his gun pointed to the man who was facedown on the concrete. "Get up and put your hands above your head," Seth commanded. "And if you decide not to comply with my orders, then I'll be happy to shoot you."

As the man rolled over on his back, Seth stifled a gasp of shock as he looked into the frightened eyes of Sam Clemmons. "Don't shoot me, man. I wasn't doing anything."

He raised his hands above his head, obviously recognizing the deadly intent in Seth's eyes. "What are you doing lurking around out here?" Seth asked as he motioned for him to stand.

"Nothing, man. I wasn't doing anything," Sam exclaimed. Seth patted him down and found no weapons, then indicated he could lower his hands to his sides. "Last I heard it wasn't against the law to stand on a street corner."

"Depends on why you chose this particular street corner," Seth replied.

Sam looked toward the house and then back at Seth. "I just wanted to see her, that's all. I just wanted to make sure she was really okay." He shifted from one foot to the other, a look of sheer misery on his features. "I just stood there, you know." His voice was soft, barely audible. "While you and my friends were digging her out of the sand I just froze. I didn't do anything to help her.

I haven't seen her since then and I just needed to see... to make sure that she was all right."

Sam's shoulders slumped forward and for a moment he just looked like a pathetic kid. "I have nightmares about it," he continued, his gaze directed at Seth's feet. "I dream that I'm riding the dunes and I ride right over her face..." He shuddered, as if the image in his head was too horrific to bear.

Seth wasn't sure what to believe. Sam Clemmons knew the dunes probably better than anyone in town. He'd been at the scene of the discoveries of both Rebecca and Vicki. He was a maladjusted loner who had come from a difficult background. All strikes against him and yet Seth wasn't sure what to believe about him.

He seemed genuinely distraught about how the events had unfolded on the day Tamara had been found. He also seemed concerned about her well-being, but for all Seth knew he could be a great actor covering his reason for being here.

Sam was right about one thing. It wasn't against the law to stand on a street corner. He lowered his gun and scowled at Sam. "Go on, get out of here and don't come back. I don't want to see you anywhere around this neighborhood again."

Sam gave a curt nod and then took off running in the opposite direction. Seth tucked his gun into his waistband, raked a hand through his hair and expelled a breath of tense air.

He knew from experience it would take a while for the adrenaline that flooded through his veins to dissipate. He entered the house the way he'd left it, by the back door. Tamara stood in the kitchen, clad in her sexy short pink nightie, her eyes wide as she clutched a butcher knife in one hand.

"Put that away before you cut off your own finger," he said. "Everything is under control."

She slowly lowered the knife. "What happened? I got up to get a drink of water and saw the back door open and you nowhere to be found."

Her eyes still held a hint of panic as she set the knife on the counter. "We had a Peeping Tom of sorts," he said. "I went outside to see who it was and what he was doing standing just across the street watching this house."

"Who was it?"

"Sam Clemmons."

"Wasn't he one of the guys who found me?" She sank down at the kitchen as if her legs were too weak to hold her upright.

"Yeah, he's the one who froze and didn't help dig you out. It appears he's suffering a bout of guilt over that and just wanted to get a look at you, assure himself that you're okay."

She narrowed her eyes. "Do you believe that?"

"At this point I don't know what to believe. All I know is that I had no viable reason to arrest him and so I told him to scram." He tried to keep his gaze focused on her face and not drifting down the length of her half-naked body. "Show's over, go back to bed." His voice was curt and sounded more like a command than a suggestion.

He could tell that his tone had irritated her by the way she whirled on her bare heels and stomped down the hallway. He felt a moment of remorse, but shoved it aside. It was time to withdraw from her, to remind both himself and her that this was all about a job and nothing more.

He slept on the sofa with one eye open for the remainder of the night and by morning his foul mood had only intensified. She was quiet during morning coffee, but didn't appear to be mad and somehow that made it worse.

"I'm sorry I snapped at you last night," he said once they were in his truck and headed for the sheriff's office.

"It's okay. I know you're under a lot of stress." She flashed him a bright smile. "This wasn't exactly what you had in mind when you came here for a vacation."

A night of his time here was far more than what he'd ever expected from a vacation, but he didn't say that aloud. He didn't want to think about the night he'd spent with her. "No, it wasn't what I had in mind," he agreed. "But I'm glad I was here. Sheriff Atkins would have probably requested some FBI presence anyway. It just made it easier with me already being here."

He turned into the parking area in front of the sheriff's office, shut off the engine and then turned to look at her. "I'm thinking of calling in some reinforcements from the bureau. I've got a buddy, Mick McCane, who I know recently finished up a case in Arkansas. Maybe he can come out and give us a fresh perspective on everything."

She unfastened her seat belt and gazed at him somberly. "You know you don't need to call in reinforcements. What you need to do is find a way to break through my mind, and if that means being hypnotized, then find somebody who can do that for us."

"Are you sure that's the way you want to go?" he asked, his heart stepping up his rhythm as he recognized once again what might lie ahead of them...of her.

"At this point I think it's the only way you're going to catch the killer. I have to go back, Seth. I have to go back to the moments before I landed in the sand dune. The key to solving the murders may be there and once that's done we can both get on with our lives."

And that was exactly what he wanted...wasn't it?

THE BREAK ROOM WAS beginning to feel like home and half of the deputies on the force her family. Tamara sat at the table and stared absently at the tiny television that was mounted to the wall in the corner. A morning talk show was playing but she paid it no attention.

It had begun...the distancing from her by Seth. She'd known it was coming, knew it had to happen, but she hadn't realized just how bereft she'd feel when it began.

The night they had spent together had obviously changed things for him, made him realize things between them were out of control, that her feelings for him were out of control and now he was backpedaling as fast as he could to get on firmer footing.

Despite the constant presence of the officers coming and going, she'd never felt so alone.

It was just after noon when Deputy Billy Broadwick came in carrying a fast-food bag that he set in front of her. "Agent Hawkins told me to get you some lunch." He sat down in the chair opposite her as she opened the bag. "I got you a chicken sandwich and a side salad. I hope that's okay. It's what my wife always orders."

"It's fine," Tamara replied. She liked Deputy Broadwick. The young man was ridiculously in love with his wife, Haley, and they were expecting their first child in a month. "Since you and Haley decided not to learn the sex of the baby, what color did you decorate the nursery?" she asked, eager for any kind of conversation after being alone for so long in the room.

"Yellow. Haley calls it buttercup, but to me it's just plain yellow. How are you doing? Must be pretty boring just sitting in here day after day."

She smiled at him ruefully. "Thank goodness there's a television in here. Otherwise I think I might go stark raving mad."

"I'll bet you're eager to leave this all behind you and get home."

Tamara opened the wrapping on the chicken sandwich and nodded, because she knew it was the response he expected. But the truth of the matter was she had yet to feel any urgency, any homesickness at all. What did that say about her former life? Had she been unhappy? Lonely?

Deputy Broadwick sat with her while she ate her lunch and they talked about Amber Lake and the Fourth of July celebrations set to occur in the next five days. There was always a huge firework display put on by the town out by the dunes, but he wasn't sure it would happen this year because of the dunes being closed.

Even though Tamara knew it wasn't her fault, she felt half-responsible for robbing the town of its annual celebration fireworks. If she could only just remember.

Damn her mind for attempting to keep her safe from whatever she'd experienced.

It wasn't long before Deputy Broadwick had to return to duty, leaving her alone again with only her thoughts.

The fact that Seth hadn't popped in at lunchtime to check in on her spoke volumes of how far he'd backed off from her. She told herself it was all for the best. It was possible by the time they left here today he'd have the name of a hypnotist who would be able to retrieve the memories she'd repressed.

It was possible within the next day or two she'd have her memories back and would be saying goodbye to the FBI agent who had saved her life…the same man who had stolen her heart.

She moved from the table to one of the two easy chairs in the room. There was also a cot shoved against one wall, she assumed for lawmen who found themselves working overtime and needing a quick catnap.

She eyed it longingly. Boredom made her sleepy and she was bored and disheartened and already grieving the loss of this small town and Seth.

The chair embraced her with comfort and she must have fallen asleep, for she was instantly trapped in a dream. Once again she was in the sand. She knew the sun was high in the sky for she could feel the heat of it on her exposed skin.

She knew she was in trouble, but she couldn't help herself. Her muscles refused to obey her brain's commands. She wasn't just paralyzed from the neck down. Her eyes were closed and as hard as she tried, she couldn't open them.

I should have never stopped at that rest area just

outside town. I should have never lingered to chat with the man walking the cute little dog. Thoughts, regrets, shifted through her head along with the sound of the scrape of the shovel against the sand.

"An ostrich, that's what you are," a deep voice sounded from nearby. "You should have stopped him, but you didn't do anything. You're nothing but a damned ostrich and you belong in the sand."

Her mind screamed her terror as she heard the scoop of the shovel and then the plop of the sand falling into place…on top of her…burying her.

No, no, please! Her brain screamed the words her mouth refused to form, and she tried desperately to open her eyes, at least to catch a glimpse of the man who was responsible for her death.

But her eyes wouldn't open, her mouth couldn't move, and there was no way to halt the imminence of her untimely death. As she heard the scoop of the shovel once again her mind raced down a rabbit hole, into total darkness.

"Tamara."

The sound of her name brought her out of the darkness and up off the chair, fight-or-flight adrenaline spiking through her.

"Hey, it's okay. You were asleep."

She stared at Seth's face and she wanted to weep because his handsome features instantly calmed her racing heart, the concern in his eyes immediately pulled her from the dark hole where she'd fallen. "I was dreaming," she finally said. "Bad dreams about the dunes."

His eyes darkened. "Then I'm glad I woke you up.

It's almost four. I decided to call it an early day. There's nothing more I can do here right now."

She nodded, still a bit dazed from her dream as she followed him down the hallway and out the front door of the building.

"I have the sheriff checking out Sam Clemmons a little more closely," he said when they were in the truck and headed back to the house. "I told them to see if he or his parents owned any other property around the area. They've already checked out his place, but his family might own an old farmhouse or acreage just out of town."

"Let's hope they find some answers," she replied. "I laid out some hamburger to defrost this morning so I'll make a meat loaf for dinner." She paused a moment, playing over her dream in her mind. "He called me an ostrich."

"Who did?" Seth shot her a quick glance.

"The man who buried me. He called me an ostrich and said I belonged in the sand." Her heartbeat accelerated as she consciously willed herself back to the nightmare he'd pulled her from.

She saw Seth's hands tighten on the steering wheel. "Was it just part of a crazy dream or do you think it was a real memory?"

"Definitely a memory," she replied. "I don't know how I'm sure about that, but I am. And something else, I think he took me from the rest area outside town. I remember stopping there and I remember a man with a dog."

She could feel the tension that suddenly wafted off Seth as he pulled into the driveway. "Is there a rest area outside town?" she asked, sudden doubts making her wonder if it was just a dream or a true memory.

"Five miles outside the city limits on the north side. It's a little park area with bathrooms and a place to walk your dog." He shut off the engine and his eyes glowed with excitement. "If we know he took you at the rest stop, then we have the initial crime scene and hopefully that's where we'll find some kind of evidence."

He was out of the truck before he'd finished speaking. "I need to talk to Atkins. We need to get his crime scene deputies out there immediately."

Tamara got out of the truck and hurriedly followed after him. Maybe this was truly the break they needed to solve the case. Perhaps the killer had been careless at the rest area and there would still be some evidence there.

Once they were in the house Seth immediately got on the phone and Tamara busied herself preparing the meat loaf and then popping it into the oven. She found a box of scalloped potatoes, followed the directions on the back of the box and stuck them into the oven, as well. All she needed to do was add a can of green beans and dinner was complete.

Seth had disappeared into his sister's bedroom and she could hear that he was still on the phone, coordinating whatever search was about to take place.

He was gone almost an hour and by that time Tamara had pulled both the potatoes and the small meat loaf from the oven and had the green beans simmering on the stove.

"We've got everyone ready to head to the rest stop. Want to take a ride?" he asked.

She should have known that he'd want to be in the thick of things. Not only was it his job, but it was always who he was as an FBI agent, as a man. She glanced helplessly at the food and then back at him. "Just let me cover things up—we can microwave it later—and then I'll be ready."

She wasn't ready. Minutes later as she got into the truck with Seth, she could feel the excitement wafting from him, but a sense of dread filled her as she thought about returning to the place from her dreams.

It had to be real. She couldn't have dreamed about a rest stop she'd never been to, and the idea of going back to the first scene of the crime created a tight pressure in her chest. Whatever had happened there had occurred before she'd been found in the dunes.

Did the man with the dog have anything to do with what had happened to her? Or were they just meaningless elements in her dream?

When they got to the rest area would she suddenly remember the face of the man who had tried to kill her? Would she remember those horrifying moments when he'd laid her down and then begun to methodically cover her with sand?

Was she about to come face-to-face in her mind with the Sandman?

Chapter Eleven

Seth was hoping that if her dream was right, then the rest area had been the point of her abduction. Nobody had checked the area because it wasn't in the city limits and there had been no reason for them to even consider it as having anything to do with the crime.

He hated taking her back, but was hoping that by being there, by retracing some of her steps, she might remember something important.

"I was on my way to visit my Aunt Rose in Tulsa," she said suddenly.

He looked at her in surprise. "Then why hasn't anyone heard from your aunt when you didn't show up there?"

"It was a surprise visit. I hadn't told her I was coming. I just got up one morning and decided to take the drive and stay with her for a couple of days. She's not my real aunt…she was a friend of my mother's and while we aren't super close, we try to stay in touch every couple of weeks by phone." Her face was pale, her features filled with tension in the waning daylight.

"Is this too hard on you, Tamara? We can go back to the house if you can't do this." He'd hate to miss the initial crime scene investigation, but he'd do it if she wanted to.

"No, I need to do this," she replied, the force of her words at odds with the frailty of her body language, the sheer vulnerability that shone from her eyes.

As he drove he couldn't help but shoot surreptitious glances at her, trying to gauge her emotions as the miles clicked off. Would the scene of her abduction unlock the last of her memories? And would she be able to handle those memories if they came rushing back?

He realized he was scared for her…afraid for her mental health…afraid for her very sanity.

"An ostrich. Why would he call me an ostrich? Did I see something I shouldn't have? Or not see something I should have?"

He felt her gaze on him, intense yet bewildered. "I can't imagine," he replied. "I wish I had all the answers for you, Tamara. I wish I could shoulder the pain of what you've gone through."

She leaned back against the seat and sighed. "I'm afraid to remember," she admitted in a small voice.

"What you must keep in mind is that you've already endured whatever happened to you and you survived. Your memories can't hurt you. You're a survivor, Tamara, and you've already lived through whatever your memories bring to you." He flashed her a forced grin. "You're tough and I know you can handle this."

She cast him a wry glance and released a tremulous sigh. "I hope you're good at reading character."

"It's one of my strengths," he assured her. However, this case had made him doubt that sentiment. In all the people he'd interviewed he'd read both strengths and weaknesses but he wasn't sure he'd sensed a psychopathic killer.

Of course, psychopaths were difficult to read because they were so adept at appearing normal. The mask they wore in their everyday life was firmly in place and only slipped when they finally lost control of their impulses and compulsions.

"I think it's almost over," she said, pulling him from his thoughts.

"What do you mean?" he asked. Ahead he could see the rest area and the congregation of official vehicles and officers awaiting their arrival.

"I just have this thrum inside me that makes me feel like something is about to happen...something is about to blow."

So she felt it, too. The ticking time bomb that he'd felt for the past couple of days.

He pulled to the curb beside the sheriff's car and shut off the engine. He was about to unbuckle his seat belt when she stopped him by placing a hand on his arm.

Her eyes shimmered as she tightened her grip on his arm. "I just want you to know that whatever happened to me was worth it since it brought you to me. I'll never forget you, Seth Hawkins, and I have no regrets about anything that happened between us."

An uncomfortable laugh escaped him. "You act like you're never going to see me again. We're just going to get out and look around and then we'll be back at Linda's to eat that dinner you made."

She nodded absently, her gaze captured on the brick building that had the men's restroom on one side and the ladies' on the other. The whole area was a parklike setting with big shade trees and short walking trails.

"I remember being here," she said. "I decided to make a quick pit stop here before heading on to Aunt Rose's house."

Seth opened his door and she followed suit. As she joined him on the sidewalk in front of where they'd parked he reached for her hand, wanting to support her through this ordeal.

Sheriff Atkins nodded at them both. "We haven't done anything yet. We were waiting for the two of you to see if Tamara's memory might be jogged by being here."

She let go of Seth's hand and took several steps toward the ladies' side of the building. "I was here. It was just starting to get dark." Her voice was faint, as if coming from a dream. "I went inside. There was nobody else around."

"No cars parked in the area?" Tom asked.

She shook her head. "Not when I went inside. I was the only one here." She stepped up to the building and placed a hand on one of the tan bricks. She raised her head as if to smell the fresh scent of the nearby pine trees.

Seth wasn't sure if she was steadying herself by holding on to the building or exploring the surroundings with all her senses. Touch…smell…she was in the moment of memory and he glanced at Tom, indicating that everyone stay quiet while Tamara experienced being here once again.

She closed her eyes and drew in another deep breath. Seconds stretched to minutes and still she didn't move.

Finally she opened her eyes and pulled her hand away from the side of the building, a deep frown cutting into the center of her forehead.

"When I came out there was a man. Even though I was alone I didn't feel a bit afraid. He was walking a dog, a cute little pup." She stared at Seth, but he knew she wasn't seeing him. "I bent down to pet the dog and…and…" A helpless expression filled her face. "And that's all I remember."

"Can you tell us what the man looked like?" Tom asked. "Short…tall…anything about him?"

The frown in her forehead deepened. "No. I remember the dog was some kind of a terrier mix, but I don't remember anything about the man other than I wasn't afraid."

"Did you see another vehicle in the parking lot?" Raymond Michaels asked with obvious impatience. "We can't exactly arrest all the people in town who have cute little dogs. We need something more specific."

"And you need to back the hell off," Seth said, a steely strength beneath his soft voice.

"Get the team together and start going through the bathrooms," Tom said to Raymond. "Maybe you'll find something specific in there."

"I'm sorry," she said miserably. Seth reached for her hand and she grabbed it, holding tight. "I remember the dog, I have no memory of the man. I remember leaning down and touching the soft fur of the dog, but after that my mind is blank."

"It's okay, you're doing the best you can." Seth wanted to take the haunted glaze from her eyes, to assure her that nobody expected anything from her. She'd lived through whatever had happened to her and that was enough.

"I'll make sure my men go over this place with a fine-tooth comb," Tom said. "We'll check the building and the surrounding area and parking lots. I doubt that the trash has been picked up out here since Tamara was here. We'll cart it all back to the office and see if our killer threw something away."

Seth nodded. "I'm taking Tamara back to Linda's place." He'd noticed that she'd begun to shiver despite the heat of the night air.

"I was a woman alone in an isolated area. Why wasn't I afraid to approach the man? Why didn't I go right to my car and leave?" she asked. But they were questions without answers at the moment.

Her shivering intensified and Seth dropped her hand and instead wrapped an arm around her shoulders. "Come on, let's go home."

"I was stupid. I let some stranger get close enough to me to take me, to drug me or something and then he took me to the sand dunes and buried me." Her voice rose with an edge of hysteria. "I heard the scrape of the shovel. I felt the heat of the sun on my face as he buried my body. 'You're nothing but an ostrich,' he said. What does that mean?" She looked to Tom and then back to Seth. "For God's sake could somebody please tell me what that means?"

Seth squeezed her closer against him. "Come on, honey. Let's get out of here." With a nod to Tom, knowing that he and his men would probably work through half the night, Seth led Tamara back to his truck.

It was a long, silent drive back to Linda's and Seth's

heart ached as he realized she'd pulled into herself, and he wasn't sure if he should attempt to interact with her or just leave her alone to process whatever was going through her head.

He didn't want to remind her that when she'd been taken from here she hadn't been taken directly to the dunes, that there was still another place that must contain horror for her someplace in this small town.

When they reached Linda's she went directly into the kitchen and began to reheat the meal for dinner. It was as if she needed to do something to keep herself whole and functioning.

It was at that moment, as she stood in front of the microwave, that Seth realized the depth of his love for her. He'd never felt this way about any woman and now he understood why people married, why they took a chance at happily-ever-after even though statistically it seemed as if the odds weren't in their favor.

His love for her filled him up, swelled in his chest until he felt as if he might explode, but instead he sank down on the sofa with a weariness of spirit.

For the first time in his life he understood what it felt like to love somebody, and if events worked out as they expected she would go back to Amarillo and he would return to Kansas City. All too quickly he would also learn how painful it was to tell that somebody goodbye.

THEY WERE BOTH QUIET as they ate their meal. Tamara had no idea what was going on in Seth's head, but in her own was a cluster of emotions and thoughts that battled against each other.

The meat loaf and potatoes couldn't begin to take

away the taste of fear that lingered in the back of her throat as the sensations of being at the rest area played again and again in her head.

There was no question in her mind that was where she'd been taken. Whether the man with his dog had anything to do with her abduction or somebody else who she didn't remember had come along and taken her, she couldn't answer. She only knew that standing in the lush grass just outside the building had shot a sense of terror into the back of her throat that she couldn't quite swallow.

As bad as that was, she felt like an utter failure. She'd remembered so much, being at the rest stop, anticipating the last of her drive to her surrogate aunt's house, even the man with his little dog. But she hadn't been able to identify anything about the man. She hadn't noticed a vehicle in the parking area.

Why hadn't she been more careful? She was a grown woman, one who rarely took chances of any kind. So why would she allow a strange man to get close enough to her to grab her or do whatever he'd done to her? It didn't make sense. Nothing about all of this made any sense at all.

It wasn't until they were finished eating and had moved to the living room that she finally talked to Seth about all that was going on in her brain.

"I'm not a careless woman. I know about personal space and checking my surroundings when I'm out shopping or running errands," she said. "Yet, I'm positive when whoever took me approached, I felt no danger."

"Maybe because of the dog?"

She hesitated and then shook her head. "I don't think so. I've heard the stories of perverts dragging around dogs to entice children and vulnerable women closer to them. There has to be another reason I felt safe enough to let him get close enough to grab me. For all I know the man with the dog had nothing to do with it. Maybe he drove away and somebody else arrived before I got into my car."

A sigh of frustration escaped her. "I feel like such a failure. I was so sure once the memories started coming back I'd have a face, or at least an impression of the man who took me. But I've got nothing. And now you have nothing."

"That's not true," he protested. "We now have the scene of the initial kidnapping. Who knows what the crime scene investigators might find that will lead us to the killer. Tamara, don't beat yourself up."

"I can't help it. I feel so stupid. How did I allow myself to become a victim?"

She grabbed his arm and held tight. "I'm not just scared, but I'm also so angry about it all. I want to find the man who did this to me and kill him, I want to stab his eyes out and bury him in the sand." Seth pulled her into his arms.

Leaning weakly against him she hit his chest with her fist, an ineffectual blow that caused him no pain but that he knew released some of hers.

She hadn't shown anger since the moment of her rescue and he considered her rage now to be healthy and healing.

He had no idea how much time passed with her hitting his chest, venting the depth of her anger at an unknown assailant who had forever changed her life. Finally she leaned against him weakly, obviously spent.

He stroked her hair and simply held her. Once again his wealth of love for her buoyed up inside him, tormenting the tip of his tongue in a need to be spoken. But he knew that telling her how he felt about her would only make things worse for them both.

He had no idea what filled her with dread about returning to her home in Amarillo, but sooner than later she'd have to go back and face it—she had to go back to the life she'd had before she'd been kidnapped from a rest area, kept someplace for hours and then buried in a sand dune in a small town where she'd just been passing through.

Finally she raised her face to look at him. The anger was gone, the fear had disappeared and the only expression on her face was naked need and a hungry desire.

"Just one more night, Seth. Make love with me one last time and I won't ask for anything from you again."

"Tamara," he began to protest despite his desire to do exactly as she asked. "We can't do this anymore. I can't do this anymore." He gently shoved against her so that she sat up rather than leaned against him.

Her lower lip trembled but he refused to be swayed by anything she did, anything she said. One of them had to be strong. One of them had to be smart, and it was smart not to get in any deeper than he was, than he sensed she was already.

"I care about you, Tamara. I care about you more than I've ever cared about any other woman, but as I've told you before, this isn't real life. You've mentioned several times that there is something or someone causing you anxiety whenever you think about going home. You have issues that obviously need to be addressed there."

He got up from the sofa, his shoulders feeling as if the weight of her entire life rested on them. "I don't know what your world was like before you were found in the dunes and nothing we do here and now is going to fix it. Only you can do that and it would be foolish for us to continue to pretend that there's nothing in this world but the here and now, the you and me."

She gazed down at her hands now folded in her lap. "I know you're right, but I don't want you to be right. Be wrong, Seth, for one last night be wrong."

God, he wanted to make the wrong choice. He wanted to hold her in his arms one last time, to taste the fiery heat of her kisses once more. His body ached with the need to connect with hers, to take her again not only for his own pleasure, but for hers.

But the fact that he wanted her so badly, the realization of how much he loved her made him strong. "I can't, Tamara. We can't play at this anymore. It's getting late and I have a feeling it will be an early morning. It's best if we just say our good-nights and leave it at that."

She held his gaze for a long moment, as if hoping to hear a different answer. He broke the gaze, looking beyond her as she finally got up from the sofa.

Only then did he look at her once again. She appeared small and defeated but he knew there was nothing more he could do for her.

"Then, I guess I'll just say good night," she said.

He nodded. As she walked down the hallway toward her room, he knew that somehow in the last twenty-five words that he'd said he'd broken her heart.

Chapter Twelve

It was time to go home. As Tamara sat in the break room the next afternoon she knew it was time to say good-bye to Amber Lake and go back to where she belonged.

She couldn't be any more use to the case and she'd allowed herself to develop a depth of feelings for Seth that obviously had no future. She had most of her memories back now, at least enough of them to return home and pick up what had been her life.

She had no idea what made her feel so anxious about returning to her apartment, but whatever it was, it was time she go back and face it.

Tonight she intended to tell Seth that first thing in the morning she planned to rent a car and go back. She'd eventually make new plans to visit Aunt Rose and would try to put all this behind her. Once there she'd have to deal with her car insurance and get some kind of wheels, she'd need to catch up on her web mistress duties and she'd have to figure out a way to stop loving Seth Hawkins.

It was for the best. There was no reason for her to continue to linger here when she wasn't helping anyone and each and every minute with Seth would be an exquisite form of torture.

The crime scene investigators had come up with little to show after spending half the night at the rest area. The problem was it was a public place and fingerprints and DNA samples were plenty.

According to the scuttlebutt she'd heard from the deputies who drifted in and out of the break room there was little optimism that the trash cans in the area would yield any clues.

There had been no more mention of her seeing a therapist or a hypnotist and she was convinced that what little she'd been able to give them last night at the rest area was all she had to give.

She couldn't give them an impression of the man, had no facial features to offer them, and maybe it was because she'd never seen him coming. Maybe the person who had kidnapped her had sneaked up behind her and somehow rendered her unconscious before she'd seen anything about him.

Breakfast had been awkward, the first awkwardness she'd felt between herself and Seth. She didn't want to hang around until things got worse than awkward.

She hadn't seen Seth since they'd arrived at the office that morning. Once again it had been Deputy Broadwick who had brought her some lunch and had sat with her and visited for a few minutes before he'd disappeared back to his duties.

As she thought of the night before her cheeks burned with a touch of embarrassment. She'd practically begged Seth to make love to her and she couldn't even be upset with him for refusing. He'd been right. This wasn't real life and she had to stop clinging to him, wanting him, pretending that somehow this life with him in Linda's house in Amber Lake could be real.

Definitely time to go, and hopefully the man who had taken her wouldn't follow her home. She hoped something would break that would allow Seth and the sheriff and his men to make an arrest within the next couple of days.

Besides, she knew the killer was a local and she had a feeling if she put some miles between him and herself she'd be safe. Unfortunately, that meant he'd turn his attention to another woman.

It was just after five when Seth came into the lounge and it was obvious by the slump of his shoulders, the terse set of his mouth, that nothing positive had happened again today.

He looked bone-weary and she could only imagine the pressure on him and all the others to solve the crime, to put the bad man behind bars.

"How about we stop by the café for some dinner before heading home," he suggested as they got into his truck.

"Sounds fine to me." Maybe it would be easier to tell him what she'd decided about leaving in the morning over a meal in a public place. At least then she hopefully wouldn't have to worry about embarrassing herself by crying or accidentally confessing that she was madly in love with him.

It took them only a few minutes to get to the café and be seated at a table in the back where he ordered the special of chicken-fried steak and mashed potatoes and she decided to have the roast beef with vegetables.

As they waited for their meals, they chatted a bit

about nothing, the awkwardness that had been between them that morning lingering on.

Again and again her attention was drawn to the sign advertising the caramel pie, her thoughts returned to those moments in the rest area and her brain worked to find any hidden details she could offer Seth as a parting gift. But there was nothing.

"I'm leaving in the morning," she said, breaking the uncomfortable veil of silence.

He looked at her in stunned surprise. "What are you talking about?"

"I'm renting a car and heading back home. I can't do anything more here."

"But there are still things we don't know. If what you remembered about the rest area is true, then you were abducted around seven or eight at night and yet you weren't discovered until the next afternoon. We need to find out about those missing hours now more than ever."

Tamara picked up her glass of iced tea and took a sip and then set the glass back on the table. "I've done all I can, Seth." She didn't look at him, but rather kept her gaze on the wooden table. "Maybe I'm never supposed to remember that time, maybe my brain will always protect me from whatever happened during those hours. All I know is that it's time for me to get home. It's time for Linda and Samantha to have their house back and for me to get on with the rest of my life."

"Are you sure you're ready to go back?"

She looked up at him and wanted to fall into the soft gray of his eyes. He cared about her. She knew that without question. She'd never forget that moment when she'd come to consciousness in the sand and her first sight had been those kind, calm eyes of his. It might have been that single second of connection that had made her fall in love with him.

"Ready or not, it's time," she replied. "I have clients ready for me to get back to work. If I remember anything else I can always call you. But it's foolish for me to just hang around here and put off the inevitable."

"But how will you get home? We haven't even found your car."

"That's what rental cars are for. I'm sure there's a place here in town or nearby where I can rent a car to get back to Amarillo. Once there I'll talk to my car insurance company and see what they can work out. As far as I'm concerned, my car is officially a stolen vehicle. I'll manage."

He looked as if he wanted to change her mind, but he leaned back in his chair and released a sigh of obvious resignation. "Of course you'll manage. You're one of the strongest women I've ever met."

As she thought of leaving him, she didn't feel strong. She felt as weak as a baby, ready to weep with a kind of despair she'd never felt before about a man. She didn't even remember feeling this way after her divorce from Jason.

Thankfully at that moment the waitress arrived with their meals and the conversation turned to the tenderness of the roast, the richness of his gravy and anything else that had nothing to do with the crimes, the killer or her leaving Amber Lake behind.

An early twilight stole over the area as they left the café. Clouds chased across the sky, portending the possibility of a rain sometime overnight.

"Surely you won't want to take off if it's raining in the morning," Seth said once they were back in his truck and headed to Linda's.

"I can drive in the rain. All I'll need your help with is getting a rental car. Once I get home and can get my banking situation straightened out, I'll make it all right with you."

"I'm not worried about that. Wally down at the gas station on Main is also part of a chain of rental cars. He's always got one or two cars available. I'm sure we can get you set up without a problem."

As much as her heart ached, she knew she was making the right decision. It was time to say goodbye to Amber Lake. It was time to say goodbye to Seth.

They hadn't been inside the house for long, and Tamara had just gotten comfortable on the sofa, when Seth's cell phone rang. He listened intently, his features suddenly tense…excited. Tamara straightened up, wondering who the caller was and what they were saying to him.

He listened another minute or two longer. "We'll be there as soon as we can," he replied, and then clicked off and slid his phone into his pocket.

"That was Atkins. They believe there's another body at the dunes, but none of them have moved in to the crime scene location yet."

Tamara's heart dropped as she realized another woman had been buried. "But maybe she's still alive. I was."

"But your face hadn't been buried. Apparently all they can see of this person is part of a hand. The good news is they caught Sam Clemmons on his ATV riding away from the scene. Atkins is sure he's our man. This is the kind of proof we've needed. He's the Sandman and he's in custody."

"That's wonderful!" Tamara exclaimed. At least she'd leave here in the morning knowing that the man who had tried to bury her alive was in jail. She just wished he'd been caught before another woman had died.

"Come on, let's go. They're waiting for us," he said as he strapped on his shoulder holster.

"They're waiting for you. You go and I'll spend my time here packing up for the morning."

He frowned and opened his mouth as if to protest, but she stopped whatever he was about to say by holding up a hand. "You said it yourself, the bad guy is in custody. I'll be fine here and to be honest, I don't want to see another crime scene like that."

His frown deepened. "You'll lock the doors? Don't let anyone inside?"

"Of course not," she replied. "But it sounds like the danger has finally passed."

For the first time since he'd gotten the call a smile curved his lips. "Yeah and Sam makes sense. He's been at the top of our suspect list since the beginning. We just needed something to tie him to the burials. Tonight we got our break. He was actually seen fleeing from the crime scene. Now, let's hope before you leave here tomorrow morning I'll know what the deal is about you being an ostrich."

She nodded. "Get out of here. They're waiting for you." She could feel his excitement, the need in him to move, to get to the scene.

He left and she carefully locked the door behind him. Alone. Time to pack up and face whatever discordant music awaited her in her real life.

She went into the guest room and realized she didn't even have a suitcase to pack with the things she'd bought since being here. She grabbed a large black plastic garbage bag from the kitchen and carried it with her back to the bedroom. She had just begun to fill it when the doorbell rang.

Her heart thumped a hard rhythm for a moment even though she told herself that Sam Clemmons was the Sandman and he was in custody, caught at the scene of the latest crime.

She hurried to the living room and moved the curtain aside an inch, just enough that she could see the khaki uniform of Steven Bradley, the lovesick puppy man. She relaxed. He was probably here to do a check-in on Samantha and Scooter.

Tamara unlocked the door and eased it open at the same time Steven offered her a bright smile and opened the screen door. "Hey, Tamara, just wanted to stop by and say hi to Samantha and her new furry friend."

"I'm sorry, Steven, they aren't here right now. Samantha and Scooter are staying at her dad's house for a few weeks."

"Oh, okay. Maybe I'll check in with them there. Or, maybe not."

Before Tamara sensed any danger to herself, she jumped as the sting of a needle plunged into her arm. "Hey," she exclaimed and stumbled backward a step.

Almost instantaneously her leg muscles collapsed, sending her to the floor in a heap. Trouble. The word screamed in her head. She was in trouble. She tried to move her arms in an attempt to get back to her feet, but nothing was working. She was paralyzed.

"Don't even try to fight it," Steven said as he stepped into the foyer and picked her up in his arms just as he probably did wounded dogs. "It's a special concoction that took me months to perfect. Your heart will keep beating, but you can't move."

He carried her out of the house and with a quick glance around the neighborhood he moved to the trunk of his car where he placed her inside and slammed the lid.

Darkness. She smelled the scent of tire rubber, of oil and of impending doom. She was in trouble and nobody knew it because they thought they had the Sandman in custody. But they were wrong.

The Sandman had her in his custody.

Chapter Thirteen

By the time Seth pulled up to the main entrance of the dunes, the last gasp of sun was attempting to shine through the thickening layer of clouds. Within the next thirty minutes or so it would be dark.

He saw Sam Clemmons handcuffed and locked into the back of Atkins's patrol car. Sam's quad runner sat nearby. Atkins approached, his face holding a mixture of the same emotions Seth felt at the moment. It was relief and elation that Sam had been caught, mingled with the dread of discovering another dead woman.

"Since we don't have the funds for fancy surveillance cameras, I've had my deputies doing drive-bys here, especially during the nighttime hours. Deputy Michaels did an evening run by here and saw that." Atkins pointed in the distance where a hand protruded from the sand. "At the same time he saw Sam riding off hellbent for leather. He went after Sam and got him in custody, then called me to let me know what was going on."

Seth looked toward where the hand appeared to glow almost translucently in the last pale glow of sunlight. "He didn't take much time to hide this one. Anyone coming in this way would see the body part. What's Sam saying?"

"That he had nothing to do with it, that he was just sneaking in a quick ride. He's sobbing and snotting his innocence all over the back of my car, but him being here again is the kind of coincidence I just don't believe in."

Seth thought about the night he'd caught Sam lurking across the street from the house. Apparently he'd been casing out the house, seeking a new entrance in an attempt to grab Tamara. He'd definitely fooled Seth, who'd believed his story about feeling bad because he hadn't helped dig her out of the sand.

Atkins clapped Seth on the back. "We've got him now. He's not going to hurt anyone again. Finally my town will be rid of the Sandman."

Seth nodded. "And now I guess it's time to do the hard part. Find out who his latest victim is. Let's get photographs of the scene first, especially ones of Sam's quad and any of the tracks he made in the sand. We've only got a few minutes of daylight left—you might want to get some artificial lighting in place and ready."

"We're a small town. We don't have any special lighting for night work, but I'll see what I can do." As Atkins left Seth to take care of the initial business, Seth stared out over the dunes and tried not to think about the fact that tomorrow morning Tamara would be gone.

Maybe it was a blessing that she couldn't remember what had happened to her after she'd been kidnapped from the rest area. Maybe she'd never have to remember whatever happened in those missing hours. Her brain had obviously kept those memories from her because they were too heinous to remember.

There was nothing more he'd like than to explore a

true relationship with her, invite her to Kansas City to share his life. But more than once she'd mentioned some unpleasant, unfinished business awaiting her in Amarillo. He couldn't ask her for a future until she knew all there was to know about her past. There might be something in Amarillo that would halt her from having any kind of a future with him.

Besides, she might get away from this place, away from him and realize that her feelings for him were formed in that single instant of eye contact when he'd pulled her from the sand, that what she felt for him all along was nothing more than gratitude and a sense of safety she'd needed while she'd been here.

He shoved thoughts of Tamara out of his head as Atkins had the deputies park their cars so that their headlights shone directly on the crime scene area.

With feet weighted by dread, Seth and Tom advanced toward the macabre scene where the hand protruded from the sand. Who were they going to find beneath the sand? For sure a brunette. Seth vaguely wondered what brunette had done such damage to Sam that it had turned him into a killer. Did he get a kick out of riding his quad over his own personal cemetery? Were there bodies out here that hadn't even been discovered yet?

Seth didn't even want to go there. The idea of this playground for dirt-bike riders and quad runners being a burial pit just beneath the surface made his stomach queasy.

As he waited for everyone to get into place and the photos to be taken, he walked over to Atkins's car and opened the back door.

"I didn't do it," Sam cried. "I was just out here sneaking in a ride before I have to go to work at the bar. It's been tough since they closed the dunes. I'm, like, addicted to riding." He bent his head to wipe his nose on his shirt shoulder. "I saw that hand and totally freaked. I was driving away to get to my truck so I could get help when Deputy Michaels came after me. I stopped to tell him, but he threw me down on the ground and cuffed me."

Sam's sniffling stopped and his eyes narrowed. "He kicked me in the side a couple of times even though I was down and already cuffed."

Seth wasn't surprised and he intended to speak to Atkins before he left Amber Lake about Michaels's penchant for bullying. But if Sam really was the Sandman Seth could understand Michaels's added touch of finesse to the arrest. Seth fought his own desire to punch the kid as he thought of Tamara's face shining up from her sand grave.

"What's up with the ostrich?" Seth asked.

Sam stared at him in what appeared to be genuine puzzlement. "What ostrich? What are you talking about?"

Sam looked like nothing more than a scared, barely legal-aged kid, and Seth slammed the car door closed, a disturbing uncertainty simmering inside him.

He wanted to believe that Sam was guilty. It made everything so neat and clean. Bad guy caught, case closed and no more danger of horrendous live burials to the women in Amber Lake, no more danger to Tamara.

Desperately, he wanted it to be Sam, but there was just a sliver of uncertainty in his mind about the kid's guilt. It was just a gut feeling that he hoped was wrong.

But when he'd asked Sam about the ostrich, Sam's look of total incomprehension had appeared so genuine.

By the time he walked back to Atkins, it was time to get closer and check out who, exactly, was buried in this latest murder. "I was thinking earlier that hopefully there aren't bodies out here that we don't know about," Seth said as they walked.

"Bite your tongue," Atkins replied and a deep sigh escaped him. "I'll tell you one thing—if there are bodies out here they aren't locals. We've got no missing persons reported in Amber Lake."

"Tamara was taken from the rest area," Seth reminded him.

"I know, and hopefully she's the anomaly and really was the third victim in the beginning of this nightmare. Sam fits the profile for a serial killer. He's about the right age when they begin to kill, he comes from a bad background and he's pretty much a loner."

Seth flashed Tom a terse grin. "That could describe half the men I work with at the FBI." His grin fell as they drew closer to the hand sticking up out of the sand.

It looked odd…the fingers fatter than normal female fingers. "Something's not right," he murmured more to himself than to Tom. As he reached an area close enough to lean down and look closer, he cursed beneath his breath and grabbed the hand. It came loose easily from the sand.

"Hey!" Tom yelped in protest.

"It's not real," Seth said. He stood up and held out the detached forearm. "It's a damn prosthesis."

He stood up and stepped aside, indicating that some of the other deputies complete the dig to see if anything

else had been buried there. His mind raced with sup-
positions. This had been a well-executed trick. Every
law enforcement person working for the town was here.

Heart starting to pound an uneven rhythm of fear,
he yanked his cell phone from his pocket and quickly
punched in Linda's phone number.

One ring. *Pick up, Tamara,* he thought urgently. Two
rings. He clenched the phone more tightly to his ear.
Three rings. Why wasn't she answering? Four rings
and then the click of the answering machine coming
on. Linda's voice filled his ear with her prerecorded
announcement to wait for the beep to leave a message.

"Tamara, it's Seth. Pick up the phone," he said when
the beep had sounded. He was vaguely aware of Tom
stepping closer to him. "Tamara, please, pick up the
phone."

The urgency inside Seth grew to mammoth propor-
tions. Where was she? Why wasn't she answering him?
Because the Sandman had fooled them all. Because
she wasn't there to answer the call. She was with the
Sandman.

His heart crashed against his ribs in sheer terror. "He
bluffed us. He set it up so that all of us would respond
to a body in the dunes so he could get to his real target." Seth could barely keep the tremble from his voice.

"Tamara." Tom said her name flatly, as if she were
already nothing but another tragic victim in a madman's game.

"Send somebody over to my sister's house," Seth
said, although he was certain they would find the house
empty…Tamara gone.

He didn't want to leave here. He needed to think. He

needed to crawl into the mind of the clever man who had set up such a ruse to obtain his ultimate goal. He desperately needed to figure out if he had Tamara, and, if so, then where was he going with her? And how long did Seth have left to try to save her life?

Seth had to do what he did best, delve into the mind of a killer.

Chapter Fourteen

If Tamara wasn't certain she was going to die, she might have found her current situation almost peaceful. She couldn't move, there was no question of somehow escaping or fighting back. And with final resignation all the missing pieces of her memory came rushing back to her.

Steven had been the man with the dog at the rest area, and she hadn't been afraid because he'd been wearing his khaki uniform. He'd looked official and respectable and worked for the city of Amber Lake. Why would she have any reason at all to fear him?

She'd made it so incredibly easy for him, bending over to pet the cute little terrier she now remembered seeing in the animal pound. She also realized that when she'd been in the pound and had needed to get out, had felt as if she was suffocating, it had been because on some deep level she'd recognized the scent that had clung to Steven...a scent of dog and heat and feces.

When she'd gone with Seth, Linda and Samantha to the animal pound to pick out Scooter, it hadn't been her first visit. She'd spent a night and half a day locked in a cage in a back room next to a caged German Shepherd that looked like he'd like nothing better than to tear out her throat.

Each time she'd started to come around, to get the feeling back in her body, Steven would appear to give her another shot, rendering her helpless all over again.

The next afternoon when he'd taken her out of the cage and moved her to the trunk of his car, he'd muttered to her as if she were somebody else…as if she were his mother.

"Just like an ostrich," he'd said. "Bury your head in the sand, that's all that you did when he beat me to within an inch of my life. Mothers are supposed to protect their kids, but you just hid your head in the sand and now I'm going to hide your head for you."

She'd wanted to scream at him, to tell him that she wasn't his mother, that she'd never done anything to harm him, but she couldn't speak. Her lips wouldn't move, her mouth refused to form a single word. She was trapped in her own body with only her brain working overtime.

Along with the memories of what had happened to her immediately following Steven grabbing her came others, as well. Her unhappy marriage to Jason, the final straw that had broken their marriage and finally the reason she'd dreaded going home, the reason for the core of grief inside her.

The casket had been white and barely bigger than a shoebox. The baby had been a little girl, born too early and never having drawn a breath of life.

Grief tore through her and it was impossible to blink away the tears that filled her eyes. It had been that sorrow, along with an abiding loneliness that had filled her apartment in Amarillo, which had made her reluctant to go home.

It had been Seth who had filled up that loneliness, eased any pain that might have been left behind and made her want a future with him, a future filled with all the things that had been absent in her life.

And now it was too late. It was all too late.

The Sandman was going to put her to sleep forever. Her heart beat a slow rhythm despite the fear that filled her as she thought of the scrape of a shovel against the sand, as she thought of the weight of that sand falling first on her feet and legs, then on her midsection and finally covering her face, smothering her to death.

She wished she'd told Seth she loved him. She wished she'd said the actual words to him. Even if he didn't love her back, she wished she had given him the gift of knowing that he was deeply loved.

Too late. Now it was all too late. She hoped it wouldn't be him who found her. She hoped he wouldn't frantically dig in the sand to find her, to try to save her when it was evident she was gone. She didn't want his last image of her to be her dead body.

She forced her thoughts away from Seth and to her current situation. Steven was driving relatively slow, an occasional bump shifting her body. The last bump had shifted her into a position where something sharp poked her in the back, but there was no way for her to move into a more comfortable position.

Was this what it had been like for Rebecca Cook and Vicki Smith? What had been their final thoughts as they'd been driven to their deaths? Had they entertained regrets? Clung to happy memories? Or simply wished for another bump to allow their body to get more comfortable?

The car slowed and the whine of asphalt beneath the tires was replaced by something softer and more bumpy. The dunes? Surely he wouldn't take her there. That's where Seth and Sheriff Atkins and all his men were working a crime scene.

But Seth had mentioned at one point or another that there was more than one way into the dunes and that the area was big enough that it couldn't all be seen by mere eyesight, and by now it was surely dark. Nobody would see him bury her.

Tears once again filled her eyes and fell down the sides of her cheeks as the car came to a stop and the engine was cut. No more time. She'd heard that drowning was a relatively painless death. What about drowning in sand? She had a feeling it was going to be a terrible way to die.

The trunk lid opened, the small light inside radiating out enough that she could see Steven's face. The smile on his lips read of pleasure, but the darkness in his eyes spoke of the need for revenge.

I'm not your mother, her brain screamed inside her head. *Please Steven, don't do this. Don't kill me for any sins you think your mother committed. I didn't commit them.* She tried to put all those emotions into her eyes as he bent over and picked her up in his arms.

"Time for the ostrich to bury her head, just like you did when I was little and Dad was beating the hell out of me," he said as he began to walk.

She could hear the whisper of sand beneath his feet and the terror inside her peaked to where she wished she'd lose her mind, prayed that her heart would stop beating before she heard the very first scrape of the shovel against the sand.

He bent down and dropped her onto the grainy surface and then walked away. They were at the dunes. Someplace, perhaps not so far away from where Seth and the other lawmen were working. If only she could just scream, if she could just crawl, but she could do neither.

"Let's get this show on the road," Steven said from nearby and she heard the first rasp of the shovel against the sand and she knew he had begun to dig her grave.

IT DIDN'T TAKE LONG for Seth to get the information that Tamara wasn't at Linda's place and the front door had been standing wide open.

She was with him. The Sandman. He'd already directed several of the deputies to get in touch with Henry Todd and with Jerome Walker and Ernie Simpson, the other two young men who had been with Sam when Tamara had been discovered.

Raymond Michaels was officially off Seth's suspect list. He couldn't be here and with Tamara at the same time. The one thing Seth refused to do was run out of here half-cocked, with no specific suspect and no known location in mind.

He knew the key to the whole thing was an ostrich. That memory that Tamara had of the perp calling her an ostrich held the key to the killer's identity.

There was no way he could run fast enough to catch a person he didn't know; he couldn't knock on doors and try to gain answers. The time bomb had exploded and if he didn't figure something out fast, Tamara would be dead.

Ostriches. As he paced across the sand, he considered what he did know about the oversize birds. They were too big to fly. They could kill a man with a kick of their powerful legs. He frowned. What else? There had to be something else.

With each tick of his heart, with every blink of his eye, he felt as if time had run out and Tamara was gone and when he thought about that the absence of her nearly cast him to his knees.

Darkness had fallen complete across the dunes, the only lit area being the main entrance where the deputies' car headlights provided illumination.

Ostriches. *Don't bury your head in the sand.* The descriptive saying jumped into his consciousness. "Don't bury your head," he muttered aloud. He'd heard that somewhere recently. Where? Where had he heard something along those lines?

You'd be surprised by how many people just bury their head in the sand. It had been at the animal pound. Steven Bradley. Thoughts flashed through Seth's brain, processing like a minicomputer. Steven in his official uniform would appear safe to a woman alone. Steven had access to a dozen different dogs…dogs to walk in a park…dogs to lure a woman closer.

Seth remembered how the dogs had silenced at Steven's command, how the little terrier had instantly rolled over on his belly when Steven had approached. Had the little pup been looking for a belly scratch or had he been showing complete submission?

The killer liked power and who better to have power

than an animal control officer who wielded authority over cage after cage of helpless animals?

"Steven Bradley," Seth said to Tom as the sheriff approached. "I think it's Steven Bradley. Get somebody to the pound and to his house. See if he can be found at either place." Seth spoke at warp speed, his brain still processing.

"What should I do about Sam?" Tom asked.

"Cut him loose…no, wait." The killer had a pattern. Like an ostrich. Bury their heads in the sand. Seth shot a glance out into the darkness of the dunes beyond where they stood.

"Hold him in custody," Seth said as he hurried toward Sam's quad runner. He heard Sam shout a protest through the closed car window as Seth started it up with a roar.

How cunning, to have all the law in town gathered right here while the Sandman completed his work in another area of the dunes. It was the kind of in-your-face thing that Steven would enjoy…just like leaving the little pile of sand behind when he'd tried to break into Tamara's bedroom.

Seth gunned the engine, grateful that the machine had twin headlights. He powered them on and then began the search, certain in his heart, certain in his very soul that Steven was here someplace with Tamara. The only thing he didn't know for certain was if it was already too late.

Chapter Fifteen

Tamara wished the stars were out. As she lay unmoving on her back, listening to the sounds of her grave being dug she wished there were stars twinkling down on her, a full moon to witness the very last moments of her life.

Steven had been silent as he dug, the scuff of the shovel against the sand a rhythmic white noise as she focused on the last thoughts she wanted in her mind when he buried her.

Seth. She wanted to be thinking about being wrapped in his arms as her feet were covered with sand. She wanted to fantasize that it was his weight covering her as the sand weighed down her middle. She wanted to remember the glow of his eyes, the taste of his lips as the sand finally fell over her face and she drew in her final breath.

She'd been afraid to embrace her love for him fully because of her feeling of something hanging over her head back home. But now she remembered what that something was and realized there was nothing holding her back from loving him completely and forever.

She would die loving him.

Her heart squeezed tight in her chest as the sound

of the digging stopped and Steven's face loomed over hers. "Time for bad mommies to face their punishment."

He crouched down beside her and even though the only light source came from a flashlight he held in his hand, she could see the madness that radiated from his eyes. "You shouldn't have pretended that you didn't see when he beat me with that belt, when he broke my nose. You shouldn't have buried your head in the sand when he twisted my arm until I screamed, when he kicked me so hard I couldn't walk for two days."

Tears oozed from her eyes and she realized they weren't only tears for herself, but also for the little boy Steven Bradley had been, for the torment he'd apparently suffered when he'd been young and helpless.

He'd obviously been a victim of an abusive father and a mother who wouldn't protect him, but that didn't excuse the choices he was making now. That didn't excuse the fact that he was trying to heal his past by killing innocent women.

He'd become a monster and now the monster was about to strike and she couldn't move a muscle to stop him. As he grabbed her arms and began to drag her across the sand to the pit he'd prepared, terror blasted through her head. *Seth,* her brain cried out. She brought into focus in her mind a picture of him smiling, that crazy, sexy grin that filled her with warmth.

She hung on to the vision as she felt herself fall into the pit and as the first shovelful of sand covered her feet.

SETH DROVE WITH RECKLESS abandon, seeking a light, a vehicle, something that might give him a clue as to where in the dunes the Sandman was at work.

Was it already too late? So much time had already passed. He couldn't even be sure how quickly Steven had moved in to take Tamara from Linda's place. She would have opened the door to him. She would have assumed he was stopping by to check on the dog and see Samantha. There would have been no sense of danger because she thought the Sandman was already in custody.

He couldn't stand the thought of having to dig Tamara out of the sand again, only this time too late to save her.

The thought of having to dig her up, of never seeing her smile again made his stomach roil as if he needed to vomit. They had to be here somewhere and he had to find them in time.

Back and forth he raced in a gridlike pattern, hanging tight over the bumps, flying over the tops of the dunes as his heart beat a heart attack rhythm.

He'd been riding for only about five minutes or so when it struck him. Deadman's Bluff. He had a feeling Steven would find it amusing for Tamara to be buried at Deadman's Bluff after the bluff he'd pulled off with the fake arm.

Seth headed in that direction, praying that his instincts were right and he wasn't wasting precious minutes going in the wrong direction.

He had to go with his gut instincts; it was all he had left. His heart had been ripped out the moment he'd realized that the hand in the sand was plastic and the Sandman wasn't seated in the back of Tom's patrol car.

Although he had a need for speed, he also knew that if he approached Deadman's Bluff too fast in the dark he'd fly right over the edge and could be seriously injured. Despite the urgency that drummed inside him, he eased back on the gas.

As the bluff approached the clouds momentarily broke up and a faint shaft of moonlight filtered down. In that moonlight, Seth saw him...Steven Bradley in his uniform, a shovel in his hand.

With a roar of rage, Seth jumped from the quad, which continued to race forward and flew off the edge of the bluff. He raced toward Steven and the young man turned, his face radiating a killing rage. Steven raised the shovel and swung it, managing to connect with Seth's shoulder.

Pain seared up his arm, but the pain was minimized by the fact that he could see Tamara in the sand, her legs covered, but the rest of her sand-free.

He'd gotten to her in time and knowing that numbed the pain and gave him a strength that surged up inside him. But Steven had the strength of madness, of nothing to lose shining from his eyes.

He advanced toward Seth again with the shovel but this time when he swung Seth sidestepped the blow and dove for Steven's legs. Steven fell to the ground with a grunt and let go of the shovel handle.

Instead he used the end of a flashlight in an attempt to pummel Seth's head and shoulders. A hard smack to the side of the head had stars dancing in Seth's head and he realized if he didn't get control of the situation, there would be a double tragedy tonight.

Seth managed to grab one end of the flashlight and together the two men wrestled. Sand flew into Seth's eyes, making them burn and tear. Any skin that was bared became quickly abraded by the rough land surface.

He punched Steven, an uppercut to his jaw that snapped his head upward. Steven's hold on the flashlight momentarily released. Seth threw the light to the side of where they lay, precariously close to the edge of the bluff.

Steven appeared stunned as Seth pulled himself to his knees and went for his gun in the holster. He should have had it out and ready before now, but all he'd been thinking about was finding Tamara alive. Now he had to make sure he lived to keep her alive.

Before he could grab his gun to end the fight, Steven was on him again, punching and kicking as they once again rolled on the ground, first Steven on top of him and then him on top of Steven.

Panic welled up inside him as he recognized that they were so close to the edge of the bluff a single wrong move, a simple half turn would plunge either one or both of them over the edge.

In the distance, sirens sounded. Backup was on the way, but there was no way to guess if they'd arrive in time. Tamara had yet to make a move, which meant some kind of drug still possessed her body and as a light rain began he worried that the sand around her might shift, that she would end up dead despite his greatest efforts.

"She has to be buried," Steven screamed at the same time lightning slashed the sky and a second later thunder clapped overhead. "She spent my whole childhood with her head buried in the sand. I'm just finishing the job."

Seth had no idea who he was talking about, but at that moment he bucked and rolled and Steven slid off the lip of the bluff, the only thing visible his fingers digging into the sand to keep him from falling.

A patrol car pulled up and light filled the area. Seth scrambled to the lip of the bluff and grabbed both of Steven's wrists in an effort to keep him from falling.

Below where Steven hung the quad runner lay on its back, the headlights still on and steam hissing from some ruptured hose.

"Please help me. Don't let go," Steven said. There was nothing of a crazed killer in his eyes as he looked up at Seth. He looked like just a scared kid, afraid to fall, afraid to die.

And yet at least two women had met heinous deaths at his hands. He'd tried to kill Tamara. An emotional battle momentarily warred inside Seth's head.

It would be so easy to just let go. If the fall didn't kill him it would probably severely injure him. The crime scene photos from Rebecca and Vicki's murders flashed through his head. The memory of digging Tamara out of the sand was forever etched inside his brain.

Just let go, a little voice whispered inside Seth's head. Let him die in the dunes where he'd left two women dead.

But Seth wasn't a murderer, and intentionally letting go would be murder. With all the strength he possessed, he attempted to pull Steven up.

As he worked, he was conscious of the sound of footsteps running toward him and a moment later Tom knelt beside him and together they got Steven onto safe ground.

Tom rolled him over to cuff him while Seth ran to Tamara. The rain had begun in earnest, but he scarcely noticed as he dug the sand away from her legs and then picked her up in his arms.

She was deadweight, the only emotion on her face radiating out from her eyes. Relief and love, they were both there. He held her tight and at that moment Raymond Michaels arrived in his car.

Seth carried Tamara there and once he and Tamara were loaded in the backseat, Michaels took off for the hospital.

"It's over," Seth murmured to Tamara. "It's over and you're safe."

Her head gave a barely imperceptible nod as her fingers flexed outward. Seth's heart jumped as he realized whatever drug she'd been given must be wearing off.

Raymond said nothing on the drive and Seth was grateful for his silence. Seth didn't want to hear the deputy run his mouth. He just wanted to focus on the woman in his arms, and to listen to the slow even breathing that let him know Tamara was okay.

They were met at the hospital by orderlies and a gurney. Apparently Tom had called ahead to let the hospital staff know that they were coming.

Tamara was whisked away, Michaels left assumedly to return to the crime scene and Seth sank down in a chair in the waiting room, his heart still pounding with residual adrenaline.

She was safe and the case was over. He'd done his job and now the town of Amber Lake would never have to worry about the Sandman again.

The hardest part was yet to come. He loved Tamara,

but he intended to tell her goodbye. She had to go home and figure out her life and how this experience had changed her. There was absolutely no doubt in his mind that she had changed. Everyone who was touched by murder, by terror, was somehow transformed.

He loved her and he knew she believed herself to be in love with him, but her feelings for him had to be all muddied by this experience. He couldn't trust that she knew right now if what she believed she felt for him was real.

It was time he cut his losses and run, head back to where he belonged and maybe with time he'd forget about Tamara and his time with her here in Amber Lake.

He'd been seated in the waiting room about an hour when the doctor came out. Dr. Kane took one look at him and frowned. "She's doing fine, but you look like you need a little cleanup and maybe an ice pack or two."

"I'm fine. Can I see her?"

"Not until you let me clean you up. One look at your ugly mug and Tamara might go into shock. Come on." Dr. Kane gestured for Seth to follow him in through the emergency room doors.

Seth followed him to a small cubicle where he winced as Dr. Kane cleaned off his face with an antiseptic swab. "You're already bruising on the side of your face. Are you dizzy? Feel sick to your stomach?"

"I'm fine. I just want to see Tamara." He needed to see her, to assure himself that she was really okay.

"She's being moved to a room for the night. Whatever drug she was given seems to have worn off but I'm keeping her for observation for a night. You know that cut on your chin could probably use a stitch or two."

Seth couldn't even remember how his chin had gotten wounded. The fight with Steven now seemed like a distant dream with fuzzy parts he didn't care to remember. All that mattered was that Tamara was okay.

"I'm fine," Seth said with a touch of impatience.

Dr. Kane stood from his little stool. "Okay, she's in room 124."

With that information Seth was out the door and hurrying down the hallway. He just needed to make sure she was all right. He now understood the need that had driven Sam the night he'd been standing across the street from the house…the need to assure himself that she really was okay, that the sand hadn't swallowed her whole.

There were still unanswered questions. What had driven Steven to do what he'd done? What kind of drug had he used on the women and where had he kept them before taking them to the dunes? But Seth didn't care about that. With Steven in custody, Tom and his team would soon find the answers to those questions.

Apparently Tamara had already had a shower for she looked clean and comfortable and was clad in a blue-flowered hospital gown. She smiled as he entered the semidark room. "My two-time hero. I have to admit I was starting to get worried out there on the dune. What took you so long?" Although her voice was light, her eyes held the darkness of that time when she'd been alone with Steven on the dunes.

"Oh, you know, I had to change my shirt and give myself a quick shave. Heroes have standards to uphold."

"Looks like you shaved a little too close," she replied. He sat in the chair next to her bed and she automatically reached out her hand for his.

He hesitated a moment before taking hers, but when her fingers curled around his, he felt the connection deep in his heart. "You scared me," he finally said, speaking around the large lump that had formed in the back of his throat.

"I was scared for me," she replied. "I was foolish. I opened the door to him. I just assumed he was there to visit with Samantha and Scooter and then he stuck me with a needle and I went down."

"None of us suspected Steven. He wasn't even on our radar. It was just dumb luck that I found you when I did."

She finally let go of his hand and propped herself up higher in the bed. "How did you find me? What made you realize it was Steven?"

"The ostrich thing." He explained to her how he'd figured it out and that he knew Steven would be some-place on the dunes to complete his job.

"It was his mother," Tamara said. "He blamed his mother for not protecting him from his abusive father and he was burying her over and over again. When I was in his trunk and he was driving me to the dunes, all my memories came rushing back."

He listened as she told him what she remembered of the night she'd spent in the animal pound and couldn't imagine the horror of that time.

"I also thought of what has kept me from wanting to go home," she said.

"And what's that?"

"Grief and self-pity." He raised an eyebrow in curiosity and she continued. "My apartment was filled with it for the past two years. I'd buried myself in loneliness, wallowed in the grief of a lost child."

"A lost child?" He reached for her hand once again, unable not to touch her in some way as she spoke of the trauma in her past.

"Jason wasn't particularly happy when I got pregnant after we'd been married for almost a year, but he seemed to resign himself to the fact that he was going to be a father. There were already cracks in our marriage, but like so many fools I thought maybe a baby would help, that somehow we'd be better as a family than as a couple."

He felt the tension in her fingers as a deep sadness filled her beautiful eyes. "Something happened in my seventh month, the doctors aren't sure what, but the little girl that I carried died. They induced labor and I gave birth to her and then picked out a casket for her to be buried in."

Seth's heart ached with her pain, although there was no way he could feel the depth of agony such an experience would produce. "I'm sorry, Tamara."

For a moment her eyes shimmered with tears and then she swallowed hard and seemingly willed them away. "It was a tough time, but the worst part was that I knew deep in my heart that Jason didn't really grieve the loss, that I thought he was more relieved than sad. I filed for divorce the very next day. I moved out of our house and into the apartment and brought all my pain, all my grief with me and I never really moved past it.

That's why I didn't want to go home, because there's nothing there for me."

She looked at him expectantly, but he knew he couldn't allow himself to get caught up in the emotion of the moment. He let go of her hand and stood, needing to distance himself before he did something they both might regret.

"Now you can go home and build a better life for yourself. You're such a strong woman, Tamara. It's time to let your grief, your fear and all of your baggage go and learn to live with happiness."

Her gaze remained locked with his, and she went so still it was as if she was once again drugged. He knew what she was thinking, that there had been no offer of anything for them in his words. He took a step toward the door.

"Will I see you tomorrow?" she asked as she raised her chin.

"I don't know," he replied. "Tom will be in to see you and wrap up all the details. I'll make sure he has all your things from Linda's place. I'm not sure when I'll leave to head back to Kansas City. Maybe it would be best if we just said our goodbyes now." His chest hurt, as if her arms were wrapped too tightly around him.

"I don't want to say goodbye...ever," she said, her eyes simmering with emotion. "I'm in love with you, Seth."

Her words were like a knife in his heart. He didn't want to hear them. He didn't want to know them. He definitely didn't want to embrace them as real.

"Tamara, I care about you deeply, but I've never made any promises. We both knew this...us...was just a temporary thing. I'm built to travel alone and you need to go home and face whatever demons haunt you there. Find happiness, Tamara, that's what you deserve."

He didn't wait for a reply, but hurried out of the room. He made it almost to the front door of the hospital before he sagged against the wall, a grief he'd never felt before washing over him. It was the grief of what might have been if they'd met at a different place, at a different time.

When she'd told him about the loss of her baby, he'd wanted nothing more than to pull her into his arms, to hold her until the pain inside her stopped, but that was a heart pain that would haunt her on some level forever.

He lingered only a minute and then shoved off the wall and headed for the exit. There would be loose ends to tie up and then he could head back to Kansas City, where he belonged.

It was time for this vacation to be over and for him to somehow reclaim the life he'd left behind…a life without Tamara.

Chapter Sixteen

It had been a week since Tamara had returned to her apartment in Amarillo. Her car had been found in Steven Bradley's garage, along with her purse containing all of her identification and credit cards.

She now sat at her kitchen table and tried not to think about the man who had consumed her thoughts since returning home.

She hadn't seen Seth after he'd left her hospital room that last night. Sheriff Atkins had checked her out of the hospital the next morning and then had taken her into his office to get her official statement. Once that had been done he'd taken her to Linda's house to get her things and then had driven her to get her car from the impound lot.

Just like that it was over. There wasn't even expected to be a trial as Steven had confessed to everything, including the murders of Rebecca Cook and Vicki Smith.

The first thing Tamara had done when she'd gotten home was write a long, heartfelt note of thanks to Linda and Samantha for welcoming her into their home when she'd had no memories of where she belonged.

After that she kept busy catching up on her web work, cleaning her place with a vengeance and working past the grief of the past so she could begin to find some sort of happiness in her future.

If there was one thing her time with Seth had taught her, it was that she was capable of loving, that she was ready to have the family she'd once dreamed of. The grief of the little girl she'd called Danielle would always be in her heart, but it no longer was an obstacle working against her as she tried to move forward.

All she had to do was forget all about Seth Hawkins.

He was still too fresh in her mind to even begin to think about another man. She still tasted him, still felt his arms around her. Life would be so easy if she could repress her memories of him as easily as she had repressed her memories of Steven Bradley and the horrendous events that had happened to her at his hands.

Seth had thought her love was just gratitude. He'd believed that her love had been born solely due to the circumstances they'd found themselves in, but he'd been wrong.

She hadn't loved him because he'd saved her life and she didn't love him because he'd been the one person she'd trusted during the most stressful time of her life.

She'd fallen in love with his charming, sexy grin, with his sense of humor and those gray eyes of his that made her want to fall into them.

Taking a sip of her iced tea, she stared out the window where her view was of a perfect, cloudless blue sky. Seth had told her to go home and find her happiness, but he hadn't realized that he was an important component of her happiness.

She got up from the table, dumped the last of her tea down the kitchen sink and then went down the hallway to her office. Work. It had been what had gotten her through the loss of her baby, it had taken her mind off her failed marriage and now hopefully it would snatch thoughts of Seth out of her brain.

She didn't know how long she'd been working at the computer when a knock sounded at her door. Probably the delivery man with the new fancy backlit keyboard she'd ordered.

She opened the door and her breath caught in her chest. He leaned against the doorjamb, clad in a sinfully tight pair of jeans and a white T-shirt that showed off his biceps. As Seth smiled at her, that achingly sexy grin, she didn't know whether to scream or cry.

He was probably here to tie up something to do with the case, a little voice whispered inside her head. *Just because he's here doesn't mean he's here for you.*

"What a surprise," she said, pleased that her voice held none of the tumultuous emotions his very presence wrought inside her.

"I was in the area and thought I'd stop by. Are you going to invite me in?" He raised a dark eyebrow.

"Sure...of course." She stepped backward to allow him entry. The scent of his familiar cologne wrapped around her and made her remember once again what it had felt like to lie in his arms, to feel so safe and warm.

"Would you like something to drink? I've got some iced tea in the fridge." She led him into the kitchen.

"That sounds good."

As she went to the refrigerator, he leaned against the doorjamb between the living room and kitchen. "Are you working a case in Amarillo?" She frowned as her hand shook when she poured the tea.

"Nah, I'm finally taking that vacation that I was going to take when I went to Amber Lake."

"And you decided to vacation here in Amarillo?" She held out the tea and when he didn't take it from her she set it on the table, her heart beating faster than it should. "What are you doing here, Seth?"

"When my boss told me to take a vacation I thought of all the places I'd like to be and this was it." He jammed his hands in his pockets, looking oddly vulnerable as he stared down at the floor. "Maybe now that you're back here things have changed. Maybe you've sorted out your emotions now and don't feel the same way that you did, but I had to come here and find out." He raised his gaze to meet hers. "Because, honestly, I can't stop thinking about you, Tamara."

Her heart that had been beating too fast seemed to stop in her chest as she stared at him, wanting to... needing to hear the words from him.

He pulled his hands from his pockets and shifted from one foot to the other. "I'd decided a long time ago that I wasn't going to get married, that I didn't need the hassle that came with love, but something crazy happened to me from the moment I saw you at the dunes so helpless and vulnerable again."

She took a step toward him. Her heart beat once again rapidly, leaving her half-breathless with sweet anticipation. "Something crazy?" she echoed.

"I didn't just want you to be safe. I wanted to smell the scent of your hair, taste your lips, feel your body against mine. But more than that I wanted to see your smile and hear your laughter. I wanted you to be the first person I saw each morning and the last person I saw at night. I love you, Tamara, but I understand if..."

He got no other words out of his mouth for she threw herself into his arms and covered his lips with hers. Their kiss was filled with hunger, but also with a tenderness that found any darkness that might have lingered in Tamara's heart and lit it with fiery warmth.

"Nothing has changed," she finally said when the kiss had ended. He tightened his arms around her. "I was hopelessly, desperately in love with you when I drove away from Amber Lake and I feel the same way right now."

This time his mouth captured hers she tasted home and the promise of love and family and future all wrapped up in his kiss. He moved his lips from hers and blazed a trail of fire down the side of her neck.

"Now *this* is a vacation," she whispered.

He gave a low, husky laugh. "No, this is so much more."

She laughed, knowing that this was a vacation that was going to last a lifetime. She was finally where she belonged...with Seth, the man who had saved her from death and brought love and meaning to her life.

* * * * *

REQUEST YOUR FREE BOOKS!
2 FREE NOVELS PLUS 2 FREE GIFTS!

HARLEQUIN

INTRIGUE

BREATHTAKING ROMANTIC SUSPENSE

YES! Please send me 2 FREE Harlequin Intrigue® novels and my 2 FREE gifts (gifts are worth about $10). After receiving them, if I don't wish to receive any more books, I can return the shipping statement marked "cancel." If I don't cancel, I will receive 6 brand-new novels every month and be billed just $4.49 per book in the U.S. or $5.24 per book in Canada. That's a savings of at least 14% off the cover price! It's quite a bargain! Shipping and handling is just 50¢ per book in the U.S. and 75¢ per book in Canada.* I understand that accepting the 2 free books and gifts places me under no obligation to buy anything. I can always return a shipment and cancel at any time. Even if I never buy another book, the two free books and gifts are mine to keep forever.

182/382 HDN FVQV

Name	(PLEASE PRINT)	
Address		Apt. #
City	State/Prov.	Zip/Postal Code

Signature (if under 18, a parent or guardian must sign)

Mail to the **Harlequin® Reader Service:**
IN U.S.A.: P.O. Box 1867, Buffalo, NY 14240-1867
IN CANADA: P.O. Box 609, Fort Erie, Ontario L2A 5X3
**Are you a subscriber to Harlequin Intrigue books
and want to receive the larger-print edition?
Call 1-800-873-8635 or visit www.ReaderService.com.**

* Terms and prices subject to change without notice. Prices do not include applicable taxes. Sales tax applicable in N.Y. Canadian residents will be charged applicable taxes. Offer not valid in Quebec. This offer is limited to one order per household. Not valid for current subscribers to Harlequin Intrigue books. All orders subject to credit approval. Credit or debit balances in a customer's account(s) may be offset by any other outstanding balance owed by or to the customer. Please allow 4 to 6 weeks for delivery. Offer available while quantities last.

Your Privacy—The Harlequin® Reader Service is committed to protecting your privacy. Our Privacy Policy is available online at www.ReaderService.com or upon request from the Harlequin Reader Service.

We make a portion of our mailing list available to reputable third parties that offer products we believe may interest you. If you prefer that we not exchange your name with third parties, or if you wish to clarify or modify your communication preferences, please visit us at www.ReaderService.com/consumerschoice or write to us at Harlequin Reader Service Preference Service, P.O. Box 9062, Buffalo, NY 14269. Include your complete name and address.

HII3

SPECIAL EXCERPT FROM

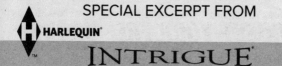

HARLEQUIN

INTRIGUE

THE MARSHAL'S HOSTAGE
by USA TODAY *bestselling author*
Delores Fossen

*A sexy U.S. marshal and a feisty bride-to-be must go on
the run when danger from their past resurfaces....*

"Where the hell do you think you're going?" Dallas demanded.

But he didn't wait for an answer. He hurried to her, hauled her onto his shoulder caveman-style and carried her back into the dressing room.

That's when she saw the dark green Range Rover squeal to a stop in front of the church.

Owen.

Joelle struggled to get out of Dallas's grip, but he held on and turned to see what had captured her attention. Owen, dressed in a tux, stepped from the vehicle and walked toward his men. She had only seconds now to defuse this mess.

"I have to talk to him," she insisted.

"No. You don't," Dallas disagreed.

Joelle groaned because that was the pigheaded tone she'd encountered too many times to count.

"I'll be the one to talk to Owen," Dallas informed her. "I want to find out what's going on."

Joelle managed to slide out of his grip and put her feet on the floor. She latched on to his arm to stop him from going to the door. "You can't. You have no idea how bad things can get if you do that."

He stopped, stared at her. "Does all of this have something to do with your report to the governor?"

She blinked, but Joelle tried to let that be her only reaction. "No."

"Are you going to tell me what this is all about?" Dallas demanded.

"I can't. It's too dangerous." Joelle was ready to start begging him to leave. But she didn't have time to speak.

Dallas hooked his arm around her, lifted her and tossed her back over his shoulder.

"What are you doing?" Joelle tried to get away, tried to get back on her feet, but he held on tight.

Dallas threw open the dressing room door and started down the hall with her. "I'm kidnapping you."

Be sure to pick up
THE MARSHAL'S HOSTAGE
by USA TODAY *bestselling author Delores Fossen,*
on sale April 23 wherever
Harlequin Intrigue books are sold!